J J RICHARDS

The Icehouse

DCI Walker Crime Thrillers (Book 1)

Simulacrum Press Publishers

First edition

ISBN: 9798399348902

Editing by Hal Duncan
Cover art by Tom Sanderson

This book was professionally typeset on Reedsy.
Find out more at reedsy.com

Contents

"For you were made from dust, and to dust you will return." Genesis 3:19-14.

CHAPTER ONE

S*o many stars*, he thought. One thing about living in the country was seeing the night sky on a cloudless night, and this one was one of the clearest: so radiant and boundless, even more so than usual.

On a starry night like this, Tom Woods often looked up at the inverted bowl of the sky, marvelled at it hanging there like the blackest of blankets, one pierced with tiny pinholes allowing specks of incandescent light to shine through. It gave him a deep sense of calm, especially when he'd just smoked a doobie.

Tom had never really taken the time to learn the names of these mysterious floating orbs right enough. He did recognise the unmistakable constellation of Orion, though, which he'd learned of as a teen when he'd gotten into Metallica—with their song of the same name. Not that he could do much headbanging anymore, with his thinning, short, slightly greying hair, nor would he want to. He'd mellowed a bit in middle-age, preferred a bit of light rock these days. The National was his current favourite, fitting perfectly into this more refined musical wheelhouse. He often stepped out into the back garden after dark to take a breath, contented with a full belly, listening to the beautifully scratchy lead vocals

1

of Matt Berninger in his Bluetooth earbuds, or something equally melodious, gazing at the infinity of the sky, getting some perspective. That wasn't where he was now though. This was somewhere else.

It was deathly quiet except for the distant sound of night creatures—an owl hooting, something rustling in the nearby foliage, and the buzz of cockchafers in the mid-May air. *Cockchafers.* Such a funny name. But Tom didn't feel like laughing right now. He had no earbuds in this time, felt peaceful, almost like he was floating. He thought he might be dreaming. He'd had dreams like this before, ones where he could fly at will, lucid dreams, where he became conscious of the fact he was dreaming and could change what he was seeing. It was like taking a journey into the unconscious and finally being in charge of what went on there, if only for a short time. He couldn't do anything like that now though, so it seemed he *was* awake.

He looked at the sky some more while he tried to get his bearings and saw the North Star. Or was it Venus? The one his wife was always convinced was an airplane because it was so bright. He'd got a Night Sky app on his iPhone once, showed her exactly what it was called, but he'd forgotten now. He also had no recollection of her name—which was strange. That had never happened before. Or, at least, he didn't think it had. *Was she called Kate, or Cathy?* He knew he was married, was sure of it, could even see her face, but her name eluded him. His head didn't feel right, his thoughts wonky. Something was very wrong.

He became aware that the sky was moving faster than it should be. He thought of how, sometimes, when clouds are blown, it can give the illusion you're on the move; but this was a cloudless night. It wasn't the night sky that was moving at all—not at this speed, anyhow. It was him. He was lying on his back, that much he knew, but he wasn't in bed; he was certainly outdoors. He could smell something too, something earthy. Sheep muck. That was it. Reminded him of camping holidays in the Lake District in his youth, a smell he didn't completely dislike as it brought him back to simpler, happier times. *Where was he?* An uncomfortable feeling started to well up in the pit of his stomach, rising higher and higher, slowly snowballing into anxiety and beyond.

He needed to get it together, figure out what was going on. He was definitely moving. He also realised his head kept bobbing up and down, but the ground wasn't so hard—if he was on the ground, that is. He wasn't sure. There was some kind of padding. Something soft, but harder below. He knew that feeling. *What was it?*

He tried to lift his head to look at his feet but couldn't move—couldn't move anything except for maybe his fingers. This was also very disconcerting, and his anxiety levels began to rise further. He felt grass. That was the feeling that had just eluded him: the feeling of soft grass on dry, rock-hard ground!

He stopped trying to move, submitted to it—it seemed pointless.

'Hello?' he said, hardly recognising his own voice, it being hoarse, barely audible. 'Is anybody there?'

The night sky settled, becoming static once more. He was stationary again, which came as something of a relief: the jerky movement was starting to make him nauseous, like he sometimes felt when he rode in the back of a car for too long along winding country roads.

'I think I need some help here,' he tried to say, but he wasn't sure it came out quite like he intended. He wondered whether he was seriously ill, whether he might have had a stroke. He was hyperventilating now, panic grabbing hold of him, not letting go. His wife would be worried sick, whatever her name was. He missed her. He needed to get home, or to a hospital. He needed to get better.

'Help,' he said again, sensing someone was there—perhaps a paramedic—and then hearing someone breathing, confirming his suspicions. There was another sensation too: *cold*. And he thought his head hurt. Or it was numb, or wet, or both. He definitely didn't feel right, but the panic started to subside a little knowing he wasn't alone, as people were usually all right, he thought. They were typically happy to help. And he didn't feel *so* bad. He expected the someone to tell him to try to relax, that he was being taken to an ambulance, that he would be okay. He'd probably just had an accident or something, blacked out.

'What's happening?' he asked.

A figure stood over him, but Tom couldn't really see their face in the darkness, only the backdrop of the night sky, the half-moon silhouetting them.

'I want to go home,' said Tom, but the figure didn't respond. His heart started pounding now, even more than before, in fear, and confusion, sensing that something was badly amiss. *Why weren't they answering him?*

'Where am I?' he asked, desperately seeking an answer.

He could now see the figure was holding something. Tom recognised what it was, but his brain was sluggish, and he couldn't put it into context.

How had he got here? Memories were pushing their way

4

back. He'd been out walking. With his wife? No. They'd been arguing. He went with the dog: Eubank. An English boxer that wasn't the best looking, which hoovered up any bits on the carpet, always looking for food. It hadn't been with them long though, him and his wife. *Why could he remember the dog's bloody name but not his wife's?* He was getting properly frustrated now, his brain feeling clogged up, moving too slowly, in need of a good oiling.

'Please,' said Tom. 'Who are you? I need help.'

The figure stood over Tom lifted their arm in the air, the one that was holding something. He knew what it was now—the object. Of course. It was something he used every day at work, as a handyman.

The object was a *hammer*.

He tried to put his hands out to protect himself but couldn't. Only his fingers wiggled, impotently, the rest of him paralysed.

'No, please,' said Tom again, but this time in a more desperate, pleading tone, one devoid of hope.

CHAPTER TWO

Detective Chief Inspector Jonathan Walker stepped out onto the wet farmer's field just adjacent to Rufford Park Lane and pushed his gold-framed Aviator Classic Ray-Ban sunglasses further up his noticeably deformed nose. They were the ones his wife had gotten him for his fortieth birthday, the ones he'd never worn, the ones she said looked 'cool'. He didn't feel *cool* right now though. With his black work suit and tie, and shades, he looked like an amateur dramatics' actor performing in a Blues Brothers play. Either that or something out of a 1980s American cop show. Except rather than being in the Californian sunshine, riding snazzy Kawasaki KZ1000s, he was in overcast, chilly Lancashire in the North-West of England, riding a shitheap of a car, and wearing an outfit that was now two sizes too small. And the only 'CHiPs' that could be found anywhere near him were the ones smothered in salt and vinegar. Still, the sun specs were doing their job—the bright daylight was killing him.

Ironically, it hadn't actually rained properly in the district of West Lancashire for a few weeks, which was unusual, and lucky, or said shitheap, the unmarked Vauxhall Corsa he was currently driving, might have gotten bogged down in mud.

Right now, though, the rain was finally starting to come down some, so he didn't want to waste any time. He still had to drive out of there. As a senior officer in the Criminal Investigation Department (CID), DCI Walker usually got a more upmarket pool car, an Audi A6 being his last, which the other detectives had learned, over time, not to use. Sadly, his enforced leave of absence meant he'd have to make do with what he had. It seemed he'd lost his dibs on that one, for the time being.

He went around to the passenger's seat of his car, opened the door, and grabbed a waterproof poncho from his backpack. It was still in its packaging, so he tore it open and slipped it on. This one was blue. He'd ordered a pack of ten, all transparent, but he'd somehow got a selection of colours and hadn't wanted the hassle of returning them. Still, it was better than being in damp clothes all day, and they fitted perfectly over his suit jacket. He'd have to make do.

Despite the rain, the field still felt hard underfoot, but it was littered with sheep muck, and he'd already stood in some. He checked the bottom of his shoe to assess the damage.

'Damn it,' he said, wiping it on a spot of clean grass.

'Try not to compromise the scene, sir,' said an approaching uniformed officer, smiling. She looked familiar. They'd probably met before, but he couldn't quite put a name to the face. The Lancashire Constabulary had thousands of staff in an extensive network of stations and posts; he couldn't be expected to remember everyone, despite working in most of these stations at some point during his over three-decade long career. He looked at her, right in the eyes, waiting for an introduction.

'DCI Walker, I'm familiar with your work. The way you cracked the Jody Shaw case was fascinating. We covered it during my policing degree a few years ago,' she said, before holding out her hand. 'I'm PC Shelly Briggs. I've seen you around before, but we've never been formally introduced. It's nice to finally meet you.'

Walker shook and nodded to acknowledge the compliment.

PC Briggs, early thirties, was short at about five foot four, with long straight dark brown hair and skin that was a bit darker than the average Lancashire lass, which made Walker wonder whether she had mixed race ancestry, though he couldn't quite put his finger on what. It wasn't obvious. She was attractive though, Walker thought, but then again, most women her age looked good to him these days, what with their almost flawless unwrinkled skin—not that he was really interested, not like that, anyway. At least, he didn't think he was. It was good to be out and about again though, quite literally in the field. He'd missed it, having a purpose, having a reason to get up in the morning. His latest recovery had been long and hard, and he'd spent most of it alone, in bed.

There were several squad cars parked nearby belonging to officers who'd already secured the scene.

'Let me take you to the Duty Officer,' said PC Briggs.

They'd entered the farmer's field, known informally by locals as the 'Deer Park' due to its historical usage, via some slightly dilapidated Victorian gate posts at the Rufford New Hall residential estate. This was, apparently, the best way in and down the stretch of open fields, as it contained a grassy pathway of sorts lined on both sides by field maple trees, which was relatively flat compared to the rest of the extensive rough grazing area and plenty wide enough for a vehicle to drive down. It only took a minute or two to get to the crime scene from the gate posts, while it would have taken ten or more minutes if navigating the muck on foot. The farmer had already been contacted by Police Community Support Officers (PCSOs) and had been happy to cooperate, advising them of the best way in; he'd already removed the livestock from the field in order to try to preserve the crime scene and facilitate ease of entry.

'What animals come in here?' asked Walker. 'Just sheep?'

'Correct, sir,' said PC Briggs. 'You know your muck.'

Walked nodded. 'Should do. I've been in it for thirty-two years, Constable,' he said.

They walked across to a mounded area that had been taped off with a wide perimeter, so Walker knew that was where he'd find the body. There were several officers stood nearby, making sure the scene was secure, and one of them approached—another familiar face, and this time one that Walker could put a name to.

'Sergeant Finch. It's good to see you again,' said Walker. 'I'll be the DCI assigned to this case, and the Senior Investigating Officer.' Walker knew they'd worked together before, was sure he'd got the name right, but couldn't exactly remember when and where. PS Finch, a middle-aged male, clean shaven with short dark hair, was largely unremarkable in appearance except that he was physically fit, and the sort who hit the gym at least three times per week. Walker always remembered when an officer caused problems with an investigation, and Finch wasn't one of them; not yet anyway.

'Very good. I'm the Duty Officer who called it in to CID. We have a fresh one, Chief, a day or two old—male, middle aged. His wife called it in. She lodged a missing person two days ago and then went out looking for him, eventually found this. The Divisional Surgeon will confirm once you're happy with everything,' said PS Finch. 'But it is more than likely who we think it is. Lived just across the road, through the woods. A Tom Woods, oddly enough.'

'Oddly?' said Walker, before realising. 'Oh, I see: the *woods*. And who do we have here? PCSOs?' he asked, turning up his nose. He wasn't a fan of the Police Community Support Officers, as they didn't have the same training or mentality as actual police officers and could easily mismanage a scene. He was hoping there wouldn't be any on site; it would make things a whole lot easier.

'Yes. But they're good ones—Officers Blithe and Willocks,' said PS Finch. 'They know what they're doing, sir.'

'Well, I hope they made sure those bloody sheep got penned in and remain untouched,' said Walker. 'They may contain evidence.'

'I'll check,' said PS Finch, with a notably sheepish look on *his* face. This told Walker this detail might have been overlooked, and that he might well remember PS Finch next time for the wrong reasons.

Sergeant Finch looked across to PC Briggs, who was still stood close by, listening in. 'That will be all, Constable. Please man the perimeter.' PC Briggs nodded and stepped a few meters further away, but still close enough to hear some of what they were saying.

'How many ways in and out does this place have?' asked Walker.

'We have a PC checking the perimeter as we speak, sir,' said PS Finch. 'I told him to also tape up any entry points, but really anyone could just jump over a fence from anywhere. It's quite a large area—might take him up to an hour to get around it. It's very secluded, isn't it? Reminds me of that film,

The Village, the one where they start a new life, away from crime and the dangers of the world.'

'Time is of the essence, PS Finch,' said Walker, not getting the reference and wanting to move things on. 'I don't have time for chit-chats. Show me the body, eh?'

'Yes, sir,' said PC Finch, a bit abashed, leading the way, politely helping Walker under some of the blue and white police tape marked 'POLICE LINE DO NOT CROSS'.

As he approached, the mound in question just looked like a little hill covered with foliage, weeds, and brambles. The rain had started to come down a bit heavier now, and Walker shielded his face so he could see where he was going better. He wished he'd brought his wellies now, something the other officers had all evidently had the foresight to do. He was grateful none of them had mentioned his inappropriate footwear, at least—or him wearing sunglasses in the rain, for that matter. Not yet anyway. Forgetting the boots was a rookie mistake though. He'd clearly been out of action for far too long. He wasn't organised yet.

As he navigated his way around the mound, it soon became clear to Walker that the small hill had some kind of entrance going in it—an old doorway of sorts with an open gate made of strong, cast iron. There was a little stone wall to climb up to get to it, which surrounded the base of the mound, but scaling it wasn't too difficult, and just required a little care.

'What is this place?' he asked.

'We looked it up while we were waiting,' said PS Finch. 'It's called an *Icehouse*. Apparently, it's what they used back in the day instead of a fridge-freezer. They'd load it up with big blocks of ice in winter, and then they'd store food in there. Must be a body of water somewhere nearby they'd cut the ice

11

from. Or there used to be, at least.'

'I see,' said Walker. 'Rufford Old Hall is near here, isn't it?'

'It is, sir,' said PS Finch. 'But it's a little far. This would have been a part of the New Hall estate, near where you entered. In fact, I know it is—saw it on a *Wikipedia* page, sir.'

'And the body is inside here?' he asked as they got up close to the entrance.

'That's correct, sir,' said PS Finch.

Walker peered inside. It was gloomy, but he could just about see that it dropped down vertically after a few feet. 'Wasn't it locked?' he asked. 'Looks dangerous.'

'It was indeed, sir. We contacted the local council. It's a protected heritage site or something. Said they had the key to the padlock that was put on there, but it hadn't been inspected for a number of years. The one locking it appeared to be new, though. So, we used bolt cutters to get it off and save some time.'

Walker looked more closely, squinting. It was dark, dank, and he could already smell the decay of the body. They wouldn't have needed to inspect it up close to check if the person was still alive. It was already fairly clear to him that they weren't. That was good for the investigation, though, Walker thought—less chance of contamination, what with all the paramedics traipsing everywhere when a victim was still alive. Of course, he'd prefer they *were* still alive; but if they were going to die anyway, unconscious, on the ambulance ride, then it was better if they were already gone—more chance to catch and convict the killer that way, more chance of him actually doing his job.

'There's a ladder,' said PS Finch. 'But I've only been halfway down. Used my torch, could see enough. Deceased male matching the description of the missing person.'

Walker removed his sunglasses and placed them in the inside pocket of his suit jacket, before taking his poncho and the jacket off. The Supe had asked him to return earlier than scheduled due to his experience in leading such murder investigations, which weren't launched too often in these parts. He wasn't entirely ungrateful either—he'd be going a bit mad rattling around at home by himself. Although one of the other DIs would have been suitably qualified, they wouldn't have had Walker's know-how or expertise. So, Walker had jumped at the chance. It was an interesting case, for sure, and he was more than intrigued. 'Can you hold these?' Finch nodded and took the poncho and jacket, while Walker removed a small torch from his belt and turned it on. He held the torch out in front, flashing it this way and that, carefully surveying the terrain, before entering the icehouse.

The inside of the building was ironically, given its frosty name, much warmer than the outside air, while it also shielded Walker from the increasingly unpleasant wind and rain. These benefits were quickly dwarfed by the increasing intensity of the putrid stench coming from below though, which dominated the senses, thick in the air, overpowering, and beyond unpleasant. Even from here, it would have been nauseating to most normal people, but Walker had learned to become comfortable with being uncomfortable, to tolerate that which most folks could not. It had become his natural habitat.

There was a small passageway to begin with, which he'd already seen from the outside—that Walker had to navigate while stooping down low. It reminded him of a trip to Egypt he once had, inside the Pyramid of Khufu at Giza, a place where he'd felt the most claustrophobic in his life. This wasn't as bad, but he got the same sensation, a feeling that the old structure could suddenly come crashing down and crush him at any moment.

After the initial passageway, the structure then suddenly dropped downwards, accessible via a more modern, aluminium ladder, just like PS Finch had described, so Walker carefully clambered on to it and was able to still hold his torch between the thumb and index finger of one hand while keeping the rest of his fingers on the ladder for stability. There wasn't much light once the descent started, even with the torch on. He wouldn't be able to see much at all without it—if anything—so the killer would have had to come prepared if they'd descended at all, and Walker soon saw that they had.

The body had not been haphazardly thrown down into the pit. Or, at the very least, it had been rearranged after being dumped. It was carefully laid out, the deceased lying on their back, arms by their sides, just as you'd find in any morgue. Walker stepped off the ladder and got onto solid ground again, closer to the body. He shone the torch, going from the toes of the corpse towards the head, covering his own mouth and nose with his free hand the best he could. He squeezed his nostrils tightly closed with his index finger and thumb, using his palm to cover his mouth while breathing via a tiny gap he left at the bottom of his hand, trying not to gag at a stench that had, as expected, become ever more potent the closer he got. Some of the younger, less experienced detectives would be throwing up by now, unused to such strong smells, the sort of stink that seemed to somehow find its way into the very mucous of the nose and refused to budge. Over the years, Walker had gotten used to it, to a degree, even at such close proximity, and didn't need to wear a mask anymore, which he found was of very little help anyway. He found his own hand to be both more convenient, and more effective.

He continued to scan the body, and when his torch finally reached the head, Walker froze, his heart pounding. If the Superintendent had known about this, he never would have brought him back early, let him work the case.

The body Walker was looking at had a cross of ash, carefully drawn on the forehead—the very same symbol and material that his Mandy had been marked with all those years ago, when her body had been found in similarly macabre circumstances. His sister's murder was why he'd gotten into policing in the first place, and now, it seemed, he'd gone full circle. He registered that the head of this man had been violently struck and was badly injured, but he wasn't focussed on that right now. He knew the body would need to be inspected to determine if it had been damaged in being thrown down onto the base of the icehouse, but that wasn't his main concern right now.

He was focussed on that cross of ash—mesmerised by it.

Walker found himself hyperventilating and stumbled backwards, almost tripping and falling over in the confined space. This was it. This was his chance to finally catch that murdering bastard, his sister's killer, put them behind bars, once and for all. Either that, or he'd kill them himself.

'It's you,' he said in a whisper. 'I don't believe it. It's finally you.'

CHAPTER THREE

Walker sat down at his desk with a cup of decaffeinated coffee in the Incident Room at Skelmersdale Police Station. He was still a little shaky, could really have done with a stiffer drink to settle his nerves, but he'd have to make do with what he had. He hadn't drunk caffeinated products in years, couldn't—gave him a bad stomach—but he liked a little red wine or even a shot of Talisker whiskey in the evenings, his smoky favourite, to help him sleep. That was when he wasn't working or on medication, though, which he currently was, on both counts. His poor health and long-term prescription of valaciclovir as antiviral meds meant he hadn't been able to have any alcoholic beverages for several months, which hadn't really bothered him that much, until now. This was the first time he'd really had any sort of craving. He could almost smell that sweet, rich, smoky goodness.

'You really going to drink that stuff?' asked PC Briggs, who'd come in to write her report, gripping on to her strong black *caffeinated* coffee. 'It's probably been there for years. No one I know touches the stuff. It's pointless.'

Walker just rolled his eyes and took a sip. 'How many people do we have over there?' he asked, perhaps a bit too sharply. As soon as he'd examined what they had, he'd get back out there himself. They needed all hands on deck. Plus, he was bloody well going to personally leave no stone unturned on this one.

'Pretty much every available officer we have,' said PC Briggs, as she handed Walker a piece of paper, her hand steady, her demeanour respectful. 'My report,' she said, to clarify what she was giving him.

Walker added the piece of paper to the pile he already had on his chosen desk. As the Senior Investigating Officer, it would be his job to formulate a strategy for the investigation, based on the information they had, and to log actionable items. He hadn't really organised everything as he'd like yet though, having been on leave for so long. It took time to get things in order. It had been about eight months since he was last on active duty this time, before his second episode of viral meningitis and associated encephalitis. He still felt a little dizzy and fatigued from it some days, like today. But apart from that, and the light sensitivity issues, he'd pretty much recovered by now, apart from the psychological effects of having to cope with a rare recurrent form of an illness that could strike again at any time. Still, he wasn't thinking about that now for the first day in quite some time. He'd taken his pills and was fully focussed on the case in hand, which was turning out to be possibly the biggest and most important of his career to date—the most important as far as he was concerned at least.

He gave PC Briggs's statement a quick read. There didn't seem to be anything of immediate note, except what he'd already been told: that the padlock on the icehouse looked new and had been cut off by officers attending the scene.

'Can you give this lot to the Admin Team?' said Walker, holding up the pile of paper to PC Briggs. 'I'm getting back out there. I want to be on site with this one.' That was if the Supe allowed him back out there at all. His own report wasn't in the pile, having been handed in to Superintendent Hughes the moment it was ready. It all depended how he took the news that the murder might be connected to Walker's sister's cold case.

'Sir?' asked PC Briggs, as there were plenty of officers ready to conduct interviews and search the immediate area, which was around a twenty-minute drive away, *if* traffic was light.

'I need to be out there. The young DI can handle things from here, when he finally turns up,' Walker said, blowing on his coffee and taking one final sip. But, before he could leave, one of the female admin staff popped their head into the Incident Room.

'DCI Walker,' she shouted. 'Supe wants to see you.'

Walker nodded, having already been expecting to be summoned sooner, rather than later, and headed to the office of the very man who'd called him in: *Superintendent Ronald Hughes.*

* * *

'You have to let me stay on this one, Ron,' said Walker.

'Let's stick with Superintendent Hughes this time,' said Supt Hughes. Walker raised his eyebrows. 'It sends a message to the others,' he clarified. 'And to ourselves. Please, sit down.'

Walker took a seat and looked around the office of Supt Hughes. It was exactly as he remembered—*unspectacular* was the word, a dismal little place that was no better than the concrete laden exterior of the station. The only thing that made it even remotely homely was a framed photograph of Supt Hughes's family, which sat on his desk in front of him.

Supt Hughes picked up Walker's report from his desk and took a good look at it, his face serious, worrisome.

'You really think you can take this on, remain objective?' asked Supt Hughes. 'I would never have called you in if—'

'Of course, sir. How long have you known me?' said Walker. 'It's not a problem.' Supt Hughes gave it some thought but didn't look convinced, so Walker went on. 'It was decades ago. It's probably just a coincidence or a copycat. It's very unlikely to be the same person at this stage. I know that.'

Supt Hughes mulled it over some more.

'Either way, I'll handle it,' said Walker, and Supt Hughes put the report back on the desk.

'Well, you'd better,' said Supt Hughes. 'Or my career is on the line.'

Walker nodded and looked outside. It was still raining. 'I appreciate you bringing me back early. I was starting to climb the walls back there.'

'Nonsense,' said Supt Hughes. 'How long have we worked together, Jon?'

'Let's stick to DCI Walker for now,' said Walker. 'It sends a message to the others. And to ourselves.'

Supt Hughes smiled. They'd developed a good repartee over the years and enjoyed working together. Hughes was a little older than Walker, but not by much.

Walker eyed the back of the framed photo he'd seen many

times on the desk of Supt Hughes. 'The family okay?' he asked, not really so interested deep down—as he knew Hughes wouldn't have been there if there were any major problems—but wanting to show concern anyway.

Supt Hughes glanced at the picture and smiled. 'All good,' he said, before looking like he regretted appearing so pleased about it. 'And you?' he asked, in a more serious tone.

'I guess so,' said Walker, meaning he had no idea—his wife and kids rarely contacted him at all these days.

'Old dogs like me still remember the Amanda Morris case. What happened to your sister was terrible, and her killer is still out there. So, who better to have on this case than you, I suppose?' said Supt Hughes, though he sounded like he was trying to convince himself as much as anything.

'Look, if there is a connection—and I'm not saying there is, it's very unlikely—but *if* there is, then I'm probably the best person to establish that, aren't I, sir?' said Walker. 'You know how much I've studied that case.'

'I do,' said Supt Hughes, with some reluctance. Walker had been obsessive about the case over the years. 'How similar was the marking to the Morris case?'

'There were some notable similarities. Appeared to be drawn with ash again, or something similar,' said Walker, leaning forward, then sitting back again, not wanting to appear too eager. 'We'll need to get forensics to confirm the material used.' He scowled. 'But if it is him...' He'd felt close a couple of times over the years when he'd been working on cases involving killers with similar profiles. But there'd never been another one with that marking. This was different. This had to be him. But he couldn't let the Supt know he was thinking that.

'Take it slow, Detective,' said Supt Hughes. 'You know these things rarely pan out as you'd expect. DI Riley should be back at the Incident Room any second. Wisdom tooth. He's been in agony with it for weeks. Couldn't change the appointment anytime soon and now he's late coming back. Sorry about that—throwing you in at the deep end, I mean. I might have put him on it if he'd bloody been here.' It seemed Walker wasn't the only detective on the case with health distractions.

Walker shook his head, dismissing the apology, and put his hands on the arms of the chair, exerting some downward pressure, not enough to lift himself up yet, but enough to tip off the man opposite him that he was eager to leave. Supt Hughes got the message.

'You may leave now, DCI Walker,' he said.

Walker stood up and headed for the door, but before he could leave, Supt Hughes said, 'And Jon, Michaela says when you have some time, you should come around and have tea with us.'

Walker turned around one last time, suddenly feeling like the main character in a Lethal Weapon film, only with the addition of a notably northern English accent. 'Tell her that's very kind,' he said. 'But I think I'm gunna be busy on this for a while.'

Supt Hughes, nodded. 'Well, let's hope you get your man—or woman—sooner rather than later,' he said. 'Good luck.'

'Yes, let's hope so, sir. And thank you again,' said Walker, before he left the office.

* * *

'Is that DI Riley back yet? I need to get out there. Help with enquiries,' said Walker to PC Briggs, back in the Incident Room.

'Not yet, sir. We called the dentist. They said there'd been some complications getting the tooth out,' said PC Briggs. 'So, he's going to be delayed some. He sends his apologies. At least, they *think* that's what he said.'

Walker noticed a Merseyside lilt to PC Brigg's speech this time, not much, but it was there. She wasn't a Lancashire lass. Or, at least, she was from somewhere around Skem—as Skelmersdale was unaffectionately called by the locals and their neighbours in the region—which although officially in Lancashire, was largely populated by generations of people spilling over from further west in Merseyside.

'*You* can come and assist me then,' said Walker. 'Come on.'

'What? Me?' said PC Briggs. 'I've never worked with CID on a murder case before. I'm not—'

'Then you'll be perfect,' said Walker. PC Briggs raised her eyebrows, evidently not quite sure what he was getting at. 'No preconceived ideas,' he said. She nodded her complaisance.

They got moving, navigating the corridors and staircases of Skelmersdale Police Station, descending from the fourth and top floor, where its Criminal Investigation Department and the Incident Room they were using was located, down to ground floor level. There was no conversation while they made their way. Walker was busy thinking about the case, and he was pleased PC Briggs wasn't unnecessarily chatty and seemed to understand this. Early indications were that they'd get on well.

'Heading out already?' asked a female officer on Front Counter Service, manning the front desk. She'd seen them come back and had heard about the case, was no doubt curious about what was happening.

'We're helping out with enquiries,' said PC Briggs. 'It's all hands on deck time.'

The officer at the front desk suddenly fumbled with something beneath the desk and presented it to them. It was an unmarked tin box.

'Blueberry muffins,' she said. 'One of the officer's wives made them. Take some. There are loads.'

PC Briggs took the tin box and held it out in front of her, making sure they didn't get damaged.

'Thank you. It's always good to keep well fuelled while working a case,' said Walker, hoping that would end the conversation, and it seemed to do the trick.

'Any good?' asked Briggs, shouting back to the woman as they were exiting the building.

'She's a chef!' said the officer, which meant that they were. 'She's written a book and everything.'

The parking lot was just around the corner and Walker still had the keys to the unmarked Vauxhall Corsa pool car he'd driven earlier. He pressed the key fob and it bleeped, reminding him where he'd parked it among the other cars there, some of which looked almost identical.

'Where are all the bloomin' Audis?' he asked. 'I'm a goddamned DCI, for Christ's sake. I should be driving better than this.'

'I guess there are a lot more dicks working around here at the moment,' she said. She had some humour and delivered it well. Walker liked that. It kept him grounded. But this was no time for jokes, and he didn't want to encourage it. Not for now, at least.

'Get in, PC Briggs,' he said. 'We have work to do, and lots of it.'

CHAPTER FOUR

Walker parked on Rufford Park Lane, not too far from where the victim had been found. It was a long, straight road with only one entry, off the main road—the B5246, also known as Holmeswood Road, the road where the victim had lived. He intended to speak to the deceased's wife later in case the other officers missed something. But those recently widowed, he found, tended to give better information sometime after the initial news came in, once they'd had a little time to let it sink in, let the seismic shock subside, just a touch. So, he'd give it an hour or two, at least, before that; let her get herself together a bit first, the poor woman.

There were already a number of officers conducting house-to-house enquires, trying to get information about goings-on leading up to the murder of Tom Woods, so Walker decided to make a start on the two estates at the far end of Rufford Park Lane, where enquiries hadn't been made yet—these being the Rufford New Hall estate and Springwood Drive.

'Nice place,' he said, looking around properly for the first time. 'Must be some money here.'

The Park Lane was lined with majestic Scots pine trees either side of the road, beyond which were farmers' grazing fields fenced off just beyond the trees, one of which was connected to the Deer Park they'd found the body in. The lane was more like the entrance to some grand mansion, a horse racecourse, or some expensive private golf course than it was to a housing estate. It was impressive. Of course, it *had* been the long driveway to a grand mansion at one time, before Rufford New Hall had been reappropriated—something Walker had discovered while looking into the place.

'I sometimes get coffee at one of the cafes at the Marina in Rufford,' said PC Briggs. 'The Tastebuds is the best. Great cakes. Always plenty of nice vehicles in the car park there.'

'Well, anything would look nice compared to this,' he said, slamming the door of the Corsa as he got out. 'And we're supposed to be inconspicuous in these, eh? Ridiculous. Shall we?'

He'd already noticed the sheep penned in near the entrance to Rufford Park Lane and figured these were probably the same sheep that had been roaming around the Deer Park. *Good*, he thought. *PS Finch seems to have sorted that one. And best of luck to the inspector who gets that actionable item—to search the sheep. That's gunna be a real pain.*

They came to a large, detached property on the corner of Springwood Drive, which was situated just before the Rufford New Hall estate. The two estates were markedly different, with Springwood Drive being a row of modern detached brick-built buildings, while Rufford New Hall was cream coloured, a collection of flats and terraced properties that had been converted from the eighteenth century Rufford New Hall estate and its stables, an estate originally owned by the Hesketh family—former lords of the manor of Rufford—later used as a convalescence hospital, before finally being sold and converted into their present state.

'Number one. As good a place to start as any,' said Walker, looking at the first house on Springwood Drive. It was a gated property, so he pressed the buzzer next to the gate and waited.

'You been on a lot of cases like this?' asked PC Briggs.

'A few,' he said, solemnly, shifting his sunglasses up his nose a touch, despite it being typically overcast.

The intercom crackled into life. 'What?' said the voice on the other end. Sounded like an old woman, and a cranky one at that.

'Hello, madam. I'm DCI Walker. I'm here with my colleague, PC Briggs. We would like to speak to you for the purpose of gathering information about a crime that's been committed nearby. May we come in?'

'I'm in the middle of something,' said the woman. Walker looked at his colleague and frowned. 'Dusting,' she elaborated. After a few seconds, the woman on the end of the line huffed and the gates started to open.

'To some people, dust *is* a crime,' whispered PC Briggs. 'My mother for one.'

Walker smiled. He knew exactly what she meant. His mother-in-law had been just the same, before she passed away. She used to run her finger along the mantel shelf of their fireplace, driving his wife nuts.

They walked up to the front door of the house and Walker knocked on it, only for it to be opened before he could finish his customary three raps.

'Okay, okay, give me a minute,' said the woman. She had one of those faces that looked like it hadn't smiled in years, looked like it couldn't even if she tried—with those particular facial muscles having long since atrophied. 'What's this all about?'

'I'm afraid there's been a crime of a serious nature, madam. Could we come inside? We're conducting house-to-house enquiries. Trying to find out if passers-by might have seen anything,' said Walker.

'I see,' said the woman, suddenly looking interested, and somewhat concerned. 'Is it a burglary?'

Walker looked at PC Briggs. 'I'm afraid we're not currently commenting on the nature of the crime,' he said. 'We're just collecting information at this stage.'

'I suppose you'd better come in then,' the woman said, still holding a duster and putting it down on a side table in the hallway. She closed the door after them and showed them through to a well laid out sitting room with expensive furnishings. Walker took off his sunglasses and put them in his pocket, squinting as he did so, getting used to the light in the room.

'Would you like something to drink?' she asked. She looked about seventy, or more, Walker thought, and she walked with a bit of a bend in her back, like a lot of older people.

'Not for me,' said PC Briggs.

'How about you go fetch those cakes from the car?' said Walker. He wasn't hungry, but he knew it was often useful to offer interviewees something first, if possible, whether it be some information, a compliment, or a *cake*.

'But Chief...' said PC Briggs, before seeming to think better of it. 'Back in a sec.'

PC Briggs excused herself, while Walker took a seat. 'I'll have a cup of tea, if you don't mind,' he said. 'No sugar. I'm sweet enough. Just a touch of milk. Decaf is even better.'

'Fine, I'll put the kettle on,' said the woman. 'But we don't have decaf.'

Walker took out a pen and a notepad. Although all information eventually went into the HOLMES database—the *Home Office Large Major Enquiry System* used to aid in large-scale investigations—it still all had to be handwritten first in case any data was corrupted or lost, so there was always a hard copy to hand.

'Before you do that, could I take your name first?' asked Walker.

'Yes. Of course. It's Mrs Robinson. Patricia Robinson,' she said.

'Didn't Simon and Garfunkel write a song about you?' Walker blurted out, perhaps a bit too abruptly, trying to be funny, make some kind of a connection, forgetting for a second about her solemn face. He looked up from his notepad and was immediately reminded. It seemed his social skills had become a bit off-kilter over the past few months as well, not surprising given his lack of visitors and general contact with the outside world while recovering. He'd been on his own too much.

'What are you trying to say, Officer? Are you suggesting I'm making advances towards you because I've offered you a drink? Is that why you sent that female officer on her way?' the woman said.

'No, no. I...' Walker tried to remember what that song, *Mrs Robinson*, was about. Was probably something to do with a woman next door having an affair, he thought. Maybe an older woman. 'Sorry, I didn't mean anything,' he said.

'Well, I'm tired of that old one. Ever since I married Stephen,' she said. 'Is that what passes for funny these days? Really.'

'Stephen. Is that your husband?' asked Walker.

'Yes. He was anyway. He passed away last year. Lung cancer. Hadn't even smoked for thirty years. Can you believe that?'

'I'm sorry to hear that,' said Walker, making a few more notes.

'I'll get the tea then,' she said, without much emotion, and left the room.

Walker eyed the place. It was pristine. Everything was in its place, and there was very little clutter, if any—just a few ornamental pieces, a coffee table, and two sofas on top of an oak wood floor, which was also perfectly polished. Mrs Robinson clearly kept a clean house. Either that, or she had reason to keep it especially clean right now. Walker also made a quick note of this.

It wasn't long before PC Briggs returned. She'd left the door open and let herself back in.

'Got them,' she said, placing the tin of cakes on the coffee table and sitting next to Walker.

'I'll do the talking. You just observe for now,' said Walker.

'Will do, Chief,' said PC Briggs. 'She making drinks?'

Walker nodded and got back up, took a look around. He gazed out of the front window. 'Space for... four... five cars out there in the driveway. It's big.'

'But only one car is present, sir,' said PC Briggs. She'd noticed too.

Mrs Robinson came back in holding a tray containing one teapot and three cups with saucers.

'We'll need to let it brew a bit longer,' she said, placing it on the coffee table next to the tin. 'What's that?' she asked. She sounded constantly annoyed, like it was her default setting.

'That's a tin of blueberry muffins one of the officer's wives gave us,' said PC Briggs. 'Apparently, she's a chef.' Walker scowled at her, so she looked down in her lap and got out a notepad to focus on instead.

'Well, I don't eat other people's homemade products,' said the woman. 'Anything could be in there. But you're welcome to eat some if you like, as long as you don't make any crumbs.'

'As you wish,' said Walker. It didn't matter that she'd rejected the offer, so much. Not to him, anyhow. What mattered was that they'd offered her something first before asking her to tell them what she knew.

'So...' said Walker. 'Two days ago, on the thirteenth of May: did you witness any activities, anything at all, that you thought may have been suspicious?'

'Well, you'll need to be a little more specific than that,' said Mrs Robinson. 'I did think I saw one of the neighbours put some polystyrene in the blue bin. That's not allowed, you know. But I'm guessing you're looking for something a bit more serious than that.'

Walker cleared his throat. 'Yes. Do you ever walk around what the locals call the "Deer Park"', he asked. 'This is the area we're most concerned with.'

'Oh, thank God!' said Mrs Robinson. 'At last. Someone is finally doing something about that. It's been driving me mad.'

Walker glanced at PC Briggs, whose eyes went just a touch wider, before looking down again at her notepad, steadily holding her pencil, ready to take more notes.

'What has?' asked Walker. 'What, exactly, has been driving you mad, Mrs Robinson?'

'Well, the trespassing, of course. Isn't that what you're talking about? Only residents of Springwood Drive are supposed to be walking out there. It's written into our leases. We pay a fee each year, and in return, the farmer allows us access to his land, for walking and such. Nobody else should be going out there,' she said. 'We pay almost £300 per year! £293, to be exact. It's scandalous! And there's nothing we can do about it. We have to pay for what everyone else gets for free.'

'I see,' said Walker. 'And have you seen anybody who shouldn't be there recently?'

'Oh, no. I don't go into the Deer Park itself anymore. There are too many strangers there. And it's often too muddy and full of sheep muck. I'm too old for that now. The ground is uneven too. Hurts my feet. I just go into the woodland area at the edge of the park these days. That's the farmer's land too. I walk my dog in there, my little Choo-Choo.' For the first time, Mrs Robinson's sullen face turned upwards into what Walker assumed passed for a smile.

'And where is your... *Choo-Choo* now?' asked Walker. PC Briggs suddenly cleared her throat, fighting a smile, trying not to laugh.

'My Choo-Choo is out in the garden, playing,' said Mrs Robinson. 'Do you need to interrogate her too?'

'No, that will not be necessary,' said Walker. 'And in the past week or two, you've not seen anyone around here that seemed out of place. Anything like that? Anyone who concerned you?'

Mrs Robinson looked up, giving it some thought. 'Well, there was some kid in the woods one day. Wearing one of those hoodies, he was. Scared me half to death so I left and went home. I didn't recognise him from our estate. Don't think I'd have recalled him even if he was. Could hardly see his face at all what with the hood, and sunglasses too.'

'This is really useful information, Mrs Robinson. Do you remember the colour of this hoodie?' asked Walker, knowing the detail could be important. She hesitated. 'This would be a person of interest to us that we'd like to rule out as a possible suspect.'

'It was a dark colour, I think. Perhaps a navy blue. Or dark grey. I'm not sure,' she said.

'And his approximate age?' asked Walker. 'You said he was a "kid"?'

Although this information was highly relevant to the current case, Walker was also thinking about how old his sister's killer might be if they were still alive. He—and Walker was pretty sure it was a *he*—certainly wouldn't be a kid anymore. The murder had happened in 1987 when Walker was just sixteen. Although he'd never completely ruled out a very young killer, like in the murder of James Bulger just a few years later—a case that, unlike his sister's, had been extensively covered by national newspapers—the cigarette ash cross suggested a more adult mindset, and statistics were also strongly in favour of it being someone older. Walker's best guess was the current age range of Amanda's killer was somewhere from the late forties at the very youngest, up until the sixties or seventies, or even older. Most likely, he thought, they were somewhere between their early fifties to their late seventies. This, disappointingly, didn't fit with Patricia's initial description of the person in the wood though, which was another reason why Walker was digging for more.

Patricia Robinson wavered at Walker's question regarding the person's age, appearing unsure. 'Well, at my time of life, everyone looks young, don't they? I'm really not sure. My eyes aren't what they once were. He could have been an adult, I suppose. He did look a bit familiar, but I couldn't place it. I only had a glance, you see—I was too shaken up. But like I said, people go in there from all over, so it could have been anyone. I'm tired of it. It's not fair that we have to pay, and they don't. I should give them a piece of my mind,' she said. 'It's not right.'

Walker looked across to PC Briggs again. 'That wouldn't be wise, at the moment, Mrs Robinson. I would strongly advise against that. In fact, it might be better if you stayed closer to home, for the time being.'

'I'm not scared of any burglars,' said Mrs Robinson.

'It's not...' said Walker. He wanted to keep the nature of the crime on the downlow for now, if possible. It would give them the best possible chance of finding a lead. 'It's up to you, but, for the record, we *are* advising that you stay home as much as possible for now.'

'Well, I need to walk my Choo-Choo,' she said, stubbornly. 'She gets a little stiff if she doesn't get regular exercise.'

'That's your choice,' said Walker. 'But I'd advise you to stay on the lane or around this estate for now.' He looked at the window once more. 'There's just one more thing,' he said. 'Does anybody else live here with you, or visit regularly? I just ask because it's such a large, beautiful house.'

'Why, yes. My son and his wife, and his little girl live here, along with my daughter, who isn't married,' she said. 'They're all out now.'

Walker raised his eyebrows. 'Oh. Doesn't the little girl have any toys? I didn't see any—'

'All in the back,' snapped Mrs Robinson. 'I'm sick of tidying. Her mother leaves her stuff everywhere.'

Walker took a deep breath, preparing to leave. He didn't see anything here worth chasing for the time being. 'Well, thank you. That will be all for now. I'll see myself out. Please provide the details of everyone living here to PC Briggs before she leaves,' said Walker, before looking at PC Briggs and saying, 'We'll put that in the Action Book when we get back—to get an officer to return and interview them too.' PC Briggs nodded her understanding.

On the way out, Walker shouted back, 'Take care of yourself, Mrs Robinson. We'll be in touch if we need anything more.'

CHAPTER FIVE

D I Riley held the side of his face, pressing it slightly, checking to see how the pain was from his recent wisdom tooth extraction. It still wasn't great. He could feel his cheek had swelled and it was still a bit numb from the anaesthesia, meaning if he smiled only half his face responded, making him feel like he was being sarcastic. He guessed the pain would only get worse as the anaesthesia continued to wear off—something he was not looking forward to. But apart from that, he felt fine and would rather have the distraction of work than moping around at home. At least he could count on his colleagues to keep him grounded, stop him being such a moaning Minnie. He was a bit soft when it came to physical pain, he knew.

He'd come out to Rufford Park Lane to meet with the farmer, the one who owned the Deer Park and the surrounding land. One of the items in the logbook was to talk to him and examine his sheep for evidence pertaining to the Tom Woods case. It was unlikely there was any evidence on any of the sheep, Riley thought, but it was still an item that needed to be cleared, and it seemed he'd drawn the shortest straw what with him not being around when the tasks had been assigned. That's what tended to happen when someone was out of the office for a while—all the best jobs got taken, leaving the dregs and donkey work for those returning. And this time, that *someone* was him. Fair enough. He'd have done the same. He'd just have to take it on the chin.

Riley had arranged to meet the farmer, Eddie, at the end of Park Lane, where the sheep were currently penned in. He was waiting for the man to arrive, arms on fence, looking at the sheep, breathing in the farm smells, his car parked just a short distance down the lane—an Audi A6. He looked at his watch. The farmer was already ten minutes late.

'Come on. Where are you?' said Riley, getting a bit impatient, but right on cue, a vehicle arrived, a white Ford Ranger pickup truck with the windows rolled down, despite the chill.

The truck drove across the pavement towards a large gate that provided entry to the field. The man driving it got out. He was fairly young, in this mid-twenties or early thirties at most, fit, and dressed like you might expect a farmer to dress—old jeans splashed with bits of mud tucked into some green wellies, a black woolly sweater, and a flat grey cap. He looked at DI Riley, eyeing him up and down. Riley was dressed smartly in an off-the-peg suit that fitted him well despite a developing beer belly, and a green North Face raincoat. He was affable with a friendly face, and most people took to him with little trouble. At twenty-nine, he was also at an age where he could relate some to both the youth and the middle-aged.

'You the bobby?' asked the farmer. 'You said you wouldn't be wearing a uniform, right?'

'I'm DI Riley, yes,' said Riley. 'Eddie?'

Eddie nodded and proceeded to open the gate, before getting back into the truck and driving, rather quickly, into the field and abruptly stopping again. He got out.

'Come on then,' said Eddie, smiling. 'Let's be having you.'

DI Riley walked into the field and Eddie closed the gate again, his truck still running with the door open, fumes going everywhere. Thankfully, Riley had also been smart enough to bring a pair of black wellies, which he'd put on before leaving the car and tucked his suit trousers into, and it was now clear just how much he'd need these rubber boots. At least he would keep relatively clean and dry—or, at least, that's what he thought. That was the plan.

'Terrible, what happened, isn't it?' said Eddie. 'Just awful.'

'It is,' said Riley. 'That's why we're being so thorough, to try and catch whoever did this.'

Riley preferred to get people in their natural habitat, whenever possible, where they felt more comfortable, rather than getting them straight into a sterile police interview room, an environment where most people tended to stiffen up. He thought he had more chance of getting something out of them when they were comfy, of getting some valuable information, although he was well aware that any evidential value would diminish in an unrecorded environment like this. As a preliminary information gathering exercise though, he definitely preferred it—it suited his personality better, allowed him to establish a relationship first. Plus, he had the sheep to search anyway, so he might as well kill two birds with one stone, he thought, try to have a bit of a chat to the farmer at the same time, if he was willing. Turned out, he didn't have to try too hard. The farmer was a talker.

'Serves 'em right in a way though,' said Eddie. 'They shouldn't have been in my bloody field to begin with if they don't live on Springwood. Only that lot have a legal right of access to our land.'

'Is that so?' said Riley, trying to look disinterested, but really being *very* interested.

'Yeah. People keep knocking down my fences when they're climbing over or damaging them enough for the sheep to escape. Or they leave the bloomin' trail gates open. They can't even put a simple piece of rope over the posts! I even make it easy for 'em, make a nice little loop. And then I get flak cos the sheep get out on the roads, or in someone's garden, damaging their flowers. It's a pain in the arse,' said Eddie, getting visibly annoyed. 'I get calls all the time, day and night.'

'I see,' said DI Riley. 'And do you ever get into any altercations with any of these people?'

'*Altercations*,' said Eddie, as he moved towards the pen the sheep were tightly enclosed in. 'You mean a fight?'

'Yes. An argument or conflict,' said Riley. 'Anything like that?'

'No. I just tend to leave 'em to it if I see anyone on our land, as chances are they're from the estate, and even if they're not, a lot of 'em alert me if one of the sheep is injured or in danger. People pass my number around, you see. They tend to look out for the flock, let me know when one has got out or whatever, as I said.' said Eddie, backing up a bit. 'So, there are pros and cons, I suppose. Although...'

'Although what?' asked Riley.

'I do sometimes wonder whether it's a dog that's injured one of my sheep, and not a fox or some other wild creature. I've had a few go down recently—a bit more than usual. If people let their dogs run off the leash in there, they could definitely do some damage. I'm not saying they are, but they could. I'm not in there that much though. I can't police an area of that size all the time. I'd never get anything done,' said Eddie. 'Fact is, sheep die all the time, for whatever reason. At least a handful every year. It's a real shame. We just leave the carcasses out there, let Mother Nature do her thing. They disappear eventually, but they do smell a bit. If I ever find out someone's dog has killed one of 'em, though, I'll go mad, I will.'

DI Riley looked at Eddie, raised one eyebrow, just a touch.

'I don't mean it like that,' said Eddie. 'I 'ad nothing to do with this. I'd just shoot my mouth off, that's all. And then I'd call you lot.'

Eddie seemed to realise that he'd been a bit harsh on the victim, perhaps hadn't painted himself in the best light. He frowned, thoughts clearly churning.

'I didn't mean that guy deserved to die or anything. I just meant he shouldn't have been there. He was trespassing, after all,' said Eddie. 'Hey, you don't think we 'ad anything to do with this, do you? Just because it's our land, that doesn't mean anything. If we'd have killed anyone, we'd have buried them deep. You'd never have found 'em. We can dig a hole ten feet deep in no time with our machinery, then fill it up again, grow crops on top. You'd never know the difference. We could do it before sunup, get the tractor lights on it. We have all kinds of equipment like that. No one ever bothers us when we're working. We wouldn't stick them in that old icehouse, that's for sure. A body would just rot in there, attract too much attention—animals and the like. And people go up there sometimes, checking it out, history buffs. We ain't stupid.'

DI Riley raised both eyebrows now. He'd never known anyone to dig themselves in so deep and attach themselves to an investigation so unnecessarily. 'Good to know,' he said.

'Who is *we*, by the way?'

'Me and my two brothers,' said Eddie. 'And me dad. But he doesn't work anymore. He's retired.'

'Well, we'll have to interview you all in due course, eliminate you from our enquiries,' said DI Riley.

'No problem at all,' said Eddie. 'Any time. We've all been away the past few days. Went down to Oxford for the farming conference there. We'd only just got home and put the sheep back in the Deer Park from the other field when I got a call about this, and we had to take 'em out again. It's been nonstop.'

'I see,' said DI Riley. It seemed almost too convenient, but a strong alibi nonetheless if it could be verified, and he didn't really get any vibe that Eddie had anything to do with this. In his experience, the guilty tended to be much tighter lipped and careful about what they were saying. Whereas *he* was anything but.

Eddie and DI Riley were right up to the sheep pen now, looking inside, the noise from the flock getting notable louder as they became more nervous, probably wondering what was about to happen.

'So, you need to search all of the sheep then?' asked Eddie.

'Yes. For evidence,' said Riley. 'Just in case something got stuck to their fur.' He knew he'd made a mistake as soon as he said it.

'You mean, their *wool*?' said Eddie, smiling, before Riley could correct himself. 'Sheep don't have fur. They have wool.'

'Yes, of course. That's what I meant,' said Riley. 'Sorry. I've not been around animals much. I tend to deal with people, on the whole—although you could argue that some of them are animals too.'

'Right. I guess I'm the opposite,' said Eddie. 'That's probably why I'm so bloody knackered from that conference—talking to so many people! I'd rather be digging ditches, alone.' Eddie unlocked the pen and held the door. 'Ready then?' he asked.

'Ready for what?' asked Riley.

'Well, ready to search all of these sheep,' he said. 'That's what you came here for, ain't it?'

Riley froze, not sure what was happening. 'Yeah, but... I'm not going in there,' he said. 'It's packed.'

'Well, of course you're not,' said Eddie. 'I'm gunna let them out, one at a time, and you can search them all you like. Sound good?'

Riley had never touched a sheep before, not unless he was eating it. He wasn't sure how to handle them.

'Just show 'em who's boss,' said Eddie. 'You'll be all right.'

DI Riley wished he'd brought a colleague along now to aid with the search. He'd not really thought it through, just assuming the farmer would handle the sheep for him.

'Can you at least hold them for me?' asked Riley.

Eddie thought about it and then spat in the dirt—the grass being all worn away near the pen.

'Go on then,' he said, grinning. He was just playing with him. 'I suppose.'

Eddie took out one reluctant sheep, grabbing it by the back legs and pulling it through, before locking the pen again. Riley looked all over the nervous animal while Eddie held it, parting its wool here and there, making sure nothing had got lodged in deep, especially near its backside, which smelled of shit, not surprisingly. Bits of faeces were matted in.

'Nothing on this one. Next,' said Riley, just before Eddie lost his grip on the sheep's legs. It kicked out and caught Riley, right on the side of the face, on the same side as his recently extracted tooth. He yelped. It seemed the anaesthesia was already wearing off, and significantly so.

'*Mother-f-f-f... Argh!*' shouted Riley, holding his face. It was only a glancing blow, but enough to bloody hurt.

'Come on. It only just caught yer. You'll be all right,' said Eddie.

'Had a tooth out today, right where it just kicked me!' said DI Riley. 'Shit, that hurt.'

'Oh. I see. Sorry about that,' said Eddie. 'Too bad. Only another two-hundred and twelve to go.'

DI Riley's eyes went a little wider. He pulled his two-way radio from his belt and was just about to use it to call for some extra help, when Eddie said, 'Wait. I've got an idea. This lot are just about ready for shearing anyway. How about I take the wool off of 'em, bag it up, and then your guys can sift through it at their leisure? Just be sure to send it back when you're done. And I mean *all* of it. Sound good?'

DI Riley put his two-way radio back in its holster. 'Why, that's a great idea. Why didn't you say anything—'

Eddie smiled again, indicating that he hadn't just come up with the idea. He had a mischievousness about him that a lot of young men had, although his was perhaps magnified, Riley supposed, due to him being on his own so much and getting bored with his own company.

'Sorry,' said Eddie. 'I should have thought of that sooner. It was funny seeing you with that sheep though.' He started to laugh. 'You looked terrified. It's just a sheep, for Christ's sake.'

'Mr... Eddie. This is no laughing matter. A man has died, and it's our responsibility to gather evidence as quickly as possible so justice can be done. If there's any more of this,

I'm charging you with obstructing our investigation,' said DI Riley. 'Is that clear?'

'But I didn't do anything,' said Eddie. 'I'm just trying to help.'

DI Riley looked at Eddie, closely, now not sure whether Eddie had been messing with him or not. 'Please shear the sheep and bag up the wool for inspection, as you suggested,' he said. 'I'll remain here to oversee the operation, to bag anything that you find whilst doing it.'

'Fair do's,' said Eddie. 'I'll get me stuff out from the truck.'

While Eddie was busy organising some equipment for sheep shearing, DI Riley stood in the muck just outside the sheep pen, the single sheep he'd already searched now running free, deep into the field. He rubbed his cheek again and looked up to see a car approaching, a dark blue Vauxhall Corsa—same make and model as many of their unmarked pool cars. It slowed down and came to a stop. Inside sat PC Briggs and an older guy in plain clothes who Riley didn't recognise.

PC Briggs put the window down and leaned out. 'DI Riley! You skiving off again? Stop playing around in the muck.'

'Examining the sheep,' said DI Riley, shrugging his shoulders with a forlorn expression. 'Actionable item.'

The guy sat next to PC Briggs looked serious, said something to her, but DI Riley couldn't hear what it was. He wondered whether the man might be the new DCI who'd been assigned to the case—the one with health problems who he'd never met, for one reason or another.

'Find anything yet?' asked PC Briggs.

'Not yet. Only just started,' said DI Riley. 'It's gunna take time. The farmer will shear them, bag up the wool, and then we'll send it off to forensics for analysis. I'll stay here while he's shearing though, see if he finds anything while doing it, if you know what I mean.' He meant he'd also be keeping a close eye on the farmer, just in case, as well as bagging any larger items as soon as they were found, for immediate consideration.

PC Briggs said something to the driver again, before saying, 'Very good.' The car left, leaving DI Riley to his sheep and the muck, muttering to himself, holding that swollen cheek again.

CHAPTER SIX

'**K**athryn Woods?' asked Walker, but he was pretty sure it was—her hair was dishevelled, her eyes red, like she'd been crying. After conducting several more interviews on Springwood Drive, Walker and PC Briggs had now come to the house of the deceased's wife on Holmeswood Road, hoping to shed some light on the circumstances leading up to the death of her husband. On the way over, Walker was pleased to see DI Riley had been searching the sheep taken from the farmer's field where Tom Woods had been found and was hoping it would turn up some evidence to use. He was less pleased that he'd seen an Audi A6 parked nearby though, which he assumed was one of the pool cars, one that he, as a senior inspector, should be driving.

'Yes. Come in,' she said. She led them into the living room, this time a more typical British setup with a Berkeley cream leather sofa set, coffee table, and a large Samsung TV in the corner—at least, such a TV *used* to be large, Walker noted; these days it seemed par for the course. They all sat down, Walker and PC Briggs on a three-person sofa, one of them on each end, and Mrs Woods in a matching single sofa chair.

'So, I'm DCI Walker and this is my colleague, PC Briggs. We're so sorry for your loss, Mrs Woods.'

'Thank you. "Kathryn" will be fine,' she said.

'As you wish. I understand someone has already been to speak with you?' said Walker. 'But we're here to gather more detailed information, given the circumstances in which your husband was found.'

'I understand,' said Kathryn, bursting into tears. PC Briggs looked across to Walker and stood up, going over to Mrs Woods and comforting the woman by putting an arm around her. There was a box of tissues nearby, half used, so PC Briggs grabbed a few and handed them to Kathryn.

'It's going to be okay,' said PC Briggs, giving Walker a look that said Kathryn Woods would never be okay. 'You just have to get through this and then it will get a little bit easier.'

When Kathryn's tears subsided a little, PC Briggs sat back down.

'Are you alright to answer a few questions now?' asked Walker. 'Kathryn slowly nodded. 'Okay. So, we already have some basic details that the other officers collected,' he said. 'But on the day your husband disappeared, was there anything out of the ordinary that you remember? Anything at all?'

'Well... we'd just had an argument. I can't even remember how it started now. We've not been good recently,' she said. 'That's why we got Eubank—our dog. He's in the garden. Tom was taking him for a walk.'

'I see,' said Walker, not sure how the dog had got back without its owner, but simply waiting to find out, not wanting to lead the conversation too much.

'He went out just after seven, I think, just before it went dark. Never came back. I thought he'd left me, at first,' she said.

'Because of the argument?' asked Walker.

'Because I can't have children,' she said, looking down at herself, her expression suggesting she was still bitter about it, angry even at her body's barrenness. 'He wanted to be a dad. We were hoping the dog, Eubank, would make us closer, but he's hard work, and it just caused more friction in the end. Tom was trying to train him. He got a book and everything.'

Walker looked at his notepad, at some notes he'd made earlier from the reports of other officers. 'And... I'm told you called this in the morning after he went missing, reported it as a missing person.'

Kathryn nodded. 'At first, I was angry, thinking he'd left me. I was convinced of it. But as the hours passed, my anger slowly turned to worry. I don't think I slept at all. I made the call first thing in the morning.'

'I see. So, this was reported as a missing person, and officers did a preliminary observation of the area. And then I have it that you found one of his shoes?' said Walker. 'Can you explain how this occurred?'

'Yes. Not much was done at first. The officers that were sent to me said they get people reported missing all the time; that people often leave their wives, or husbands, without saying anything, especially after an argument, and then get in touch a few days later. But his van was still here, and so was all of his stuff. Something felt off.'

'The officers were correct,' interjected PC Briggs. 'I think the figures are about a quarter of a million missing persons reported in the UK every year, and, if memory serves, about eighty per cent of these turn up okay after around twenty-four hours.' She was defending her colleagues, probably trying to make sure no official complaints were made, or that any legal action was taken, so Walker let that one go.

'I see,' said Kathryn. 'They said they'd be in touch soon, but I was going out of my mind. I had to do something. I walked around all the areas I knew he walked Eubank. I couldn't find anything. But when I got home, like some miracle, Eubank was sat there, waiting for me at the door,' she said.

'But the dog was alone, I take it?' said Walker.

'Yes. And he had something in his mouth—one of Tom's trainers,' said Kathryn.

'No leash?' asked Walker.

'No,' said Kathryn. 'It was off.'

'Has the dog ever displayed any aggressive tendencies?' asked Walker. He was wondering if Eubank might have attacked Tom's assailant first, perhaps angered them enough to lash out, with fatal consequences.

'No. He's a sweetheart. Just, he's young, still a pup, about six months, so he's a little exuberant. That's why Tom was trying so hard to train him,' she said.

Walker looked across to PC Briggs, who was busy writing. 'Are you getting all of this, PC Briggs?' he asked. She looked up, just for a second, and nodded, before going back to her scribbling.

'And that's when you called the police again?' asked Walker.

'No. I thought he might still be alive. I don't know what I was thinking, actually. I was in a panic. I thought he might be in trouble, and needed help, so I immediately took Eubank out. He led me to this place, through the woods over the road, and into a field filled with sheep. He couldn't wait. I could barely hold him the way he was pulling on the spare lead I'd put on. I got to some kind of old structure, a ruin with a locked gate leading into some kind of underground man-made cave. I'm not sure what it was, I don't usually go in there, but Eubank sat down in front of it and started pining, and that's when I called the police,' said Kathryn. 'I could smell it you see, *death*. I knew that smell from when my dad died—we only buried him last year. While I was waiting for the police to arrive, I was trying to convince myself it was just a sheep carcass or some other dead animal down there, but deep down I knew.'

'I see. Well done, Kathryn,' said Walker. 'That can't have been easy. And thank you for explaining everything for me in such detail. It's a great help for our investigation.'

'So, he was killed?' asked Kathryn.

'We cannot make any assumptions, but it is very much looking that way, and rest assured we're treating it as a serious and violent crime,' said Walker. 'Please, if at all possible, keep this with your nearest and dearest for now, as we don't want the media compromising our investigations—they have a habit of doing that. So, that would be very helpful, if you could. We're going to do our very best to catch whoever did this to your husband, Mrs Woods.'

'Thank you. I just don't know who would want to do that to Tom,' she said. 'He was just so... likable, most of the time.'

'That was going to be my final question: if you could think of anybody who might have had any sort of conflict with your husband, any argument or friction, or any work-related issues?' asked Walker.

'No. Not that I can think of. Nobody except myself,' she said. 'But every couple argues, right?'

Walker and PC Briggs both knew that a large percentage of homicides were committed by intimate partners, but they also knew that one woman, alone, could not have pulled a body of her husband's size across a main road, over a stone wall, through a woodland area and farmer's field, and into an old icehouse—not alone, anyhow. Even if they'd gone for a walk together, and she'd killed him there in the field, it would still have been extremely difficult to pull him up into that icehouse all by herself. She was a skinny, small lady, with low muscle mass. It was very unlikely.

PC Briggs nodded, and both her and Walker stood up, Walker just ahead of her, getting ready to leave.

'We'll be in touch soon, Mrs Woods, keep you updated,' said Walker. 'In the meantime, if you think of anything else, anything at all, then please give me a call, day or night.' He handed Kathryn a card with his mobile number on, and she took it with two hands.

'He was a big man, but he wouldn't have hurt a fly you know,' she said.

'I'm sure he wouldn't. Good day to you, Mrs Woods,' said Walker, instantly regretting his phrasing, as a good day was the last thing she'd be having for quite some time.

CHAPTER SEVEN

Emily Watkins got off the bus that had taken her from Scarisbrick Hall School and stepped out onto Holmeswood Road. She wore her predominantly boysenberry-coloured Whittakers pinstriped school blazer without her red coat, which she'd stuffed in her bag as it was no longer very cold—at least, not to her. She noticed some of the olds walking around still wore jackets, but she didn't need it, despite her mum telling her she must carry it. *As if she didn't have enough to carry*, she thought, with all her books and folders and whatnot. Her shoulders ached as the straps from her backpack dug in, and she quietly cursed.

She looked up and wondered whether something might be going on at one of the houses across the road. A car was parked in front of it, and a man and a female police officer were getting in some crappy old car. She looked at them and got eye contact from the man for a second, so she looked down, not wanting any attention. She'd had enough of that recently—*attention*. She didn't want any more trouble. She was in enough already. Her parents would freak if they saw her coming home with a police officer. It didn't look like a police car though, so she thought maybe the woman officer was off duty, with her husband or something, maybe just visiting someone.

At sixteen years old, Emily was starting to feel like an adult, and she could certainly look like one in the right outfit, but she was still treated like a child. As her birthday was in October, she was one of the oldest in her class. She couldn't wait to leave school, go to college, stop wearing that horrid uniform. But she still had a few months to go yet. She'd already done her mock GCSEs, and had done better than expected, even getting a couple of A-grades, and she was now preparing for her final exams, the first one being next week. She was already getting nervous.

She put her head down, trying to look inconspicuous, and walked towards home, which was just off Holmeswood Road on to Rufford Park Lane, and then left onto Springwood Drive. Another police car drove by, and she noticed there was also some police tape covering a section of the stone wall up ahead, the one she was walking next to. It was taped in a place she knew people often jumped over to get into the wood, a place where the ground on the other side was a bit higher, where someone had conveniently put a rock to use as a step. She'd used it herself many times walking home, as it was nicer to walk through the wood than by the main road, which often got very blustery next to the open crop fields on the other side, agricultural land which started just after the short row of houses that the police car was parked in front of.

You could exit the woodland path at the entrance to Rufford Park Lane by jumping over another wall near the corner, but she wouldn't be using that route today, what with the police tape and all. Even without the police and the tape, she still wouldn't have used it, as her parents didn't like her going in there alone, and she was in so much trouble already—when she hadn't even done anything, not really. They'd kill her if they found out. She thought they were so uptight.

She wondered what might have happened in there for it to be taped up like that. *Had someone died? Or been mugged?* Rufford was usually a quiet area—boring, actually. Nothing ever happened there. It wasn't even a town, just a tiny village on the south-west side of Lancashire. It didn't even have a proper shop; just an old petrol station selling a few household things next to a gun shop, of all things, and a pharmacy. *Why were the police here?* There was probably just a dead sheep in the wood or something. She'd seen them get in there sometimes, from the farmer's field. Her dad said they were worth a bit of money. Maybe someone had stolen one. Or perhaps one had gotten onto the main road, and someone had hit it. That would make a real mess.

She made it on to Rufford Park Lane and felt the weight of the world slowly push down on her shoulders. She didn't want to go home. She couldn't breathe there. They'd make her do chores and study for her exams, like they had done every day for the past few weeks. They were tyrannical. It wouldn't be fun—far from it. The pressure of passing her GCSEs was really getting to her. Well, passing them wouldn't be too difficult, but making her parents happy with her grades was another matter. They wanted her to get into college and then go off to university—said she should be aiming for one of the red brick universities. At least she'd get a bit of freedom if she did that though, away from everyone, so she was trying. But it was tough.

Normally, she'd spend a bit of time texting her friends on the way home, maybe even sit down for a while on one of the benches in the wood—the ones a local had been making out of fallen trees—but she couldn't even do that as her parents had taken her phone away as punishment. She hadn't even done anything wrong! She'd been covering for her friend at school, had taken the rap for some graffiti on one of the school walls. They'd all had their stuff searched, and her friend Katy had begged her to hide the spray paint cannister in her bag, as Katy's father had said he'd put her in a public school if she got in trouble again. Katy just loved the street artist Banksy. She adored him. He was her hero... if he even *was* a "he". Katy thought he was a rock star, and she was addicted to doing her own public displays of art—trying to emulate his style. Emily thought her creative friend might have a problem, thought she was crazy for painting on the back of one of the school buildings. But she loved her friend, who was in the year below, didn't want her to get expelled. Katy'd already had two warnings. She wouldn't get a third. So, with her previously clean record to protect her, Emily had taken the rap, had explained it as being due to the pressures of her exams. But her parents were coming down on her harder than she'd expected, and it sucked.

It wasn't that her parents were bad people—they just worried too much and pushed her too hard. People seemed to think children from wealthier families had it easy, born with a silver spoon in their mouths, but as far as Emily was concerned, they didn't understand the pressure and the lack of free time some get compared to other children. Although Emily had spent her formative years in a semi-detached house in Ashurst near Skelmersdale, in a much less affluent environment, her father's property renovation business had taken off at some point, and they'd moved to this big, detached house in Rufford. Their lives had changed. When it was time for her to leave primary school and go to high school, her parents had made the decision to send her to Scarisbrick Hall School, a well to do private affair in Scarisbrick, just south and west of Rufford. It was where all the rich kids went. And although she liked her school, and the people there, she sometimes missed her old life as she'd had more freedom and time to herself back then. It had been a much simpler life.

She entered her estate on Springwood Drive and slowly walked down to the cul-de-sac where she lived, looking at her shoes, for the most part. Once there, she found her mum waiting outside her house just a step away from the front door, which was slightly ajar. Emily checked her watch—she was a little later than usual, but not by much: just a few minutes.

'Emily! Where have you been? You're late,' said her mum.

Her mother was dressed immaculately, as usual, and wore make-up to hide her age. Not that she was that old, but in her forties, she now had to do what she could. Emily thought it wasn't fair her mum wore so much make-up all the time, as they wouldn't even let her wear a bit of lipstick, like some of her friends did. They were making her look not cool.

Emily huffed. 'Sorry. The bus was late,' she said.

'I called the school, young lady. They said the bus left on time, as usual. Where have you been?'

'I'm tired,' said Emily. 'I guess I was walking a bit slowly. I saw some police doing something on the main road.'

'I know,' said her mum. 'Something's going on. That's why I was getting worried. Get in here.'

Emily sighed and hung her head, hooked her thumbs under her backpack straps, lightening the load a tad.

'Come on.' Her mum pushed the front door open a bit more. 'Now!' she said.

CHAPTER EIGHT

PC Briggs rode next to DCI Walker in their unmarked dark blue Corsa as they headed back to Skelmersdale Police Station.

'So, what do you think, Chief?' she asked.

She'd never worked a homicide case before—if it even *was* a murder—and she wasn't entirely sure what they were looking for. She found DCI Walker unusually intense at times, despite his obvious efforts at being friendly. The case felt almost personal to him, although she couldn't quite put her finger on why or how. It was more a feeling. It was like he needed to catch this killer more than anything in the world, but he was holding himself back, trying to go through the right processes, be patient, but not always quite getting there. She wondered whether he was always like this, on every case, whether that was why he'd been so successful in his career.

'I think we need to get back to the station and collate all the information we currently have,' he said, sounding a bit annoyed. 'Like I already said.'

PC Briggs didn't want to push it, but she knew, with DI Riley being back on active duty now, that she'd soon be on traffic duty again or attending burglaries in Skem or whatnot. She knew this might be her last chance to learn anything tangible about such CID operations, at least for the time being. She'd thought about studying to be a detective herself one day, but it was just a rough career plan at present; she hadn't actively looked into it in any great detail yet. She'd not been in the police force for that long really, compared to some of the other officers, and still had a lot to learn. She wasn't even sure if she was cut out for that yet, never mind detective work. But she was curious about what the CID did, day-to-day, and whether that might be a better fit for her.

'Any hunches?' she asked, knowing she might be pushing it, but wanting to carry on the conversation anyway.

'*Hunches?*' said DCI Walker, glancing at her and raising an eyebrow while he was driving. 'Have you been watching too many TV crime dramas?' he asked. 'Let me guess. CSI, is it? That American one. Don't expect us to have a forensics lab like that—all high tech, modern, and pristine.'

'How green do you think I am?' asked PC Briggs, faking sounding insulted. 'And I'm a British girl. *Luther* is more my cup of tea. I think I might have a thing for Idris Elba.'

'Idris who?' said DCI Walker. 'And what kind of a name is "Idris" anyway?'

'I think you'd like it,' said PC Briggs. 'He's a DCI, like you.'

PC Briggs got the distinct impression that although DCI Walker was conversing with her, he wasn't really there, was otherwise occupied, thinking about something else, multitasking. He seemed to have that ability to hold a simple conversation with someone while simultaneously mulling over something else. It made sense though, she thought, as interviewing people often required saying one thing, while thinking another.

'Who would do such a thing?' asked PC Briggs as DCI

Walker carefully turned on to Lancaster Lane in Parbold, just off from Robin Lane, a blind junction that often caught motorists out. 'We have to find out who that kid in the hoodie was, right? If they even were a kid. They might know something or have seen something. Or...'

'Or it might have been them,' said Walker. 'I'm well aware of how this works, Constable.' He seemed irked about something—not so much about what she'd said, but something more, something she couldn't quite pin down.

'How are we going to find out who it was though?' asked PC Briggs. 'It could have literally been anyone. I even have a hoodie like that myself.'

'Well, the *why* is actually more important to focus on than the *who* at this stage. It's motive that will lead us to the killer and the evidence we require to make a conviction,' said DCI Walker, slipping into a mentoring type persona and tone. PC Briggs grabbed the opportunity with both hands. She wanted to learn more, and a Detective Chief was the perfect teacher.

'Okay. Then *why* would somebody do something like this?' asked PC Briggs.

'That is what we intend to formulate a hypothesis for. Or several,' said DCI Walker. 'But first, we must collect as much information as possible, so we can do that.'

PC Briggs never expected anything like this to happen today, of all days. It just happened to be her birthday—her thirty first—but she hadn't mentioned it to any of the other officers. She didn't want the attention. It was already one she'd never forget.

They made it on to Higher Lane, heading towards Dalton, which was technically in Skelmersdale, but it was a well to do area and not really associated with downtown Skem at all.

'Have you ever seen anything like this before?' asked PC Briggs. 'I mean, I know you've worked on other homicide cases. But have you ever seen anything similar to this specific case?'

She was thinking of the old, historical building the deceased was found in. It just seemed odd. Walker clenched his jaw and said nothing for a moment.

'I'll look at what we have and brief the team when we get back,' said DCI Walker. 'You will be a part of that top-tier team, PC Briggs, as you were one of the first on the crime scene. You're part of the investigation now.'

'I am?' said PC Briggs. 'I mean... thank you, sir.'

'*Chief* will do just fine,' said DCI Walker.

'Chief,' said PC Briggs. *Wow.* She was working a case—a proper case—and she couldn't wait to continue to be a part of it.

* * *

Back at Skelmersdale Police Station, DCI Walker was going through all the information they currently had about the case of Tom Woods. There was already a lot—interview transcripts, photos, initial forensic analyses, police reports, and more. There would be boxes of the stuff by the time they finished, but he didn't care about that, just as long as they got the killer.

Early indications were that the offender was most likely male, given the strength needed to drag a man of Tom Wood's size and throw him down the bottom of that icehouse. Either that, or more than one person was involved—which was unlikely, Walker thought. He knew the vast majority of murders in Britain were carried out by a single killer, and he was also aware that of these, most of them were male perpetrators, with two thirds also being white. These also happened to be the probabilities that defined the profile of his sister's killer. In that particular case, the killer was also deemed to be highly organised, exhibiting some element of psychopathy, and carrying out the murder in a planned way rather than it being spontaneous. Some elements of control in the violence of the injuries were also indicative of an anger-excitation typology, in which the offender is driven by anger whilst also exercising constraint and able to experience gratification from the victim's suffering. But with the peak age for criminal convictions being in the early twenties, and with those in their late teens being most likely to carry out a crime, this significantly reduced the chances of this being the same killer; plus, the description of the guy in the hoodie did nothing to support this hypothesis. This didn't stop Walker from hoping though. He'd seen deviations from the norm many times before, knew there were outliers. What he held on to was that the two murders shared the same ritual and signature, in the cross of ash on the forehead, which demonstrated some case linkage. The disposal of the body in the current case did concern Walker in connecting the two cases, as this kind of hiding of the body was not present in his sister's case—though he had an idea that a young man might be bolder and more prone to take risks, while an older man might be more careful, and have more to lose. He certainly wasn't giving up on such a scenario just yet; it was way too early in the investigative process for that.

What they had so far was 226 interviews at 134 households in the surrounding area, taken from residences in the immediate vicinity of the Deer Park where Tom Woods's body was found. Having said that, 114 of the occupiers were either out or not answering, which meant that there were already 114 actionable items in the logbook for officers to follow up. And those were just the preliminary house-to-house calls. There would be more. This would be a wide-scale investigation and Walker knew the key to unlocking it would be the dogged perseverance of all the detectives working the case, along with extreme professionalism and diligence in following up every single possible lead. Nothing could be overlooked. Missing one thing might be the difference between success and failure with the case. And even though it was statistically unlikely this was Amanda's killer, the cross of ash suggested some kind of a connection—a son or an apprentice of some kind who'd taken up the same M.O., perhaps. Or maybe Amanda's killer had been banged up for some petty crime at some point, had bragged about their exploits to a cellmate who was now copycatting them. The possibilities were endless. His sister's isolated murder was only covered in one or two little known books that Walker knew of, so a personal connection was maybe a more likely scenario where a copycat was concerned. But if it wasn't the same person, and there was such a connection, he knew finding this killer could lead to Amanda's. One way or another, it felt like this was his chance to finally find his sister's killer, and Tom's, and God knows who else, and he wasn't going to let that go without the mother of all fights.

'A couple more for you, Chief,' said one of the officers, throwing some more paperwork on Walker's desk. Walker didn't know the officer—a male in his mid-thirties—but he would by the end of the case. He'd know everyone. The man was rough around the edges, a little brash. 'All have returned now, or are back out on active duty,' said the man.

Walker nodded without looking up again, having already seen enough, chewing over what they had, and what he was going to say to the team they'd assembled to work the case. Some of them wouldn't have any experience of working a homicide case like this, just like PC Briggs, while others might have gotten set in their ways, having worked too many. He'd need to loosen them up, make sure they were flexible enough to be open minded and see the evidence for what it was, without any preconceived ideas, whilst also being rigid and disciplined enough not to miss anything. With the cross of ash on the victim's forehead, just like his sister all those years ago, he felt there was enough to at least join the dots and include this cold case in their early investigation discussions via a linkage analysis.

He studied the photos of the cross of ash on Tom Wood's body, and then compared it with the official cold case photos of that of his sister, which he'd pulled from the database and printed; something he wouldn't have been able to so easily do in the pre-digital era. He was wearing his reading glasses—his eyes weren't what they once were for close up detailed work like this—and he pushed them further up onto the bridge of his nose, squinting. The room was bright, with several fluorescent lights overhead casting a white glow, making him uncomfortable and a little dizzy. He couldn't wear his sunglasses because they weren't fitted with lenses. Plus, he didn't want his colleagues to know just how much his illness was affecting him.

After all these years, seeing his sister like that still made his heart beat that little bit quicker, although he'd seen the pictures so much that he'd become a bit mentally numb upon viewing them. The same photos had been on the wall of his office for years, along with numerous case notes and theories. His wife had hated it, had wanted him to let it be. But he just couldn't let it go. It was his sister, after all. It was why he'd gotten into police work in the first place. And now, he finally had a real shot at either finding her killer or getting a substantial lead that could crack the case. He couldn't let emotion cloud his judgement on this. He knew if it did, he'd be taken off the investigation, or worse.

Walker stood up and moved to the front of the Incident Room, where there was a whiteboard. He grabbed a black pen.

'Attention everybody,' he said, loudly enough to make sure everyone stopped what they were doing. He'd been doing detective work for a while now—over two decades, in fact—and had a confident authority about him.

The team that was assembled, all twelve of them, including PC Briggs and DI Riley, stopped what they were doing and looked at Walker. He started by writing the name of "Tom Woods" on the whiteboard.

'As you know, this man is dead, and we need to find out who was involved, and why,' said Walker. He underlined the name several times, then grabbed a magnet and fixed a photo of the deceased Tom Woods next to his name. It was a close up of his face, with the cross of ash clearly visible and his head all bashed in, dried blood around the wound.

'This is a photo of him as he was found. As you can see, a marking has been drawn on his forehead, a cross. We're waiting for confirmation from forensics, but it looked like it was drawn using some kind of ash or dirt,' said Walker, fixing another photo to the whiteboard, this time of Tom Woods's full body, carefully laid out on his back with his arms by his sides.

'Someone arranged him like this,' said Walker. 'And put him in this.' He fixed one more photo to the whiteboard, this time an external photo of the icehouse. 'They locked it with a new padlock and left him there. The old one was most likely cut off with bolt cutters and discarded. We have yet to find it. So, bear in mind that bolt cutters are another item to look out for when doing your rounds.'

Next, he took a photo of his dead sister from his file, held it in two hands, looked at it, the back facing the other officers for the time being.

'I'm going to show you something from a cold case now, one from 1987. Note the similarity,' said Walker, as he put the photo on the whiteboard with another magnet. There was a notable shift in the room, with one or two taking in a sharp intake of breath as they all realised they might be dealing with a serial killer, and a long-standing one at that. Next to the photo of his dead sister, Walker wrote 'Amanda Morris.' Walker had changed his name when his mum had remarried, after his father's death. He also found it useful for his fellow officers not to know that he was the brother of Amanda Morris, as it was a well-known case in the area amongst some of the older officers and residents. Even after all these years, there were still people who remembered.

'Amanda Morris's killer was never found. So, we need to consider the possibility that whoever did these murders might be the same person, or that it's a copycat killer. If it's not the same person, there might be a personal connection. As such, information from this cold case will also be included in this investigation,' said Walker. 'Of course, there might also be no connection at all, as the symbolic marking of a cross of ash on the forehead is widely used in Christian ritual. But we must consider this as a possibility given the obvious similarities.' He was trying his best to remain objective, but it wasn't easy. 'You'll each be given individual tasks to complete on a daily basis. And as always, please make sure everything gets input into the HOLMES system at the end of the day for review.'

The Home Office Large and Major Enquiry System was the computer system used to assist in major inquiries like this, so large amounts of information could more easily be referenced and analysed. Walker hadn't been a big fan of the system in its early years, had preferred the old ways, when a Statement Reader would have been the centre of such an inquiry process and would personally dissect every statement as they came in, finding patterns in the data. But despite that, the new computerised system had developed a lot over the years and had become more sophisticated and reliable than any single person, so he'd started to rely on it, as they all had.

'We're most likely looking for a young white male, at this stage, based on statistical probabilities, but if it is the same killer as the Amanda Morris case, then we'd be looking for someone in their late forties onwards—most likely early fifties up to seventy or so. So, bear that in mind. We've also had a description of a stranger loitering nearby wearing a dark-coloured hoodie, thought to be a teen or someone young, although the witness wasn't entirely sure and seems to have assumed this from the style of clothing worn. This, of course, could just be a youngster hanging around, smoking weed or drinking or something, but it is a person of interest for now that we need to follow up on. Above all, please maintain an open mind at all times. If this isn't connected to the Morris case, then it really could be anyone,' said Walker. He wasn't sure if he was talking more to himself, or the team sat in front of him. 'That's all. Any questions?'

DI Riley put up his hand like a school student in front of a teacher. He was young for a detective at twenty-nine and had that exuberance and enthusiasm about him that many new detectives on the job had. He was likeable—perhaps too much so for a detective.

'DI Riley,' said Walker. They'd already met and introduced themselves when Walker had returned. 'Good to have you back. Let's hope you can bring some *wisdom* to the case.' Some of the team quietly chuckled, not sure if they should be laughing or not. Walker knew that team spirit was important, even if he didn't feel like cracking jokes. He had to keep them close and maintain a good relationship with them.

DI Riley smiled, but it was a pained one and only half of his face moved properly. He also had a bruise forming on his cheek.

'Thank you, Chief. So, if the two cases are connected, then the killer, like you said, must be pretty old by now,' said DI Riley.

'Pretty old? Like me?' said Walker.

'No, I meant...' stuttered DI Riley, not wanting to insult his new DCI.

'It's okay, Inspector,' said Walker. 'Carry on. They'd have to be my age or older, correct. I assume you have more. I think we already have a handle on the arithmetic. What is that smell, by the way?' He knew damned well what the smell was—he'd seen him amongst all those sheep.

Everyone chuckled again, also knowing what DI Riley had spent his morning doing.

DI Riley smiled again and nodded. 'Some scuff marks were found in the field, possibility indicating the body was dragged some distance. So, this would have been someone in good shape then. Maybe someone in their fifties or even sixties fits, just. But older than that—it gets more unlikely.'

'This is yet to be confirmed with forensics too,' said Walker. 'So, for now, we assume the victim died close to the scene. Those marks could have been made from the farmer. I don't suppose you asked him when you saw him, did you?'

DI Riley shook his head. 'Afraid not. Didn't know about the scuff marks until I got back here. It can be followed up, though.'

'Anything else?' asked Walker. 'Did you find anything on the sheep yet?'

'Just a couple of items,' said DI Riley. 'One used condom, one beer cap from a bottle of Heineken, and one piece of rubber.'

'Sounds like you had quite the party,' said Walker, which got another chuckle from the group.

'Hardly,' said DI Riley.

'Well, that's three items then, not a couple,' said Walker. 'Let's keep things as precise as possible. And by rubber, you don't mean another bit of condom I take it? What did it look like?'

DI Riley gave it some thought. 'No. Best guess, a piece from a tool or some machinery, something like that. The farmer didn't recognise it as something they'd use though.'

'Then find out then, DI Riley,' said Walker. 'As soon as you can. And leave a photo of it on my desk. Is that it?'

'Yes. That's all,' said DI Riley. 'Except this…' He took a box from under his desk, got up, and went over to where PC Briggs was sitting, placing the box in front of her. 'We got a tip off from one of your colleagues.' He opened the box and folded the sides down to reveal a birthday cake. 'Happy birthday!' he said, smiling. On the cake was written 'HAPPY BIRTHDAY Briggsy!', accompanied by a picture of some handcuffs and a truncheon shaped like a dildo. She laughed, and most others followed or clapped a little.

'Oh, thank you, everyone,' said PC Briggs. 'That's really kind. Let's eat some together later, when we've got some work done.'

'Here, here,' said Walker, clapping his hands to signal the end of the meeting. He suddenly realised that Superintendent Hughes had been stood outside the door to their Incident Room, a door which had a window in it. He wasn't sure how long he'd been there, as Walker had been focussed on his team.

Supt Hughes saw that Walker had seen him, opened the door, and slowly walked inside, standing next to Walker.

Walker held out his palm to introduce his old friend. 'Superintendent Hughes, everyone,' said Walker. 'In the flesh.'

'Thank you, Inspector,' said Supt Hughes. 'Good afternoon, everyone. And happy birthday to you, PC Briggs.' He looked out at the people in front of him, regarding them. The room was quiet, waiting for his next words. 'Now, I don't need to tell you that this is one of the biggest cases we've had in quite some time,' he said. 'We're going to try to keep this one from the media for as long as possible, but you know how they are—they'll find out sooner or later; usually sooner. If you feel compelled to warn your own nearest and dearest about this, that's your call. I can't stop you. But make sure it doesn't go any further than that for now, for the sake of the investigation. We're going to need your very best work on this, and it may require some considerable overtime. If any of you have any doubts about whether you can handle this, any at all, then please tell me now, and we'll get someone else in to replace you.' He gave it a few seconds, giving each member of the team some time to reflect. Nobody answered. 'Good,' he said. 'Carry on then.'

The room started to increase in noise again as everyone went about their business.

Supt Hughes ushered Walker over to the side of the room, and then out into the corridor, closing the door to the Incident Room behind him. It was quieter there, and private.

'You okay?' asked Supt Hughes. 'Can you handle this?'

'I'm fine,' said Walker. 'Never been better.'

Supt Hughes sighed, clearly having some second thoughts about putting DCI Walker on the case. Normally, if a case involved any personal circumstances of a Detective, someone else would be put on it. But this was different, and the case was yet to be evidentially proven to be linked with the cold case of Walker's sister. He'd known Walker for a long time and knew exactly how much it would mean to him to finally apprehend his sister's killer. It would mean everything. Plus, he also knew that nobody else would know more about the Amanda Morris case than Walker. He was obsessive about it, and his extensive knowledge could break the case.

Supt Hughes frowned and stared at Walker. 'If you get too deep into this, and start to lose your objectivity, I won't hesitate to—'

'I won't,' said Walker, resolutely.

Supt Hughes eyed him some more, looking deep, his gaze boring into him, Walker felt, searching for any hint of doubt. 'Very good then, DCI Walker. Very good. As you were. And go home and get some rest soon. This is a marathon, not a sprint. You need to take care of yourself. You've done a long shift today on your first day back. I don't want to see you before two in the afternoon tomorrow, or you're off the case. Got it? There are plenty on the team to take care of things until then.'

Walker paused for a second, wondering whether he might be able to persuade his Superintendent otherwise. His boss's expression told him not to push it. 'Got it,' he said. 'I'll head home soon.'

He did feel somewhat jaded from the day's events, actually, not being used to working, not used to doing much of anything really. His Superintendent was right. If he was going to be successful and find the killer, he needed to pace himself, get some strength back first. But he also knew he needed to take the chance, to capitalise on it, or he'd regret it for the rest of his life. It was a delicate balancing act and one he really needed to get right. On this occasion, though, he'd listen to Supt Hughes, haul his arse back home, get some rest. He'd need all of his strength tomorrow. Plus, he'd have to choose any opportunities for insubordination or rule breaking wisely—save them for when he really needed it. He knew he might have to resort to that at some point if he was to get what he wanted. He wasn't going to hold back on this one. But now was not the time. Not yet.

CHAPTER NINE

PC Shelly Briggs wasn't just a cop—although that defined much of her current identity. She was also a sister, an auntie, and a daughter, and she loved all of those jobs just as much, thought they were just as important, if not more. It was the morning after she'd been assigned to work with a DI for the first time, and a chief at that. She was very proud. But the case she'd been requested to help with made her think about her loved ones even more than usual, to worry about them. That was why she'd dropped by her sister's place before work today, as it was on the way anyway and she knew how the kids liked to see her in uniform.

'I'll come quietly, Guv,' said Sam, holding out his wrists to be handcuffed. Her eight-year-old nephew had a cheekiness about him that many his age did, if they had the confidence. And he did.

'It's Constable Briggs to you,' said Shelly, reaching for her cuffs and placing them on Sam, much to his delight. It was something she'd done many times before, a ritual he never seemed to get bored with.

'He's a criminal!' said Sam's ten-year-old sister, Lucy. 'He left the cereal box on the table. Lock him up!'

Sam giggled as his sister started to tickle him and he was

unable to defend himself. 'Enough! Get them off!' he said. 'I'll put the cereal back in the cupboard, honest.'

Shelly removed the cuffs and put them back on her belt. 'You all ready for school then?' she asked, glancing at a clock and looking at the pyjamas they were still wearing. It was a Tuesday, and they'd usually be in their school uniforms by now. Lucy and Sam looked at each other and started to laugh. 'What? What's funny?'

'The teachers are on strike today,' said her sister, Sue, huffing. 'Union action again.'

'Oh,' said Shelly. 'I hadn't heard. Been busy with this case. It's—'

'Just be careful, whatever it is,' said Sue. 'Don't take any chances.'

Shelly had much admiration for her sister and how she'd overcome her victimisation. Not everyone did. When Sue was young, not long after her thirteenth birthday, she'd somehow made her way to a nightclub wearing makeup, so she'd look older. There, she'd met an older boy who'd taken her outside to the car park, where he'd proceeded to beat and rape her. Shelly had been just ten at the time and hadn't really understood what her sister had gone through until much later. Now she did know, she wasn't sure she'd have recovered quite as well as Sue had. In fact, she often wondered whether, if it had happened to her, she'd have turned to drink or drugs—taken a darker path. But, thankfully, her sister hadn't. She'd held it together as well as could be expected and got on with her life. Shelly would just die if anything like that ever happened to Sam or Lucy. She wanted to protect them. It was one of the many reasons why she'd decided to become a copper in the first place—that and the money, of course. Everyone had to earn a living. Or, at least, most of them did.

'Could I have a word, in private?' asked Shelly. Sue nodded and headed into the kitchen, leaving Sam and Lucy to play.

'What is it?' asked Sue. 'Have you finally broken up with him?'

'What, Jamie? No. He's… No. That's fine. I mean, it's not great. But it's fine,' said Shelly.

'Sounds fine then,' said Sue, sarcastically.

'No. I just wanted to… I'm working on this case at the moment. I'm not allowed to say too much at this stage. But someone has been murdered, and I've been helping the local DCI with it,' she said.

'Well, that's great!' said Sue. 'I mean, not the murder, of course, but the case. Look at you, moving up in the policing world.'

'Yes. That part is great, and I'm really excited about it. But the murder was pretty brutal, and it's not that far away from here, so I just wanted to give you the heads up about it. I was going to call you last night, but I knew you'd all be in bed by nine and didn't want to wake anyone. Can you all be more careful? Nobody going out alone, if possible, that sort of thing. Stay within public visibility at all times. No country walks alone—that's a *must*,' said Shelly, a bit out of breath, speaking too quickly.

'Well, okay then,' said Sue. 'We'll be careful. Thanks for putting the holy fear of God into us.'

Shelly smiled. It was just a little sisterly banter they enjoyed. 'You're welcome,' she said. 'And could you keep it to yourself, for now—we're only allowed to tell our nearest and dearest yet, to safeguard the integrity of the investigation.' Sue nodded. 'Actually, could I just pop into the conservatory and call Jamie as well, let him know?'

'You haven't told him yet?' asked Sue. 'Wow, you two *are* close. Go on then, you'd better warn your boyfriend about the psychopath on the loose.'

Shelly smiled again, but this time it was a pained one. Her sister had a point. She'd not really thought about Jamie's safety yet, what with her thoughts focussed so much on Sue and the kids. She stepped into the conservatory, flipped open her phone case, and called him.

'Hiya sugar lumps,' he said. She hated it when he called her that, and she rolled her eyes. 'What can I do you for so early int' mornin'? You wanna come ova, sweeten me tea?' Jamie was from an area of Wigan called Beech Hill, near to where the old football stadium was, Springfield Park, which had since been bulldozed over and had a housing estate built on top of it. He wasn't 'thick', as he called it, not stupid by a long chalk. He was a Heating Engineer, a tradesman with his own van and everything—self-employed. Except his social skills were... less than desirable, Shelly thought, most of the time. She'd thought it cute when she'd first met him, but it got old real soon. And now she was stuck with him, at least for now.

'No, Jamie. I do not want to *sweeten your tea*. I'm starting work soon. I just wanted to... check in. Make sure you're okay.'

'Well, of course I'm alreet. Why wouldn't I be?' he said. His accent made him sound tough to Shelly. But he really wasn't. Like most proper Wiganers, he was a little rough around the edges. Not really one for fine dining or trips to the theatre. A pie and a game of footy was more his kind of thing.

'Look Jamie, I've been working this case recently—'

'What? Being a detective now, are we? Should I call you Sherlock from now on instead of Shelly?' he said. He was just teasing, trying to be funny. But his brand of humour didn't really do it for Shelly. It never had, although there were times when she'd pretended. One of those times was not now. 'Is that why you didn't come and stay with me last night, on your birthday? I got your text saying you were working overtime. I've still got your card and present.'

'Yes. I've been working with a DCI, Jamie. Can we be serious for a moment?' asked Shelly. 'There's something I want to tell you.'

'What? You *like* him? Are you breaking up with me?' asked Jamie.

'No, of course… Well, I do like him, yeah, actually. But not like that. He's in his fifties,' said Shelly, getting exasperated.

'Then what then? You're working overtime again tomorrow, aren't you?' asked Jamie. 'I bloody knew it. You know how important this game is to me.'

Jamie had got them tickets to see his beloved football team, Wigan Athletic, at their new home at the DW Stadium. Said it was a big one, a play-off game first leg or something—not that she really knew what that was or what it entailed. But he'd said she just had to come. She didn't really like football though, wasn't that interested, although she tried her best to pretend, for his sake.

'Er, when was that again?' she asked.

'Wednesday,' he said. 'Tomorrow evening at 7:45pm! How many times have I reminded you?'

'Oh. Well, I'll try my best, but I can't promise anything now. Not with this case I'm working on.'

'But you already promised!' said Jamie. 'You can't promise

and then say you can't promise.'

Shelly paused. 'I'm sorry, Jamie. It is what it is. Can I tell you about the case now? It's important.'

'No. This game was important. That's just... *work,*' he said.

'Jamie. Just listen, will you? You can't tell anyone yet, but there's been a murder in Rufford. Just promise me you won't go out alone, will you? Don't go anywhere secluded. No country walks. Can you do that? We're doing our best to find the killer, but until then...'

Now it was Jamie's turn to pause, taking in what she'd said.

'Well, since I was going to the game with you, I'll have to go out alone now, won't I?' he said. He was a child. Shelly couldn't stand it.

'That's fine. You'll be in a crowd. Just don't go anywhere without people,' she said. 'And make sure you keep this to yourself, will you? I'll be in deep trouble if—'

'Whatever,' said Jamie. 'See you then.' He hung up.

'*You be careful too, Shelly,*' she whispered to herself, sarcastically. 'Idiot.'

She wasn't sure why she was staying with him at this point. She guessed it was comfortable, that it was too much work to find someone else, or to adapt to being single. Plus, he had his good points. He was pretty fit, and he was decent in bed. But that was about it. Those were *all* his good points. Damn. Those things don't last, she thought. They never do.

Shelly made her way back into the kitchen, where Sue was tidying a few dishes.

'You told him?' asked Sue.

'Yup,' said Shelly.

'And?'

'Kept going on about that stupid football game', said Shelly.

'There's a good chance I won't be able to make it now. Might have to do overtime.'

Sue gritted her teeth and started to laugh. 'Oh, no! What a tragedy!'

They both took a few seconds to think before Sue took out a plastic bag from the understairs cupboard.

'Your birthday gifts and cards!' she said. 'There's a few from some of our aunties, uncles, and cousins, plus ours. Hope you like them. I thought you might pop around yesterday. I wasn't sure when you'd be finished.'

Shelly took them and nodded. 'Aw, thanks, sis,' she said, giving her a hug and a kiss.

'You do anything last night?' asked Sue.

'No. I was bushed. Went straight to bed,' she said.

'With Jamie?' said Sue.

'With *Netflix*,' she said.

Sue smiled. 'Seriously though, sis. Be careful at work, eh?' she said. 'I don't know what we'd do without you.'

Shelly nodded. 'Will do. And remember what I said. I'll see you all very soon.'

CHAPTER TEN

Detective Constable Chris Lee swung by the offices of West Lancashire Borough Council on Derby Street in Ormskirk. DC Lee was short and stocky with short, shaved hair, and despite being just thirty-eight, he had an old school approach to detective work, preferred using his brain rather than a computer. The council offices were contained in a large building that might be mistaken for a block of new build flats if the sign hadn't said any different—so much so that the soon-to-be middle-aged detective had almost missed it.

Inside, DC Lee was asked to wait in a small waiting room, before a pale-looking woman appeared, sporting a tidy ponytail and round glasses.

'DC Lee,' she said, holding out her slender hand to shake. 'It's a pleasure to meet you. Now, what can we do for you?'

DC Lee stood up and shook the woman's hand. 'And you are?' he asked.

'Oh. Sorry. I'm Claire. Claire Gordon. I'm the office manager for the Heritage and Environment Team. I understand you have some questions about one of our buildings of historic interest. Please, come through to my office.'

'I don't think that will be necessary,' said DC Lee.

'Actually, it probably will be,' said Claire. 'We have so many sites it's impossible to remember them all. I'll need to look up whatever it is you're interested in.'

DC Lee nodded. 'As you wish then.'

They entered the office of Claire Gordon, with her title clearly labelled on the door, and DC Lee sat down in another chair while Claire got organised.

'Now, where is the site in question located?' asked Claire. 'And what is the nature of it?'

'It's an old icehouse just off Holmeswood Road in Rufford,' said DC Lee. 'At least, that's what I'm told it's called. It's in some kind of deer park that's now used as a grazing area for sheep.'

Claire tapped on her computer keyboard for a few seconds, and then paused.

'Oh,' she said. 'It looks like a police officer has already been in touch about this—the *Rufford New Hall Estate Outbuilding Three: Icehouse*. Someone called to try to get a hold of the key to the padlock securing it. The notes say that officers decided to cut off the padlock to save time, and we've been informed the building is currently a crime scene under investigation. Wow,' said Claire, her eyes going a little wider. 'I've been on holiday for a couple of weeks. Only just got back today. Barbados. It's a lovely—'

'Can we just focus on our business here, madam?' asked DC Lee.

Claire nodded, a little embarrassed. 'I'm sorry. I've not had time to get up to speed yet. The person who was covering for me is now also on holiday. I guess a lot can happen in a fortnight.'

'Indeed,' said DC Lee, getting a notepad and pen out. 'Can

you show me where the key to this structure is kept?'

'Certainly,' said Claire. 'They're kept in a locked storage cupboard in the basement. Come with me.'

Claire led DC Lee through the Council building, across a corridor and down some stairs to a small basement area that was being used as a storage room.

'Here we are,' said Claire. She was looking at a glass fronted cupboard that contained masses of keys on metal hooks. It was locked with a numerical keypad and Claire punched in a number and opened it up. Inside, it was all organised in alphabetical order and she soon found a hook labelled 'RNH 3: Icehouse'. Unlike all the other hooks though, this one did not contain a key.

'Miss Gordon?' said DC Lee, as she stared at the empty hook.

'It's Mrs,' said Claire. '*Mrs* Gordon. I'm married.'

'Apologies. Mrs Gordon?' corrected DC Lee. Although she wasn't that old, she presented herself something like an old spinster, which had made DC Lee wrongly presume she was unmarried. He'd pictured her with a house full of cats. 'Is there a problem?'

'The key doesn't seem to be here,' said Claire. 'Perhaps it's already been removed and disposed of, as the police had said they'd destroyed the padlock.'

'I see,' said DC Lee. 'That's unfortunate. Please could you find out and get back to me ASAP to confirm?'

'Yes, I will,' said Claire. 'Absolutely.'

'It's important,' said DC Lee.

'I understand,' said Claire.'

'Then, that will be all,' said DC Lee, as Claire closed the glass doors on the unit containing the keys, which automatically locked it again.

'Glad to be of help,' said Claire.

Before DC Lee left and went back up the stairs, he turned around and said, 'There is one more thing, Mrs Gordon. How many people would have access to this cupboard, and know the code to the lock?'

'Oh,' said Claire. 'Just about everyone who works for the Council would be able to guess the code on this thing. We use the same code for everything. The code is—'

'There's no need to tell me what it is, Mrs Gordon. Thank you,' said DC Lee. 'I'll see myself out.'

CHAPTER ELEVEN

Jonathan Walker's home these days, if he could call it that, was a modest-sized two-bedroom maisonette flat on Silverdale Road, a typical middle-class housing estate in Orrell. It had previously been one of the three rental properties he and his wife had bought, but after they separated, he ended up in this one as the tenant had just vacated. It seemed simpler to live there himself than instructing the lettings agent to find another tenant, then also having the inconvenience of finding a place for himself. So, with his wife's agreement, that's what he did.

The flat was a first-floor affair, a self-contained unit with a staircase leading straight up from the front door into a living room, kitchen, two bedrooms, and a bathroom. It wasn't that bad, but it was definitely a step down from the more spacious detached house he was used to living in. He'd spent more time here than intended, now wished he'd given it a repaint and cleaned it up better after the last tenant, who'd made a bit of a mess. Hindsight was a funny thing though. He wished he'd done a lot of things differently in his life.

The agents clearly hadn't done a great job of maintaining the flat. But in a way, the shabbiness of it matched his mood, and maybe his body too. He'd similarly neglected himself in recent years, got into a right old state. He hadn't had time for decorating and DIY shopping at B&Q, that's for sure. He was a DCI. He'd been busy, with work. And then he'd been ill. He wondered whether the state of the flat might be an outer representation of his inner world? He wasn't sure. What lay in his unconscious mind, so tantalisingly out of reach, was a continual and frustrating mystery.

He sat on the three-seater cream-coloured Emmen leather sofa him and his wife had got from DFS a couple of years ago—the one they were still paying for on interest-free credit. It was still in a nearly new condition, having hardly been used at all until recently, although there was a small discolouration on one of the arms where his wife accidentally spilled some nail polish remover just after they'd bought it—something they'd had a typically stupid argument over, one that spiralled into something else entirely. That seemed like a long time ago now they'd separated though.

Things had changed a lot, and not for the better as far as Jon was concerned, despite the fights. He was certainly using the couch a lot more these days, finally getting some money's worth out of it, what with his illness, being off work, and having months of recovery time at home. In fact, he thought he hadn't sat around and done less in his life. It had all been driving him a bit barmy, especially with living alone now and not having that day-to-day social contact anymore—until his Superintendent had called him yesterday, that was, telling him about the case.

It was still only eleven in the morning—still three hours to go before Supt Hughes would let him clock in—so he turned on the TV. His leg was jiggling, involuntarily, itching to get going. But he knew he needed to rest first to get the best out of himself. At the very least, he needed to make sure the Superintendent didn't kick him off the case before he'd even gotten started, and that meant towing the line.

There wasn't much on the telly. He'd never got properly set up when he'd moved in—hadn't been bothered—so he didn't have Sky or Netflix or anything, just a basic Freeview box. He settled on a show called 'Loose Women' on ITV. He'd never realised how mundane and yet utterly addictive daytime television could be, had always been out working, most of his life, and when he wasn't, he kept busy at home. So, he'd never seen such programmes until the last couple of years when he'd started to become unwell. He'd never watched that much telly at all really unless it had some kind of educational or research value. This certainly did not, but he had to pass the time somehow. Plus, he began to see the value in trying new things. Perhaps it would spark an idea later, help him think outside of the box. It certainly couldn't hurt.

After finishing watching the Loose Women discuss whether, "Is there an epidemic of PTSD in Britain?" Jon got up and tried a few push-ups. He managed just sixteen before stopping for a breather, then did a few sit-ups with his feet hooked under the heavy sofa for stability. He managed twenty of those, then stopped, climbing back on the couch. He had to slowly build his body back up somehow. He'd try again later. Little and often was his motto. He was getting there physically, for sure. But it was his mind that he really needed to take it slow with. He needed it fresh, ready for the case ahead, but decided a little light reading couldn't hurt. He needed to build that up slowly too.

He picked up an academic journal on a side table next to the sofa, one called *Medicine, Science and Law*, a journal that claimed to 'advance knowledge of forensic science via the publication of research articles and peer reviews'. He sometimes used Google Scholar to conduct such research, but he preferred to hold a physical book in his hands whenever possible. It felt more intimate, somehow, the smell of it, the weight.

He'd ordered this volume as there was an article in there of particular interest, one entitled, 'Forensic analysis of cigarette ash using ATR-FTIR spectroscopy and chemometric methods', which would provide researchers with the tools to identify a particular brand of cigarettes from cigarette ash at a crime scene. It was a major breakthrough for cases involving cigarette ash, which could be used to reopen a number of cold cases, he thought—including one in particular, the one so very close to his heart. He also thought it might come in useful with the current case, which was why he was taking another look.

After reading it, he lifted himself back off the sofa and stood up. He hadn't weighed himself for a while, but he knew he'd put weight on the last couple of months—probably the result of eating too much junk food and being less active than usual. He'd lost a lot of weight during his last hospital visit, and initially wanted to replace it. So, he'd allowed himself to eat anything and everything in the recovery phase, the so-called 'see-food diet'. He'd overcompensated, though, got stuck in unhealthy habits. His arms and legs were fine, but his belly was something else. He'd really felt it when going up the stairs at the police station yesterday. In a word, he'd gone too far, and now he had to reel it in.

Jon felt his energy drain as he started to move, something he'd become accustomed to—another long-term effect of meningitis—and went into the kitchen. The previous day had been particularly gruelling: his first day back on the job. Supt Hughes had been right to send him home early. He was trying to appear to be okay, but really, he was struggling.

He opened the fridge and looked inside, seeing what was left. Not a lot. He grabbed some Arla LactoFREE semi-skimmed milk and made himself a cup of decaffeinated tea, finding some custard creams in one of the cupboards, taking those too. He needed a bit of energy. He'd have to get some groceries later, if he had time.

He wasn't sure if he was even fatigued anymore, or whether it might be depression, or a lack of vitamin D. Whatever it was, he generally felt a bit shitty and couldn't really get a handle on it. Probably he'd been too focussed on his own malaise—not enough distractions. He'd fallen out with his body, for sure, no longer had any confidence in it. It had betrayed him, and he wouldn't be forgiving it in a hurry. Every time he got the slightest of headaches, he freaked the hell out, thinking the virus was coming back to finish him off, whatever it was. The doctors didn't even know. Something just kept getting up into his brain that shouldn't be, messing him up.

He'd lost the power of speech the first time, couldn't even walk. It was a long recovery. The second time wasn't much different. In the end, he'd been diagnosed with *recurrent benign lymphocytic meningitis* of an 'idiopathic' nature—meaning the cause was unknown. That's all they'd come up with after all those tests, the endless blood samples, the numerous lumbar punctures collecting cerebrospinal fluid: 'CAUSE UNKNOWN'. It wasn't that he was afraid of dying, either. What he was scared of was not finishing his life's work by catching his sister's killer, leaving them out there somewhere to attack again.

With the curtains drawn and the windows closed, the flat was beyond stale. It didn't bother Jon much though. He'd gotten used to it and didn't get many visitors. So, he thought, what the hell? He'd just leave it. Before today, he'd thought it wasn't worth opening a curtain and a window to get dazzled by blinding light, which would inevitably give him some head pains and leave him anxious for the rest of the day. *Photophobia*—light sensitivity—was yet another after-effect of his condition. And if he'd opened the windows at night, to avoid the light, then it would be too cold. So, no, he'd just left it as it was, lived with his own rancid miasma.

It was only today, when he'd been faced with going out for an extended period that he'd remembered those old sunglasses, the ones his wife had bought, and dug them out. They'd been invaluable yesterday. He didn't know how he would have gotten through the day without them, squinting his way through tasks, shielding his eyes, no doubt, as he had whenever he'd gone out previously. He'd be wearing them again, today, and every day from now on. He didn't care what people thought.

There were dirty dishes everywhere in the flat too, here and there on shelves and side tables, along with half eaten takeaways and pizza boxes piled up in the corner. If he had any excuse, it was that the two-weekly garbage collection couldn't keep up with him now he was there 24/7, and he knew it was already currently full.

He sat back on the sofa with his tea and biccies, without even so much as a small bread and butter plate to catch the crumbs, as everything was already dirty. His wife wouldn't have been impressed if she was there. She'd be getting on at him. But he kind of missed that too.

One of the few decorative elements of the flat were some photographs strategically placed on top of a bookshelf in the living room, photos of his sister, his wife, and his kids. He missed them all, dearly, and didn't know how he'd ended up like this. His sister had been taken from him when he was just a kid himself, of course—at sixteen years old—and more recently his wife had left him because of his obsession with finding Amanda's killer. It seemed everyone left him in the end, for one reason or another. He knew he hadn't been present as a husband, and as a father, for many years. But he still missed them.

His children were in their teens now. He didn't know when they'd grown up. They didn't seem interested in him anymore. The cold truth was they didn't really know him all that well. They'd visited him in hospital when he'd been ill, but he didn't remember much about that. He'd been out of his mind, hallucinating, struggling with headaches that felt like running into a brick wall as fast as you can, over and over. Not a good time. He'd become a burden to them, something he deeply regretted.

He got up and grabbed one of the photos—one containing his wife, Dawn, and two kids, Harry and Amelia. The kids were only little in the photo. They'd gone to Chester Zoo, one of their few good days. They were happier back then. His obsession had taken a back seat for a few years, before coming back with a vengeance, like an addiction he simply couldn't shake.

He looked at the photograph of his sister next, taken not long before she'd died, still in the same metal-effect plastic frame his mum put it in, the silver paint coming off, the glass all scratched up. He picked up the frame and removed the photo from the inside. The colour had slightly faded, and on the back, it said, 'Amanda Morris, aged 8, Summer 1987'. He'd seen it a thousand times before, maybe more. But he liked to look at her and see her name. She looked happy, smiling, beautiful, completely unaware of the fate that was soon going to befall her. She didn't deserve that. No one did. It was a tragedy most of the world had forgotten. But not him. Not ever. Whenever he felt the more potent regret of not saving his sister's life, which he still did, he remembered that his life would have taken a different path if he had, that he wouldn't even have met his wife, that his children wouldn't be alive. It gave him some solace, but not much.

He'd met his wife through one of the guys on the Force—Mike. She was his sister, and Walker had met her at Mike's wedding. A few years later, it would be them who were getting married, with Mike as the best man. Not that he saw Mike much these days. His old friend had lost faith in him as well, took his sister's side, as he *should.* She hadn't been happy at all these past few years, Walker knew, had been emotionally starved, shut out by him. The breakup had come as no surprise to anyone, not least Walker.

One of the reasons he thought he got so immersed in his work was so he didn't have time to feel like this. Whenever he wasn't working a case, and he had too much time on his hands, he tended to wallow and agonise over past mistakes. He grabbed his pills, the antivirals he was still taking, and swallowed one down with his cooling tea. He couldn't tell his colleagues about any of this though. He needed to appear to be strong, so they'd follow him, no matter what. He needed to be a leader and project confidence—which he did, in his job.

In private, he was a broken man, both mentally and physically.

He'd pushed his family away, and the stress of those broken relationships, combined with overworking and not taking care of himself properly, had led to a decline in health that had now become chronic. The doctor had also said if he didn't start looking after himself better, the chances of the virus reoccurring increased, meaning he could be struck down again at any time. This had a psychological effect though, as every time he got a headache, he worried it was happening again. Still, he'd downplayed his illness at work, told them it wasn't serious—even though it was. He pretended he was okay.

He went into the second bedroom, which was smaller than the main one, but still big enough for its purpose—another makeshift evidence board of his sister on one wall, and one more for the case he was currently working on. The board for his sister was significantly more complex and extensive compared to the current case, containing a variety of photographs, newspaper articles, maps, and documents, all stuck to the wall with tape, all connected here and there with red string pinned to the plasterboard walls. The board for his sister's case and the current case were also connected with one piece of string, with a large question mark, penned on the wall with a black marker, just under this line of string.

Walker stood, looking at the two evidence boards, running his fingers through his hair, exhaling deeply. He shook his head, not finding any new insights, and went to the wardrobe in the corner. Inside, it was filled with work clothes consisting of several identical shirts and suits, all off the shelf. He had little else, although there were a couple of worn-out jumpers and T-shirts, some of which he currently wore. At the bottom of the wardrobe, and also dotted around the room, were boxes of information he'd compiled over the years relating to his sister's case. He opened one of them, which had various photos on top of a pile of paper. He grabbed a few, looked through them. They were pictures of his dead sister at the crime scene, lying there with that cross of ash on her forehead, looking calm and serene. He'd gotten copies of the photos at some point. He couldn't remember when. He wasn't supposed to bring case documents home, but he'd managed to cadge a favour from someone in the evidence locker, before everything had been digitised, someone he'd told his story to, someone who'd gone through a similar thing. If he could find the person who killed his sister, once and for all, he imagined it would change everything. He'd finally be free from it and could get on with his life—make things up to his wife and kids. Until then, he'd always be wondering, chasing every lead he could get his hands on. It would never end.

He put on some work clothes and went to the main bedroom, sat down for a minute. He grabbed the landline telephone and looked at it, hesitating. His wife often didn't answer his mobile number, less and less in recent weeks, so he thought he'd give the landline a go.

'Sod it,' he said. 'What have you got to lose?'

He called Dawn's number and waited. He wanted to talk to his kids, hear his wife's voice. He hadn't spoken to any of them in a while, although he did get the occasional text reply when he tried to check in. He'd heard some schools were on strike today, so thought he'd take a shot at Harry and Amelia being off.

'Hello? It's me,' said Jon.

'What's up, Jon?' It was his wife's voice. She'd answered, at least. But she sounded annoyed and short of patience. 'Why are you using this phone?'

'Hi Dawn. I just wanted to… How are you doing?' he said.

'You called to ask me how I'm doing?' she huffed. 'How do you think I'm—' She took a moment to take a breath. 'I'm fine, Jon. The kids are fine. We're all fine. Now, if there's nothing else?'

'Yes, I just… Are they there? I wouldn't mind a quick chat if they are,' he said.

'They're at school, Jon. It's a Tuesday! It's the same old shit with you, isn't it? Goodbye.' It seemed his kids' school were not participating in the strike action after all.

'Goodbye, Daw—' The line went dead before he could even finish her name. If he didn't find his sister's killer soon, he reckoned his relationship with her would be cut off just as coldly.

Feeling jaded again, Jon lay down on the double bed for a second. It was the one they'd kept in their garage when they'd got a new, bigger, Super King Size at home. They'd kept this one just in case it might come in useful. *Useful* for what, he wasn't sure. Perhaps they'd both known, deep down, that they'd be breaking up soon.

He checked his watch: 11:37am. He still had some time to kill, so decided to take a nap, really get himself in A1 condition ready for the day ahead. He had to be prepared, give it everything he had, whilst also doing everything Supt Hughes said so he didn't get kicked off the case. And if his Superintendent wanted him well rested, then that's what he'd be. Roger that.

Jon closed his eyes, saw his sister's face burning into his eyelids, as always, and fell into a dreamless sleep.

CHAPTER TWELVE

'W hy am I still with you, Chief?' asked PC Briggs, fixing a few strands of hair behind her ear after a chilly gust of wind had dislodged them.

Walker had met her not far from the deceased's home in Rufford, outside a building declaring itself Clarkson Tiler Funeral Care on Burscough's main shopping strip, which, with Burscough being a small town, wasn't much—though it was quaint and likeable under normal circumstances.

'Because you haven't suitably pissed me off yet,' said Walker. 'Plus, I find it useful to sometimes get a female perspective, if that's not too much to offend the modern PC brigade.'

'Why would that offend us police constables?' said PC Briggs, her brow furrowed in mock confusion.

'Not... I meant "political correctness",' said Walker, not sure if she was winding him up or not. She was.

'Got you!' she said, laughing. 'No. Not at all. You blokes often miss what's staring you right in the face. Hey, wouldn't DC Riley have been expecting to accompany you with your investigations?' asked PC Briggs. 'He was originally assigned to work with you before his dentistry delay, I think. I don't want to step on anyone's toes.'

'DC Riley is a big boy,' said Walker. 'Don't worry about

him. I don't want him whining on about his goddamned teeth every two minutes. I need someone focussed, not distracted with pain and pill popping. Do you want the gig or not?'

'Yes, of course,' said PC Briggs. 'I really appreciate the opportunity. Thank you.' She looked up at the building in front of them. 'I've never been to one of these places before though.' She seemed a bit nervous. Having been a police constable himself at one time, Walker expected she'd have seen dead bodies, at least, whilst on duty—people who'd passed away in their homes and in road traffic accidents and the like—but this was something different. She'd never have been present during an up close and detailed examination like this.

'You'll be fine,' said Walker. 'You get used to it.'

Inside, they were met by the Funeral Director, and the owner of the company.

'Mr Clarkson?' asked Walker.

'Yes. We've been expecting you. Please, come this way,' said Mr Clarkson, a middle-aged man who was fast approaching old age, grey and slightly balding, but clean shaven and well groomed, wearing a creaseless black suit and tie with a white herringbone shirt.

The funeral home had been instructed by the deceased's wife and, now the post-mortem was complete—having been expedited by Walker and the Lancashire Constabulary—Tom Woods's body had been released to the family, despite the ongoing inquest and criminal investigation. Walker had been in touch with the coroner assigned to the case and had been assured that all due diligence had been done in examining the corpse. Still, he wanted to meet them at Clarkson Tiler's to discuss and review further, as he wanted to see for himself before the body was buried or cremated. Although the coroner's offices for Lancashire County Council were located a thirty-minute drive away in Preston, the coroner assigned to the case was more than happy to meet them at the body on this occasion due to the unusual nature of the case and the need for brevity.

'The Coroner, Mr Park, is waiting for you in the mortuary,' said Mr Clarkson.

'Very good,' said Walker. 'You can leave us with him, for now.'

'Sir?' said Mr Clarkson.

'This will be a private discussion,' said Walker. 'Information about the investigation is only to be divulged to those involved.'

'Of course,' said Mr Clarkson, speaking in hushed tones. 'Just let me know if you need anything then. It's just through the door on the left.'

Walker nodded and went to the door, labelled 'Mortuary', with PC Briggs close behind. Inside, Mr Park was sat down, waiting.

'Hello,' said Mr Park, seeming in a hurry, immediately standing up. 'DCI Walker?' Mr Park was a middle-aged man of East Asian ethnicity—maybe Korean, Walker thought—but he spoke with a strong northern accent that caught Walker off guard for a second. It wasn't what he'd been expecting as they'd not spoken on the phone yet and had only communicated by email. The accent didn't seem to match the face.

'Correct,' said Walker. 'Mr Park. It's good to meet you.' He held out his hand to shake, and Mr Park reciprocated.

'You too,' said Mr Park, before also holding out his hand for PC Briggs, and shaking her hand as well. 'And you are?'

'PC Briggs. I'm assisting with the investigation,' said PC Briggs.

'Okay, let's get started then, shall we?' said Mr Park.

Tom Woods's body was lying on a metallic trolley close by, covered by a black body bag. Mr Park slowly unzipped it and pulled it back, revealing the white naked body of the deceased.

PC Briggs seemed not to react at first, but seeing Tom Woods up close, with his head all bashed in, must have been a bit of a shock. It was much worse in real life than in the photos in the Incident Room and Walker noticed her starting to breathe a little heavier. The smell was probably also something new for her. All the bodies she'd previously seen would have been relatively recently deceased.

Walker looked at her, understanding her discomfort. 'You okay?' he asked.

'Yeah, course, Chief,' said PC Briggs. Walker wasn't buying it. She was trying to sound okay, but she looked far from it.

Mr Park glanced at Walker. 'Newbies, eh?' he said, smiling. 'There's a sink in the corner if you need it,' he said, 'and some tissues.'

'I'll be fine,' said PC Briggs, with the slight sharp tone of someone annoyed and trying not to show it. She'd probably imagined that kind of thing really only happened on TV crime dramas, Walker thought. Now she'd know different though and be better prepared next time—if there *was* a next time, that was. For some folks, once was enough.

Walker had already seen the wounds on the deceased's head up close when he'd first inspected it in the gloom of the icehouse, but he'd not wanted to come to any conclusions until the body had been inspected properly by the coroner, as he knew the damage could have been done when throwing the corpse down into the building. In the bright white light of the mortuary, the wounds looked even worse, but it didn't really phase him. He'd seen it all before.

'As you can see, we have some very obvious blunt force trauma to the head. There have been four blows made, creating two contusions and two actual penetrations of the skull—two on the front, and two on the back. There is extensive subarachnoid haemorrhaging present, which is basically bleeding in the brain tissue itself, and that is likely to have been the cause of death,' said Mr Park. 'The line you see on the forehead is where the skull has been temporarily removed during the post-mortem, in order to complete the autopsy.'

'Of course. And do we have anything regarding the object that might have made these blows?' asked Walker.

Mr Park seemed to struggle to contain a proud smile and then nodded before opening a drawer in a nearby desk and removing a plastic box containing a hammer and a few tools. He brought it over, removed the hammer, and handed it to Walker.

'We're pretty sure a hammer was used, most likely from an IKEA "FIXA" 17-piece tool set, like this,' said Mr Park. 'The diameter of the head of the hammer is pretty unique in the range available in the local area, at least. We tried a few, from B&Q, Screwfix, even Asda. None matched perfectly except the FIXA. We then found a small, microscopic fleck of steel located in a sample taken from one of the wounds, a particular type of steel that is exclusively manufactured in Sweden. This confirmed it.'

Walker held the hammer, turned it around in his hand. It

seemed a little lighter than the hammer he had at home, but still heavy enough to do considerable damage.

'Not many single men in IKEA,' said PC Briggs. 'I go there sometimes, in Warrington. It's all couples and families. Most of the men look like they can't wait to get out of there too. But it's a big place to get around. That is a girlie toolbox, sir. Seriously, would either of you buy this piece of shit?'

Walker shook his head and looked at Mr Park, who smiled. He then inspected inside the toolbox the hammer had come from and put the hammer back in its plastic moulded place. Inside the box were various tools—an adjustable wrench, combination pliers, a bit screwdriver with bits—but what was of most interest to Walker was the rubber casing for the hammer. It looked exactly like the item in the photo DI Riley had left him; he'd dropped by the Incident Room before meeting PC Briggs, checked for any updates, and seen the photo amongst a pile of documents on his desk. He picked up the rubber hammer head cap, which allowed the hammer to be used as a rubber mallet, and held it between his index finger and thumb.

'DI Riley found a rubber cap just like this when he inspected the sheep that had been in the Deer Park,' said Walker. 'It was stuck to one of the sheep's wool.'

PC Briggs raised her eyebrows. 'Wow. This is huge,' she said. 'For the case, I mean.'

Mr Park gave that proud smile again. 'There's something else, too,' he said, getting closer to the body of the deceased once more. 'As noted, there are two blows on the front of the head, as you can see, and this one...' he pointed to one of them, the one that had penetrated the skull, 'is the death blow. We are able to determine that these two blows on the front of the skull were made just moments before death. We have also been able to establish though, with a degree of accuracy, that the two blows made on the back of the skull, with the same weapon, were made somewhere between one to three hours before the time of death.'

'What? You're sure?' asked Walker.

'The pathologist who carried out the post-mortem examination was certain,' said Mr Park. 'He even underlined it in his report, which he rarely does.'

Walker gave it some thought. The deceased had been attacked, from behind, and had survived for several hours. Then he'd been struck again, face-to-face this time, with the same hammer, until he'd been finished off.

'Would the first two hammer blows have been enough to render him unconscious?' asked Walker.

'Yes. Almost certainly,' said Mr Park. 'He could easily have been out for a couple of hours or more with that. He may even have still been unconscious when the final blows were made, or not.'

'Was there any alcohol or drugs in his system?' asked Walker.

'No. The toxicology reports came back negative on those. He was clean,' said Mr Park.

'Any wounds on the hands or arms?' asked Walker, thinking the deceased would have been fighting for their lives if they did regain consciousness, and would have naturally raised their hands to defend themselves when the final blows were made.

'Negative again,' said Mr Park. 'There was some other damage made to the body, but these were post-mortem injuries, not ante-mortem ones, and there was nothing significant to the hands or arms anyway.'

'So, more likely to have been killed when he was uncon-scious then,' said Walker. 'Which is something, for his family, at least.' Walker looked closely at the cross mark on the victim's forehead. 'And this?' he said.

'Forensic analysis has confirmed that this marking has been made with ash,' said Mr Park, raising an eyebrow. Walker knew he had more. He was milking it.

'What is it, Mr Park?' asked Walker. 'What do you have?'

'The ash. It has been ascertained that it's from the cremated remains of... *a human body*,' said Mr Park, looking pleased with himself.

Walker stood up, tall, folded his arms. 'Can it be dated?'

'I'm afraid not. Radiocarbon dating won't tell us anything useful here. Such techniques wouldn't allow us to estimate, with any degree of accuracy, exactly how old the ashes are. All we'd be able to say is that they're the cremains of someone who died in the last five hundred years or so, if that's the case, which means they could be from a cremation half a millennia ago, or from last week. It would be pointless to run such a test, which is why I have not.'

Walker rubbed his chin, a tad disappointed at not being able to date the ash, but also pleased they had something to go off. 'Well, I'd wager more towards the last week end of things. Or at least the past few years,' he said. Now they had a real lead to narrow their search a little, and the make and model of the murder weapon. PC Briggs was right. It was a major breakthrough for the case. It was something they could work with. 'Thank you, Mr Park. This has been very helpful.'

CHAPTER THIRTEEN

Patricia Robinson fixed a lead to Choo-Choo, her white Pomeranian dog, and headed out towards Rufford Park Lane, a sudden gust of wind whipping at her face as she went. If her little Choo-Choo was good, she'd climb over the wall into the woodland near the main road where she could take the dog's lead off and let her run around a little. Her Choo-Choo liked that, sniffing around the leaves and exploring somewhere different.

It wasn't the best day, but at least it wasn't raining, as it so often did in Lancashire. It had been an unusually dry May so far until the recent rain had landed, which had been something of a blessing, but forecasters predicted storms would soon be moving in. For now, though, it was a crisp spring afternoon, so Patricia had worn a thick woolly sweater and covered it with a raincoat, just in case it started to come down again. She didn't like to be caught out.

There were four cars parked in a row on Rufford Park Lane—even more than the usual spill-over from the Rufford New Hall estate when there weren't enough parking spaces available. It wasn't something she liked to see, as it spoiled the countryside views.

'Somebody should do something about this,' she muttered

to herself as she walked by the cars, looking inside for any clues as to who the owners might be. One of them was filled with boxes of stuff that she could see through the windowed hatchback boot, and there were some empty snack wrappers on the dashboard too. She tutted. 'Messy folk,' she grumbled. 'Lazy.'

She got to the end of Rufford Park Lane and her Choo-Choo still hadn't done her business, so Patricia popped her dog onto the stone wall at the end of the lane and climbed over. It wasn't easy at her age, but at least there was a large bush in front that covered her ungainly manoeuvring. Fortunately, the wall wasn't very tall either, so she was able to sit on it and then slowly swing her legs over. She'd learned how to do this pretty well without hurting herself or causing any discomfort, having done it countless times already.

Choo-Choo hopped down next to her onto a well-trodden path that had naturally been made leading into the woods, and they moved deeper in. There wasn't much sunlight in there today—it was gloomy, for sure, but at least the trees shielded her from any wind, which was a plus.

Once they'd made it into the woodland proper, they got onto a wider path, which had been lined with felled tree trunks and a seemingly endless supply of branches, clearly marking the path for users. It was private land, owned by the local farmer, but she and all the other residents on her estate had legal access to it due to the annual fees they paid as part of their lease, something she'd recently explained to that detective who'd come to see her. She wondered for a second whether the DCI would do anything about the trespassers she'd told him about, but quickly decided it was unlikely. If she saw anyone in there who shouldn't be, she wouldn't be shy in letting them know. She'd done it before, and she'd do it again. Unfortunately, there were many possible access points—way too many to police, even if such a police force was willing to sacrifice resources for such a relatively menial offence.

It was generally fairly quiet in this particular woodland, which was why she liked to walk there. On an average day, she'd be surprised if she saw even two other people in there. It wasn't unusual not to see anybody.

Patricia had liked to stroll in this wood with her husband, Stephen, before he passed away. He was such a lovely man, so kind and considerate—and he'd never once gotten annoyed about her complaining; or at least, he never showed it. When he'd been diagnosed with cancer and had all the tests done, the doctor hadn't sugar coated it, had told them straight he wouldn't make it. It was too far gone. It wasn't fair. She felt cheated, watching her Stephen quickly fade from the man he was to one riddled with pain, mostly incoherent due to the strong painkillers he was taking. She'd nursed him at home, herself, with the help of her family—if she could call it that—and managed to keep him out of any hospice. At least that was something, anyway. He'd died at home surrounded by the people he loved.

She moved a little deeper into the woods and Choo-Choo started to pull at something poking out of the soil and rotting leaves.

'What's that?' asked Patricia. 'Choo-Choo! Leave that alone!'

Choo-Choo tugged a little harder, revealing some fabric—an old woolly hat that had become soggy and dirty.

Patricia smacked her dog on its side, not too hard, but hard enough to make it stop.

'Bad dog!' she said, annoyed. 'Dirty!'

Choo-Choo gave up on its discovery and moved on. Patricia, though, was startled as a figure walked by, his footsteps soft and featherlike—which must be why she hadn't noticed him approaching during the distraction. She didn't know who he was, but she'd seen him before—the one she mentioned to that detective—that kid who'd scared her. She could see his face a bit better this time, up close. She was sure he wasn't from her estate. She knew almost everyone on there. And he seemed to be smirking too, like something was funny. But there was nothing funny about it for Patricia. That was twice he'd frightened her now. He was wearing one of those hoodies again that she thought all the young louts wore these days, a dark green one this time, the hood up over a black beanie hat, and sunglasses—which Patricia thought odd as it wasn't even very sunny. It looked suspicious, like he was up to no good.

She glowered at him, but decided not to say anything, just in case. As he walked further away and disappeared into the trees, Patricia's disconcertion turned to anger, simmering at first and then rising up, more and more, laying on top of the annoyance she was already feeling about her misbehaving dog, along with the more substantial grief and sense of injustice she was still experiencing over her dead husband.

'They have no bloody right, coming in here,' she spat. 'Why doesn't the farmer *do* something?'

She continued on with her walk, shaking her head, quietly simmering, hoping she wouldn't see anybody else, wondering whether the young hoodlum she'd just seen had anything to do with the police visit she'd had earlier.

CHAPTER FOURTEEN

'Cremated remains?' said PC Briggs, shaking her head. 'Drawn on the body. This case just gets weirder and weirder.'

DCI Walker and PC Briggs had just got back into their unmarked police car, having now left Mr Park and the mortuary at Clarkson Tiler Funeral Care.

'You stay on the force,' said Walker. 'You'll see a lot more *weird* in the next twenty years.'

'But why would the killer draw a cross of ash on the victim's forehead in the first place, and why use the ash of someone already deceased?' asked PC Briggs. She was just talking out loud, but, despite this, Walker appeared to want to give it a shot anyway.

'Ashes to ashes, dust to dust,' said Walker. 'It's symbolic.'

'Sir?'

'It's biblical. Or, at least, it has biblical connotations. Do you know what Ash Wednesday is?' he asked.

'Yes, of course. I mean, I've heard of it,' said PC Briggs. 'Everyone has. It's a religious thing, isn't it. Doesn't it come just before Easter? Around February or March?'

'Ash Wednesday marks the beginning of the forty days of lent, which come before Easter on the Christian calendar.

It's known as the *Day of Ashes*, a day of repentance when Christians confess their sins and profess their devotion to God,' said Walker. He seemed to know a lot about it.

'Sorry, are you a Christian, Chief?' asked PC Briggs.

'Well, I was baptised as one, but no. I have little belief in God,' said Walker. 'Nor did my family. It was just something that people did back then. Many people are though, so it's prudent to know these kinds of things when you're a detective.'

'You mentioned something about this in your briefing, didn't you? I was thinking about it. Don't they put a cross of ashes on their foreheads in church?' asked PC Briggs. 'I think I've seen that somewhere. Just like the markings on the body.'

'That's correct, Constable,' said Walker, glancing across at her as he drove. 'You do know something, after all. It's during mass, on Ash Wednesday, when the priest places such ashes on worshipers' foreheads in the shape of a cross. That's what I'd been referring to. It's a reminder that we're all made from dust and that one day, we shall return to that dust. It represents mortality and penance for one's sins, and many Christians choose to keep the cross on all day.'

PC Briggs sighed. She knew she had a long way to go if she ever wanted to become a detective. 'You know your stuff, Chief. But it's been weeks since Ash Wednesday, hasn't it? So...' She was just thinking out loud again and this time Walker chose not to respond. 'Religion is a bit funny when you think about it, isn't it?'

'You could say that,' said Walker. 'But it weirdly has some scientific support, this one. When you consider that we're all made from *stardust*, to be precise, it's a great insight for its time. Remarkable, in fact.'

'Sorry, Chief. You've lost me,' said PC Briggs. 'I've never really been interested in all that space stuff. There are too many problems to worry about down here on Earth.'

'It's a bit hard to get your head around, I know, but according to science, it seems most of the elements that make up our bodies were formed in various stars over the course of billions of years. Some of them may even have been formed during the Big Bang itself,' said Walker.

PC Briggs took a few moments to think.

'You're right,' she said. 'It is pretty hard to get your head around. I'm fairly sure I came from my parents, you know, after they—'

'But the *elements* that make up... never mind,' said Walker. 'The point is that this idea in the Bible—that we are made from dust, and that we shall one day return to the dust—has some literal truth to it, at least from one angle. We can't assume one particular reading. We have to try to get in the killer's head, figure out what they were trying to say with this, what they were thinking. Is it as straightforward a religious statement as it seems, or is there some more personal meaning in play? We know the cross of ash is a major symbol in one of the key Christian festivals, the symbology of mortality and penance for sin. So, is the killer using this in a simplistic way to say the victim had to die to pay for their sins, or have they incorporated that symbol into some more elaborate personal delusional system? Are they marking them for heaven, for example, with the murder seen as a way to save them from the sins of the world? We have to consider all possibilities.'

'Well, there's certainly that, sir. Or they could just be stark, raving, bonkers,' said PC Briggs, 'and they've got the idea off the telly.'

'Or that,' said Walker. 'But I'd wager there's more to it'.

Walker accelerated as a green light turned to amber, made it through just a split second before it turned red.

PC Briggs eyed him. 'Where are we going now, Chief?' she asked.

'Back to Patricia Robinson's house on Springwood Drive,' he said. 'I want to know if her husband was cremated or not.'

PC Briggs nodded her understanding.

'Call DI Hogarth for me and get him on speaker,' said Walker. A predominantly desk-based DI, Hogarth was an expert in research and information gathering. 'Me and Hogarth go way back. I wouldn't want anybody else working on this with us.' PC Briggs complied, and the phone started to ring.

'Skelmersdale Police Station,' said the voice on the other end of the line. PC Briggs turned the speaker up to near full volume. 'What can I do for you?'

'Shannon. It's PC Briggs. Can you put me through to DI Hogarth, please?' said PC Briggs. 'If he's there.'

There was a pause. 'Will do,' said Shannon, before the line started to ring again.

'Hogarth,' came the voice on the other line.

'Hello, DI Hogarth. It's PC Briggs here. DCI Walker would like to speak with you now, if that's okay.'

DI Hogarth cleared his throat. 'Of course. Put him on.'

'Hogarth, I need you do something, ASAP. I need a list of cremations… let's say in the past five years within a three-mile radius of Holmeswood Road. We'll start there, but we may have to cast a wider net down the line,' said Walker. 'Check Kathryn Woods's father as well though. She said he was buried last year, but we need to double check that information. And then check one Stephen Robinson, also recently deceased.

We're going over to his wife now to ask her, but we'll still need it confirming as well. You got that?'

There was another pause on the line. 'I think I can probably manage that, sir,' said DI Hogarth in an unusually laid-back attitude for a DI. 'Found something, have we?'

Walker ignored the question and pushed on. 'And when you have that list of deaths, log it in the Action Book to get officers out to each and every one of those households for interviews, ASAP—barring the Robinson and Woods homes. We'll deal with those. And let me know when you have the list,' he said. 'It's important.'

'Got you,' said DI Hogarth. 'I'm on it. Talk soon.'

The line went dead.

'So, do we have an actual lead now, sir?' asked PC Briggs.

'We certainly do,' said Walker. 'From now on, we'll focus most of our resources on all those in the area who recently had a relative cremated. We need to narrow it down, get a list of possible suspects. This is how the process works. It's like a funnel: we start wide, then narrow things down.'

'I see,' said PC Briggs, glad to be learning anything from someone as experienced as Walker.

'But for now,' said Walker, 'our list consists of a list of one—that of Patricia Robinson and everyone who lives in her house, as we know she recently lost her husband, and he may have been cremated. So, let's focus on that first.'

'Can one thing even be considered to be a list, sir?' asked PC Briggs, as they rounded a corner, perhaps a little too quickly for her liking.

'No,' said Walker, without the trace of a smile. 'But for now, it's all we have.'

CHAPTER FIFTEEN

With Choo-Choo now having done her business, Patricia held the remains of some of her pooch's Forthglade Grain Free dog food in a biodegradable dog poop bag, which she'd tied and double tied, just to make sure, and then put in one more bag for good measure. She headed back to the stone wall she'd climbed over earlier as she wanted to get back home to watch some afternoon telly—the *Antiques Roadshow* was on first, and she didn't want to miss that.

She was just approaching the path that led to the stone wall, when the figure from earlier started to approach her again, coming from the opposite direction. He startled her once more, so she went off into the trees and foliage to one side, pretending Cho-Choo needed to go to the toilet, getting out of his way. She suddenly felt quite afraid, especially with the police coming around earlier looking for that burglar, or whatever it was about—but this only served to stoke her anger again, what with all the injustices in her life already.

She waited for the man to pass—if he even was a man yet—as she could no longer see him from her current vantage point, but he never did. *He must have hopped over the wall*, she thought. Except when she got back on the woodland path, she saw him, up ahead, sat on a large tree stump, one of three large trees that had been cut down after one had started to fall last winter. She would have to walk near him to get out of the woods as he was just sat there, looking at his phone, hood still up, sunglasses on. *What is he doing?* She thought, now getting even angrier, just about ready to explode, glaring at him as she approached. The man looked up, right at her, but he wasn't grinning this time.

'Who are you?' she blurted out, no longer able to keep her mouth shut. 'Where do you live?'

The man stood up, so she tried to get closer to her exit route, but they were about equidistant from it. She wished she'd gotten a little closer before saying anything now.

Choo-Choo wasn't on her lead yet and she went over to the man, sniffing around him.

'I said *where do you live?*' said Patricia again.

The man pointed somewhere, like that should explain everything.

'You have no right coming in here. This is private land, for residents of Springwood Drive only,' she said, feeling a bit better for having said something. 'I don't like seeing strangers in here. Makes me feel uncomfortable. I'm an old lady.'

The man took a few steps forward, his demeanour aggressive.

'I'm *not* a stranger,' the man said.

Patricia didn't like his attitude. She thought perhaps this was the very person the police were looking for. She'd report it when she got back. She'd had enough of their little exchange and started to walk towards the smaller path that would lead her out.

'Well, you look strange to me. Come on, Choo-Choo. Let's

go,' she said, making sure the dog was following, and she did, quickly going on ahead of her.

But, once Patricia's back was turned completely, she heard the man start to run at her, his feet no longer featherlike, now pounding over the dead leaves and dirt like sledgehammers. As she turned to look back, her heart caught in her mouth. She saw he was holding a hammer, raising it up. He tried to hit her with it, and although it was glancing blow, it was still hard enough to knock her off her feet. She fell to the ground, on her back, everything hurting, the pain in her head and back sharp and present. Her anger quickly dissipated, replaced by pure fear.

'Choo-Choo, *run!*' she said, worrying for the safety of her dog, one of the few things she had left that she really cared about.

The man staring down at her took off his sunglasses and rolled the hammer over in his dominant hand.

'Wait... I *do* know you,' she said.

'Why can't you people just leave me alone?' spat the man, twisted full of rage, before bringing the hammer down, hard, one more time.

CHAPTER SIXTEEN

Walker pressed the button on the gate of Patricia Robinson's home for a third time, this time mashing it a little harder and repeatedly. There was no answer.

'I guess she went out,' said PC Briggs.

'I suppose so,' said Walker, looking around the neighbourhood. There was a car driving by so Walker held his hand out, motioning for them to stop. It was a BMW 7 Series sedan, black, and a tanned young woman wearing Armani sunglasses put the window down a few inches.

'Yes?' she asked.

Walker flashed his ID. 'I'm DCI Walker of the Lancashire Constabulary. We're looking for the elderly lady who lives here. Do you know her?'

The woman paused, put the window down a bit more. 'Not really. But I often see her walking her dog, up and down the lane. I saw her there a few hours ago actually, when I drove past.'

'Okay. Thank you,' said Walker, nodding, before the woman drove off again. He looked around some more, smelling the air.

'So, now what?' asked PC Briggs.

'Let's take a look around,' he said, surveying the perimeter of the property.

'Sir?' asked PC Briggs.

'You know these old people… she could have fallen down the stairs, or had a heart attack, or anything. She may need our help,' he said. 'Best to check it out, be on the safe side.'

He found a spot where the ground was a little higher and he was able to haul himself up onto a wall and drop down the other side. It wasn't easy, as Walker wasn't in the best physical shape, and it wasn't pretty, but he somehow managed, his pride forcing him through it. Once down, he found a plastic panel on the wall next to the gate and flipped it open. Inside, there was a button, which he pressed, and the gate opened, allowing PC Briggs to easily enter with him.

They both started to look through some windows of the house and knock on the door, trying to find out if Mrs Robinson was home.

'Mrs Robinson!' shouted Walker. 'It's DCI Walker. Are you there?'

'Patricia,' said PC Briggs. 'Are you okay?'

There was no response.

They tried a few more times. Still nothing.

Walker tried the front door to see if it was locked. It was. He looked through the living room window one more time, using both hands to shield any glare this time. He couldn't see anything out of place and that was the kind of house she kept.

'If she was home, I'd expect the dog to be barking by now,' said Walker. 'And several hours is too long for a woman her age to be walking the dog. So, either she's gone out again somewhere, with the dog—which I suppose is the most likely scenario—or... something's wrong.'

'Shall we come back a bit later?' asked PC Briggs.

Walker thought about it. He didn't like to go on feelings, but something was telling him to investigate further. 'Let's take a little look around the lane,' he said. 'Just in case.'

PC Briggs nodded, and they started moving toward Rufford Park Lane, crossing over the road once they got to it, looking both ways for any oncoming traffic, looking as far as the eye could see. It was deserted.

'If she is out here, I'm sure she couldn't have gotten far,' said Walker, as he continued looking around, this way and that, gazing out into the Deer Park, and back down the lane. 'She's pretty old.' With experience, he'd found that carefully surveying a scene and coming up with the most likely scenario could save a lot of time, rather than just running around like headless chickens. He liked to use his brain more than his legs, and this was one of those times. He hoped no illness-related brain fog would kick in anytime soon, and he had a few heart palpitations as the thought brought on a flash of anxiety, before passing again.

'Shouldn't we be getting back or interviewing more residents?' asked PC Briggs. 'I'm sure she'll be back soon. She's probably just gone for a drive with a friend somewhere, doing a bit of shopping, maybe? Or some afternoon tea at one of those farm shop cafés they have around here? Those retired people love that kind of thing.'

'Yeah. You're probably right. I just...' said Walker. 'Just a few more minutes, just to be on the safe side.'

He looked up and down the lane again. There was a nice strip of grass down one side next to a footpath, running all the way to the bottom of the lane towards the main road. 'If I was walking a dog from this house, I'd go along that footpath there and let it do its business on that strip of grass,' he said. 'But if it didn't go, I'd keep walking, right to the top of the lane. Let's keep going, just a bit further.'

'What's that?' asked PC Briggs. Walker had no idea what she was referring to.

'I don't—'

'Shh!' said PC Briggs, putting her index finger on her lips. Walker glared at her. 'Sorry, sir,' She said. 'I just thought I heard something, that's all.'

But then Walker did hear something. It sounded like the distant sound of a yapping dog.

'Come on!' he said, starting to walk quickly, jogging here and there.

By the time they got to the end of the lane, the sound of the barking dog had gotten louder.

'That way,' he said, pointing to his left, towards a wooded area. 'It's coming from in there.'

He peeled back some shrubbery to reveal a stone wall with a well-worn path leading up to it and beyond. He had to take a moment, placed his hands on the wall, let it take his weight while some dizziness passed.

'Sir?' asked PC Briggs, wondering what he was doing.

'It's nothing. Come on,' he said.

He hopped over the wall and PC Briggs followed.

'Wait. It's stopped,' said Walker, halting and trying not to make a sound. The dog barked again. 'This way,' he said, pointing to their left again.

He started to break into a run now, with PC Briggs trailing behind him.

'This way,' said Walker. 'Hurry! I think I just saw it, over there near those bushes.'

When they got closer to the bushes, they found there was an opening at the side that led into an internal space. And there, in that space, was one agitated white Pomeranian dog, yapping away next to a large piece of white styrofoam wrapping covering something, the kind used to protect large pieces of furniture packed in boxes. Between the barking, every now and then, Choo-Choo tugged on the wrapping, but not enough to pull it out from under the several heavy rocks it was held down with. Walker removed the rocks, one by one, before taking a deep breath, preparing himself for what might lie underneath.

He carefully lifted up the styrofoam wrapping.

Underneath was the dead body of Patricia Robinson.

CHAPTER SEVENTEEN

'Oh, no,' said PC Briggs, putting her hand over her mouth. Choo-Choo tried to get closer to the body, but Walker grabbed the little dog, firmly, almost getting nipped by the little bugger, and then assertively tugged it back.

'Don't let it touch her!' said Walker. 'We can't compromise the crime scene.' The body had a cross drawn on the forehead again, with what looked like ash, just like the other case. It seemed it was the same killer.

PC Briggs put her hand down in front of Choo-Choo, dorsal side out, letting the dog sniff her. Then she got down on her knees and patted her, before picking the little dog up under her arm. Walker thought she handled the situation well and was glad he'd brought her along. She had a calming way about her at the exact moment it was needed.

'Go back to the car and call it in and take the dog with you,' said Walker. 'Mobilise a team. Now!'

'Is she dead?' asked PC Briggs. 'Shouldn't we—'

Walker had some experience with this sort of thing. He could tell with the expression on her face and the smell. She was gone. Had been for at least a few hours. He checked her pulse, just to make sure and follow protocol. He shook his head. 'Go,' he said.

PC Briggs started heading back to the car with Choo-Choo, leaving Walker crouched down next to the body. He looked all around it, careful not to move or touch anything, his eyes scanning everything in great detail. After some intense scrutiny, he spotted something sat on top of a leaf that looked out of place. It was only small, easy to miss, but it seemed man-made. He got up and tentatively took one step over, first making sure there was nothing where he was placing his feet, and crouched down again, leaning in. He squinted and focussed his eyes. He was right. Sat right there was a small piece of rubber with a hole in it. He took out a pen and an evidence bag, took the top off the pen, and delicately inserted the nib into the hole of the rubber, picking the item up, before placing it in the bag. Then, he zipped up the bag and held the object in the air, scrutinising it. It was black on the top, but red underneath, round and about the size of a generously sized blueberry. Although it looked familiar, he wasn't quite sure what the thing was yet. But, by hell, he intended to find out.

* * *

By the time Walker emerged from the wooded area, a team had already assembled and cordoned off the body with tape marking the police line. He'd seen what he needed to see, for the time being, so he let his colleagues do their jobs, got out of their way for a bit, gathered his thoughts.

PC Briggs was stood next to their unmarked car, still

holding Choo-Choo.

'I think she needs to go,' said PC Briggs.

'So, let her go,' said Walker.

'But I don't have any doggy baggies,' said PC Briggs, now seeming visibly shaken after handling the situation so well. It was just hitting her—the proximity of death and violence. Walker had seen this before in rookies. She needed to talk about something normal for a few seconds to reset herself, so he reluctantly obliged.

'Doggy bags are what we use to take leftover food home from a restaurant,' said Walker. 'What you want is a dog poop bag. Just use your initiative. I think there are some empty crisp packets in the car. Use those.'

'Yes, sir,' said PC Briggs.

'But not the smoky bacon ones,' said Walker, trying to ride the train of normalcy a bit longer. He needed her focussed and together. 'There's still a few left in there.'

PC Briggs didn't seem to know what to do, how to react. Walker knew this kind of thing—investigating a serial murder—would be new to her. She'd have to adapt, and quick, or he'd have no choice but to take her off the case. He didn't have the luxury of carrying anyone, regardless of how much potential he thought she had. From the time he'd already spent with her though, he was confident she could handle it, find some kind of rhythm. And when those important moments came, he felt he could count on her, like in the woods just now, and that was priceless.

'Can I tell my family, Chief?' she asked. 'Some of them don't live too far away, and... I'd like to warn them, you know—keep them from harm. I mean, I already mentioned the first murder, asked them to be careful, and told them to keep it to themselves, like the Supe said. But this is different. A serial killer? This is getting really serious.'

Walker took a few moments to think. He wondered if they'd done the right thing—not informing the media about the first murder yet and failing to tip Mrs Robinson off that they were investigating a homicide. If they had, she might still be alive, he thought. Then again, doing so would have risked muddying other lines of inquiry, what with the rumours that would have inevitably started flying around the local community, causing scaremongering and more. In the end, if someone wanted to kill, they'd find a victim—someone who wasn't being careful enough, or who was vulnerable in some way. And he'd had no reason to believe that the killer would kill again so quickly. That was unusual. But now was different. They had a confirmed serial killer on their hands, and one who had a quick turnaround time and who stuck to the same area—at the moment, anyway. They had a responsibility to warn people.

'Yeah. Talk to your family, by all means. We're going to need to release a press statement, ASAP, so everyone here can be more careful from now on. The people have a right to know. We need everyone in the local area to be diligent and stay in public visibility, preferably with one or more people, until we catch the killer.'

'And do you think we will? Catch them, I mean,' said PC Briggs.

'Two murders in the space of a few days,' said Walker. 'They're out of control. Someone must have seen something. We just have to find out who, and what.'

* * *

Outside Skelmersdale Police Station, a crowd of local and national journalists had gathered, ready for the statement of DCI Walker. They'd been told of a major incident in the area and the need to report to local people to warn them about the possible dangers. There was even a film crew present from ITV Granada Reports—ready to film whatever Walker was about to say.

'Are you okay?' asked PC Briggs as she and Walker exited the station. Walker had told her to stand next to him while he spoke, but he'd firmly instructed her not to say anything, and was just inviting her along for the experience. This kind of thing wasn't an everyday occurrence in Lancashire.

'Course,' said Walker, lying. He'd done this kind of thing a few times before—holding press conferences—but he'd never really got comfortable with it. He wasn't one for public speaking, wasn't especially articulate; but he got the job done. He'd learned to tolerate such tasks, at least. Or, he had before his illness, anyway.

PC Briggs held out a clipboard with a statement attached. 'They prepared this for you,' she said. 'Some of the DIs. You just need to read it.'

Walker took it and scanned through, before handing it back to PC Briggs. 'Don't need it,' he said. 'Don't worry. This won't last long. I want to keep it a bit briefer than this.'

They had officers over at Patricia Robinson's house as they spoke, talking to her family, informing them about what had happened, and what would happen next. The officers had also been instructed to tell them about the press conference they were having now as well, to assure them that no names would be given regarding the victims at the present time. Kathryn Woods, the wife of the first victim, had also been told the same.

Walker cleared his throat, ready to speak.

'Two steps to your left, please,' someone shouted, so Walker obliged. 'Er, half a step back and a step forward.'

Walker huffed and reluctantly did as requested, holding his arms out slightly to ask if he was suitably positioned now. No response came, so he began, already feeling more than a little irked. It was going dark, and some lights were abruptly put on him. It didn't help with his light sensitivity issues, what with him not wearing his sunglasses now the sun had gone down. He squinted, trying to get used to it, his annoyance levels rising. He thought about reaching into his inside pocket, grabbing his Ray-Bans, putting them back on, but decided against it. That wouldn't be a good look in front of the media for a DCI.

'Good evening, everyone,' said Walker, trying to be as professional as he could. PC Briggs stood next to him, head slightly down, respectfully, like she'd been told. 'There have been two major criminal incidents in the Rufford area of West Lancashire in the past few days. Two people have been killed in separate attacks, which we believe were carried out by the same offender. One of them, a middle-aged man in his thirties, was out walking his dog in a nearby field just off Holmeswood Road, and the other was an elderly woman, also out walking alone in a woodland area in close proximity to the same field the first victim was found in, just off Rufford Park Lane. Both were found with blunt force trauma to the head, and both were DOAs. The attacks were carried out just a few days apart. The names of the victims will be kept confidential at the present time, but our thoughts are very much with their families. We may release more information soon if we deem it necessary for the public safety, or for moving our investigation forwards. In the meantime, the general public, especially in the area of Rufford, are advised not to go out alone in rural locations, and to remain in public visibility as much as possible if they are by themselves. I repeat, residents in the Rufford area, and beyond, are advised to *not* go out alone in areas of low pedestrian traffic whenever possible. Rest assured we're doing everything we can to apprehend this dangerous individual as quickly as possible. Further to that, we'd also like to appeal to anyone who's seen anything suspicious in the area to come forward. In particular, if anyone has seen a white male in a dark coloured hoodie in or near the woods just off Holmeswood Road, adjacent to Rufford Park Lane, or knows who that person might be, this would help eliminate them from our enquiries. And if that sounds like you, please come forward. You're not a suspect at present, just a possible witness we need to talk to. That's all for now. Thank you.'

Walker nodded to the assembled crowd and started to walk back to the station with PC Briggs as cameras continued to flash.

'Do you have any leads on the serial killer?' asked one of the journalists.

Walker and PC Briggs continued on their way, without looking back.

'Does the killer have any rituals?' asked another, just before they got inside and closed the door.

'Good job, sir,' said PC Briggs. 'Very professional.'

'I have my moments. But next time you can do it,' said Walker. 'Your apprenticeship is over.'

'Thank you, but I don't think—'

'I'm joking,' said Walker. 'But I might let you say a few words, if you're good.'

'That would be great for my resume actually,' said PC Briggs. 'Thank you, sir.'

'You're welcome,' said Walker, rubbing his head. The lights from the cameras had given him some sharp head pains.

'You okay, sir?' asked PC Briggs, obviously noticing him wincing.

'I'm fine. Just a little headache. Now, let's nip out the back way and get over to Patricia Robinson's house again—have a chat with her family, see if they know anything. We need to get this investigation moving before this bastard attacks again. And judging by the duration between the two killings, we don't have a hell of a lot of time.'

CHAPTER EIGHTEEN

Robert Harris climbed the dusty, dirty carpeted stairs of his flat in Skelmersdale with his mucky trainers still on as usual, slipping his dark green parka jacket off at the top of the stairs and throwing the hood over the newel post, letting it hang there. The décor of the inside of the building matched that of the outside—a colourless ugly grey with no personality, at least, not one that any person in their right mind would want to spend any time with. Luckily, most people who knew Rob would argue he *wasn't* in his right mind, so he felt quite at home there.

Although little Robert had shown some potential at school, he'd never really taken to academic life, couldn't focus for more than five minutes, and this same issue had plagued him in adult life too, never being able to hold down an actual steady job, for one reason or another. He'd tried when he'd been in his late teens—did a brief apprenticeship as a mechanic at the local garage, which he was quite proud of at the time, stacked boxes at Poundland, that kind of thing, but nothing ever stuck. He didn't have the discipline. He also found the benefits system to be a meandering, bureaucratic mess, which was why he'd fallen into selling drugs. After all, everyone had to survive, somehow. There was always at least some demand in the drugs trade—especially in the Digmoor area of Skem; it was fairly easy work, most of the time, and there were plenty of people who needed help selling it. Plus, he really liked a good old smoke himself, so it was win-win for him.

When he'd been a bit younger, in his early twenties or so, his lifestyle had been exciting and something to envy for some folks in the local area—at least, *he* thought so. He'd had his own car, a cute girlfriend, and enough money to enjoy himself day and night. But things had changed. The party was now over, and, deep down, he knew it. He was the last one there, as usual, not wanting to go to bed. And he was getting old, already feeling the brutal aches and pains of years of self-abuse. He was tired of the lifestyle and the loneliness, but still addicted to the former, always needing a dopamine release to stave off the latter.

His girlfriend, Wendy, had left him, of course. Why wouldn't she? He was a slob, no longer as slim and fit as he used to be when they'd first met. He'd become podgy, a result of a bad diet of high saturated fats and processed foods, and not enough exercise. It wasn't rocket science, but he simply couldn't be bothered doing anything about it. At least one good thing had come out of his relationship with Wendy though, apart from the mind-blowing sex, of course, and the fact that she used to let him do whatever he wanted—and that meant *anything*, providing Wendy had been suitably 'medicated' with his range of goods beforehand. The good thing, the really good thing, was his daughter, Eve, which ironically was the result of the other good thing. Wendy had gotten pregnant before she'd left him, and he still occasionally got to spend some time with the kid, which gave him a lift, made him feel like his life wasn't completely worthless. Except when it was, which was most of the time.

Rob sat in front of his desktop PC computer—which was about twenty years old now—and turned it on. The fan sounded like an old hairdryer powering up, but at least it still worked, *just*, and if he was patient, he could still surf the Internet and get off on the increasingly niche adult entertainment he'd become accustomed to viewing. He'd have bought another computer if he could afford it, but business wasn't quite as good as it once was, and this, coupled with high levels of inflation and rising living costs, meant he wasn't usually left with much surplus cash. Plus, he wasn't working as much as he used to. He didn't have the appetite for it anymore.

Once the computer had fired up and the various programs had finished loading, he double clicked on a folder he'd called 'Fotos' and scrolled through the thumbnails. He selected a bunch of them and double clicked again, bringing them up to full screen, before scrolling through, one by one. There were various photos of Eve, with her mum, Wendy. She was only little in the first few, but later, when she got older, there were some with her new family—the Robinsons. He brought another photo up, a close up containing only his daughter, and left it there while he started to roll a joint. He opened up his marijuana stash tin, which said 'Keep Calm and Smoke Weed' on the front, and started to take out some skins. He liked looking at his daughter, but she was increasingly looking like her mother when she'd been a bit younger. This weirded him out a bit, made him think and feel things he knew he shouldn't, that he was uncomfortable with, and which confused him—if only for a second.

He sometimes wondered whether his brain had become

porous with all his drug taking or wasn't wired properly anymore. But it was too late now. He'd taken his path in life and there was no going back. He'd long since conceded that he couldn't find a way back even if he wanted to. The path he'd taken had been bulldozered over behind him, covered over by myriad housing estates, ones too new to show up on Google Street View. It was a metaphor, and probably not a very good one at that—which highlighted his decline in brain function. The point was, he was completely lost. His life wasn't supposed to turn out like this. It was just so... sad.

Now with a fully rolled joint in his mouth, as yet unlit, Rob scrolled through the photos some more and came across one containing Eve's mother-in-law—the one his kid called 'Granny'—Patricia Robinson. The old bag. Always giving him a hard time, saying he should dress better and talk properly, not walk like a teenager, and clean his friggin' car. Some people deserved to die, the stuck-up clean-freak bitch, thinking she was better than everyone else just because she had a nice house. Harris bet she'd screwed her way into it when she was younger, just like his Wendy was doing now. *Women*, he thought, *are all the same.*

There was an empty glass on his desk, already used and dirty, but he pulled it forward anyway, opening one of the drawers and taking out a ten-year-old bottle of Jack Daniel's whiskey, the one he only drank on really special occasions. There were still a good few shots left in the bottle, so he poured himself a generous triple or so, before replacing the cork stopper and stuffing the bottle back in the drawer.

He zoomed in on the photo on the screen, focussing on Patricia Robinson, until he had her full profile covering the screen. Then, he took the joint from his mouth and popped it on the desk, before raising the glass of whiskey to the computer monitor. 'To your death, bitch!' he said, with dead eyes, before glugging down a generous amount and making a satisfied noise. He started to laugh, let out a few chortles, enjoying the moment, before stopping and looking serious again.

He pulled out another drawer, but this time he pulled it all the way out, completely off its runners, putting the drawer and the random contents of it on the floor. Then, he reached inside the void, right to the back of the desk where the drawer didn't fully house and took out a roll of cash. He looked at it, took the rubber band off and flicked through it, counting the money, a mixture of twenties, fifties, and tens. It took a while to count, as there was close to two-thousand quid there. He smiled. It had finally been a good month. Maybe he'd buy that new computer after all.

He put the cash on the desk and stood up, dragging the computer monitor closer to him at groin height, just a few inches away. After popping the joint in his mouth, lighting it, and taking a puff, keeping it there, he pulled down his trousers and well-worn boxer shorts and began to pleasure himself. He stared intently at Patricia Robinson's face on the screen, hate in his eyes. 'Take that, bitch!' he said, as he continued tugging. 'You're no better than me, bitch! To your death!' He was outside of himself now, distracted from the tedium and loneliness of his life, if only for just a few seconds. And then, just as quickly, it was over.

He pulled up his pants and puffed on the joint some more, took a deep inhale, holding it there, letting it burn his lungs, before looking up and releasing the smoke. There was a half roll of toilet paper conveniently placed on the desk, ready for such occasions, so he grabbed some and wiped everything down.

'What's wrong with you, Harris?' he said to himself, having a rare moment of clarity, realising what he'd just done. He breathed a heavy sigh, not feeling that good about it—and not really getting the hit he'd craved either. He wished he'd used Wendy's photo now as a visual aid, like he had so often, and so successfully, in the past. He thought he'd call her, hear her voice, maybe give it another shot that way. He grabbed his phone, rang her. Nothing. She rarely answered his calls at all these days, except when she wanted something like weed, or something else—which was why he thought she'd answer this time. He knew she was almost out of ganja, waiting for more. But she wouldn't answer if she was with *him.* He put the joint down in an ashtray as the smoke started to burn his eyes, and coughed up a lump of phlegm, slowly and carefully spitting it into the tray next to the reefer without contaminating it.

Rob then went through the contacts on his phone some more, trying to find someone he could chat with. He didn't like to admit it, not even to himself, but he was lonely, needed someone to talk to. All he really had in there were clients, so he called one, someone who'd been a good customer over the years, who he'd gotten to know a bit.

'Hey, Spud. It's Rob. How's it—'

'Rob. I'm taking a bit of a break at the moment. Chest is all messed up,' said the guy called Spud.

'Aw, come on, man! If it's money I have loads of the stuff. Come over and I'll give you a free hit of somethin'. I have some stuff you don't need to smoke too at the minute,' said Rob. 'Or we would just have a drink?' He knew he was coming across as a bit needy now, a bit desperate, but he didn't much care.

'Not now, Rob. But thanks.'

Spud hung up and Rob threw his phone onto the sofa cushion in frustration.

'Bollocks to you then,' he said, grabbing the spliff and joining his phone on the sofa, lying back, and taking another long, slow inhale.

CHAPTER NINETEEN

Having been informed of the death of her mother-in-law, Patricia, by two uniformed police officers, who'd now left, Wendy had just gotten off her phone. She'd told a few friends about it—what had happened. She'd needed to get it off her chest a bit, to someone other than her husband, who'd been typically unemotional and taciturn after being informed about his mother's death. It was like talking to a brick wall, and a cold one at that. Why couldn't he just talk to her, tell her what he was feeling? Why couldn't he ask her how *she* was feeling? He had his good points of course—that was why she'd married him. But this emotional stonewalling was driving her nuts, and it had gotten worse in the past couple of years. He'd never been prepared to listen to the very real complaints she had about his mum. He'd never taken her side, always in the middle. And now Patricia was gone, he never would take Wendy's side. He'd put his mother up on a pedestal, eulogise her. That was just what people did with the dead.

Wendy wasn't sure she could stand it, at the funeral and all—the praise, talking about Patricia like she was perfect, like they always did at funerals. Still, she'd have to get through it somehow. She'd have to bite her lip and pretend she was sad that Patricia was gone, even if she really wasn't. Her mother-in-law had made her life hell over the past couple of years, complaining and criticising her, arguing with her. As if her life wasn't already stressful enough, bringing up a young child and having to do that in someone else's house with their own rules. How was it even possible to keep a house spotless when you have a toddler? It was impossible! But Patricia had expected her to do so all the same. Well, she was gone now, and Wendy thought it was probably for the best, once the dust had settled—and settle it would once she'd been gone for a while, both literally and figuratively: after all, it was Patricia who'd been doing all the cleaning.

At least they could get on with their lives and start to enjoy themselves again, Wendy thought. It was actually quite a relief. Patricia hadn't been enjoying life anyway—she'd been a grumpy, sour-faced old lady who was just waiting to die anyway. Once they'd all gotten over it, they'd see it was for the best, in a utilitarian sense. Sometimes, things had to get worse before they got better.

Wendy had been talking on the phone in the garden, taking a breath, finally able to smoke a little weed there without her mother-in-law's prying eyes. She needed it, to relax. It was her way of self-medicating. Feeling better, she came back inside and popped a mint in her mouth—not that this would cover anything: her hair smelled of smoke, her clothes, everything. She often just ate it, but with Patricia gone, she figured, what the hell? It would be fine to have a little smoke. It was more enjoyable that way. She'd have a quick shower, wash it off before anyone noticed.

She came back inside, but her husband was now in the kitchen, pouring himself a shot of whiskey. He wasn't a big drinker, but he did like a tipple now and again.

'Just to take the edge off,' he said. 'Just the one.' He took a sip, and then some more.

'I'm going to have a quick shower,' said Wendy. 'I need to feel human again.'

Carl nodded, but then got a whiff of the weed as she was walking past.

'What's that?' he asked. 'Are you back on that shit?'

She wasn't going to be able to deny it and decided not to even try. 'I'm sorry, I... I had an old spliff left, and I really needed something to help me calm down, just like you're doing now with that whiskey.'

Carl looked at his glass. He'd normally be furious with her, for going back to her old life—one of drug taking and partying. But these were exceptional circumstances.

'Fair enough,' he said. 'As long as it's the last one. Don't be getting any more now.'

Wendy nodded. 'Course not,' she lied. 'I didn't even know I had it. I just found it in my jewellery box. I was looking for the broach Patricia gave me.'

'And did you find it?' asked Carl, as she wasn't wearing any broach.

'Yes. I'm going to put it on after my shower.' She wasn't, of course. She'd just made that up. But she would now.

Wendy put a hand on her husband's arm. She knew he was hurting and wanted to make him feel better somehow.

'We'll get through this,' she said. 'You'll see. Things will get better, in time.'

There was a cold, uncomfortable silence before Carl broke it. 'What do you mean? My mother is *dead*. She's been murdered. How on Earth are things going to get better after this?'

He'd taken it the wrong way, like he always did. 'I didn't mean... I just meant... Look, maybe something good can actually come out of all this. We'll get half the house, sell it, and be able to start a new life all by ourselves, just like we wanted. You know it's been tough here. And you could use some of that money to really get your new business up and running too. You'll see, things will get better once all of this starts to pass over.'

'*Pass over?*' said Carl, starting to raise his voice. 'How can you think about money at a time like this? She only just died! Are you completely stoned?'

'I'm just trying to be practical,' said Wendy. 'We're parents. We have a child to think about. Look, I'm gunna take a shower. Let's talk about this later. I don't think this is a good time.'

Wendy left the kitchen and started to go upstairs, but Carl followed, right on her tail.

'You're glad she's dead, aren't you?' he shouted. He'd completely lost it now. 'You hated her. She was right about you. You're nothing but a money-grabbing whore.'

Wendy turned around, halfway up the stairs, fury rising. He'd gone too far this time. 'What? She said *that*?'

'Not in so many words,' said Carl. 'She had a bit more class than that. But yeah. She thought you married me because our family has a bit of money.'

Wendy continued to climb the stairs, right to the top, with Carl following. He grabbed her, by her blouse, stopping her from going any further.

'Well? Didn't you?' asked Carl.

'Didn't I *what*? Marry you because you had some money? Of course not. What do you think I am?'

'A money-grabbing whore,' said Carl, through gritted teeth, clearly unable to stop himself now, grief and anger probably overpowering any rational part of his brain, making him unable to accept what Wendy had said.

Wendy slapped Carl in the face, hard, making him lose his balance for a second. She was furious now.

'You are. You're glad she's dead,' said Carl again, in a calmer tone this time, which somehow sounded even more aggressive.

'And why shouldn't I be glad?' she said. 'She made my life a living hell!' Now Wendy had gone too far too.

Carl took in a deep breath, one of shock, and held it. He looked in disbelief at what she'd just said. He probably hadn't meant his accusation, hadn't really believed she was that callous, had just wanted to hurt her. But she couldn't take it.

'I… need some time alone,' said Carl, letting go of Wendy, defeated.

Wendy began to panic. He'd done this before, threatening to leave her—using his power. He knew she had nothing without him. 'And what does that mean?' she asked, eyes wide, shaking. Carl was still stood at the top of the stairs, a couple of steps from the top, while Wendy was on the landing, on firm ground.

'It means… I don't know what it means,' said Carl. 'Maybe I don't want to be with you anymore. Can I just deal with my mother's death first? Can I *do* that?'

Now Wendy was really entering panic mode. Her heart was pumping, fast, her thoughts spinning. Everything was going foggy. She felt out of control. If Carl left her before he got the inheritance money, she'd get nothing. They were broke. And even if he did get it, and then he left her later, she might still be left with nothing. These rich families were good at dodging taxes and the like, good at making the system work in their favour. He'd find a way, somehow. She'd be back living in Digmoor in Skem, or somewhere equally depressing and dangerous, without a penny to her name. God knows what she'd do. She'd probably end up working the streets or selling drugs with Rob. Her life would be over. Best case scenario, she'd get some shitty job, packing boxes at Asda or cleaning toilets or something, maybe she'd have to get a second job too, kill herself working just to be able to raise her daughter, just like her mother did. She couldn't allow that. That wasn't the life she wanted for her little girl, or for herself. She'd finally escaped that life. She couldn't go back. She didn't know what she was doing. Her panic spiralled and she put out a hand, ready to push Carl. Maybe, in his grief, he'd fall down the stairs, hit his head on the newel post and accidentally die. Then, any inheritance would come to her. Her daughter would be saved. She'd live a good life.

Wendy wasn't thinking straight at all. Her thoughts were racing, going into overdrive. She was just about to summon the courage to shove Carl when her daughter appeared at the bottom of the stairs, looking up at her.

'What's happening, mummy?' she asked. 'Why are you shouting?'

Carl turned around. 'It's nothing, darling. We're just a little upset about Granny, that's all.'

'I'm sorry,' said Wendy, taking a deep breath, her daughter's beautiful face helping her calm down. 'I'm sorry about everything.'

CHAPTER TWENTY

Walker and PC Briggs sat in Patricia Robinson's sitting room once more. Choo-Choo was lying next to the couch they were on, not seeming very happy in her periodic whining, and they were faced with the grieving family of Mrs Robinson.

'Okay, so we have Carl Robinson—you're the son of Patricia. And Wendy Robinson, who is your wife, Carl, and your six-year-old daughter, Eve. And Ronda, I understand you're Carl's sister and Patricia's daughter,' said Walker. He was writing everything down in his notepad, making sure nothing was missed. 'Correct?'

'Yes. But Eve is not my daughter,' said Carl, who still looked a little shaken.

'Daddy?' said Eve.

'Yes, I'm your daddy, sweetheart,' said Carl, touching the side of her face, reassuringly. 'But I'm not your biological father, that's all. Robert is.'

'Robert?' said Walker.

'Robert Harris,' said Carl, in a tone that suggested they didn't get on.

'Divorced?' asked Walker, looking at Wendy.

'Never married,' said Wendy. 'It was a mistake.'

Eve now looked at Wendy. 'Mummy? Am I a mistake?'

Now it was Wendy's turn to touch Eve, gently on the back this time, pulling her close. 'You are *not* a mistake, darling. Never. You're the best thing that ever happened to us.'

'Then it wasn't a mistake, meeting Wobert?' asked Eve, butchering her biological father's name, something Carl seemed to take great pleasure in.

Wendy thought about it. 'It was a mistake, but a lucky one,' said Wendy. 'Because we got you.'

Eve seemed happy enough with the explanation, so Walker took the opportunity to move things on.

'We're going to need to speak to Robert. Someone will get his details when we're done here. One of our officers will call. Now, has there been anything unusual you've noticed in the past few days? Any odd characters hanging around? Anything that Patricia might have said?'

Carl shook his head. 'Not really,' he said. 'Not that I can think of.'

'Anybody?' asked Walker. 'Anything at all, even if it seems insignificant.'

Ronda was very quiet, upset, but Walker thought there might be something else too. She seemed uncomfortable about something but was holding back.

'Ronda?' he asked. 'Do you have anything to say?'

Ronda shook her head, gripping on to a tissue, and wiped her nose.

Walker took a deep breath. 'Okay then. If you think of anything at all, please get in touch. We're very sorry for your loss, and we'll do everything in our power to catch whoever did this.'

'I'll show them out,' said Ronda, getting up, so Walker and

PC Briggs followed her to the front door, leaving everyone else in the sitting room.

Ronda opened the door and stepped outside with them, closing the door behind her so there was just a small crack still ajar, allowing her to get back inside without getting locked out.

'There is something,' she said, in a hushed tone, 'but I didn't want to say in front of the others.'

'What is it?' asked Walker, moving in, getting closer. Ronda hesitated, opened her mouth to speak, but stopped. 'If you know something, Ronda, you must tell us so we can catch your mother's killer.'

'Well… I heard them arguing, one day—mum and Wendy. Something stupid about toys not being laid up all the time. They had words. Anyway, when it was over, Wendy came through the hallway to go upstairs, and on her way, I heard her mutter something while I was in the sitting room with the door open. She mustn't have known I was in as I got back while they were in the middle of their argument.'

'Oh. And what did she say?' asked Walker.

'She said… "*when are you going to die, you stupid bitch!*", said Ronda.

'I see,' said Walker. 'I'm sure it's nothing. People get upset and say awful things, sometimes. Have you talked about this since? Cleared the air?'

'No. I don't like to get involved in these things,' said Ronda. 'But I didn't like it. I've hardly spoken to her since. I know my mother could be difficult sometimes but… she is… she *was*… my mum.' Ronda started to get upset again.

'Well, thank you for telling us,' said Walker. 'It's not easy, I know. If there's anything else, please don't hesitate to get in touch or drop by the station in Skelmersdale. We must go now, I'm afraid, as the first twenty-four to forty-eight hours of any investigation are vital.'

PC Briggs put a hand on Ronda's back, consoling her. 'It's going to be okay,' she said. 'If there's anything we can do, just let us know.' Ronda nodded, appreciatively.

'Actually, could we get the details of Mr Harris now?' asked Walker, if you have them.

Ronda nodded, took out a mobile phone from her pocket, and searched through it. She stopped on the contact details for Robert Harris and showed the screen to Walker, who wrote the number down in his notepad.

'I never use it. I only have it at all because my mum said I should keep it in case of emergencies,' said Ronda. 'He's really rough. Unlikable. I think he's a druggie.'

'I see,' said Walker. 'Well, thank you.'

Ronda nodded again and quietly moved back into the house, closing the door behind her.

They waited a few seconds until she was completely gone and started to walk away. 'What are you thinking, Chief?' asked PC Briggs in a hushed tone, once they'd got a little distance. 'You think the wife is involved in this somehow?'

'Well, anything is possible at this stage,' said Walker. 'We can't rule anything out. Come on. Let's go find this Harris character. See what he's all about.'

* * *

'Mr Robert Harris?' asked Walker. They were in Digmoor,

one of the less desirable places in Skelmersdale and an area where police officers were often called out to due to the higher than average crime rates.

A man was stood at the door of a prefabricated reinforced concrete house, one of many in the local area which many people thought were an eyesore—ugly, outdated buildings that showed no consideration towards aesthetics. But they were cheap, so people like Rob Harris could at least afford a place to live. This one looked like a rental rather than an owner-occupied property though. It was a mess, and house owners tended to take more pride.

'Yeah, I'm Rob,' said the man. He looked like he hadn't shaved or washed in days, and he wore some stained grey sweatpants and a T-shirt with a picture of a marijuana leaf on it. His place stank, or he did, or both. 'What is it now?' He glanced down at his T-shirt and rolled his eyes. 'Don't you have nothin' better to do? I'm tired of this shit.'

'Mr Harris. I'm afraid we have some bad news,' said Walker. 'It's your daughter's grandmother. I'm afraid she's been the victim of a brutal attack. She's dead, Mr Harris.'

Rob didn't seem to know how to react to such news. He appeared to grapple with it, trying to find a suitable reaction, but then visibly gave up, shrugging it off.

'And I'm supposed to care because?' asked Rob. 'Didn't like the woman. Posh bitch. Snooty as hell.'

Walker had seen most responses when giving people this kind of news, but this was a first, even for him. It was cold in the extreme. He glanced across to PC Briggs, raised an eyebrow. 'Well, we just thought you should know,' said Walker. 'And we're currently questioning everybody involved with the family anyway, as a matter of course. May I ask what your current involvement is?'

'With that family? Not a lot,' said Rob. 'My ex sometimes asks for a few favours. And I see my kid, Eve, from time to time. I don't like it over there much though. They're all a bit stuck up.'

'May we step inside for a moment, Mr Harris?' asked Walker.

'Er, I'd rather you didn't,' said Rob, looking around the neighbourhood. He had some wired earphones dangling down from an iPod Shuffle that was clipped to his T-shirt. Walker followed the wires down and looked at the earbuds.

'Could I see those for a minute?' asked Walker.

'What? These?' said Rob. 'I didn't nick it, for Christ's sake. I got it at a car boot sale.'

'It's fine. I just want to take a look,' said Walker. 'Would that be okay?'

Rob huffed. 'Whatever. Nothing to hide!' he said, unclipping the device and handing the lot to DCI Walker.

Walker looked closely at the earbuds. There were little soft earbud tips attached to them—about the size of a *generously sized blueberry*, rubber, or silicone maybe. He pulled at one and it came off, with ease.

'Hey!' said Rob. 'Easy. I need those.'

It was definitely comparable to the one Walker found near the dead body of Patricia Robinson. They were undoubtably common these days, even if they didn't feature in Walker's world. All the kids seemed to be wearing them, insulating themselves from the outside world. But that was two strikes on the man now—those being his connection to the family and the wearing of earbuds very similar to those found at the crime scene. Walker didn't like coincidences and his policing whiskers were starting to twitch.

'Do you like to wear hoodies, Mr Harris?' asked Walker.

'What's it to you?' asked Rob. 'Are you gunna ask to see me kecks as well next?'

He seemed young enough to wear that kind of clothing, definitely seemed like just the dodgy type who might want to conceal their face with a hood. Walker at least pegged him as a possibility for their unknown hoodie guy, especially given his connections to the Robinson family. Perhaps he'd thought Patricia had seen him up to no good in the woods, recognised him. It was certainly worth considering.

'Mr Harris, we're going to have to take you in for further questioning,' said Walker. 'To help us with our inquiries.'

'I ain't going nowheres,' said Rob. 'I've done nothing wrong.'

'I'm not asking, Mr Harris. If you refuse to cooperate and don't come willingly, we do have the powers to detain you for questioning,' said Walker. 'Please, come with us.'

'This is ridiculous,' said Harris. 'Arseholes. You're having a laugh.'

'Come now, Mr Harris,' said Walker. 'Any more of that and we'll have to cuff you.'

'This is bollocks,' said Rob. 'Just because I live in this shithole and like a bit of weed, you assume it's me that's done it. This is... discrimination, or something.'

'It is what it is,' said Walker. 'You're coming with us.'

'Get your keys and lock your door, Mr Harris,' said PC Briggs. 'This might take a while.'

CHAPTER TWENTY-ONE

Now sat in an interview room at Skelmersdale Police Station, Robert Harris fidgeted with a plastic cup filled with water that the staff provided. His right leg jiggled up and down nervously under the table while DCI Walker and DI Riley entered and sat opposite him.

'Where's the chick?' asked Rob. 'She was alright.'

'PC Briggs will not be attending this interview,' said Walker. 'This is Detective Inspector Riley.'

PC Briggs had to attend court for a couple of hours to provide evidence in a GBH case—something that had been arranged before she'd been assigned to work with DCI Walker—so DI Riley had joined him for now, although Walker had made it clear that PC Briggs would continue shadowing him until the case was over, once back, for continuity. He didn't like to change staff midway through a case, felt it was detrimental to the chances of success. Plus, she'd been very helpful so far, and didn't want to be without that.

'Mr Harris,' said DI Riley, meeting him for the first time.

'Are you sure you wouldn't like your lawyer present for this, before we start?' asked Walker. Harris had declined to call a lawyer when asked, had rejected to call anyone at all.

'Lawyer? I don't have no goddamned lawyer!' said Rob.

'I can barely afford a place to live. I'm two months behind on my rent.' He stank of booze and weed and other bodily stenches, but the interview room didn't have a window and the air-conditioning was still off in May. There was no escape.

'You have the right to free legal advice, Mr Harris. We have a duty solicitor available, if you'd like?' said Walker.

Harris took a moment to think about it. 'Don't need it,' he said. 'Ain't done nothin' wrong.'

Walker and DI Riley got settled the best they could, and Walker turned on the recording device.

'This is May 18th, 2023, at... 4:17pm. Can you tell me your full name please?' asked Walker.

'Youse already knows mi name,' said Rob, his scouse twang getting more pronounced as his nervousness increased.

'For the record,' said Walker.

Rob leaned forward in his chair, a bit aggressively. 'It's *Robert Harris.*'

'Is it okay if I call you "Rob"?' asked Walker. He had to remain professional, even if there was a possibility he was looking into the eyes of a killer, or an accomplice to murder. It was early days though, and there was very little evidence of anything like that just yet. The man *was* just a suspect for now. But if it did turn out to be him, he knew the man couldn't be Amanda's killer too. He was far too young for that, which made Walker hope it wasn't him.

'Yeah,' muttered Rob. 'Knock yerselves out.'

'Rob, just before this interview myself and PC Briggs detained you for questioning pertaining to the murder of your ex-girlfriend's mother-in-law, one Patricia Robinson. As things stand, you are a person of interest and a potential suspect. Have you any idea why that might be?'

'No comment,' said Rob, huffing.

Walker held up Rob's earbuds, which were now encased in a sealed and labelled transparent plastic evidence bag, and then placed them on the table in front of him, pushing them over to Rob's side.

'Do you wear these often, Rob?' asked Walker.

Rob shrugged his shoulders. 'No comment.'

The one thing no attending interviewer wanted was to have a *no comment* interview, but Walker didn't get the impression Mr Harris could keep that up for too long. He didn't seem to have the discipline or the legal guidance to do so.

'Can you see the little silicone caps on the end of these earbuds?' asked DI Riley, who'd been told to feel free to get involved in the interview where he saw fit, as he also had some experience in this area.

'What is this?' asked Rob, his curiosity now getting the better of him.

'Rob, one of these silicone caps, from a pair of earbuds just like these, were found next to the dead body of Patricia Robinson, who just happens to be your ex-girlfriend's mother-in-law,' said Walker. 'Now, if we compare the one found, with the ones you were wearing, what do you think we'll get?'

Walker knew they weren't identical, but he was going off on a hunch—that Rob had discovered a missing silicone cap when he'd got home, shortly after killing Mrs Robinson, and had thrown out any other caps matching this, bought some replacements that were different. They could certainly look into his online shopping records to try to verify this, if necessary, or look at his bank statements to examine any in-store purchases.

'You'll get sod all. Or... Look, lots of people wear those

things. It could be anyone. No comment,' said Rob, quickly backing up, seeming like he was beginning to panic, perhaps suddenly realising how much trouble he might be in.

'We're going to get a warrant to search your place,' said Walker. 'Do you have anything else to say at the present time?'

'No,' said Rob.

'Then that concludes this interview,' said Walker, turning the recording device *off*.

'We just needed help with our enquiries, Mr Harris,' said Walker. 'Due to the serious nature of the crime, the fact that we found you wearing a similar accessory to that found at the crime scene, and what with you possibly fitting the description of another person of interest we have, you gave us no choice but to take you in so we could investigate further. You'll now be held in a cell for at least twenty-four hours, while we look into this. Thank you.'

'You won't find nothin',' said Rob. 'Weren't me. Loads of people wear those things.'

'Well, that's our job to find out,' said Walker. 'If you've done nothing wrong, then you don't have anything to worry about.'

Rob's leg continued to jiggle up and down, suggesting that he did have something to worry about, and Walker noticed.

'Are you sure there's nothing else you want to tell us?' asked Walker. 'Should I put the recording device back on?'

Rob shook his head, but Walker got a strong feeling he was hiding something.

* * *

Now at Robert Harris's home again with the necessary warrant, Walker and DI Riley attended the search with several other investigators, while PC Briggs stood outside, guarding the building, having only just returned from court and not yet got up to speed. A team of officers also canvassed the area, attempting to gather further information about Harris and his activities.

'Anything?' Walker asked, having found nothing of any use himself yet.

One of the officers held up a bag and pulled out some smaller transparent bags of cannabis.

'There's quite a bit,' said the officer. 'Too much for personal use alone, I think. Was probably doing a bit of dealing.'

'I want clothes that look recently used, anything with a bit of mud on. Pictures of the soles of footwear, and any earbud listening devices or silicone earbud caps,' said Walker. 'Look under the sofa, the bed, behind furniture, at the back of drawers, anywhere he might have dropped some of those things. They're only small, and easy to miss on this charcoal-coloured carpet.'

'There's nothing like that so far,' said DI Riley. 'Although his taste in music is a bit dubious—Bob Marley, John Martyn…'

'Well, there's no crime in that, DI,' said Walker, getting a bit annoyed at the distraction. 'Keep looking.' They were running into a dead end. They'd normally have to release Harris if they didn't find anything soon, but finding the cannabis was a major plus. This would allow them to detain him for longer, if they so wished. He could be charged for that.

PC Briggs entered the small abode, climbing the steep stairs, a little out of breath, but not much.

'Chief. One of the officers was talking to one of the

neighbours. They didn't like our Mr Harris much. I have their notes,' she said, looking at a notepad. 'Said he was "a bad egg" and went on to explain that... *he once bragged, down at the local pub, after a few drinks, that he knew people who could get rid of someone for the right price.'*

'Is that so?' said Walker.

'It is,' said PC Briggs.

'Well, that's three strikes now,' said Walker. 'Charge him for the possession of a Class-B drug and keep him there a bit longer. We need to follow up on this. There might be something here. Even if he's not held until the court hearing, we can still keep closer tabs on him once he's out on bail. And we can also force him to give up his passport too, so he can't run. This is good. Really good.'

'I'll call it in and get him charged,' said PC Briggs. 'And sir...'

'Yes, Constable?' said Walker.

'It's good to be back.'

CHAPTER TWENTY-TWO

Alan Smith sipped on his PG Tips tea with milk and no sugar and let it warm his chest for a few seconds, before making a contented sigh. This kind of thing was the closest he got to happiness these day—a second or two of superficial pleasure. But he'd take it anyway. He needed it.

He was sat at his Victorian pedestal desk with green faux leather inserts on the work surface, the one that had already been there when they'd bought the property. They'd negotiated hard to keep it, that and a few other items—a Chippendale style dining table and chairs with leather seat pads, and a Palais de Versailles Damask sofa set with a hand carved mahogany frame and buttoned upholstery. They'd been quite proud of their bargaining skills at the time, getting a below market price for the flat and its contents. The desk was the main triumph though, worth well over a thousand pounds.

It was at this very desk that Alan conducted most of his work and spent the majority of his time, trading the financial markets—mostly foreign exchange, buying and selling currencies. He was a swing trader. Unlike many wannabe traders, those who came and went, he used naked candlestick charts without the indicators that so many online trading 'gurus' pushed, instead using his time to carefully draw support and resistance lines and trade off of these. It wasn't rocket science, but it was effective over a long timescale, *if* one didn't waver and used sound money management practices. And he did. He'd decades of experience by now. It would have set him up for an early retirement too, if he didn't have to plan for full-time care for his disabled daughter when they got too old to take care of her, and if his ex-wife hadn't taken half of everything *he* had earned. But he wasn't working now. He already had some trades in motion for the day and wanted to see how they'd play out first. So, he was taking a well-earned break, doing something else.

The *something else* he was doing was logging in to a new Facebook account he'd made, one that didn't contain his own name or photo, wasn't linked to his primary account in any way. His wife didn't know, of course—about the account or that he wasn't working. But that was okay. He'd made time by working faster, so this was *his* time. He'd earned it. And she didn't need to know about the account. It would just make her worry.

Alan had opened a brand-new email account with another provider called Zoho Mail and used this to make the new Facebook account. It was easy. He'd called himself 'Harry B.', for no particular reason other than anonymity, and had used a free website to create an avatar for his profile picture on the account. His avatar had a young feel to it, like someone might use if they were in their early twenties—something fun and colourful, not taking themselves too seriously: a profile of a cartoonish, almost anime-style face. He'd not put a massive amount of thought into it, but some. He wanted it to at least seem plausible, not to raise any suspicions. The end result was the kind of wacky thing that the young folks did these days. Or, at least, he thought it was.

Now logged in to this new account, he visited Nick Hawley's Facebook page and slowly scrolled through it. Although Nick had died two years ago, his page was still being maintained and moderated, something Alan had known some time ago, but he hadn't been able to view all of its content then. But now that 'Harry B.' had gotten his Facebook Friends Request accepted by whoever was moderating Nick's account, he was finally able to see the full material of the page for the first time—a page that he'd so often returned to over the past couple of years, just to see the profile photo of Nick Hawley. He didn't know why he hadn't thought of it sooner: making a fake Facebook account. It seemed obvious now. Still, he'd been busy, overly stressed. He hadn't really had a minute to himself.

Looking through the account properly, he could see that over the past two years, various people had commented on the page, and although 'Nick' had replied to some of these, it was clear from the dates that someone else was replying on his behalf, talking about Nick in the third person. It couldn't be Nick. He was dead.

After reading some more of the replies to these comments, it soon became clear that the person moderating the account was Nick's mother. If Alan, A.K.A. Harry B., went back two years, to the time when Nick had died, most of these comments were a variation of 'RIP Nick', or 'I can't believe he's no longer with us!' More recently, the comments had naturally become sparser and less frequent, but there were still a few, keeping Nick alive in spirit, at least. But that made

Alan angry—that people were still thinking about Nick in that way. He didn't want him to still be alive in spirit, or in any other way. He hated him for what he did. There were no comments about how he'd almost ran them over, about how his irresponsible drinking had ruined three lives. Alan's daughter, Amy, had already been the victim of one road traffic accident, an incident that left her in a wheelchair, and that coupled with her diagnosis of ASD already made things more than difficult. So, to almost be hit by yet another irresponsible driver, just when she'd been getting used to going back outside near moving vehicles, was unforgivable. She hadn't really been outside again since. She got stressed and anxious every time they tried to venture anywhere with her. It was an absolute nightmare. She was scarred for life. Had night terrors and everything. And his wife was obsessed with trying to help her, despite the doctors telling them to 'manage their expectations'. He barely got any attention at all these days.

Alan looked at some of the photos linked to Nick Hawley's page, which were available to view by his 'Friends'. There was a fair few in black and white, the arty type. He was a melancholy boy, for sure, but good looking. He'd obviously had some friends too, but didn't seem so happy, never smiling, always seeming preoccupied with something, staring off into the distance. Alan, not for the first time, wondered how Nick had come to drinking and driving like that, whether he'd really tried to kill himself, whether it had just gone wrong, or if he'd changed his mind at the last minute. Alan would never know, of course, but that didn't stop him from wondering. Not that it really mattered now. It was too late. It was all too late.

Alan clicked on the FB box that said 'Write something to Nick…' It felt like writing to a ghost beyond the grave. There was so much he wanted to say. He thought for a minute or two, before deciding on something and beginning to tap on the keyboard.

'Why did you do what you did?' he wrote, then slowly deleted, *tap-tap-tap*.

He tried again. 'You bastard! You almost killed my little girl!' Delete. Definitely delete, very careful not to send by accident. *Tap-tap-tap*.

Alan took a breath, tried to calm himself, waited a good thirty seconds.

'RIP, Nick. I only just found out,' he wrote, followed by a sad-face emoticon, and pressed the return key. That would do—prevent anyone from being suspicious of his virtual presence. Not what he wanted to say, but he didn't want to get into any trouble.

He went back to the photos of Nick Hawley again and brought one up just of him, magnifying the image, getting a close up of his face.

'What have you done?' he said. 'You've destroyed so, so many lives.' Two families had been plunged into chaos the day Nick chose to get in that car. They'd never be the same again.

That's what the young kids don't understand, thought Alan. That there's a domino effect—that any action, no matter how small or insignificant it might seem, can have a knock-on effect. Things can snowball all too quickly, before getting out of control. One has to be careful, or risks have to be taken in order to grapple back that control. Most people just can't see the big picture though. It's like trying to reason with a bunch of monkeys throwing faeces around. It's just a waste of time even trying to explain.

Alan opened a drawer in his desk and pulled out a folder containing some loose papers. He pushed his Apple MacBook Pro back on the desk, making space for the papers, and then set them down in front of him. He spread them out on the desk, a collection of newspaper articles documenting the recent murders in Rufford, some from the local rags, and some from national publications. A Detective Chief Inspector Jonathan Walker had held a press conference, talking about it, two murders within a short space of time, but no details had been given. It was causing quite a stir in the local community. He got up and took a couple of books from a nearby bookshelf, one called 'British Crime Stories' and one entitled 'Lancashire Murders'. There were also a bunch of crime novels on the shelf as well. He was a fan of the genre, and of crime literature in general.

He started to flick through the two books, one after the other, looking for something. There were various passages highlighted and notes made. He'd been studying them at one point or another. He stopped on a page in the British Crime Stories book, pressed down on the gutter, making sure the book would stay nicely open on the page while he read it. It was the story of a serial killer in Norfolk in the early 1950s. A guy called Bill Hawley. Bill had killed four people before being apprehended. He was a violent drunk, a messy killer who'd only gotten that far because he'd killed in a very short space of time. Alan tapped the page with his finger, having found what he was looking for, and made some more notes inside the margin of the page.

'Father of Darren?' he wrote. *'Grandfather of Nick?'*

Alan saw himself as something of an amateur detective. If the police came again, he might inform them of this possible connection, do their jobs for them. He hated the Hawleys, more and more. They were bad eggs, the lot of them—a bunch of violent alcoholics. The only good thing was that Nick hadn't, as far as Alan knew, fathered any children, so at least it looked like the end of that particular genetic line, if his father could keep it in his pants. *Good riddance*, he thought. Maybe he'd just post an anonymous tip off about the connection instead of telling the police face-to-face. He didn't really want to involve himself.

An alarm suddenly started to go off on his iPhone. It was already 2pm. Time to check his four-hour candlestick charts and see how his trades were going. He closed the book, shoved the papers back into the folder, and pushed the lot to one side.

CHAPTER TWENTY-THREE

CI Walker and PC Briggs sat across from Wendy
Robinson inside of another drab interview room
at Skelmersdale Station, having asked her to come
in to help with their enquiries. After what her sister-in-
law, Ronda, had said about her arguing with Patricia, it was
important to get more information, as this implicated her as
a possible suspect and provided motive.

'Mrs Robinson, may I call you Wendy?' asked Walker.

'Yes, of course,' said Wendy.

'Thank you for coming down to the station at such short
notice,' said Walker. 'It's much appreciated in aiding us with
our investigation.'

'That's okay,' she said. 'I'm happy to help. She was my
mother-in-law, after all. But why didn't you ask my husband
or his sister to come down as well?' She didn't know yet that
Ronda had spoken to them about the friction between her
and Patricia.

'We'll get to that in good time,' said Walker, pressing the
recording device and waiting a few seconds. 'This is May 18th,
2023, at... 6:57pm. Can you tell me your full name please?'

'I'm Wendy Robinson,' said Wendy, leaning slightly towards
the recording device, as many people did.

'You don't need to do that, Wendy,' said Walker. 'The mic is very powerful.'

Wendy nodded, seeming a bit embarrassed.

'There are a couple of things I want to ask you about today, just so we can clear things up. We have to explore all potential possibilities you see, in a case like this,' said Walker.

'As I said, I'm happy to help,' said Wendy.

'Okay. So, we had a chat with your sister-in-law, Ronda,' said Walker. 'She had a few concerns about your relationship with her mum. Is there anything you'd like to tell us about that?'

Wendy swallowed, hard, and her head shook, ever so slightly, her neck muscles likely tightening up due to the tension of the situation. 'Not really,' she said. 'You know how mothers-in-laws and daughters-in-laws tend to get on. We were no different.'

'And what exactly do you mean by that?' asked Walker. 'Could you clarify?'

Wendy looked at PC Briggs. 'Are you married?' she asked.

'No,' said PC Briggs.

Wendy sighed. 'We had our conflicts,' she said. 'To be honest, she gave me a lot of stress. Do you think I want to live there in my mother-in-law's house? Carl lost his job and is trying to start a new business, you see. But it's going slow. It was supposed to be temporary, living there. But then Stephen was diagnosed with lung cancer, and then died a few months after that, and Carl took some time off. We've been there for two years now. We were only supposed to be staying a few months.'

'I see. And did you ever argue with Carl's mum?' asked Walker. 'Was there conflict between the two of you.' He knew damned well there was, according to Ronda, at least. But he wanted to hear it from her.

'Look, like I said, we had our moments,' said Wendy. 'But doesn't everyone? I didn't wish her dead. Her husband, Stephen, was a lovely man. I miss him. And so is Carl, most of the time. But Patricia was difficult. She probably didn't mean to be. But she was. She was a bit… stern, and harsh, and complaining.'

Walker took a deep breath. 'Your sister-in-law, Ronda Robinson, says she heard you arguing with her mum one day. Can you tell us about that?'

'Not really,' said Wendy. 'There was more than once.'

'Well, she said she overheard you saying something, and I quote… *"when are you going to die, you stupid bitch!"*, in reference to Patricia Robinson. Is that what you said, Wendy?' asked Walker.

Wendy's face suddenly drained of all colour—she looked like someone had just looked in on her deepest, darkest, secret. 'I don't… Do I need a lawyer?'

'You are welcome to call a lawyer and get legal advice at any time,' said Walker. 'Or we can provide one for you, free of charge. But you are just helping us with our enquires for now. Nothing more. We're not arresting you.'

'Frigging bitch!' said Wendy, spittle flying everywhere as she spoke, suddenly losing it, transforming into a different person, going back to her rougher, tougher roots, her Skem accent also becoming more pronounced. 'She's always trying to get me in trouble. What's wrong with her? Jesus. This isn't a game.'

'You need to calm down and explain to us what you said about your mother-in-law?' said Walker. 'You have to admit it doesn't look too good in the present circumstances.'

'I don't even remember saying it,' said Wendy. 'She's probably lying. And if I did say it, I would have just been venting to myself, letting off some steam. People don't always mean what they say, you know. You have to let it out sometimes.'

'That's true, Chief,' said PC Briggs. Walker had told her to play the "good cop" a little bit. 'I used to say things like that to my older sister all the time when we were little—without the 'B' word, of course. Or the 'F'. People just say stuff. They don't really mean it. I mean, *most* of the time.'

'Okay. Look, we've also spoken to your ex-partner about this, a Robert Harris. What can you tell us about your relationship with him?' asked Walker.

'What? There's not much to tell,' said Wendy. 'Like I already said, we used to go out together, and then I moved in with him and got pregnant. It was a mistake. I was young. I was drinking a lot at the time, like young people do. And then I left him and met Carl. Rob still sees his daughter, Eve, about once per month. But that's about it.'

'So, he sometimes comes over to your place of residence?' asked Walker. 'In Rufford.'

'Yes. I prefer he sees Eve at the house, or somewhere close, nearby,' said Wendy.

'And Carl and Patricia were okay with this?' asked Walker.

'Not really. They didn't like him. But he's Eve's father,' said Wendy. 'So, we decided to give it a go. We all agreed, as a family.'

'I see. We also found a large amount of cannabis at Rob's home,' said Walker. 'Did you know about this?'

'Well... not that specifically. But I know he smokes weed.

He's proud of it. It's no secret,' said Wendy. 'But what does this have to do with Patricia?'

'We're just following up on all possible leads,' said Walker. 'Sometimes, when people get involved in the drugs world, violence can often be found nearby in the fallout.'

'What? You think Rob had something to do with this?' asked Wendy.

PC Briggs leaned forward now, getting as close to Wendy as possible. 'Wendy, if we search your home, will we find anything?'

Wendy started to cry.

'It's okay,' said PC Briggs. 'It's better if we know everything from the get-go. Then you can go home.'

'Look, I sometimes get a couple of joints off of Rob, just to take the edge off,' said Wendy. 'I get stressed living there, with a kid as well. Patricia was a bit of a clean freak. Do you know how difficult it is to keep everything clean and tidy when you have a little kid? It's impossible. She was always on at me—saying she used to keep everything spotless, and that she had two kids to deal with. So, yeah, I have a little smoke in the woods now and again, across the road, or in the back garden. Or I just eat some if I need to immediately hide the smell of the smoke. That's not a crime, is it? It's better than drinking.'

'Well, technically, possession *is* a crime, actually,' said Walker. 'But we only usually issue a warning for small amounts.'

'Oh, I didn't realise,' said Wendy. 'I thought that was okay now.'

Walker took a deep breath and turned the recording device *off*. 'Well, thank you for being so honest and upfront with us,

Wendy. That couldn't have been easy in the circumstances. You may return home for now. We'll be in touch if we have any more questions'

* * *

With Wendy now gone, Walker assembled his team back in the Incident Room and stood at the front, ready to speak.

'Okay, everyone. We may have a couple of possible theories on what may have happened here; but note, they're just theories at present. We have no solid evidence to support these ideas as yet,' said Walker. 'First, it seems Wendy Robinson disliked her mother-in-law to the point where she wished her dead, and she hated living in the same house as her. And we also have an ex-partner in Robert Harris, who has been witnessed as stating he *knows people who can get rid of people for a fee.* Now, putting two and two together, we might be coming up with five, but we have to investigate further anyway. There's a possibility that someone has been paid to kill Patricia Robinson, but that doesn't explain the first murder—and both cases had the same signature and M.O., so that doesn't quite fit yet. It's possible the killer was out looking for Patricia though, as both bodies were found in the same general area, and Tom Woods just pissed the killer off somehow, was at the wrong time at the wrong place, and became an unplanned target. Then the killer tried to throw us off by making it look like a serial killing rather than a contract one? I don't know about that. But it's certainly a line of inquiry worth following.

'And what's the other idea?' asked DI Riley.

'The second theory is that Harris is drug dealing, and he's been using those woods, dressed in a hoodie perhaps, as per our sighting, to conduct some deals. We already know he's a dealer who brags about knowing contract killers, so whether that part's true or not, he's certainly an unsavoury character at best. Maybe Tom Woods stumbled into one such deal going on in there, or perhaps he was a part of a deal himself, and things went awry, got violent, and he was killed by either Harris or one of his criminal contacts. And if Patricia had seen Harris, or one of his associates she'd seen him with in the past, in that area, and there was a possibility of her tying them to the Woods murder, this would be reason to kill her too. Maybe Wendy is involved in these criminal dealings too, somehow, since they can't even afford a place of their own. So, we have to consider that too.'

'Romantically separated, but criminally involved,' said DI Riley.

'Exactly,' said Walker.

'It certainly seems more plausible than the first idea,' said DI Riley, who'd quickly emerged as one of the more vocal members of the group.

'Agreed. It's not quite as exciting as the idea of hiring a hitman, but these things rarely are. They're usually mundane. I can't really see a pro using a signature like this, even to try and throw us off. This seems to fit more with a spontaneous non-professional killing, something done in a fit of rage in the first instance and then again to cover up the first murder. They'd likely panic, perhaps coming up with the cross of ash thing as a way to paint Woods's murder as some lurid ritualistic killing, and then using it again to frame it as a serial killer, to steer us away from the mundane reality: murder over drugs or money, good old-fashioned greed and anger,' said Walker. He didn't want it to be mundane, of course, he wanted it to be his sister's killer, coming out of retirement. But with what they had so far, that was becoming more and more unlikely. 'Nevertheless, having said all that,' he noted, 'all we have at present is circumstantial evidence, and a couple of witnesses creating motive and means. What we need is hard evidence, and all we have with regard to that at present is a silicone earbud cap—so we're looking for someone who listens to music; *probably*, unless that thing just happened to already be there where the body was dumped.'

'Or they listen to podcasts,' said one of the less outspoken DIs, an overweight middle-aged fella with round glasses that Walker knew very little about yet.

'Or audiobooks?' said DI Riley.

There were sounds of agreement in the room.

'Or guided meditation?' suggested PC Briggs, seeming to want to contribute. There were a few chuckles at that one. '*What?* We all need to unwind after this job.'

'Point taken,' said Walker. 'Someone who listens to something on an audio player then. We need a match on those earbud caps. Forensics are looking carefully at it as we speak, trying to see if they can get DNA or any fingerprint samples. In the meantime, be on the lookout for any such devices or earbud caps during your rounds, and make sure to log it in the book if you observe anything like that.'

'And how does this feed into the theory that the current killer was also responsible for the Amanda Morris homicide?' asked DI Riley. 'The cold case?'

'Well,' said Walker, his voice cracking a bit, his throat getting dry. 'It wouldn't be such a stretch to imagine that someone who did something like that when they were younger could also go on to do such work—contract killing or drug dealing, I mean. So, we can't completely rule out a connection yet.'

'But, as you said, it wouldn't be very professional to use a signature, would it, if they were a contract killer?' said DI Riley. 'The cross of ash on both the victims' foreheads, and the ash of human remains at that. It's a bit weird. Unnecessary? And it makes the combined serial killer case a higher priority, meaning they have more chance of being caught.'

DI Riley was right, but Walker wasn't quite ready to give up on the idea that he might still have a chance at catching his sister's killer.

'It's more than weird,' said PC Briggs. 'It's macabre.'

'Has someone been reading?' said DI Riley, grinning. 'Or did that come to you through meditation?'

There were a few chuckles in the room, but only briefly, which Walker let go to break the tension, before getting back to business. He knew that keeping a team loose could help spark insights into a case. An uptight, stressed-out crew was no good for anybody.

'They are not necessarily professional,' said Walker. 'Perhaps they just need the money. And are a bit... you know... loopy. Or maybe the guy in the hoodie is one of Harris's associates, an older man dressed young for disguise, who could have been Amanda Morris's killer. '

'Noted,' said DI Riley. 'But just to underline that the cross of ash on the cold case victim, Amanda Morris, was drawn with cigarette ash—so notably different.'

'Also noted. But an evolution is to be expected when so many years have passed,' said Walker, stubbornly not wanting the team to dismiss that connection just yet. 'So, we'll keep that on the table for the time being. Now, what else do we have and what are we focussing on today?' asked Walker. 'DI Hogarth?'

Detective Inspector Derek Hogarth was one of the older DIs, in his early sixties, grossly overweight, and his expertise lay in research and analysis, which meant he spent most, if not all of his day either on a computer or on the phone, or both. He was so obese now that he wouldn't be able to do much else anyway. It wasn't clear whether it was desk work that had led to his weight issues, or whether it was his weight issues that had ultimately led him into desk work. Nevertheless, what everybody did know is that he was damned good at his job, and his work had led to countless arrests and prosecutions.

'Yes. I followed up on the request to provide a list of cremations in the past five years within a three-mile radius of Holmeswood Drive,' said DI Hogarth, in his customary slow drawl. He was more laid back than a diazepam user. 'There were sixty-two in total but note that number doesn't include any extended family members who live outside of the area. Also, this did not include Kathryn Woods's father either, who has been confirmed as buried. It did, however, include Stephen Robinson, who was cremated. In addition, I've also documented any violent crimes in the same area, also within the past five years. There have been several notable incidents, but most of them have already reached a conclusion.'

'Most of them?' asked Walker.

'Yes. There was one mugging that went unsolved, involving some degree of GBH—although not too serious. And there was also a hit and run with a bicyclist, who was killed on Holmeswood Road, but with no cameras in the area, we never got a conviction for that either,' said DI Hogarth.

'I see. Anything else?' asked Walker.

'Just… one suicide,' said DI Hogarth. 'On Rufford Park Lane: a *Nick Hawley*. This is also on the list of those deceased and he was cremated. Some young man who got drunk and slammed into a tree. Killed themselves. The family said he had a history of depression and suicide attempts.'

'Yeah. I was actually present for that one,' said PC Briggs. 'About two years ago. One of my first call outs. Hard to forget, really. I almost mentioned it to DCI Walker when we were there.'

'I wish you had,' said Walker, glaring at her, warning her not to keep anything back in future. 'Right. Let's follow up on all of those as well, see if there's anything there—see if there might be any connection. And I want the rest of the interviews carried out, so we've got everything covered in the immediate vicinity. Nothing gets missed. And if it does, you'll have me to answer to.' He made sure he had a look in his eyes that told everyone not to mess up—a hard, unwavering, determination. 'Now, get to it.'

CHAPTER TWENTY-FOUR

E mily Watkins stood in the back garden, waiting for Daisy—the family tan cocker spaniel—to do her business. She'd been revising hard for three hours straight, preparing for her first GCSE exam. It was a history exam, but she'd also done some studies for her next one too, which was math, which just happened to be the subject she had most trouble with. Equations and vectors weren't her thing. Her head was spinning.

She looked up at the stars and took a breath. The sky wasn't completely clear, but there were some stars out. Since her mum had taken her phone away, she'd started noticing more around her—like the night sky. But she was tired now and wanted to go to bed. Supervising Daisy's toileting was her last chore of the day. She just needed her to do her business, and quick.

'Come on, Daise,' she said. 'Get on with it.'

Emily sat down on a garden bench, waiting. Her thumbs involuntarily twitched. She'd normally be chatting to her friends on WhatsApp at this time of night or scrolling through her various social media feeds, probably posting something herself, doing a quick TikTok video or something. She hated her mum for taking her mobile phone away, but there wasn't much she could do except try to pass her exams and get them back on side.

Daisy barked a couple of times and Emily looked around, trying to find the source of her complaints.

'There's nothing there, Daise. Come on. I'm getting cold,' said Emily, who hadn't even bothered putting a jacket on, and just wore a T-shirt and jeans.

Daisy barked again and went over to the garden gate, started scratching around. Emily usually walked the dog along Rufford Park Lane, right to the end, near the main road—just as many other residents did—and back again. But her mum had told her not to leave the garden today. The police had spooked her. Emily thought her mum worried too much. It was probably just a dead sheep, or someone got their phone nicked by a teen who'd had their own taken away by their parents! Nothing much ever happened in Rufford. She didn't see what the big deal was. She was tired of adults overreacting to such things.

Emily looked at her watch. She'd only been out there for seventeen minutes, but it seemed like an hour, and it would be if Daisy didn't get a bit of actual exercise and get her system moving. All the fuss was just stupid. Her mum knew nothing. Either that or she did, and she was just torturing her, Emily thought. She considered her options. She could pop out for ten minutes, take the risk, get it done quicker? Her mum would never know. She was taking a shower. And her dad was doing some accounting or something—which probably meant he was playing those stupid computer games he played, those violent retro ones. She couldn't get in any more trouble than she already was anyway. What else could they do to her? They had her bloomin' *phone*! Her most prized possession. It was the only thing she couldn't really live without, that and her dog, who she loved dearly. So, she put Daisy on the lead and opened the gate.

Emily took a look around on the street they lived on. It was deathly quiet. Nobody was around. She knew if she didn't take Daisy out, she could be sat there in the garden for at least forty-five minutes, or more. She'd just be quick—up and down. Daisy would be satisfied and get things done. She always did it in the same place, about halfway up the lane. And then she'd pee at the end of the lane too, do a bit of scratching, yelp that cute, satisfied yelp she always did, and all would be right with the world. It was the same old routine every evening. Her mother was crazy if she thought Daisy would be happy just going out in the garden.

'Come on, Daise. Let's go. Just don't tell mum,' said Emily, looking up at the house, checking that the bathroom light was still on. It was. Her mum would take at least an hour to go through her shower routine. She had all kinds of exfoliating products and after-bath creams, and she always shaved for like ten minutes, at least, too, before her shower. She'd be ages yet. She wouldn't suspect a thing.

Daisy shot ahead of Emily, pulling her towards Rufford Park Lane, getting excited.

'Easy, girl,' said Emily in a hushed tone. 'Wait for me.'

It wasn't unusual to see one or two people strolling around Rufford Park Lane in the evening, but today was a little later, and it was completely deserted. That suited her though. She didn't want any neighbours seeing and then mentioning it to her mum. She hadn't thought of that. *Stupid.* But it was too late. They were out and Daisy wouldn't accept going back now.

'Come on, girl. We have to be quick today,' said Emily, soon getting to the spot where Daisy usually did her business. The dog sniffed around, got settled, and Emily rooted in her pocket for some biodegradable poop bags, getting one ready, anticipating a good result.

She was right. The dog did its business, as per usual, right in its usual spot.

'Oh. Good girl,' said Emily, patting Daisy affectionately on the head and torso. 'Well done.' She held the bag and scooped the poop up, before carefully turning the bag inside out, locking it inside. Then, she tied it off and threw it on the grass to one side. She didn't like carrying poo—especially at first, when it was all warm and squishy—so she always picked it up on the way back. Daisy would want to go to the end of the road yet and take that pee-pee, but they had to get a move on before anyone noticed they were gone. Her parents would go crazy if she wasn't there, but what the hell? They deserved to freak, the way they'd been treating her recently, Emily mused.

'Come on, sweetie,' she said. 'Before mum notices we're gone.'

Daisy suddenly felt the headlights of a car approaching. She hadn't heard it coming because it was a hybrid vehicle travelling slowly enough to be on electric mode. She decided not to turn to see who it was yet as she didn't want them to see her properly, in case it was one of the neighbours. She crossed her fingers on her free hand, head down, facing away, waiting for it to pass. But the car didn't go past. Instead, it kept travelling at walking speed, staying alongside her and Daisy as they moved further up Rufford Park Lane. Emily stopped and looked at the car now, conceding that they'd probably recognised her. She was going to be in so much trouble if they told her mum. The car also stopped just as she did and whoever was inside put the window down.

'Pick that up!' It was a man, and an agitated one at that. He seemed familiar, but she couldn't really see him well in the gloom. As for the car, she wasn't sure she'd even recognise it if it was from just a couple of doors away from her own house. They all looked the same to her—all white, or grey, or black, some red or blue, some bigger, some smaller. She wasn't really interested. She'd rather be looking at her phone.

'What?' asked Emily.

'The dog shit. Pick it up!' said the man. *'Fucking people,'* he muttered.

'Leave me alone,' said Emily, getting upset, getting tired of being picked on.

'I said... *pick it up!'* said the man.

Emily stormed off. She was furious. It seemed everyone was giving her a hard time at the moment. The whole world seemed to be on her back.

The car stayed where it was, and Emily continued on to the end of the lane. If Daisy didn't pee before bedtime, she'd do it on the carpet, or worse still, in one of the beds. And then her mum would really be on her again. She couldn't have that, even if some creep was giving her a hard time. He'd probably shout at her again on the way back, and then she'd tell him she'd just been leaving it there temporarily, so she didn't have to carry it to the end of the road.

She got to the end of the lane and Emily looked back to see the car was still there, in the same spot. Freak. He was probably gunna pick it up and put it in his own bin—the loser. Fine by her. He'd save her a job.

Daisy started scratching around at the end of the lane, found her favourite little piece of grass just behind the bush there. There was some police tape on that wall as well now, stopping people from climbing over. She started to get a bit freaked out herself. *What if it was more than a dead sheep?* she thought. *What if someone really got hurt? What if her mum was actually right about something?* Daisy started to pee and looked up at Emily with those big, beautiful eyes she had. God, she really did love that dog. She didn't know what she'd do if anything happened to her.

When Daisy was finished, she yelped like she always did, to communicate she was done. 'Nice,' said Emily. She took a deep breath and started to turn, ready to navigate back around the bush, ready to walk past that bloody car again. But as she was turning, she saw a dark figure in the corner of her eye. It was the man from the car. She hadn't heard it coming again and it was parked right there, door open; and he was stood right behind them.

Emily's heart skipped a beat. *What the hell did he want from her?*

Daisy growled. They were cornered, and Emily's hand instinctively went to her pocket to fish for her mobile phone, to call for help—to call her mum—but it wasn't there. Of course not. Her mum had it. Nobody was going to help her. She was all alone.

She was completely trapped.

CHAPTER TWENTY-FIVE

DCI Jonathan Walker woke to the sound of vibrations. He was a light sleeper, and virtually any sound would be enough to wake him up, despite wearing a sleeping mask and foam earplugs that made his lugholes itchy. It was his mobile. Someone was calling. He fumbled around, slipping the mask onto his forehead and grabbing his iPhone, removing one of the earplugs.

'Hello?' he mumbled, his mouth dry. 'This is Jon.'

'Could I speak to…' The caller on the end of the line fumbled with something. 'Ah. DCI Walker. Sorry to wake you up. This is PS Finch. We met the other day near that icehouse in Rufford—the Tom Woods case? We have something I think you're gunna want to be here for.'

Walker put his bedside light on and sat up in bed, rubbing his forehead and eyes. He'd had a whiskey before he'd gone to bed this time—a double—just enough to help him fall asleep, but not too much that he wouldn't be thinking clearly in the morning. He shouldn't have really. He hadn't since he'd last been ill, as his meds advised against drinking due to the excessive strain on his liver. But he'd figured one would be okay, just this once. He'd needed it to help him sleep. His brain had been too active. He looked at the time on his phone—he was still groggy. It was 2:37am.

'What is it?' asked Walker. 'Is it about the case?'

'Maybe,' said PS Finch. 'I mean, it looks that way, possibly. A young girl has gone missing on the nearby estate. No body… *yet*. But she's missing. Her parents are beside themselves. Seems too much of a coincidence, what with them living so close to the other two victims.'

'I see. I understand. Thank you, PS Finch. I'm on my way,' said Walker. 'Text me the address and I'll see you there soon.'

'Will do. Oh, and DCI Walker,' said PS Finch. 'I believe you've had PC Briggs working on this with you?'

'That's right,' said Walker. 'Is there a problem?'

'No. No problem,' said PS Finch. 'Quite the opposite, in fact. I've worked with her many times. She's good with distraught members of the public. Has a way of calming things down, you know, the female touch or something. Very empathetic. See if you can bring her along if she's willing. We could use a little extra help here. We're short staffed.'

'Will do,' said Walker, already up and preparing to leave. 'Be there as soon as I can.'

* * *

'We've got to stop meeting like this, Chief,' said PC Briggs, smiling. She was stood outside Walker's blue unmarked Corsa with the door open. She climbed in.

'Believe me,' said Walker. 'I'd rather not.' PC Briggs looked a bit offended, so Walker went on. 'I mean, I'd rather people weren't going missing in the middle of the night.'

PC Briggs made an expression Walker couldn't pin down. 'I know what you meant,' she said. 'So, what do we have?'

'Young girl,' said Walker. 'Sixteen. Was supposed to be supervising the dog in the back garden but she wasn't there and didn't come back.'

'Is that it?' asked PC Briggs. 'Is that all we have?'

'She lives on Springwood Drive. Her family were interviewed for the Tom Woods case. We never told them what it was about though, and the press release has only just gone out,' said Walker.

'So, we should have warned them sooner?' asked PC Briggs. 'We were too late?'

'Perhaps,' said Walker. 'But that's the protocol we have to follow. *Maintain the public confidence*, and all that bullshit. Plus, I've had many a case messed up by the media. It's better to stay away in all but the most serious of cases. And even then, it can often do more harm than good.'

'You mean, in cases where, like… there's a serial killer who's on a binge?' said PC Briggs.

'Yeah. Like that,' said Walker solemnly. There was an uncomfortable silence while Walker drove. The roads were quiet, at least, so they made good progress. 'Sorry, about disturbing your beauty sleep,' he said.

'What? You think I need it?' asked PC Briggs, sounding annoyed.

'No, I didn't mean…'

'Relax! I'm having you on,' said PC Briggs, looking down at Walker's hand. He still wore his wedding ring, despite currently being separated. 'Gosh. Your wife must have a field day.'

'We're not… I mean… We aren't currently living together.

So, no,' said Walker, surprised at himself for mentioning anything about his personal life to a PC he'd only just met. He hadn't woken up properly yet, got his bearings. She'd caught him off-guard.

'Oh, sorry,' said PC Briggs. 'I didn't know.'

Walker put his foot down on the accelerator a bit, eager to get where they were going.

'What about you?' he asked, trying to make small talk, trying to get to know his temporary policing partner. 'Are you married?'

'Oh, God, no,' said PC Briggs. 'I've been seeing this guy but... I don't know. I guess I'm not really that into him. I'm not sure he's that into me either.'

'Maybe it's because you disappear in the middle of the night with strange men,' said Walker.

PC Briggs smiled. 'He wasn't with me today, Chief. But yeah, I get your point.'

Walker didn't know what else to say. Small talk wasn't his forte, but it felt like a strange point to stop the conversion, so he was a bit relieved when PC Briggs opened a new topic.

'So... how'd you become a cop then?' she asked. 'Just out of curiosity.'

Walker decided to give it a shot. PC Briggs was easy to talk to—perhaps a little too much, which he thought might prove useful for the case. He wouldn't tell her everything though. Not yet. Just enough to satisfy her inquisitiveness.

'I... I guess I went off the rails a bit when I was a kid, after I left school. I drank a lot, took drugs, some misdemeanours, that sort of thing, same as a lot of kids in northern Britain in the eighties I suppose. I was heading down the wrong path for sure. Then, one day, I was arrested for breaking into a car.

My mates had dared me to get this little furry tiger toy that was hanging from the mirror. It was stupid. The officer who arrested me gave me a good talking to, put the idea of joining the police force in my head and turning my life around, and that was that. He let me go on a promise I'd never do anything like that again. I guess the kindness of that officer may have saved my life, set me on a different path,' said Walker.

That wasn't everything, of course. Not the whole story, not even close. He didn't know her well enough to tell her that. It was too soon. What he was holding back was that the officer who'd arrested him that night had recognised him from his sister's case. That was why he'd put the idea of joining the force in young Jon's head. That was why he'd been so lenient.

'Wow. That's amazing,' said PC Briggs. 'I just joined for the money!' she jested, but there was something else too, something Walker couldn't pin down—a deep sadness in her eyes. It seemed she had her own cross to carry. He'd leave it for now though. She'd tell him when she was ready, as would he.

They travelled in silence for the rest of the ride, except for when Walker offered PC Briggs some Trebor Extra Strong mints when he popped a couple in his mouth because he'd forgotten to brush his teeth, but she declined. They rounded the corner off of Holmeswood Road and onto Rufford Park Lane once more, the very place where Patricia Robinson had recently died just beyond in the woods, and then took a left onto Springwood Drive. They found the Watkins house at the end, in a cul-de-sac. They were all impressively large, detached houses, and the Watkins had one of the biggest.

'Here we are,' said Walker. 'Number 32.' There were a couple of police cars already parked nearby, so it wasn't difficult to find.

They got out and slammed the car doors. The air seemed cleaner in Rufford, and it was a crisp, clear night. An officer came out of number 32. It was PS Finch.

'DCI Walker and PC Briggs,' said the ever fit-looking PS Finch. 'Thank you for coming so quickly.'

'Still no contact?' asked Walker.

'No,' said PS Finch. 'She didn't even have a phone.'

'A teenaged girl without a phone?' asked Walker.

'She was being punished. Her parents took it off her,' said PS Finch. 'Which is a shame. We could have used the phone's GPS data from the cell provider to view its current or last known location. We could have found her with it. I didn't tell them that, though. They're already upset enough.'

'Very good, PS Finch. Right. Let's get in then and see what's what,' said Walker.

PS Finch nodded. 'Be warned, they really are in a bit of a state. Even more so than usual.'

'Got it,' said Walker. 'Thanks for the warning.'

* * *

Sarah Watkins was gripping her husband's shirt collar, bawling her eyes out while he held on to her. 'We should have kept an eye on her. Why weren't we bloody watching?'

Her husband, Adam, looked like he'd been lobotomised. He was pale, expressionless—like the walking dead. The poor fella couldn't process what was happening.

'We were. She was in the back garden,' said Adam. 'She

would have shouted if there was any problem. I was right there, upstairs. I even had the window cracked open.'

'Then where is she then?' shouted Sarah, before another wave of tears flooded onto her husband's shirt as he pulled her closer, onto his chest. 'What were you doing?'

Walker coughed a fake cough to try and get their attention. Adam looked at him, aware of their presence for the first time. There was another PC with them, a man, one who Walker didn't know—one of the night shift lot. Some officers preferred to do nights only, for whatever reason.

'Mr and Mrs Watkins, this is DCI Walker,' said PS Finch. 'He'll be taking charge of your case, at least for now.'

Adam looked at them and his wife calmed down for a second, giving Walker the opportunity to speak.

'Mr and Mrs Watkins,' said Walker. 'We're going to do everything we can to get your daughter back safe and sound. But in order to do that, it's imperative we get as much information as we can, and as quickly as possible. And for that, I'm going to need you both to calm down and think as clearly as you can. Can you do that for me? Your daughter's life may depend on it.'

PC Briggs stepped forward. 'Mrs Watkins, how about you and me go and make a nice cup of tea while my colleague talks to your husband. Would that be okay?'

Sarah wiped her nose with her hand, obviously not caring what she looked like on this occasion even though it seemed she usually did—what with her perfectly manicured nails and stylish haircut—worry for her daughter consuming her. She nodded as PC Briggs moved in close, putting a hand on Sarah's shoulder and slowly ushering her away from her husband and the room they were in. Nobody spoke until PC Briggs and

Sarah had fully exited the room.

'Can we sit down now, Mr Watkins?' asked Walker.

'Of course. It's Adam,' said Adam, who was also still clearly in shock, just like his wife; but he seemed the more likely of the two to provide some clarity on the situation.

They all sat down, Adam perching on the edge of a single patterned fabric sofa chair, Walker in a matching chair opposite, while PS Finch and… the other PC who Walker had never met sat on the three-seater sofa.

'So, I'm DCI Walker, and you've already met PS Finch and…'

'PC Tyler,' said the other constable. 'Nice to meet you, sir,' he said to Walker. PC Tyler was neat and tidy, well groomed, polite, although a bit skinny. Walker wondered how far he might climb up the policing ladder. He seemed like the kind of young bobby who had his head screwed on right, who would do well someday.

'I don't know what happened,' said Adam. 'She was supposed to stay in the garden. She was just getting Daisy ready for bed.'

'Daisy?' said Walker, guessing Daisy was the family dog, but wanting confirmation anyway.

'Our dog,' said Adam. 'She's upstairs, in her bed.'

'So, the dog was there, but not your daughter?' asked Walker, abundantly aware of the similarity to the first two cases. All three of the cases involved dog owners out with their dogs, and all of the dogs had been unharmed—or perhaps this one had not left in the first place, given it was exactly where it was supposed to be.

'Yes, that's right,' said Adam. 'But the gate was off the latch.'

PC Tyler was taking it all down in his notepad—a fancy one with a black leather cover.

CHAPTER TWENTY-FIVE

'I see,' said Walker. 'And is there anything else?'

'Yes,' said Adam. 'Daisy was wearing her lead, dragging it around everywhere. We told Emily to stay in the garden, and we don't use the lead in the garden. So, it seems very likely she went out.'

'Okay. Can you tell us where she would normally walk Daisy?' asked Walker.

'Of course,' said Adam, wiping his nose. 'We always used to go together, up Park Lane on the footpath, and Daisy would do her business on the grass at the side, and then pee at the top of the lane behind the bush. Same thing every night. Then Emily started taking her by herself—said she didn't need me to come with her anymore—until we had your lot round the other day, that is, so we told her to stay in the garden this time, just in case. We didn't know what the problem was?' He looked at them with fear in his eyes. 'What *was* the problem?' he asked.

Walker sighed. He couldn't lie to the man. He'd find out soon enough anyway as they'd done the press statement now.

'Two people have died recently, close to here. Both were attacked,' said Walker.

Adam took in a deep breath, one of shock and panic. 'Attacked!' he said. *'Dead?'*

'Yes. But that doesn't necessarily mean your daughter has been attacked too. Children run away all the time. Have you been getting on recently? Is she under any stress or have you experienced any behavioural issues?' asked Walker. 'There could be a whole number of reasons for her disappearance.'

'Actually, yes,' said Adam, with a little more hope. 'But shouldn't we all be getting out there, looking for her? Can't you send a team out? A search party?'

'It's important we gather as much information as we can first, Adam. If we spend ten minutes talking now, it could save us hours later on,' said Walker. 'So?'

Adam's shoulders slumped down even more than they had been, accepting the situation. 'She's been in trouble recently, at school—got bloody caught spraying graffiti on the school walls. We've been disciplining her, took her damned mobile phone off her as punishment and grounded her. She's studying for her GCSEs at the moment, so she's been under some stress, but that's no flipping excuse now, is it? My poor baby,' said Adam, going from anger to a full on melt down in a breath. 'She can't be hurt. She just can't. What happened?'

'Okay. Hold on there a little bit longer, Adam. Just a few more questions. Have you been out already? Did you look for her anywhere?' asked Walker.

'I ran around the neighbourhood,' said Tom. 'Looked everywhere I could think of, where she might be. Called her friends too. Nobody has seen or heard from her.'

'And how long has it been since you last saw her now?' asked Walker.

'About five hours,' said Tom. 'We thought she was just acting out again, trying to worry us on purpose or something—sneaked off to the pub or something. I'm sure she'd get in, the way she looks. We've caught her drinking before. So, I checked out the local too, but she wasn't there. We called the police after two hours, and then they questioned us and took a look around. And then you came.'

'Okay, Adam. Here's what I'm going to do,' said Walker. 'I'm going to get as many officers out looking for your daughter as possible, and we'll certainly be able to get even more once the morning comes and we have more officers on duty. And in the meantime, I'm going to personally look around the area myself, see if I can find anything. What I need you to do, is stay here, by the phone, in case your daughter, or anybody else, rings. Does she know the landline number, or your mobile?'

'I made her memorise the landline when we moved here,' he said. 'For emergencies. She knows it.'

'Good. Then make sure you answer that landline if it rings,' said Walker. 'And take good care of your wife. We'll be in touch soon and keep you updated.'

Adam nodded. 'Thank you,' he said. 'Please find my daughter.' He looked at Walker, deep in his eyes, pleading. 'Promise me you'll find her.'

Walker looked at the man—he was completely vulnerable, consumed by guilt, desperate to get his daughter back safe and well. Except he knew better than to make such promises.

'I mean it, Adam. Stay near that landline. It's important,' said Walker.

Adam nodded, resigned to his task. Walker didn't want the man going out there, doing anything stupid, and he was now fairly satisfied that he wouldn't. He looked at PS Finch. 'Do we have a photo?'

PS Finch nodded and handed a photograph of Emily Watkins to Walker, one taken in her school uniform, a close up of her face.

'That will do,' said Walker. 'Did you get a digital copy of this too?'

PS Finch nodded. 'Yes, sir,' he said.

Walker took a good look at the photo, and then carefully put it in his suit jacket pocket. 'Now, let's go find her.'

* * *

DCI Walker strode along Rufford Park Lane with PC Briggs once more, with the street-lamps illuminating the path this time, lamps that were a bit different than the run of the mill British street-lamps. These were a bit more ornate and fancier. It really was a nice area, minus all the murders and the kidnapping, that was.

'There,' said Walker, stopping and pointing at something on the grass—a plastic-looking bag.

'More doggy poop?' said PC Briggs. Walker looked at her. 'What? You want *me* to pick it up?'

'No,' said Walker, bending down to grab the bag of poop. Instead of just using his fingers, though, he took out a pen and hooked it in the loop where the bag had been tied, and then lifted it up. 'But I do want you to carry it,' he said, holding it out. 'Put it in an evidence bag.'

PC Briggs did as asked, but couldn't completely hide her disgust when she popped it in her pocket.

'All dog walkers,' she said. 'Interesting.'

'What?' said Walker.

'The first two victims and the missing girl,' said PC Briggs. 'They were all out walking their dogs.'

'Are you sure you've not done this before?' said Walker, dryly, not appreciating her stating the obvious. 'You seem to have a real knack for it.'

'I'm just saying,' said PC Briggs. 'It's a bit odd. Do you think they're dog haters?'

'Look, everything about this case is odd,' said Walker, still looking around, trying to find any possible clues as to what might have happened to the girl. 'But since all the dogs are fine, I'd wager that the person who did this does not intrinsically hate dogs, no. It may just be a coincidence. People who walk dogs often tend to do it alone, at night—make easy targets. We'll check the poop bag when we get back to the Watkins's house, see if it matches whatever they buy. And then we need to check with Mr Watkins to see if this is a typical spot where Daisy might do her business. He did say Daisy usually did it on this strip of grass. So, this might well be it.'

'Maybe the killer has an issue with littering,' said PC Briggs. 'I hate it when people do that—leave their shit everywhere. It's disgusting. Especially in these bags. It seems even worse, somehow, than just throwing it in a bush or something.'

'It's possible,' said Walker, as they got near to the end of Rufford Park Lane. 'There does seem to be a spontaneous element to these killings. They aren't very neat and tidy.'

They stopped when they got to the end of the lane. 'Well… we've been here before,' said PC Briggs. They were near the low stone wall they'd recently hopped over when they'd found Patricia Robinson's body.

'Indeed,' said Walker. 'We'd better take a look in the woods again.'

PC Briggs's face went a shade paler, Walker seeing fear in her eyes as they prepared for what they might find. Walker hoped, for her sake, that Emily wasn't there. It was so much worse when they were young.

'Okay, Chief. Let's take a look,' she said.

CHAPTER TWENTY-SIX

'We need to take a break,' said Walker. 'Get some drinks and snacks—*refuel*.'

DCI Walker and PC Briggs had been out all night, along with a team of other equally jaded officers and DIs, searching everywhere for Emily Watkins. They'd found nothing. It was actually good news though—it meant there might actually be a chance she was still alive, although given the events of the past few days, that chance remained slim unless she'd just run away somewhere.

Walker didn't really want or need to eat—although he could have used some more energy for the search. It was more for PC Briggs, who seemed to be seriously flagging. He was actually quite pleased with how his own health had held up the past couple of days. He realised he wasn't in quite as bad shape as he'd previously thought. Except, he needed his team firing on all cylinders if they were to apprehend the killer and find Emily Watkins. He was experienced enough to know he couldn't do it all alone. Plus, he still had to consider his health. There had been times during his recovery when he'd felt fine, just like this, and then suddenly crashed, so he needed to be wary of that. And if he didn't stay healthy, then he'd risk losing this very real chance of finally catching his sister's murderer after all these years, getting justice for the Woods and Robinson families, and finding Emily. He still had some considerable hope that it was the same killer, even if the MO wasn't exactly matching up. People changed over thirty-odd years.

They were stood nearby the bush where Daisy routinely took a pee at night-time, the place where people could and often did hop over the wall at the end of Rufford Park Lane and get into the woods. The forensic team had returned and were doing their thing—donned in all-in-one white plastic crime scene suits fresh out of sealed bags, shoe covers, face masks, and latex gloves—trying to find some evidence of what had happened there.

'We can't do much more for now, anyway,' explained Walker. 'We need to wait, see what they come up with.'

'Okay, Chief. Let's refuel then,' said PC Briggs.

'Know anywhere good?' asked Walker.

'Yeah. I told you about that café at the Marina,' said PC Briggs. 'Some detective you are!'

'The Tastebuds,' said Walker. 'Great cakes, apparently. Always plenty of nice vehicles in the car park.' He was repeating what PC Briggs had said earlier, almost word for word. He hadn't forgotten. He was just checking her consistency of thought, making sure she was functioning correctly. Not everyone did when asked to wake up in the middle of the night to unexpectedly work a case.

PC Briggs smiled. 'We should fit right in then,' she said.

'Maybe we can talk to the staff and some of the locals while we're there, see if they might have seen anything,' said Walker.

PC Briggs emitted a little sigh, not much, but Walker noticed. She was obviously tired and had probably been relieved to be taking a little rest before Walker had suggested they keep working during their break.

'Or, you can have a few minutes to yourself if you need a real break,' he went on. 'Sorry. I might talk to a few people though. The clock really is ticking for Emily.'

'No, Chief,' said PC Briggs, sucking in some air. 'You're right. There's no time to lose. We'll talk to a few folks. See what's what. We can sleep when we're dead.'

'Good girl,' said Walker, which got a raise of the eyebrows from PC Briggs. 'I mean... I didn't mean nothing—'

'It's fine,' said PC Briggs. 'Just don't be taking me for walkies later when this is all over. Take me for a proper drink instead.'

* * *

The Tastebuds café was a picturesque little café right by the Marina in Rufford, one of two such cafes, where all the boats and canal barges regularly docked. The thought crossed Walker's mind that if the killer had a canal barge, then Emily's body, if she was dead, could literally end up anywhere in Britain. Their job would be impossible. But that was unlikely, he thought, given the location the first two bodies were found—unless the killer had acquired a boat since then, of course.

Walker entered the café behind PC Briggs, who, having been there before, naturally led the way. Inside was small, and it was starting to get busy in the lead up to lunch with the local elderly population flooding in. Thankfully, most people had been served already and there were only a couple of people in the queue before them—an elderly lady was one, the other a man who was also on the verge of being "old", somewhere at the far end of middle age. They didn't seem to be together, but both stepped aside politely when they saw the uniform of PC Briggs, letting them through.

'That's okay,' said PC Briggs. 'We're just—'

'Thank you,' interrupted Walker, accepting the gesture. 'We are in a bit of a hurry actually.' He flashed his CID identity card, so they understood that he too was on the force. It said: 'Chief Detective Inspector Walker.'

'*Detective*,' said the elderly lady, her eyes going a little wider, a trace of excitement in her voice. She was small, grey mid-length hair tied back, but with fashionable branded glasses on and a classic large Chanel handbag. 'I've never met a detective before. Is this about that poor man who was found dead near here?' she asked. 'I saw the report on TV. Hey, weren't you the officer who—'

'That's him,' said PC Briggs, holding her thumb to one side, pointing at Walker with it. 'In the flesh. You're meeting a celebrity, madam.' She smiled at Walker and then looked at the cashier, who'd been waiting to take their orders. 'I'll have a black coffee and one of those scones with cream, please,' she said, in a quieter tone.

'It is you. I thought I recognised you!' the old lady said, delighted to be meeting someone she'd just seen on the television, before her face turned solemn, and she said, 'It's terrible what happened though.'

'Indeed,' said Walker, to the woman, before looking at the cashier himself and saying, 'I'll have the same, but decaf for me.' The cashier nodded and got to work.

PC Briggs opened her eyes a bit wider, communicating mild

surprise.

'The same, eh? You didn't strike me as a scone and cream kind of guy,' she said.

'I'm not. But there's too much choice these days,' he said. 'Best to delegate. Saves time to think about more important things, like this case. I'll scrape the cream off. Can't digest the stuff. Anything cake-like is fine by me though.'

PC Briggs smiled again. Walker liked her smile. It seemed genuine and it brightened up what was otherwise an often-depressing job.

The elderly woman was listening, intently, trying to find an angle to get back into the conversation.

'Nothing like this has ever happened around here,' the woman blurted out, before they forgot about her. 'The closest we've had was that suicide car crash a couple of years ago, over on Park Lane.'

Walker's ears pricked up a little, having already heard about it from DI Hogarth in the Incident Room. 'That's the one you were present for, wasn't it?' he said to PC Briggs. 'The one mentioned in the Incident Room.'

'Yes, Chief. It was a sad one. A young man. Suffered from depression. Drove into a massive pine tree on the Lane. I thought about it when we walked past earlier,' said PC Briggs. 'Hard not to, really. It was a real mess. Sorry for not mentioning it earlier. I didn't think it was relevant.'

'I live near em', said the man, who was still stood nearby. 'The parents of that poor lad. Just a few doors down.' He moved a little closer, had a stronger Lancashire accent than the woman, who seemed a bit more refined. 'I remember that day well. It was crackin' flags, it was. We were all sweating cobs. Moggies everywhere. I asked 'em if there was owt I could do after I heard, but they never did—*ask*, I mean.'

'I see,' said Walker.

'I remember them,' said PC Briggs. 'How are they now?' she asked, seeming genuinely concerned.

'They've never been reet since,' said the man. 'The lad's dad has gone a bit funny. Don't speak to anyone. I seen him staggerin' home from the pub drunk, sometimes, peeing in the bushes. Not surprisin' really, though.'

'I've seen him at Sephton's,' said the woman. 'Filling up—the car, I mean. I feel so sorry for him. It's heart-breaking.'

'Sephton's?' asked Walker.

'It's the local petrol station we keep passing on the way to Holmeswood Road, Chief,' said PC Briggs. 'The one next to that gun shop.'

'Yeah, I saw that,' said Walker. 'Funny little place this, isn't it?'

The cashier placed two black coffees and two scones with cream on the counter. 'That will be £10.80, please. The decaf is in the green mug.'

Walker took out a debit card, but the cashier started waving her hand around, having second thoughts.

'Never mind,' she said. 'It's on the house.'

'You sure?' asked Walker. It wasn't the first time this kind of thing had happened. The police were nowhere near as hated as the media made out.

'Yes. You keep our little village safe, detective. Then come back and buy more coffee,' she said.

Walker nodded and started to pick up his coffee. 'Well, thank you,' he said. 'Actually, can we have these to take out?' he asked. 'Sorry, change of plan.'

The cashier nodded and started to make up some small

boxes to put the scones in and got some disposable plastic coffee cups and lids. She wrote on one of the cups, *Decaf*.

'Chief?' asked PC Briggs. 'We done here?'

'I think so,' said Walker. 'Come on.'

CHAPTER TWENTY-SEVEN

'Mr Hawley? Darren Hawley?' asked Walker. They'd come to the residence of the parents of the young man who'd killed himself two years earlier.

'Yeah,' he said, rubbing his eyes, seeming the worse for wear. 'What is it?'

Walker wanted to check him out, see how far down the rabbit hole he'd gone, assess his mental stability. He looked older than expected—older than Walker—perhaps prematurely aged by loss or poor health or both. Grief could do funny things to people, he knew, and especially when a young person died. From what the locals had said, it sounded like he'd gone off the rails a bit and couldn't find a way back. First impressions were they might be right. He looked awful.

'I'm sorry to bother you. We're just making some inquiries in the area,' said Walker. 'There's been a little—'

'Is this about my son, Nick?' asked Darren, seeming confused.

'Not really,' said Walker. 'Although that is something we'd like to talk about.'

'Hey, don't I know you?' asked Darren, pointing at PC Briggs. 'You were then when my boy...'

'I was, Mr Hawley,' said PC Briggs, in a sympathetic tone. 'How are you getting on?'

Darren looked down. He was wearing green Wellington boots and he'd gotten mud all over the wood-effect flooring in the hallway. 'How do you think I'm getting on?' he asked, but it seemed rhetorical, so Walker and PC Briggs didn't answer. 'Shit,' he elaborated.

'May we come in?' asked Walker.

'I'd rather you didn't,' said Darren. 'Got things to do.'

He didn't look like he had things to do. He looked like he could barely function at all.

'The wife's away,' he went on. 'Gone to see some friends down south. I think she's 'ad enough of me. Wouldn't blame her if she had. If it weren't for her, I'd probably do myself in.'

'You been out walking?' asked Walker, looking at Darren's boots again, trying to quickly change the subject. He'd seen people fall into the well of self-pity before and knew sympathy would be of no help. It would only send him deeper. He had to be direct, keep his attention.

'Yeah. Not a crime, is it?' asked Darren, a bit abruptly. 'Sorry. It's not you. I've just… I've had enough with all the questions, that's all. I just want folks to leave me alone.'

'Well, I'm afraid there have been a couple of incidents in the area, Mr Hawley. Two people have died. You may have seen it on the news? We just want to establish that there's no connection with what happened to your son. There's no reason that there would be, as far as we know, but as what happened to your son was one of the few other violent incidents in this area in the past few years, we just wanted to rule it out of our inquires,' explained Walker. Darren stared at him, a bit dumbfounded, so Walker elaborated. 'It's just procedure.'

'Right on,' said Darren. 'You know, my boy was alright, when he died. His meds were finally working. They said it was suicide, because he'd tried before, but I really believe it was just an accident.'

PC Briggs gave Walker a glance—nothing much—but enough to tell him that Darren Hawley was probably still in denial. His son had been drinking, heavily, at the time of his death, Walker had learned, and he'd died behind the wheel of his car. If it wasn't suicide, then it was as good as.

'Do you like music, Mr Hawley?' asked Walker, quickly changing the subject before he lost him, regaining his attention.

'Music? Well, I supposed I did before...' Darren gazed off into space again, getting lost in his thoughts, before visibly snapping back. 'But I haven't listened to much of anything since then. Now, if that's all you've got to ask me, I think I'd rather—'

'Your wife. You said she was away,' said Walker, pressing on, knowing his time was almost up. 'May I ask how long she's been gone for?'

'About three weeks,' said Darren, with some degree of bitterness. 'She was only going for one. Like I said, I think she's had enough of me. Do you want to talk to her? I can give you her number if you like. It's 07635 83...7254. She'll tell you anything you need to know.'

PC Briggs already had a notepad and pencil out and jotted the number down.

'Thank you, Mr Hawley. We'll contact her in due course. Just one final question. Have you seen anything odd, or out of place, while you've been out roaming the countryside?' asked

Walker. 'Over the last few days and weeks, I mean. Please think carefully. It's important.'

He did as asked and gave it a little thought. 'Not really. Lots of dog walkers around here, some kids messing around. Nothing much. I usually just stroll to the pub, through the woods,' said Darren. 'I used to walk there with my boy when he was little. Good memories in there. Plus, if I walk the other way, I bump into folk, and they keep yabbering on at me.' Walker and PC Briggs paused, waiting to see if there was anything more. 'I'd rather be alone,' he explained, giving them a look that told them this included the conversion they were currently having. 'Is that it?'

Walker puckered his lips slightly in frustration, knowing they wouldn't get much more out of Darren Hawley, at least not right now. 'Mr Hawley,' he said, nodding. 'We'll be in touch if we need anything more. Please be careful until our investigations have reached a conclusion and stay in areas of full public visibility.'

Without saying another word or giving any eye contact, Darren Hawley closed the door to his house and disappeared inside.

Walker and PC Briggs walked back up the driveway, towards their vehicle.

'Well, that was interesting,' said Walker, looking back at the house. He saw a curtain twitching—Darren was still watching them. Walker pretended he hadn't seen, looked up at the sky instead before turning back to the car.

'Don't look now, but he's still watching,' he said. 'Just saw the curtain twitch.'

'Chief? What you thinking?' asked PC Briggs. 'He probably just wants to make sure we go.'

'I'm thinking we should follow this trail a little more, especially since we know his son was cremated. I saw this show recently about Post-Traumatic Stress Disorder. People who've been through what he has can suffer with it for years. And there's a positive correlation between PTSD and elevated rates of anger, aggression, and... violence. Do you remember the folks that his son almost knocked down before he died?' asked Walker.

'I think so,' said PC Briggs. 'I'll double check the info with the station. But yeah. I remember them. Nice family.'

'Good. Do that now—get their current address. That will be our next pitstop,' said Walker. 'Let's see what these folks know about our Mr Hawley.'

CHAPTER TWENTY-EIGHT

Walker pressed the bell to Number 1A at the Main Hall of the Rufford New Hall estate and waited, massaging the bottom of his skull with one hand, ironing out some tension. The building and the rest of the estate, originally a former country house that belonged to the Hesketh family, the former Lords of the Manor of Rufford, was still imposing, but things had changed a lot since the eighteenth century. The building had since been used as a convalescence hospital for several decades in the twentieth century, before being converted for residential use in the 1990s. The Main Hall part of the residence now consisted of six spacious flats with high ceilings and original period features. The restoration of such historical buildings for residential use had become all the rage in recent years and were being snapped up by developers like hot cakes.

'It's beautiful here, isn't it?' said PC Briggs. 'I'd love to live in a place like this. You're gunna really like it inside. I remember it well.'

Walker pressed the bell again, and this time, someone answered and spoke on the speakerphone.

'Hello? Can I help you?' said the voice of a woman.

'Mrs Smith?' asked Walker. 'I'm DCI Walker, here with my

colleague PC Briggs. We'd like to ask you a few questions, if that's alright.'

There was no response from the woman except for a buzzer, signalling that the main door was now unlocked. Inside the iconic portico entrance, the lobby area opened out into a wide-open space containing a grand cantilevered staircase with wrought iron balusters, lit by a large domed oval skylight.

'Yes. I remember this alright,' said PC Briggs. 'Impressive, isn't it?' she said, in a hushed tone, gazing around.

Walker looked about too. The place was spotless. There were no muddy footprints here. Evidently, the communal area had a cleaner.

The door to Number 1A, which was to their left on this floor, opened, just slightly, and a pale-looking woman peered out through the crack, saw Walker and PC Briggs, and opened the door a little wider.

'What can I do for you?' she asked, seeming nervous, looking around behind her. 'We've already had some officers round.'

'We need to ask you about an incident you were involved in a couple of years ago, the one concerning Nick Hawley,' said Walker. 'May we come in?'

The woman hesitated, but then said, 'Of course,' letting them step inside. She seemed to Walker like a quiet lady, a bit shy, someone who tended to keep to herself, and a little older than the average mum—perhaps in her mid-forties.

The hallway they now found themselves in was comparatively tight compared to the lobby. There were no pictures hanging on the pale soft peach-coloured walls, and the bottom of these walls, which were painted in a different darker colour below a decorative edging, had dirty marks and various scratches. In contrast with the pristine finish of the lobby area, it badly needed redecorating.

Mrs Smith led them into the living room, which was roomy, and felt even more so with the four-metre-high ceilings and wooden windows almost as high, flooding the room with light. The sun's rays also highlighted some dust in the air. The place hadn't been cleaned in a while.

'Please, take a seat,' she said, ushering them to a wooden antique dining table.

They all sat down and got settled, before the woman asked, 'I'm sorry. Would you like a drink?'

PC Briggs started to open her mouth to speak, but Walker said, 'No, that's quite alright. Is your husband home?'

'Yes, but he's just working on something. He doesn't like to be disturbed when he's doing work,' she said. 'And my daughter. She's taking a nap.'

'Working?' asked Walker.

'He trades the financial markets, works from home,' said Mrs Smith. 'I don't really understand it myself, what he does, but he makes money from it. I'm Mary, by the way.'

'I see,' said Walker.

'Wait a minute. I know you, don't I?' said Mary, eyeing PC Briggs, seeming to see her properly for the first time. 'You were there when that car almost hit us.'

'I was, indeed, Mrs Smith,' said PC Briggs, getting reacquainted. 'How are you holding up?'

'We're… okay,' she said, but she didn't look okay. Not by a long shot.

'And your daughter?' asked PC Briggs in a comforting tone. 'How is she doing?'

'She…' Right on cue, Mary's daughter began to cry, having

woken up from her nap. 'Excuse me a moment,' said Mary, looking exhausted and in desperate need of some respite.

When she left the room, PC Briggs leaned in to Walker and whispered, 'Her daughter's disabled. If I remember right, when the near miss happened, Mary told me how her daughter had been put in a wheelchair by another car, previous to that, a couple of years or so before. They couldn't believe it almost happened again. And with her daughter also being autistic, she wasn't equipped to handle reliving the trauma. I don't think she could even speak, poor girl. At least, not when I met her. It was heart-breaking. They really seemed to be struggling, as you can imagine. It's always harder for the older parents anyway even if things are normal. I have a neighbour who had a kid in her forties and she's always talking about how she wished she'd done it earlier. But in this kind of situation…'

Walker nodded his understanding while the crying contin-ued, with Mary also being heard trying to calm her daughter down. 'Looks like things are still tough,' he said.

PC Briggs sighed. 'Maybe we should just—'

Walker held out his hand, telling her to wait. If they didn't do this now, they'd only have to come back and disturb them some more later. It was better for everyone just to get it over with so they could cross it off their list of things to do.

Mary soon came back, carrying her daughter, but only just. Her girl seemed to be getting too big to be carried and judging by how she was managing, she wouldn't be able to lift her for much longer. She sat down and put her child on her lap, the girl still sucking in oxygen, her face twitching, having still not entirely got the crying out of her system. Her daughter seemed a bit confused as to who was in her home, but other than that, there wasn't much of a reaction from her. There was no eye contact at all.

'This is Amy,' she said. 'Say "Hello", Amy.' With some prompting, Amy waved her hand, but gazed off into space as she did so. 'She still doesn't speak, but we're trying, aren't we honey.'

Amy mumbled something incomprehensible.

'How old is she now?' asked PC Briggs.

'She's seven,' said Mary.

'So, she must have been about five when I last saw her then, after the accident on Park road,' said PC Briggs.

'Yes. That's right. It really shook her up, you know—the car crash—it shook us all up. It was such a near miss. It brought it all back from the first accident, you see, when Amy was paralysed. I think I told you about that at the time, didn't I? It took so long to start to get over, and then it almost happened again. She had night terrors again for weeks,' said Mary, stroking her daughter's hair. 'Poor thingy. She was making good progress before that, with her autism, and with processing what happened. But she seems to have gone backwards since.'

A door opened and then slammed at the far end of the flat.

'What's all the noise, Mary? What's going on now?' said the voice of a man with a curious mixture of annoyance and worry. It was Mr Smith. 'Is she biting you again?'

Walker and PC Briggs shared a look, waiting for Mr Smith to enter the room.

'She sometimes bites me,' said Mary, quietly, looking at her daughter with nothing but love. 'She doesn't mean it. She just gets frustrated sometimes.'

Mr Smith cautiously entered, having now realised that

CHAPTER TWENTY-EIGHT

Mary had guests.

'Oh. Hello. I didn't know...' said Mr Smith.

Walker stood up. 'DCI Walker.' He held out a hand and shook Mr Smith's hand. 'And my colleague, PC Briggs.'

Mr Smith's eyes went a little wider. 'Yes. I believe we've already met, a couple of years ago during that car crash incident. And we've already had some of your folk here this week, making inquiries about something else. We told them everything we know already, right Mary?'

'That's correct, yes. I was just about to say,' said Mary. 'Sorry, I should have said earlier.'

'It's quite alright. We're now making some more detailed enquiries, that's all,' said Walker. 'We'd like to know more about the car crash you witnessed a couple of years ago. There's no reason to suspect it's connected to the current incidents, but we'd like to tie off any loose ends, if possible. It's—'

'It's just procedure,' said PC Briggs, glancing at Walker with a small, almost imperceptible smile, but Walker noticed.

'Yes. Thank you, Constable. It's just part of the process,' said Walker.

'I see,' said Mr Smith, with some suspicion. 'And they sent a Detective Inspector to tie off this, probably unimportant, loose end?' The man had an intelligence behind his eyes, but it seemed diluted with anxiety and worry, and dark circles under these eyes dominated his otherwise flawless, pale face. He had thin black hair, cut neat and tidy, and was clean shaven.

'Don't like the office,' said Walker. 'I like to muck in with the other officers. Get my fingers dirty. I don't think I got your full name, Mr Smith.'

'It's Alan. Alan Smith,' said Alan.

'Like the footballer?' said Walker, sitting down again.

'Yes. Like the *footballers*,' corrected Alan, also taking a seat next to his wife. 'There were two with that name. One played for Leeds, and one for Arsenal. A while ago now, though.'

'Right, yeah. Forgot about him—the Arsenal one. Lanky chap weren't he?' said Walker. 'No beauty queen either.'

'I don't have time for football these days. Can we get on with this?' asked Alan, looking at his wife. 'I still have more work to do yet. It's time sensitive.'

'It seems everyone's in a hurry today,' said Walker.

'People have busy lives,' said PC Briggs. 'We'll be as quick as we can.'

'Have you been talking to the neighbours too?' asked Mary, who was still struggling with Amy's constant fidgeting and moving around on her lap.

'We've been talking to Darren Hawley,' said Walker, looking at Alan and Mary, trying to gauge their reactions.

Alan started to lose it. 'Oh, *him*. That maniac. No wonder his son killed himself,' he said, his face getting redder.

'*Alan*,' said Mary, sharply. 'Please. Don't be unkind. We have guests.'

'Sorry, but…' said Alan, at a loss for words.

'He harassed us for a while,' explained Mary. 'After the car crash. Suggested we were in some way responsible for his son's death. But we were just walking on the footpath. He drove right at us. We didn't do anything.'

'He almost bloody killed us!' said Alan, getting even angrier. 'And then his dad starts having a go at us? Shouldn't he be apologising to us? Seriously?'

'Grief does funny things to some folk, Mr Smith,' said PC Briggs. 'He was probably out of his mind, looking for someone to blame. It wasn't your fault.'

'No, it wasn't,' said Alan. The flames of his emotions having been extinguished a little. PC Briggs *was* good with people. She knew the right things to say, and at the right time—something that couldn't really be learned. It was instinctive. 'He had no right...'

'When was this?' asked Walker.

Mary looked at her husband. 'It stopped about a year ago, didn't it?'

'Something like that,' said Alan, looking at his daughter, who was now making some odd vocalisations. 'As if we don't have enough to worry about.'

Alan and Mary were both clearly stressed. They might have had a nice place to stay, but their lives seemed complicated, and caring for their daughter evidently took its toll.

'Did you report this harassment?' asked Walker.

'No. Alan didn't want to,' said Mary. 'And it wasn't that serious. He didn't actually *do* anything to us. Just kept ringing the bell and shouting things through the window.'

'I wouldn't say that's nothing. God knows what he'd have done if we'd reported him,' said Alan. 'He'd probably have run us over, just like his bloody son tried to!'

'That's enough, Alan,' said Mary.

'Well,' said Alan, before swallowing whatever he was going to say next. 'Did you remember to offer them drinks this time?'

Mary nodded.

'We won't be staying long, Mr Smith,' said Walker. 'If Mr Hawley bothers you again, could you let us know?'

'Of course,' said Alan. 'As long as you don't tell him that we reported it.'

'I think we can manage that. Well, that will be all then,' said Walker. 'We can see you already have your hands full here. Thank you for your time.'

Alan saw them out and closed the door, leaving Walker and PC Briggs to walk back to their car, which they'd parked in the small car park just across from the Main Hall. As they were leaving the lobby, they could hear Amy start to cry and shout again, and her mum struggling with her once more.

'Poor souls,' said PC Briggs, as they walked away from the portico entrance towards their car. 'I don't know how they cope.'

Walker glanced back at the living room window to Number 1A. There was nobody watching them this time. 'People tend to do what they have to,' he said. 'Find a way to survive. Or not, as the case may be.'

'I know. But even so. That's tough,' said PC Briggs. 'What do you think about Hawley?'

Walker wondered how old Hawley might be. Looked like he was in his sixties at least, maybe an older-looking fifty-something if he'd not been taking care of himself, which appeared to be the case. That would put him in the right age range for Amanda's killer too.

'I think we need to keep him on our radar, at the very least,' said Walker. 'Especially knowing his son was cremated. But first...' He checked his watch. 'We need to get back to the station. Our Mr Harris has been locked up for forty-eight hours now. He should be suitably uncomfortable—ready for a good interrogation.'

'Got yer, Chief,' said PC Briggs. 'Sounds like a plan.'

CHAPTER TWENTY-NINE

D C Lee stood, hands on hips, in front of a mass of water inside of the Deer Park near Holmeswood Road. It was a considerable body of water, but not so big it could be called a lake—more a large pond. It might once have provided the frozen blocks of ice, in winter, that the icehouse used to preserve food, as it was the only major source of water in close proximity. But not anymore. Those days were gone. DC Lee rubbed at his shaved hair, wondering what secrets might lie below, hoping they weren't about to find the body of Emily Watkins in there.

'Let's make a start then,' said one of two police divers who'd come to attend. They'd just finished inflating a dinghy, one big enough for two adults and some sonar and ground penetrating radar equipment to fit in. By using sonar, the divers would first be able to use sound propagation to search for any obvious underwater objects, while the ground penetrating radar could go even deeper, if necessary, and examine the soft sediment below, just in case something had sunken into it. If they found anything suspicious, they'd then dive under the water and bring it up for further inspection. That was the plan.

'Don't leave any stone unturned, gentlemen,' said DC Lee.

'We need to clear this area, since it's so close to where the Watkins girl went missing and the only body of water in the immediate vicinity. We've looked pretty much everywhere else. It's possible she's in here.'

The two divers nodded their understanding, got in the dinghy, and went out onto the water. It was murky, so nothing could be seen under the surface with the naked eye. The equipment they had would therefore be invaluable.

'We'll do our best,' shouted the diver who was in charge, now several feet away. 'We know what we're doing, Inspector. If there's anything in there, we'll be sure to bring it out.'

DC Lee left them to it, let them get on with it. He knew this kind of thing could take a while, so he took a seat on a large rock by the side of the water. A couple of officers were also taping off the area, creating a perimeter all around the water using barrier stakes, just to make sure any ramblers out and about didn't stray too close. It was taking time to cordon off too—it was a couple of hundred feet all around, easy.

No sooner had DC Lee sat down than his phone rang. He took it out and answered.

'Hello. This is DC Lee,' he said. It was the woman from the council offices, the one that looked like an old spinster, Claire Gordon, with confirmation from her colleague that the key to the padlock had been thrown away, as the police officer who called in, she explained, had said the padlock had been destroyed. 'I see. So, it was deemed to be no longer of use. Have I got that right? Well, thank you for letting me know, Mrs Gordon. Goodbye.' He hung up the call and put his phone back in his pocket.

DC Lee preferred being out in the open than in some dusty old council building, that was for sure, or even in some dust-free *new* council building. Dealing with bureaucracy was frustrating, whatever the environment. It was a part of his job that he didn't enjoy, the paperwork and red tape. But this was one of his least favourite outdoor activities too—waiting to find out if there was a dead body somewhere. He hadn't had many experiences like this, just one or two during his relatively short career as a detective, but he hadn't enjoyed those either.

He took out a sandwich he'd bought earlier from his bag. He might not have any time later for his lunch, he thought, if they found something, so he took the opportunity to chow down. He needed to keep himself well-fuelled, just in case. It was cheddar cheese and red onion on white bread, something he'd bought on the way in at the small café at the Mere Sands Nature Reserve. He knew the café was there because he'd been before, when he'd gone for a walk with some friends one time. He bit into the sandwich—it was good. He was hungry. He wished he'd picked up some crisps as well now, treated himself.

He continued eating his sandwich, and he'd just taken the first bite from the second half of it when one of the divers called over.

'Hey! There's something here—a mass, about the size of what we're looking for. We're going under,' he said.

DC Lee stood up and stuffed the remainder of the sandwich back inside the packaging and put that in his bag. He waved his understanding, and the two divers fell backwards into the water, going under with the grace of a couple of otters. DC Lee waited, patiently. He flipped open his phone and made a call.

'DCI Walker? Yes, it's DC Lee here. I'm just there now. The

213

divers have found something. They're bringing it up as we speak. Yes, I'll call you back immediately, as soon as I know. Oh, and I don't know if you saw it in my notes, but that key to the padlock of the icehouse, the one held at the council offices: it's been confirmed as discarded due to the destruction of the padlock, and it no longer being of any use. So, that's a dead end, it seems, but I'll be interviewing whoever discarded it when they get back, regardless. Yes, that's all. Thanks.' He hung up and waited some more. If it was the body of the Watkins girl under there, he'd have to drop by her parents' house, give them the bad news—another part of his job he didn't enjoy. He wasn't even sure if he liked his job, or not, or why he did it. But here he was.

The water bubbled and the divers resurfaced, holding something—a large black rubble sack tied up and filled with something heavy. They brought it over, to the bank of the pond, and shoved it on solid ground with the help of DC Lee and one of the uniformed officers who'd been taping off the area. The divers got out of the water, dripping cold water everywhere, and they all helped drag the object further ashore onto some nearby grass.

'It's heavy,' said DC Lee. It was ominous. It had the weight and feel of a body, for sure, and there was a bad smell, like rotting meat. 'This does not look good, does it.'

They carefully used a Stanley Knife to cut the bag open, going all around it on three sides. Then, by working together, they tentatively lifted the flap they'd made, and slowly, ever so slowly, pulled it back.

The bad smell hit them like a slap in the face now, made them jolt back before their eyes could even register what they were seeing. The smell *was* rotting flesh. But more than

214

that—it was mixed in with wet, mouldy wool and muck too. It wasn't Emily Watkins. It was a dead sheep, not too long gone, but decomposed enough to make them stand back a few feet before one of them might throw up.

'Jesus,' said DC Lee, holding his arm over his nose and mouth. 'It's just a sheep! Thank God for that. Why would anybody put a sheep in here? Is that how farmers get rid of dead livestock these days?'

'I very much doubt that,' said the officer on duty who'd been helping—a tall chap, skinny, in his early twenties. 'I had a mate whose dad was a livestock farmer. They just left any dead ones to rot in the field, out in the open. Nature would get rid of them in no time. There'd be nothing left but a few bones. It's good for the ecosystem, apparently.'

DC Lee looked more closely at the sheep and popped on some latex gloves. It had blood stains on its side, matted into its wool, gone almost black. But it was blood aright. He looked closer, pulled its wool back to reveal several gaping wounds that had coagulated. It didn't look like the bite of an animal though, but rather, several clean, blade-type wounds, about an inch across. It looked, for all the world, like the sheep had been knifed to death.

'This looks odd. It doesn't look like an animal attack at all. It's too clean. We're gunna need to get this back for further forensic analyses,' said DC Lee. 'It may be connected to the case, somehow. Best guess: maybe the killer did it, had a dry run, seeing how it felt.'

'No problem. We'll get it packed and ready to transport,' said the police diver who'd been in charge the whole time. 'Then we'll make sure there's nothing else in there. But we did a full search, and that was the only obvious thing in there of any substantial size.'

DC Lee stepped away, to one side, and took out his phone again. He dialled the last number he'd called.

'DCI Walker. It's me again, DC Lee. We did find something. A dead sheep, in a large plastic heavy duty bag. I could be wrong but looks to me like it's been stabbed with a knife. We're bringing it back for analysis. Could be connected with the case. Yes, sir. Thank you.' He hung up.

DC Lee took out a pack of cigarettes and lit one, took a drag; he wasn't breaking any rules as they weren't in a public place or on police premises. He didn't smoke much at all these days, not since becoming a copper, but he kept some in his pocket for occasions just like this. He'd really thought it was her—the Watkins girl. His hand was shaking, just a touch, the relief palpable as he exhaled.

CHAPTER THIRTY

arren Hawley stepped into the garden of his four-
bedroom detached home on Springwood Drive
carrying a plastic tray, one with a little lip and
hand holes. This tray contained one ham sandwich with
mayonnaise, a packet of salt and vinegar Walkers crisps, a Pink
Lady apple, and a standard can of Coca-Cola. He popped the
tray down on the cool concrete flags outside the garden office
and unlocked the door with a key he had in his pocket. He
looked up for a second, surveying the scene, checking there
were no prying eyes. It was an unusually tranquil evening,
like the calm before the storm. It wasn't particularly cold, not
windy, nor rainy—a pretty dull day for meteorologists.

With the door now open, he picked up the tray again and
went inside, popping it on a desk in the back-right corner
of the office. He locked the office again from the inside and
checked the handle, twice, before sitting down in front of the
food, looking at it, nodding, satisfied. Next, he got up and
took a hammer off a nail on the wall, one of several that held
various tools. Then, he went over to the wall on the back-left
side of the office, which was just two steps away. This wall
was different to the rest—had a kind of lattice wooden panel
fitted over a piece of hardboard, which in turn was fixed to

some sturdy wooden beams. The office had been repaired in a makeshift fashion by a previous owner using reclaimed wood, something not unusual for British sheds—which this essentially was, although one admittedly roomier than most, having been converted into an office at some point before the Hawley's bought the property, but a shed nonetheless—which tend to get a bit weathered after a period of time and need patching up. And at about a decade old, this wasn't any exception.

Darren turned the hammer around in his hand, using the claw to prise the lattice and hardboard panel away at the edge, creating a gap for him to get his fingers into. Beyond the gap was only darkness. He pulled at the panel with two sharp tugs, making it come away even more, and then once it was loose, he slid it across. It was heavy, cumbersome, required using a bit of strength, but he put it to one side, revealing a dark void.

He squinted into the void, trying to see—like he might find the secrets to the universe in there. Then he flicked a power switch on inside the office, close by, which had a four-socket plug extension lead plugged into it, which ended in the secret room. An overhead fluorescent light flickered several times before springing into life, bathing the room, if it could be called that, in bright light. He looked down at what was before him and forced a smile, one filled with regret. He brought the tray of refreshments and placed it inside the room, on the floor, just a few centimetres in.

'How are you doing?' he asked. There was no response. 'Look, if you're okay, can you just…' Still no response. 'You know I didn't mean to… That I shouldn't have…'

Darren got down on his haunches, close to the floor, and started to cry. 'No, *no!*'

He got up again and staggered out, backwards, almost tripping up as he went. He was shaken, his emotions getting the better of him, starting to spiral into anxiety and panic. He'd killed. He hadn't meant to. It was all on him.

'Shit. I'm so, so sorry.'

He grabbed at the lattice hardwood panel once more, and frantically slid it across, blocking the light coming from the secret room, and then he banged on the wood with his hands until it popped firmly into place. He took a bottle of something strong out of his back pocket and gulped some down, trying to calm his nerves. It worked, a little, but not much.

'Please forgive me,' he said, before flicking the socket switch on the wall off, killing the circuit. 'Dear God, please, please forgive me.'

CHAPTER THIRTY-ONE

'Mr Harris,' said Walker. He was sat back in the same interview room as before, but this time, DI Riley wasn't present, or PC Briggs, at Walker's request. He wanted Harris alone this time—to try to put some pressure on him, though he'd have to do that when the recording device was off, of course, at some point, if necessary. He wouldn't normally resort to such tactics. It was ethically dubious, to say the least, and against protocol. Supt Hughes wouldn't be happy if he found out, and that was putting it mildly. But this wasn't just about the Watkins girl. It was about Walker's sister too. He wasn't entirely sure if he was thinking straight. His mind was feeling a little foggy, but he was damned sure he wasn't going to tell anyone else that. He wasn't even sure he'd go through with it, but he wanted the option, at least—it might help to save a girl's life, and it wasn't like he had anything to lose. The way his health was going, he'd be taking an enforced retirement soon anyway, or worse. But, for now, he kept things above board and turned the recording device on, left that option on the back burner. 'May 20th, 2023, at 2:12 pm. This is DCI Walker interviewing Robert Harris.'

'You can't keep me here for just a bit of weed,' said Harris.

'This is ridiculous.'

'Mr Harris. I'm afraid the quantity of cannabis found at your residence is more than enough to hold you for further questioning,' said Walker. 'Now we'd like to know where you acquired this product, and who from.'

'I'm not gunna tell… No comment,' he said, folding his arms, and then shaking his head.

'Was the place in question in the woods near Rufford Park Lane and was your supplier wearing a hoodie?' asked Walker.

'What? No comment,' said Harris.

'Do you deal drugs, Mr Harris?' asked Walker.

Harris put his head in his hands and mumbled, 'No comment.'

'Do you know people who would kill other people, for a fee?' asked Walker, pressing on, ramping up the pressure, not giving him time to think.

Harris looked up, straight into Walker's eyes. 'What is this? I thought you wanted to know about the weed? You still banging on about those bloody earbuds? I told you, I had nothing to do with that old bag dying. She probably just pissed someone off. She 'ad that way about her.'

Walker had already heard enough, felt his patience slipping. He turned the recording device off and went towards the door. It had a glass panel in the middle of it, and Walker looked out, checking nobody was watching. The room also had video cameras, but Walker made sure they were 'malfunctioning' before entering. He walked around Harris, to the back side of him, and leaned in close.

'You'd better fucking tell me what you know, Mr Harris, or I'm going to give myself a black eye and beat the crap out of you, say you attacked me and that it was self-defence.

The cameras are off, by the way. Now, enough with this "no comment' bullshit. Do you know people who would kill someone for money?'

'No... I...' said Harris, seeming a bit rattled. Walker knew he'd been in police stations before, probably had a degree of comfort there because he knew procedures had to be followed. That's why Walker had to shake him up, make him a bit more uncomfortable. Walker wasn't going to hit him, of course. At least, he didn't think he was. But Harris didn't know that. 'What are you talking about?'

Walker turned the recording device back on and picked up some notes. 'We have a witness who stated, and I quote, "He's a bad egg. We was down at the pub once, and he bragged he knew someone who could get rid of anyone for the right price". Did you say that, Mr Harris?'

'What? Did Shelley Deakin tell you that? Stupid bitch! I was just having a laugh. These two blokes were giving me some bollocks. I just wanted to scare 'em off, that's all,' said Harris. 'I didn't mean anything by it. I know some rough people, sure, but nothing like that.'

'And did you?' asked Walker.

'Did I what?'

'Scare them off,' said Walker.

'No,' said Harris. 'We got into a scuffle, and *I* got kicked out! Can you believe that? It was two on one.'

'Where were you on May 13th, Mr Harris?' asked Walker.

Harris smiled. 'You idiot. I wasn't even here,' he said. 'Ibiza. Little holiday. You can check my passport. Only got back on the sixteenth. Why didn't you just ask me that in the first place?'

Walker slammed his fist on the table and Harris jumped a

little.

'You can check mi phone too, mate. Didn't make any calls to back here. Too expensive. Check mi WhatsApp texts too if you like. Didn't ask nobody to do nothing,' he said. 'I was too busy buzzin' me head off over there, having way too much fun.'

Walker wasn't entirely sure what WhatsApp was, or what it could do, but he'd heard of it. He knew enough to know it was a means of communication that lots of people used these days and could be used over the Internet for free. Walker liked to keep things simple on his phone though—calls and texts, no apps except for those ready installed. He used the calculator and alarm, and that was about it.

'Mr Harris. You didn't seem too surprised when we informed you of the death of Patricia Robinson, whether you liked her or not. Why is that?' asked Walker.

Harris frowned, seemed to grapple with the question, his mouth ever so slightly opening and closing, like he was going to say something then changed his mind, several times.

'Mr Harris?' said Walker, urging him on.

'Fine. Look, not long after I got back Wendy called me. *She* told me,' said Harris. 'She told me Patricia had died.'

'Then why did you pretend you didn't know?' asked Walker.

Harris thought some more. 'She made me promise not to say anything.'

Walker moved in closer. 'And why would she do that?' he asked, in little more than a whisper.

Harris flinched a little. 'She said she'd stop me seeing Eve if I told anyone,' he said.

'Told anyone *what*?' asked Walker, now with his voice raised again. 'If you don't tell me, I promise you'll be going to prison for a long, long time, and your life will be sheer hell once inside. I'll personally see to it. Now, what did she not want you to tell anyone.'

Harris gulped as he weighed his options and came to a decision.

'She wanted some drugs, that's all. Said she needed something after she found out about how her mother-in-law died. That she couldn't calm down. She just wanted some weed but said her bloke would go mad if he found out. That's why I pretended I didn't know. She made me promise.'

Walker didn't like what he was hearing, but it had the smell of the truth, and time was running out.

'We'll verify everything you've said, Mr Harris. But there's still the matter of your possession of cannabis to attend to, and you dealing drugs, so I'll put you in the hands of my colleagues for that. Good day to you,' said Walker, making a quick call to get someone to collect Harris and return him to his holding cell. When everyone was gone, leaving him alone in the room, Walker closed the door and punched the table this time, and then a few times more.

'*God damn it!*' he shouted when he was done, cradling his battered fist.

With Harris out of the picture, he had nothing. It was back to the drawing board. Cases like this could take months, even years, to make any leeway on. But they didn't have months or years—not if Emily Watkins was to have any chance of surviving, not if she wasn't to share the same macabre fate as Walker's sister all those years ago, his little Mandy.

He was going to have to cut some corners on this one, make sure things got done. If it wasn't the same person that killed his sister, so be it. At least he'd get some redemption by saving

Emily. But with Harris now having a firm alibi, it did reopen the possibility that the killer could be the same person who murdered his sister, and he was well aware of that. He didn't care if this was his last job, or even if he was prosecuted for misconduct for that matter, just so long as he got the bastard that did this. But it was a fine line. He couldn't compromise the logistics of the case. If he did, then even if they arrested the killer, he might still not be charged. And if that happened, and if it was the same person who'd killed his Mandy, he'd just have to take his own justice. He'd seen too many psychopaths go free because of bureaucracy and red tape. Not that he'd done anything remotely like this before, or that he didn't believe in the criminal justice system—but he knew it didn't always work. This was going to be one he needed to close out, one way or another.

He rubbed his hand, gritted his teeth, steeled himself for what lay ahead, and exited Interview Room Five.

CHAPTER THIRTY-TWO

Well?' asked PC Briggs. 'What did you get?'

Walker had just got back to the Incident Room, cradling a cup of hot chocolate he'd made for himself from one of the vending machines. The heat from it was helping his aching hand.

'Diddly-squat,' said Walker. 'He wasn't even here. He just got back from Ibiza.'

'Oh,' said PC Briggs. 'So, now what?'

Walker clapped his hands, getting everyone's attention. 'Can we gather round, people?' he asked.

Everyone stopped what they were doing and assembled.

'Robert Harris just told me he's been out of the country—Greece,' said Walker.

PC Briggs got a little closer and whispered, '*Spain*. Ibiza is a *Spanish* island, sir. Haven't you ever been?'

'No. Why would I?' he said.

'I don't know. To dance? Don't you ever dance?' she said.

Walker shook his head, impatiently, and carried on. 'Sorry. Harris has been in Spain—out of the country, anyhow. We'll need to get it confirmed, see the stamps in his passport or whatever, but the important thing is it seems he's been away at the time of these murders. That doesn't rule out any involvement comprehensively, of course, but it seems more unlikely now. We'll also need to check his phone—see what communications he's made. But the earbud doesn't match, he's been out of the country, and... quite frankly, I doubt anyone would trust him to arrange something like this. He's a proper stoner. He can barely focus. I wouldn't trust him to tie his own shoelaces, quite frankly.'

'So, where does that leave us, Chief?' asked DI Riley. 'We don't seem to have much else coming in as of yet.'

'Well, it leaves us with a problem,' said Walker. 'Because we have a girl missing, and the likelihood of finding her decreases with every hour that passes.' They all knew that, of course, but Walker just wanted to hammer it home to keep them ultra-focussed. He walked over to the evidence board, which had evolved from the couple of photos he'd previously fixed to the whiteboard with magnets. It now had several photos on there, and more writing for each one. 'Two deceased, and one missing person, in the same area, in the space of less than a week,' said Walker, hitting the whiteboard with the palm of his hand and instantly regretting it as it was the hand that was still aching. 'And one cold case in Amanda Morris, with the same markings as Deceased One and Two. With Harris having an alibi, all we have now is one person of interest seen in the woods adjacent to Rufford Park Lane, wearing a dark-coloured hoodie, a person seen by Patricia Robinson just prior to her being found dead in the same woods herself. It might be nothing—maybe just some delinquent kid or someone taking a walk—but it's the nearest thing we have to a suspect at the moment. And that isn't much. So... what other patterns and connections do we have? Start thinking, people!' It wasn't just for show, to galvanise them. He really was getting annoyed, his frustrations boiling over.

'Deceased One and Two and the missing girl were all out walking their dog,' said DI Riley. 'Seems a bit of a coincidence to me. That's the obvious one.'

'And the dogs were all fine,' said PC Briggs. 'So, it seems the killer had no desire to hurt the animals—just their owners.'

'That has already been noted,' said Walker, underwhelmed by the response. 'But that's about it. There is no other connection between these three people other than that they live in the same area, and probably use the same shops or petrol station, maybe the same vet too. We should check all those things out, get them in the action book. But by all accounts, they don't really know each other—although when photos were shown during interviews to family members, they did say they recognised them, probably saw them around. So, what else are we missing? There must be something.'

'Wendy Robinson demonstrated some motive, and her ex, Robert Harris, claimed to have the means. But we've since learned he was away during this time,' said DI Riley, just going over things again, probably hoping it would spark something from someone, or himself. 'Although he could have pre-arranged it.'

'But like I said, I doubt this guy could prearrange a piss up in a brewery, much less a murder of this nature,' said Walker. He wrote the name of Darren Hawley on the whiteboard and put a photo of him next to it—one he'd found on the Internet and printed out, one from an old article about his son.

Before he could say anything though, one of the female staff from the front desk suddenly knocked on the door and entered, holding something. It was the same woman who'd given Walker and PC Briggs the tin of cakes the other day.

But she didn't have cakes this time.

'Excuse me, sir. We have something,' she said. 'Came in the morning post. An anonymous tip-off and a copy of an article from a book. It may be relevant to the case. Here.' She held out an envelope for Walker to take.

'Thank you,' he said, taking the envelope off her. Once she'd left and closed the door, he opened it, took a look, his eyes widening. 'Jesus. It's a story about a serial killer in Norfolk in the 1950s. Someone called *Bill Hawley*. Killed four people under the influence of alcohol. The sender has also included some notes, questioning whether Bill might be the father of one *Darren Hawley*, and the grandfather of Nick. If this is right, it's huge.'

'I'll get right on that,' said DI Riley, scrambling. 'Get it confirmed, or not.'

'You do that,' said Walker. 'ASAP. See if you can identify where this correspondence has come from too, while you're at it—although I know that might be difficult. But try anyway. And this man, Darren Hawley, is our main suspect now. I'm going to bring him in for questioning myself, maybe do some observations first, see if I can catch him doing anything untoward. So, nobody contact him and tip him off. You got that? I don't want him getting spooked and running. In the meantime, find out everything you can about him. He wasn't too eager to talk to us when we visited. When I bring him in, I want his boots cast and compared to any footprints that were found nearby the bodies. Get on it as a matter of urgency. I'll interview him myself once he's here and had some time to stew. And if I can't find him, I'll be in touch to call for reinforcements. Any questions?'

The team had none and took that as the end of the meeting

and started to get back to work. The room hummed with activity. It had gone up a notch from what it had been before Walker's speech. There was a buzz that bordered on frantic.

'What about me? Am I coming with you, Chief?' asked PC Briggs.

Walker looked at her. She looked spent.

'*You*, are going home, getting some rest,' said Walker. He looked at his watch. It was after seven in the evening. 'I'm getting you to bed.'

'Oh, are you?' she said, smiling. 'A bit presumptuous.'

'You know what I mean. You've been up since two in the morning, same as me. I need you fresh and clear thinking for the next part of the investigation. It's not over yet. I'm taking you home.'

'But... shouldn't I—'

'I'm taking you home, Constable,' said Walker in a tone that told PC Briggs there was no scope for discussion.

PC Briggs breathed a small sigh of relief. She seemed tired, had probably been holding on until now. 'Well, make sure you call me if there's any problem,' she said. 'I don't want to miss all the action.'

'Will do,' said Walker, but he intended on doing this one alone.

* * *

Walker arrived at the home of PC Briggs, having driven her straight there from the station.

'Here we are,' he said, without looking at her. 'Well done

today, Constable. You're doing a great job. We've got a really strong lead now.'

'Really?' asked PC Briggs.

'Really. You may have a knack for this kind of work,' said Walker, turning to face her for a second. 'If you can get a bit fitter.'

'Oh, come on. I am pretty fit,' she said, presenting herself.

Walker smiled. '*Go*. Get some sleep.'

PC Briggs nodded. 'You too,' she said. 'You are going to go home soon too, right? Once you've brought Hawley in? You must be as tired as I am. Are you sure you don't want some back up? It could be dangerous.'

'Course,' said Walker, but it didn't sound too convincing. 'And I'll be fine. I know how to handle a drunk. I'm an experienced copper. You'll just get in the way.' He was hell bent on doing this part himself. It was personal, and he didn't exactly know how it was going to go down yet. He didn't want PC Briggs getting involved in a situation that might compromise her career, or complicate things for her in any way. He'd grown to like her and wanted to protect her from this one.

'We need you clear thinking as well, Chief,' she said. 'Probably more than anybody.'

Walker nodded. 'Got it. Thanks for the concern. Now, *goodnight*.'

'Call me if you need me,' she said, before getting out of the car, closing the door, walking up to her home, and disappearing inside.

Walker took a long breath and rubbed his face. He opened the glove box, taking out one small bottle of a PRESS Ginger Shot that was stuffed in there amongst various rags and other bits and bobs. He'd stuffed a couple in there for occasions just like this; it was something he'd been drinking recently to both boost his immune system and energise himself. Drinking it was like getting a slap in the face, or a cold shower. It was intense, a bit like drinking a shot of vodka, neat, only healthier. He used to drink Red Bull for the same reason, but he couldn't do that anymore. He opened the bottle of PRESS and drank it down in one shot, before slapping his face a little as well, trying a two-pronged approach to waking himself up. It did the trick.

'Come on, Jon,' he said, trying to galvanize himself. 'We've got work to do.'

He couldn't let this opportunity pass—not after all those years and decades of searching for this bastard, the man who'd killed his sister, and who was now evidently killing again. He knew he'd resurface eventually, if he was alive. They always did. They couldn't help themselves. And at the moment, this Hawley character seemed the most likely.

He'd definitely woken up a bit. He was ready. He was going after him.

He put the car into gear and headed towards the home of Darren Hawley—their new number one suspect.

CHAPTER THIRTY-THREE

C amped outside of Darren Hawley's residence, just a little way down Springwood Drive, DCI Walker sat in his unmarked Corsa with the engine and lights off. He sat low in his seat, extended as far back as it would go, his eyes fixed on Hawley's house. It was dark now and getting late at 10:37pm, but Hawley still didn't seem like he was home yet. All the lights were off, and the man didn't strike Walker as the kind of guy who could fall asleep early. Plus, his car was gone. Walker wanted to catch him coming home, see if there was anything suspicious. Darren Hawley seemed like a loose cannon, and if his son had mental health problems, then it was possible Darren did as well. The apple never fell far from the tree, he thought. Either that, or Darren really was a piece of work and he'd completely messed his son up, driven him to suicide. It wouldn't be the first time a parent had destroyed a child's life. And if Darren's father turned out to be Bill Hawley, the Norfolk serial killer of the 1950s, then the jigsaw would really start to fit into place. Walker was aware that psychopathy tended to run in families, and this would provide more supporting evidence for the case.

'Come on. Where are you?' muttered Walker. He took a sip of another PRESS Ginger Shot. He was on the second bottle now and wished he'd got more or bought some supplies on the way in. Not that there were many places open at this time who catered to his specific beverage needs, but he knew some service stations that were good for a little snack at least, if he'd gone out of the way a little. No, he was better off coming here directly, he thought, instantly dismissing the regret. He didn't want to miss anything. Although they didn't actually have any strong evidence against him yet, Walker had a strong feeling and wanted to catch up to the man as soon as possible before anything else happened.

He knew he might be grasping at straws again—recognised the signs. He'd been here many times before, thinking he'd gotten a strong lead on his sister's killer. It was a lifelong obsession, something he always came back to. But this time was a bit different. The cross of ash on the two victims' foreheads was very similar to that found on his deceased sister, all those decades ago, all except for the material used to make it—which could be explained, he thought, by the killer quitting smoking at some point and needing some other kind of ash to use. It was either the same person, someone who knew about it who was trying to put them on the wrong scent, or someone who knew nothing of that cold case and was simply coincidentally drawing on a fairly well-known Christian convention. But the more he thought about it, with his sister's one-off murder not really being well documented compared to more lurid cases with multiple victims, it was more likely to be either his sister's killer or a coincidence. It was lucky his sister's case hadn't gotten on the radar of more True Crime publications. He only knew of a couple of the more obscure small presses to have featured it at all, in all of his decades digging around. So, it was very unlikely that it was a copycat. Either way though, he had to find out. Regardless of whether there was a link to his sister's case, he needed to catch whoever was doing this, before they struck again and killed more innocent people.

Walker took another sip of his drink just as some car's headlights started to light up the road ahead. Someone was coming. He got even lower in his seat, popping the little bottle he was holding deep into the cup holder without even looking. The car slowed down, a bit abruptly, and then stopped just outside Hawley's house, turning onto the driveway, erratically, hitting a black wheelie bin on the way in. It was him, driving some old Toyota Prius, one that already had numerous scratches and dents in the pearl white bodywork.

'Come on then. Show me something,' whispered Walker.

Hawley got out of the car and staggered to the rear of it. He'd clearly been drinking. He popped open the car boot and looked inside, trying to find something. Then, he took a quarter bottle of something from his pocket, unscrewed the cap, and took a sip. It seemed he'd been drink driving at the very least, so Walker knew he could arrest him for that—but he wanted to see what he'd do next, see if he'd incriminate himself in some way that would link him to the ash cross killings.

Hawley took something from the car—something wrapped in an old bath towel, a large one, and he carried it in two hands, leaving the car boot open. It didn't look so light and was quite bulky in size. That was Walker's cue to get out of the car and arrest him. He got out, hurried over, breaking into a run, startling Darren, who stopped in his tracks like a deer caught in some headlights.

'Mr Hawley. It's DCI Walker. We met earlier. Have you been drinking this evening, sir?'

"What are you doing 'ere? Are you spying on me?' asked Darren.

'We're observing activities in the area due to the two serious incidents we've had here recently,' said Walker. 'And I saw you come in, driving erratically, hitting your bin, and then taking a sip of something that looked like spirits. I'm going to have to bring you to the station to test your blood-alcohol levels, Mr Hawley.'

'I just wanna be left alone,' said Darren. 'Why can't people just stay out of my way and leave me alone. Let me *grieve*.' He almost shouted this last part, saying it through gritted teeth. 'For Christ's sake.'

'I was sorry to hear about what happened to your son, Mr Hawley,' said Walker. 'But I'm going to have to bring you in now. I'm also going to need to see what you have wrapped in that old towel.'

'What... this? No. This is nothing,' said Darren. 'It's just...'

'Let me see, Mr Hawley. Open it up.' There was what looked like blood on the towel, which Walker could see now, under the light of the porch. 'Put the towel on the floor,' he said, more urgently. If British cops carried guns like their American counterparts, he'd have gotten his out at this point. What he did have though was a baton, so he took it out from his strapped-on baton holder. 'Do it. *Now!*'

Hawley did as asked, getting down to his knees, carefully placing the towel and its contents on the ground.

'Now stand back,' said Walker, and Darren got back up and staggered backwards, along the line of the house, before finding the windowsill of the living room window and gripping on to it for dear life.

Satisfied that Hawley was now a suitable distance away, Walker put his baton on the ground and placed his hands on the towel. It was covered in oil, blood, and dirt. He didn't know what to expect and got ready to act should he find something truly horrific, his mind conjuring up an image of a dismembered human body part, hoping that it wasn't.

He opened up the towel.

Inside, was an organic mess, but there was nothing human in there. It was a fox, badly injured, but not dead. Walker knew this because the fox suddenly twitched and made a sound that a happy animal never makes. It was in distress—in pain. Its back legs were bent in an unnatural position, twisted around, and it had a huge gaping wound in its chest that was bleeding and matted up its fur.

'Jesus!' said Walker. 'What the...'

Hawley started to cry, or something like that.

'I did it!' he said. 'I'm a murderer. I just can't help myself. Death follows me.'

'Mr Hawley, what happened to this fox?' asked Walker.

'Aren't you going to arrest me?' asked Hawley.

'What happened?' asked Walker.

Hawley opened his mouth to say something, but nothing came out. He hesitated... and then ran.

'*Shit,*' said Walker, who was still on his haunches in front of the dying fox, unable to react quickly enough.

Hawley was much quicker than he looked. He was nimble. He ran across the small front lawn in a flash and jumped over the low-lying brick wall surrounding it, bolting down the street. Walker got after him, grabbing his baton first. If it had been a century ago, he might have been wearing a full police uniform, holding a whistle in his mouth and blowing it as he ran to alert others. But it wasn't, and he was just one guy chasing another on a dark, quiet night. Everyone seemed to be sleeping. Most lights in the neighbourhood were already off. He was on his own, and that was just how he wanted it.

'Mr Hawley...' shouted Walker, his voice echoing off the houses and road. 'Stop! You're just making it harder on yourself.'

Hawley kept running, getting even more distance on Walker, crossing over the road and into the wood that adjoined Springwood Drive, through an opening that he obviously already knew was there. Walker followed. It was naturally much darker in the wood, but he had a torch on his belt, so he flicked it on while he was running so he could see a bit better.

'Mr Hawley!' shouted Walker again. He was losing him. He almost wished he'd brought along PC Briggs now. She could have blocked him, helped. He realised now that it might have been a mistake coming alone. He'd made it too personal, gotten in too deep. If he lost Hawley now, he'd never forgive himself.

There was no one distinct path in the wood, but several that went here and there, splitting and meandering, then disappearing completely, before returning again. Hawley clearly knew the woods well. He wasn't hesitating, even under the influence of alcohol—muscle memory guiding him—while Walker was tripping up on protruding tree roots and stubbing his toe on broken branches and the like.

Walker saw him go around the next bend. He had to keep the man in his sights, or he was going to lose him. But Walker wasn't as fit as he once was. He used to play rugby league regularly. He'd played ever since he was a teen, carried on as an adult to keep fit and strong, to stay hard. He'd not played at all since his illness though and doubted he could last for much longer than ten minutes of a game right now. He was huffing and puffing, feeling a little light-headed and dizzy even—but he couldn't think about that now. He had to get his man. He couldn't fail.

When Walker rounded the corner that Hawley had gone around, he could no longer see him. He was gone, damn it. Walker kept running regardless, soon came to a little path that led out of the wood, onto a long straight lane, wide enough for one car to drive down, or a tractor. It was a path next to some farmer's field, ones used for growing crops. This one had leeks growing in it, the pungency heavy in the night air.

Walker looked down the path, towards the main road—nothing—and then up, which carried on alongside more crop fields. There he found the dark figure of Hawley, but he was no longer running. He looked back over his shoulder and saw Walker, then started to run a few more steps, before slowing down and walking again. He clearly had a stitch, or was exhausted, or both.

'Getting tired, are we?' said Walker to himself, gruffly. 'Not like in the movies, is it?'

Walker got after him again with an unwavering determination. But it wasn't long before he got a stitch of his own, and he was out of breath too, so he also slowed to walking pace, just until he could breathe again. He still had Hawley in his sights, on a long straight path on a wide-open landscape. This was a marathon, not a sprint. There was nowhere to go. Nowhere to hide. He simply had to keep on after him. He didn't even need his torch now—the brightness of the moon illuminated plenty, and he was close enough to Hawley to see his silhouette moving.

Walker kept after Hawley like this for some time, with Hawley running for a few steps, before walking again, and Walker doing the same. They were both taking a well needed breather. There was a bend up ahead as the road went up toward a farmhouse, but Hawley took a left, down a long straight path that seemed to go on forever, through row upon row of farmer's fields used for various purposes.

'Bad move,' said Walker. 'I've got you.' Now that he'd got his breath back, and the stitch in his side had eased off a bit, Walker was ready to give it one more concerted effort. He inhaled deeply and started to run, focussing on his breathing this time and pumping his arms and legs as rhythmically as he could.

He started to reel Hawley in, only fifty feet or so from him now. Hawley was trying to run too, having seen that Walker was gaining on him, but he was out of gas, running on fumes. He kept looking around, each time finding Walker that bit closer. Eventually, he headed out into one of the crop fields, one filled with corn. The corn stalks weren't yet fully mature though, at only around four feet tall, so Walker could easily spot Hawley moving around in there.

Hawley turned around once more and saw Walker hot on his tail now, only twenty or so feet away, so he got down, below the top of the corn stalks, out of sight, scrambling around. Regardless, Walker could still see the corn stalks moving, this way and that, and he was able to catch up with Hawley pretty easily, until he could actually see him pathetically crawling around like an animal in the dirt, hiding. He was the prey, and Walker was the predator, about to go in for the kill.

'Mr Hawley, *enough!*' said Walker. He was right on him now, baton in hand, raised and ready to hit. Hawley stopped, turned around, looked at him, eyes wide, fearful.

'Just arrest me and get it over with then,' said Hawley, shaking his head. 'It was just a goddamned fox, that's all. People kill them all the time.' He got out the bottle he had in his pocket and gulped some liquor down, greedily, this time throwing the cap away in the corn field and finishing the drink off, dropping the bottle on the ground afterwards and burping.

'Mr Hawley. I'm arresting you for drink driving, and for evading arrest. You don't have to say anything, but anything you do say may be given in evidence. Do you understand?'

Hawley could hardly stand up now, much less comprehend the extent of the pile of shite he found himself in. He wasn't just drunk, but looked exhausted and malnourished as well.

'I didn't mean to... I just couldn't stop myself,' said Hawley. 'I can't stop.'

Walker grabbed Hawley by his clothes, ushering him out of the corn field. He did it a little too forcefully though and Hawley tripped up, landed on his arse, hurting himself.

'Hey! Isn't this police brutality? *Can anybody hear? This pig is kicking the shit out of me!*'

'Look around. Nobody can hear you out here. Now, get up,' said Walker, pulling the man to his feet, which wasn't easy—he was still a big fella, despite looking gaunt and probably losing some considerable weight over the past couple of years.

Walker cuffed Hawley's hands behind his back and shoved him back towards the woodland path he'd chased him down. It took a while, with much encouragement, pushing, shoving, cajoling, pulling, and even some threats, but they slowly made

241

it back through the woods they'd run out of and back on to Springwood Drive. Hawley wasn't making a lot of sense now. He was too drunk to string a coherent sentence together, and had trouble walking, wobbling, falling over several times. But, with much effort and a steely resolve, Walker finally got the man back outside his house and into the back seat of the unmarked pool Corsa, before safely fastening the seat belt around him.

After Walker closed the door, Hawley slumped over, his face sticking to the side window, drooling down it, his eyes starting to glaze over and close. He was absolutely wasted, smelled like he'd pissed himself at some point too. It was going to take hours before he was in any state to do an interview. Walker would have to let him sleep it off.

First though, there was the little matter of the fox. It was still alive, but barely, and in a lot of pain. It wouldn't make it. It was a real mess. Walker trudged back to the house, grabbing a heavy ceramic plant pot filled with compacted soil and weeds on the way, and looked with some sympathy at the fox.

'Sorry, little guy,' he said, before bringing the plant pot down, hard, on its head, and then once more—just to be sure.

CHAPTER THIRTY-FOUR

'Stick him in a holding cell and let him sleep it off,' said Walker. He was back at Skelmersdale Police Station with the night staff there, Hawley slumped over, sleeping in one of the waiting chairs. 'I'll talk to him in the morning. In the meantime, get me a warrant to search his house, ASAP. Expedite it. Tell them it's urgent, and that a girl's life is at stake. I want it done as soon as the first judge is awake and on the clock.' He couldn't enter without a warrant and risk compromising any evidence, not with what he'd arrested Hawley for. But by arresting him for an immediately chargeable offence, at least they could keep him for longer, if necessary, and potentially keep people safe. It wasn't ideal, what with Emily still being missing and in danger, but Walker thought it was the best possible move, for now. So, he'd just have to wait a bit longer.

'Will do,' said the officer on duty, a plump little woman who worked the front desk, did her fair share of night duties, and had the dark bags under her eyes to prove it.

A couple of PCs entered, returning from a shift, and Walker immediately recognised one of them: it was Mike, his brother-in-law and former friend, the one he rarely saw these days due to how things had turned out with Dawn.

'Mike, hi,' said Walker, a bit taken aback at seeing him. 'How you doing?'

Mike regarded him, not too cordially, stand-offish. 'Just clocking off,' he said. 'Heard you weren't well again. 'Feeling better?' He spoke to Walker like they'd never been friends, without even the warmth one might use with a stranger.

'A bit,' said Walker. 'Back working a case—a big one.'

'As usual. Take it easy then, Jon,' he said, and started to leave, moving past Walker.

'Thought you worked at Leyland?' said Walker, not wanting to end the conversation just yet, having not seen his old friend Mike for such a long time—and wondering whether, if he kept it going, he might also get any clues about how his wife and kids were doing. He knew Mike saw them often. At least, he used to.

Mike turned around. 'Bit short staffed here. Just filling in for a couple of days,' he said, dryly. 'Go see the kids. They miss you.' And then he left, leaving Walker to his thoughts. At least he'd got something.

'Are you going home now?' said the woman at the desk, who'd been listening to the whole thing, probably not sure what else to say.

Walker gave it some thought, but not for long. 'There's a young girl missing, and the clock is ticking,' he said. 'I'm gunna look around for a few more hours, see if I can find anything. Just... don't mention it to the Supe when you see him. Or PC Briggs, for that matter.' He wouldn't put it past Superintendent Hughes to ask Briggs to keep an eye on him and report back, so he had to be careful. He didn't know her that well yet.

The woman raised her eyebrows and sucked her teeth.

'Okay, DCI Walker. But make sure you get some sleep. You'll need to be clear thinking for that interview in the morning.'

Walker started to get paranoid. Perhaps they were all watching him, the desk staff and Mike included. Or perhaps he was just tired and overthinking it. Probably. Regardless, he would need to be more careful from now on, make sure he didn't get on the wrong side of Supt Hughes.

He nodded his thanks and left the station.

* * *

'What are you doing? I'm calling the police.' It was one of Darren Hawley's neighbours—a woman, stood in front of her husband, a guy who looked like a steel worker by day and a heavyweight boxer by night.

'I *am* the police, madam,' said Walker. He was sat on the pavement wearing some latex gloves, rooting through the contents of Darren Hawley's wheelie bins, which he'd placed on their sides for ease of looking, using a torch to see. He got up, brushed himself down, wiped his hands on his trousers, and then got out his well-worn CID identification badge to show her. The woman seemed unconvinced and cautious. 'It's okay. I'm a plain clothes detective,' he said.

Still cautious.

'My husband will go ballistic if you try anything,' she said. She was wearing a silky dressing gown, and her husband was in boxer shorts and a T-shirt, and he didn't look fazed, despite the night-time chill. They both had slippers on. She stepped back and gave her husband a nudge in the ribs with her elbow.

'*Won't you?*'

Her husband rubbed his eyes. He'd clearly been sleeping. 'Yup,' he said. 'Course.'

'Here.' Walker placed his ID card on the ground in front of the woman, and then stepped back. 'Take a look for yourself.'

The woman carefully approached the ID card, and then got down, picked it up, took a good look.

'Oh. I'm sorry,' she said. 'There's been some trouble around here, so we thought... Sorry.'

'There's no need for apologies,' said Walker. 'I completely understand. You're right to be careful. It must look odd. I'm just looking for something.'

'That's Mr Hawley's bin,' said the woman. 'Is he in trouble?'

'I'm not sure yet,' said Walker. 'Why don't you take your husband back to bed, before he goes *ballistic*.'

The woman nodded and turned to go back to her house.

'Wait,' said Walker. 'Have you seen anything suspicious concerning Darren Hawley recently? What do you make of him?'

The woman took a little time to think and faced Walker again. 'He's always been a bit of an oddball, even before his son died,' she said 'Used to stare into our living room, didn't he? And then there was that time he shouted at our Sammy for kicking his football in his garden.'

'He could be a bit of an arse,' said the woman's husband. 'But they were clearly dealing with a lot. We just didn't know it then.'

'What about more recently? Anything odd?' asked Walker.

'He just drinks a lot. Comes home late, banging things and the like, waking us up,' said the woman. 'One time we found him asleep in his front garden. It's become a nightmare. We moved here to what we thought was a nice neighbourhood, didn't we, Dave? It's anything but, now. Everything has gone nuts.'

Her husband sighed, having clearly heard it all before, countless times.

The woman looked at Hawley's driveway. 'His car's here. Why don't you just talk to him?'

'Good evening, madam,' said Walker, signalling an end to the conversation. She looked a little reluctant, but nodded, turned, and went back into her house with her husband following.

There were a lot of beer cans and empty bottles of wine and spirits in the bins. But amongst that, as he sifted through, Walker found something not only of use, but something that could be absolutely crucial to the future of the investigation.

He found a *hammer*—one that was covered in what looked like blood.

Bingo. It was even better than he'd hoped. He carefully placed it in a large evidence bag. Any evidence found on the property without a search warrant would not stand up in court. Except Hawley had hit the bins on his drunken drive home, so Walker could just say some of the contents had spilled out onto the public footpath, which they had. It wouldn't be a lie. Not exactly. It would be permissible—just.

It was now looking like Hawley had killed Tom Woods, Patricia Robinson, and possibly Emily Watkins as well, but Walker needed to know if he'd killed Amanda all those years ago too. He was certainly old enough. Walker had checked the man's ID when he'd been passed out drunk in his car, before taking him inside the station: he was fifty-six years old, which made him just twenty when Walker's sister had been killed. He wondered whether Hawley's father really had murdered someone, whether the young Hawley got messed up by it when he'd found out. Psychopathy did run in families and Walker knew the late teens to early twenties was a prime age for the onset of schizophrenia. He might have had a psychotic break, and in a twisted way this would be in keeping with the religious symbol of mortality and penance used, Walker mused, with schizophrenia often being associated with religious delusions of this type. He'd never seriously considered that his sister might have been killed by someone who was a victim themselves, someone with serious mental health problems. His rage had always steered him away from that. Hawley may have eventually recovered and kept what he did hidden, tried to put it behind him, lead a normal life. But when his son died, perhaps he started to go off the rails again, got into a feud with the Smiths, and those stressors eventually sent him back into psychosis. Walker would need to look into any records of mental illness with Hawley, confirm his age, and ascertain whether Bill Hawley was his father, or not. But it was all starting to stack up and make sense. He just had to prove it.

He still couldn't search the house yet though, not until he had that warrant, as there were no reasonable grounds, other than the proximity, to assume that the Watkins disappearance was connected to the killer and that hammer. No reasonable grounds to assume she was on the premises at all, other than a hunch. And it could also be argued that the hammer could have been put in that bin by anyone passing by. So, he had to tread carefully, get everything lined up properly. But at least he felt he was on the right path now. He just had to walk down it.

CHAPTER THIRTY-FOUR

'If you are there, Emily, hang on. Just a little bit longer,' said Walker.

He put the evidence bag on the passenger seat, headed home, and slept a dreamless sleep.

CHAPTER THIRTY-FIVE

Walker woke to the sound of PC Brigg's voice.

'DCI Walker?' She was knocking on his door with some urgency. 'We've got the warrant, to search Darren Hawley's house. Are you in there?'

He opened the bedroom window of his first floor flat and looked down to see PC Briggs looking up at him, holding two plastic cups with some bright red liquid in them. 'Chief, good morning.' She held the drinks a bit higher, trying to tempt him out, but he didn't need any encouragement. In fact, he was annoyed he'd slept so long. Must have forgotten to set his alarm. Stupid. He must have been exhausted. The sun was up—well up. He looked at the digital clock by his bed. It was well past nine.

'Be right there,' he said, slamming the window closed.

When he got outside, now fully dressed in his usual suit and tie attire, PC Briggs was leaning against her marked police patrol car, sipping on her beverage.

'Can I leave my car here for a bit?' she asked. 'I'll pick it up when we're done, if you don't mind bringing me back here.'

'Alright,' said Walker, taking a drink from her outstretched hand and tentatively sipping on it.

'Don't worry,' she said. 'They're decaf. Red berry teas.

Not bad. I might stick to it myself. Plenty of antioxidants, apparently.'

Before they left in Walker's unmarked pool car, which he'd left there overnight for convenience to save some time if he wanted to get right back to work, Briggs opened up her own car's door and pulled out a bag of something. 'I almost forgot. Butties!' she said. 'For breakfast.' She'd got two sandwiches, both ham and cheese. 'We'll eat them on the way. I got brown bread. Hope you don't mind. Thought I'd keep it healthy.'

'You've got the warrant?' asked Walker, wanting to check. 'Already?'

PC Briggs smiled. 'Yeah. *Expedited*, just as you asked. And you got Hawley, last night, I heard. Well done, Chief. I was worried about you going there all alone. Wished I'd fought my corner a bit more now. Hey, that wasn't a test, was it?'

Walker shook his head. 'Wouldn't have let you come no matter how hard you argued your case,' he said. 'Sometimes I prefer to work alone. Plus, I didn't think you were the kind of girl who'd enjoy a stake-out followed by a good old-fashioned root around in some rubbish bins.'

PC Briggs smiled again. 'I've had worse dates,' she said. 'So, you find anything? You did, didn't you?'

'I did indeed,' said Walker. 'Something potentially really big for the case. Dropped it off at the station late last night for processing, before coming here. Come on. I'll tell you about it on the way.'

* * *

251

'Oh, my God,' said PC Briggs. 'Look at this. It looks like it hasn't been touched since he died.'

They were in the bedroom of Nick Hawley, the deceased son of Darren Hawley. There were some posters on the walls of rock bands Walker didn't know—Vampire Weekend and the Arctic Monkeys were most prominent—along with some photos of various Preston North End teams in their traditional black and white home kit too. Evidently, he was a football fan, or not, depending upon your point of view.

'It's pretty typical,' said Walker. 'They like to keep things as they were. Makes them feel closer after they're gone.'

Nick's bedroom looked like it had been used only that morning. The bed wasn't made and there were various items on the floor and a games console plugged in with the TV still on and the game on pause, half played. It was Grand Theft Auto Five on the X-Box—an oldie now, but still a classic. It was a typical young British lad's bedroom.

'His phone,' said Walker, picking up an iPhone 11 from the TV stand, which was also plugged in and charged. He opened it up, but there was a password.

'Try 1-2-3-4-5-6,' said PC Briggs. Walker raised his eyebrows. 'It's pretty typical. Walker tried, but no joy. Or '0-0-0-0-0-0,' she suggested. This time, the phone unlocked.

'Wow,' said Walker. 'Nice detective work there, Constable. Really? No wonder crimes are committed.'

PC Briggs smiled, seeming happy to be of some help. 'My nephew and niece both have similarly easy to crack security lock screens on their phones too'.

Walker went to the photos folder of the phone and started swiping through. He couldn't find much of any use, so he went to thumbnails and scrolled through more quickly until he found a picture of a girl. He tapped on it and magnified the image. To his surprise, staring back at him was the face of Emily Watkins. He swiped left and then right, a couple of times each way. There were more of her, dressed in her school uniform, on the school bus, stood in her front garden, and each time it looked as if Emily didn't know she was being snapped as she wasn't looking at the camera. He took the photograph of Emily out of his jacket pocket, the one PS Finch had given him, and looked closely, comparing it to those on Nick's phone. It was her alright.

'Bag this,' he said, handing the phone to PC Briggs. 'Seems he had a crush on the Watkins girl. And now she's gone missing. We need to follow this up as well.'

PC Briggs took the iPhone and placed it in yet another evidence bag. They were mounting up. 'This is looking pretty ominous,' she said. 'With the bloodied hammer you found, and now this. Do you really think this could be our guy? He didn't seem the type. He seemed too... *damaged*?'

'That is exactly the type we're looking for. Look, we have a hammer with blood on it and an admission of guilt—although he may have been talking about the fox on that one—and a general opinion that he was a bit unhinged and an alcoholic to boot,' said Walker. 'Plus, there's the possibility his father was the Norfolk killer. If he was, Darren Hawley may have had a psychotic break brought on by the guilt of his dad's killings and his son's crash and death. He might be delusional. Hell, he may even feel some guilt over his own killings, and the cross of ash is some warped expression of that.'

PC Briggs's eyes went a little wider as the realisation of the situation hit. 'He might have abducted Emily to try to redeem himself for what he sees as failing his son. Like some kind of penance. Oh my god, what's he going to do to her?'

'Exactly,' said Walker.

'That sighting we had—the person of interest seen in the woods, the one wearing a hoodie and sunglasses—maybe that was him, dressed like his dead son? Maybe he's summoning a version of Nick through himself, and he's abducted Emily so his son can spend some time with her?'

Walker hadn't thought of that. When they'd first met him, Hawley had said he used to enjoy walking in the woods with his boy. 'We don't have any time to lose,' he said. 'Everything is pointing at him at the moment. But we need forensics to show that the blood on that hammer came from one of the victims, or we don't have enough. Let's look around a bit more. See what else we can find.'

They made it out into the back garden. There, in the corner, was something of a shrine to their son. There was a small gravestone with his name on, along with the dates 1999-2020. Next to it, there was a holder with an urn standing in it. Walker moved over to it, squatted down next to the urn, opened it up. It was empty.

'No ashes,' said Walker. 'That's strange too. I think this is our guy. The weight of evidence is too much to ignore.'

'This is a very weird set up as well, isn't it?' said PC Briggs.

Walker stood back up, faced her. 'What? The shrine? Actually, it's getting more common these days. People even bury their loved ones in their garden. I guess it's cheaper, and they want to feel close.'

'I don't like it,' said PC Briggs. 'Next to the family pets, or the barbeque or whatever. Doesn't feel right.'

'Well, each to their own,' said Walker, looking around the back of the shrine. There was a spot there that looked like it had been freshly dug. The soil was less dry and there was nothing growing—not even a few weeds or grasses, unlike the rest of the untended garden, which was completely out of control. The area in question was several feet long and a couple of feet wide. He couldn't hang on while they assembled a team. It was time to cut some corners. He had to know. 'Get me a spade,' he said. 'There's probably one in that concrete outhouse, or in the shed-slash-garden-office, whatever it is. Break them if you have to and get me something to dig with. Now!'

'Chief?' said PC Briggs, not quite seeing what he was seeing, or following.

'The Watkins girl,' he said. 'I have a bad feeling she might be buried here.'

* * *

Walker had been digging for about five minutes when he hit something, hard. He fingered around in the dirt, grabbing on to an empty bottle of whiskey, looking at it, eying PC Briggs, and then throwing it to one side, clumps of wet soil stuck to it. He knew there was a possibility he might disturb some evidence by not following procedure—artifacts or remains that forensic experts would be slower and more careful to exhume—but Walker chanced that anything found would be evidence enough, and he needed to find out quickly in case he was wrong and Emily was still alive somewhere.

He continued digging, even faster, and hit something solid again. He felt all the way along with the spade. It was several feet long, whatever it was. He got the spade under it a bit, and then used it as leverage, bringing the mass up, wrapped in even stickier wet soil and clay. He was panting, out of breath now, out of everything, running on adrenaline and little else.

'Stand on that,' he said, pointing at the handle of the spade, which he now held low, near the ground. PC Briggs did as requested, keeping the object raised up for him to inspect.

Walker brushed and pulled lumps of clays and soil off of the object, until eventually, he wiped a bit and some red shone through. It was shiny, and something sharp caught his finger when he was vigorously wiping, making it bleed.

'Shit,' he said, pulling back, looking at his finger, before dismissing it and carrying on.

'What is it, Chief?' asked PC Briggs.

He knew what it was now, and he was pretty sure Darren Hawley had put it there.

'You can let go now, PC Briggs,' he said.

'What?' said PC Briggs, still not sure what they had.

'I think it's an electric guitar,' said Walker, breathing a sigh of relief. 'Young Nick's, I presume. We'll probably find other stuff in there too. He's put some of his favourite items in here, like people do in coffins sometimes.

'Thank God,' said PC Briggs.

'Oh, God has nothing to do with it,' said Walker. 'And if he does, then we're gunna have some pretty strong words one day.'

'Or *she*,' said PC Briggs. 'Bit presumptuous, don't you think?' She was looking for some normalcy, the pressure of the situation getting to her again.

Walker got up, covered in dirt, wiping himself down. If it was anyone else, he'd probably tell them to shut the hell up. But PC Briggs had something about her. 'Oh, if this is all made by some omnipotent creator, then I'm pretty sure it's a man,' he said. 'And I don't mean that in a good way.'

PC Briggs nodded, seeming relieved by their little exchange. 'So, now what?'

'Now... we talk to Hawley and try find out what this is all about, and where that poor girl is. And we get forensics to give us some results on that hammer, pronto, as a matter of urgency—as a matter of life and death. Come on.'

CHAPTER THIRTY-SIX

As DCI Walker and PC Briggs tried to enter Skelmersdale Police Station, they were accosted by a lively gathering of journalists and photographers asking about the case. It seemed the media had become a lot more interested since the last statement had been given.

'Detective Walker, have you got any leads on the whereabouts of Emily Watkins?' asked one of them.

'Do you have "The Icehouse Killer" in custody?' asked another. It was the first time Walker had heard the offender described in such a way. The media always came up with a nickname whenever there was a suspected serial killer, and that one seemed to be as good as any.

'Can you confirm that this is a serial killing?' asked another.

They were blocking their path, and Walker knew he wouldn't get inside anytime soon unless he gave them something, threw them some kind of a bone. This was exactly why he hadn't informed the press in the first place: so that they'd stay out of his bloody way.

He stopped walking, putting his hand in the air, indicating he was about to say something.

'Quiet, please,' he said, and the journalists piped down, except for some clicking of cameras and the flashing of lights.

'We're currently working a case involving two homicides and one missing person in the Parish of Rufford. However, this is time sensitive, so we must get on with the investigation now. We'll make a more formal statement in due course.'

One of the journalists, a woman, attractive, late thirties, got a bit closer, right in Walker's face. 'We understand the first body was found in an old icehouse, and the second in a woodland area. And now, a young girl in the locality is missing too? Do you have any advice for the residents of Rufford, given the obvious danger present there at the moment?' she asked. There was a television camera next to her, rolling, with a close up on DCI Walker's face.

'As I already said in my formal press statement, *stay home*,' he said, 'or go out with someone. Try not to walk around alone in secluded areas. The M.O. of the killer involves picking people off when they're alone in quiet public areas. So, try to avoid that, if possible. That's all for now. I have nothing further to add.'

The cameras ramped up on their clicking and flashing, and Walker and PC Briggs finally got inside the station and closed the door, the noise dampened, but not completely.

'Oh, my God! Have you ever seen anything like it?' asked PC Briggs. She seemed a little shaken by all the sudden attention. It had ramped up a notch since the press conference, become a bit manic.

'I'm afraid so,' said Walker. 'Just try to ignore it and focus on your job, Constable.'

'It's hard to ignore when there's a bunch of people blocking your path,' said PC Briggs. 'That was crazy! How did they find out about the Watkins girl so quickly?'

'These things have a habit of leaking out,' said Walker. He

addressed the staff at the front desk. 'How's our Darren Hawley doing? Has he sobered up yet? I need to interview him ASAP.'

'We took him some coffee earlier on, made it extra strong,' said the woman manning the desk. 'He's been banging on the door half the night too—something about a fox. We've got one there—a real nutter.'

'Well, that's the least of his worries now,' said Walker. 'I'm going to need a Psych Eval done on him.'

'I can arrange that for you,' said the woman. 'No problem.'

'Thanks. And I need to call forensics, find out about the hammer I found in his bin.'

'Oh, that already came back,' said the woman. 'It was marked as urgent. I printed a copy out ready for you. Thought it might save you some time.'

She held out a piece of paper and Walker took it, nodding his appreciation, before eagerly taking a look.

'Yes!' said Walker.

'What?' asked PC Briggs.

'The blood on the hammer,' he said, looking at her, dumbfounded. 'It's a match on *both* victims. We have a result. And a hell of a result it is too!' They had the murder weapon. They could charge him for a double homicide now.

'Holy shit,' said PC Briggs. 'That's amazing. Pardon my French.'

'Holy shit indeed,' said Walker. '*Le français c'est bien.* We have him. But what we don't have is the Watkins girl. We need to find out where she is, and fast, just in case... Let's go.'

* * *

'Mr Hawley. Good morning,' said Walker, in a hurry, but trying not to show it. 'How are we feeling today?'

Hawley didn't respond.

'You had quite a lot to drink last night. I'm going to start recording now,' said Walker, pressing the button on the machine to record their conversation. PC Briggs was next to him, while Hawley had his lawyer sat by him, looking through some files. It was a good job too. Walker thought he might kill the bastard if he was left alone with him, especially if he admitted to other, more longstanding crimes—specifically that of the murder of Amanda Morris, Walker's sister. He'd often wondered how he would react if he came face-to-face with her killer. He'd fantasised about it, had some very dark ideas over the years.

'This is May 22nd, 2023, at… 11:23am. Can you tell me your full name please?' asked Walker.

'Darren Hawley.'

'And can you tell me why you're here today?' asked Walker.

'Shouldn't you be telling me that,' grumbled Hawley, before sighing and saying, 'It's because of the fox, isn't it?'

'Mr Hawley, you returned home driving last night with very high levels of alcohol in your blood. We also found a dead fox in the boot of your car. What can you tell us about that?'

Walker wasn't interested in the Fox, but he wanted to start slowly, get Hawley talking a bit first. It *was* killing him to go so slow, what with the Watkins girl still missing, and with him chasing his sister's murderer for all these years too—his patience was tenuous to say the least—but he knew this was the right approach if he wanted to get some valuable information. He'd had it work many times before.

'My client found the fox on the road. He believes it had been

261

hit by another driver first, but he also ran over it by accident, before stopping and putting it in his boot, just in case it could be saved,' said Hawley's lawyer. 'No laws have been broken here. Only dogs and livestock hit by a car must be reported to the police.'

'And you are?' asked Walker. 'For the record.'

'I'm Mr Hawley's lawyer. My name is Robin Fletcher. My client has provided a written statement detailing this,' he said, getting a piece of paper out from a folder, and pushing it across the desk. 'There.'

Walker took a look at it. It was typed and signed off by Hawley, probably written by his lawyer, he thought.

'The majority of the alcohol in his system was also drunk after he stopped the car,' said Mr Fletcher. 'Which I believe you, yourself, witnessed? As you did not measure his blood alcohol levels immediately after he exited the car, and as he drank alcohol after this, you have no proof that he was over the limit while driving.'

The lawyer thought he was there to get his client off on drunk driving charges and evading arrest. He was in for a shock.

'Mr Hawley. The possible drunk driving charges and evading arrest are something that my colleagues will follow up. I don't deal with such relatively trivial matters. What I'm interested in, as a Detective Chief Inspector, is why you had a hammer in your wheelie bin that has the blood of not one, but *two* murder victims—homicides that we're currently investigating.' Walker stopped there, let it hang for a few seconds, heavily, letting it sink in.

'What? I...' He looked at his lawyer. 'I don't know anything about that.'

'I'd like a word alone, with my client, please,' said Mr Fletcher, his face suddenly a good deal more serious and a shade paler.

Walker stopped the recording device. 'As you wish,' he said, before leaving with PC Briggs and heading to the Incident Room. He closed the door and left them to it.

'Isn't it all a bit too easy, Chief?' asked PC Briggs, as they moved away. 'A bit too convenient? For us, I mean. I don't have any experience in these things, but it seems a bit—'

'It is. You're right. But I have a theory about that,' said Walker.

'Do you think he's blacking out, when he's on the booze?' asked PC Briggs. 'I had an uncle who used to be like that—used to wake up in odd places, not knowing how he got there, or what he'd done. My mum used to have to pick him up sometimes.'

'You read my mind. Yes, I think it's a possibility that he's doing this and not remembering. At least, he may not remember where he put that hammer. He seemed genuinely surprised about that. But it is just a theory at present. There are other possibilities to consider.'

'Such as?' asked PC Briggs.

'Well, the obvious being that the murder weapon may have been a plant, what with those bins being so easily accessible to anyone walking by. This tip we got, alleging he's the son of a serial killer, hasn't actually been verified, and we have no idea who sent it just yet. And even if it's true, having a killer for a father doesn't prove a thing,' said Walker. He was trying to remain objective. As much as he wanted it to be Hawley—not just for the present murders, but for that of his sister as well so he could get some closure—he had to make sure he got the right person.

'So, you're thinking it could have been some kind of malicious tip from the real killer, who's then planted the murder weapon in Hawley's bin to frame him?' said PC Briggs. 'Sounds a bit fanciful if you ask me.'

'Yeah. Me too,' said Walker. 'Has the feel of a good old-fashioned nut-job to me.'

They walked into the Incident Room to be met by some muted applause from the staff there. They'd seen the forensics results, which were now on file for all to see.

'Well done, Chief,' said DI Riley. 'Got the bastard. Did he squeal?'

'Not yet,' said Walker. 'Listen up everyone. We're not quite there on this as things stand. We need to figure out where the hell the Watkins girl is, and quick, just in case she's still alive. And in order to do that, we're either going to need a full confession from Hawley, or we need to discover some further evidence or clues from his place and belongings. The answer has to be there, somewhere. We just need to find it. I'm going back in there to talk to him now, see what his lawyer has to say. In the meantime, you do everything you can to find that girl.'

Things were getting frantic now, which was why Walker was speaking more quickly than usual. The clock was ticking, and soon, they'd be out of time—if they weren't already. It was unlikely that Emily Watkins was still alive by now, Walker knew, but they had to try, to do everything they could.

Having finished rallying his troops, Walker returned to Interview Room Three with PC Briggs to finish interrogating Darren Hawley. This time, he carried the hammer that had been used as the murder weapon, wrapped in a transparent evidence bag. They sat down opposite Hawley and his lawyer and turned the recording device back on.

Walker put the hammer on the table in front of them.

'Mr Hawley, we were discussing the hammer that we found in your wheelie bin, the one that has been used to kill two people. This hammer. Is this yours, Mr Hawley?' asked Walker.

Hawley leaned forwards, taking a good look at the hammer, trying to focus, still a little the worse for wear after getting drunk.

'No. I don't think so,' said Hawley. His lawyer turned and stared at him. 'I mean… no comment.'

'Mr Hawley, may I call you Darren?' asked Walker. Hawley nodded. 'Look, Darren, this hammer has undergone forensic analysis, and, as I said, we've found the blood of not one, but two people who have been killed just a stone's throw away from your house in the past week. Do you have any recollection of using this hammer during that time?'

'I do not,' said Darren. 'To be honest, I don't remember much.'

His lawyer leaned back, giving up on the briefing he'd just given his client. It seemed he was a talker.

'Is that because you've been largely intoxicated during that time?' asked Walker.

Hawley gave it a little thought. 'Yes. I've never really admitted it, not even to myself, but I suppose I'm an alcoholic.'

'Okay. Now, think very carefully before you answer this next question, Darren. It's very important. When you drink, do you sometimes black out, and not remember what you've done, or where you've been, or how you woke up in a particular place?'

Hawley started to break down and cry. 'Yes. I do. Do you think I killed those people? You do, don't you? I wouldn't… Why would I?'

'That's enough!' said his lawyer. 'You're leading my client, putting ideas in his head. This will not stand up in court!'

'Do you know that your son, Nick, was stalking Emily Watkins?' asked Walker. 'Had some kind of a fixation with her. Do you know who she is?'

Hawley nodded. 'Yeah. Course. She's Adam and Sarah's daughter. They live close by.'

'And the crush?' asked Walker, leaning closer.

'Yeah, I knew about the crush. My Nicky was always looking at her, ever since he first laid eyes on her. But how did you know?' asked Hawley, still sobbing, but dry crying without the tears.

'Darren, this young girl, Emily, is missing. She has been for two days. She was walking her dog on Rufford Park Lane one evening, and the dog came back without her. She's just sixteen years old. Please think carefully. Do you know anything about this?'

'I do not,' said Hawley. 'I don't remember anything like that.'

'Have you blacked out in the past couple of days?' asked Walker.

'I don't remember much about the past week,' said Hawley, working himself up into a panic. 'Things have been spiralling out of control since my wife went away. I just remember drinking, and falling and hurting my knee, and you turning up at my house. Everything else… It's like the memories are locked in some dark, underground cave. I can't even get a glimpse. But what you're saying… It's… It's… I just can't believe it.'

'Okay. If you don't remember, then it's not your fault, Darren. You're sick. You have a disease. You're an alcoholic.' Walker didn't really mean it, and it killed him to do so, but he needed to be Hawley's friend, so he'd help them find Emily. Finding her was the most important thing right now. 'We just need to find this girl. I know it's a very difficult thing to ask, but if you were to hide a person, or a body, where do you think you would put them?'

'I don't know,' said Darren. He thought some more. 'I really don't know.' He started to cry a bit more, but then stopped, an idea popping into his head. 'Well...'

'*Well* what? Darren?' asked Walker, more urgently. 'What is it?'

Hawley closed his eyes and scrunched them tight. 'I don't want to say.'

Walker banged on the table with his clenched fist. 'There's a girl's life at stake here,' he said. 'You need to tell us!'

Hawley opened his eyes again and looked down at the table. 'Our garden office, next to the concrete shed. There's a secret room in there,' said Hawley.

'What do you mean?' asked Walker. 'A *secret room?*'

'I don't know. I didn't make it. The previous owners must have put it there. It freaked us out when we first found it. We'd been living there for three months before we discovered it. We thought there might be a dead body in there. But there was just bits of junk and some strong florescent lights. We think they might have been growing a little weed in there or something.'

Walker looked at PC Briggs with an expression that told her they were about to leave.

'Mr Hawley. How do we get in this secret room?' asked

Walker.

'The office key should be hung on a hook near the back door. Just go in, and there's a large wall panel on the left at the far side. It's quite heavy, but if you lift and pull, it should come away. You might need to grab a tool for leverage. But that's where you'll find it,' he said. 'The secret room is behind there.'

Walker turned off the recording device.

'You'd better not be messing with us,' he spat, eyeballing Hawley, before looking at PC Briggs and saying, 'Let's go. Now! And bring him with us. I want him there in case we can't find that bloody key.'

* * *

Darren Hawley's garden office consisted of a wooden shed that had been converted and painted a willow colour, set back in the bottom left corner of his substantial garden. The garden had probably once been beautiful, but it was now so overgrown it was hard to imagine. The exterior of the garden office had paint peeling off and some rotting boards, but it was large—large enough to be a place of work if one was so inclined. It had electricity, a PVC window, and a desk. At first glance, Walker couldn't see where a secret room might be located. To the front, the garden office sat alongside a concrete outhouse, which Hawley had referred to as the 'shed' and was primarily used for all his gardening tools and the lawn mower, which evidently hadn't been used for a while. But the concrete shed didn't extend as far back as the office, which meant there was space for an extra, hidden room at the back, which couldn't easily be seen due to the backside of the office being so tight to the fence—too tight to look around.

Now inside the garden office, having already got the key, Walker muttered to himself, 'This is the panel he was talking about.' The other officers, and PC Briggs, were waiting outside, as it wasn't big enough for everyone, and Walker preferred to go in there alone anyway, so he could both concentrate better and protect them from seeing any possible horrors that might lie inside. He pulled at the heavy wooden panel, lifting out and up. It wasn't easy, but after a few jerks, it came free, just as Hawley had described. He slowly slid it over—it was heavy, but he managed. Inside, was a dark void. He got the torch from his belt, took a breath, and flicked it on.

Emily Watkins wasn't there.

What was there was something of a memorial to Darren's son, Nick. A large, framed photo of him stood on the wooden floor in the middle of the room, surrounded by various personal items—a key chain, some trophies for various sports, a Nike cap, and more: various snacks with the wrappers still on, unopened cans of a variety of soft drinks. What was more disturbing was that some of Nick's clothes had been laid out in front of the photo, as if he was lying there, with a weathered old football placed at the top, used as a head. It had a face drawn on its peeling leather with a permanent marker, a bit like Tom Hanks had done with his own blood in that movie *Cast Away.* Hawley, just like Chuck Noland—the character that Hanks had played in that film—had clearly gone utterly insane.

'Damn it!' said Walker, before punching a wall.

'Chief?' came a shout from PC Briggs. 'What was that?'

'She's not here,' he shouted. 'There's just more of Nick's stuff in here. It's a shrine. Wait…' There was something inside the sweater that was laid out on the floor. Walker rummaged inside of it, pulled out a bag of something: it was a transparent bag of ash.

Walker came out of the garden office. 'I found something,' he said, holding up the bag for PC Briggs to see. 'Looks like the cremated remains of Nick, the bag that should be in that urn over there.' He nodded towards the urn next to the gravestone they'd looked at earlier. 'He's gone bloody cuckoo too. You should see it in there. It's mad.'

'We've got him?' asked PC Briggs.

'It looks very much like this is our man,' said Walker. 'We just need a match on those ashes, if that's even possible.' If they didn't find the Watkins girl soon, they'd have to admit it was probably already too late; they'd have to concede that their task was simply to find her dead body so her parents could at least have some closure. 'Bring Hawley,' said Walker. 'Right now. I need to talk to him. And make sure security is tight.'

CHAPTER THIRTY-SEVEN

Darren Hawley was being held in a squad car in handcuffs, supervised by two uniformed officers. They brought him to Walker, who was still in the back garden.

'Leave us,' said Walker.

'Chief?' said PC Briggs.

'That's an order. Leave us!' Walker shouted, and PC Briggs and the other officers reluctantly left them to it.

When they were gone, Walker grabbed Hawley by his clothes, pinned him up against the brick wall of the house, slamming his back against it.

'Where is she?' he said. His head was beginning to throb, pounding hard on the back right side—one of the tell-tale signs of his illness, making him wonder whether his time on the case might be limited. It was time to cut corners, get things done, worry about the consequences later.

'I don't know!' said Hawley. 'I'm sorry… I…'

'Where the hell is she? What did you do to her?' shouted Walker.

Some of the neighbours heard the commotion, opened an upstairs window. 'Hey. What's going on down there? Who are you?' the neighbour asked.

'It's the police,' shouted Walker. 'Check the squad cars at the front. Leave us be, please.'

The neighbour slowly, and hesitantly, closed the window again.

'I'm going to ask you this one more time. Where is she?' asked Walker, holding Hawley even tighter, restricting his breathing a bit.

Hawley started to emotionally break down again, so Walker let him loose.

'Is Bill Hawley your father?' he asked. Di Riley still hadn't been able to confirm this, or not. Information about Hawley's father had been absent from the public record.

'What? *Who?*' he asked, confused.

'The bloody Norfolk Serial Killer, that's who,' said Walker. 'Is he your father?'

Hawley let out an exasperated breath. 'I don't have a father,' he said. 'My mum brought me up. Never met my dad. I don't think she even knew who he was. Never told me his name. My surname is from her—Hawley was her maiden name.'

'Then what do you know? The family your son nearly killed, the Smiths, said you've been harassing them. Do you remember that?' asked Walker.

'They said *that?*' asked Hawley.

'Yes. The father, Alan, was quite angry about it. Him and his poor wife already have a lot to deal with without this, just like you did with your son. Their daughter is disabled, you know.'

Hawley laughed so Walker grabbed him again, pushing him hard against the wall once more. 'This is no laughing matter, Mr Hawley!'

'No. It's not funny. It's just… If anything, it was the other way around. I only went over there a couple of times, to their house, I mean. I just wanted to know what happened to my Nick in a bit more detail, and if they had any final contact with him before he died. I wanted to know what his last words were, if he was in pain, that kind of thing. I wasn't harassing them.'

Walker loosened his grip again, rubbing his head where it hurt with his now free hand, trying to massage the pain away. If the headache wasn't continuous and long lasting, he'd be okay.

'And did he?' asked Walker. 'Have any last words, I mean.'

'They wouldn't talk to me. Said to leave them alone, so I did, after that second visit. I wouldn't have gone back at all if I wasn't desperate. That's when I really started to drink more heavily, after that, I think,' he said.

'And is that the last time you spoke to them?' asked Walker. 'What do you mean it was the other way around? If you were drinking a lot, it's very possible that you kept going there and don't remember, isn't it?'

Hawley started to lift up his shirt and pull down his trousers.

Walker wasn't expecting that. 'Mr Hawley, what are you doing?' he asked.

Hawley pulled his pants down, just a couple of inches, to reveal some scars.

'Bastard pushed me into a bush one night—a bloody thorny one. Hurt like hell!' said Hawley. 'It never really healed properly. I think it got infected.'

'What happened?' asked Walker.

'I'd been drinking again, but not so much yet because the landlord at the pub stopped me. I was walking home from the pub to drink some more, and I stopped to take a piss on a bush. I'd be drinking pints, you see. I felt someone stood behind me and I turned my head while I was peeing. It was him—Alan Smith. He just stared at me, like a psycho, and then shoved me hard, into the bush.'

'Didn't you report it?' asked Walker.

'No. I figured I owed him one, for what my son did,' said Hawley. 'By the time I got out of that damned bush, he was walking away, listening to his stupid earphones like nothing happened.'

'Earphones?' said Walker, his ears pricking up, getting ready for action.

'Yeah. Whenever I see him out and about, walking, he's always wearing those wireless, Bluetooth earbuds all the kids wear these days,' said Hawley. 'And a hoodie, and sunglasses sometimes too. He must be in his forties, or fifties even, but he dresses like a kid. He's a maniac. I'm actually quite scared of him now. He has it in for me. Haven't seen him for a while though.'

Walker ran to the garden gate. Of course. It wasn't just Darren Hawley who might be suffering from PTSD. The Smith family had also experienced the kind of trauma that could lead to this condition, and to associated anger control issues.

'Hey! Where are you going?' shouted Hawley. 'Are we done?'

Walker didn't answer, but he knew exactly where he was going—he finally had a match on their suspect in the woods, someone who was also in the right age range to have carried out Mandy's murder too. He was going to Alan Smith's home. He was going to take him in.

CHAPTER THIRTY-EIGHT

Three squad cars and two unmarked DI's cars arrived at Alan Smith's home at Rufford New Hall, ready to arrest him and search his home. There was only one small lane out of there, which the police cars road blocked, so he wouldn't be able to escape by car, at least. Walker knew they had little actual evidence on him yet, but he had a theory: that Smith was the killer and had tried to frame Hawley by putting the murder weapon in his bin. Hell, he may even have tipped them off about the Norfolk Serial Killer too. There was something just not right about him, which Walker had previously put down to the stresses of living with a disabled child, almost being knocked down by Nick Hawley, and then being harassed. But the conversation with Hawley had now put a different spin on that. What they had to do now was gather enough evidence for a conviction—if what Hawley was saying was true—and that started with finding earbud caps that matched those found at the second crime scene and linking the murder weapon to Smith.

Walker pressed the button for Number 1A and Mrs Smith answered.

'Hello?'

'This is DCI Walker. We need to come inside,' said Walker,

a bit more abruptly than the first time.

'Okay, but...' The buzzer sounded and the front door opened up, letting them through.

Inside, Mrs Smith had already opened the door to flat Number 1A, ready to let them inside. She was visibly shaken, and rightly so. Seven officers entered, with some of them wearing body armour and brandishing batons.

'What's this about?' she said, clearly alarmed at what she was seeing, putting her arms defensively across her chest.

'Where is your husband, Mrs Smith?' asked Walker in a tone that conveyed the utmost urgency.

'He's... he's not here. He's out, walking,' she said.

'Damn it!' said Walker. 'Get the cars out of here. We're gunna bloody spook him.'

Some of the officers left, leaving just PC Briggs and DI Riley on site with Walker.

'Mrs Smith, listen very carefully. We need to search your home as we believe there may be evidence here that could help us save a girl's life,' said Walker.

'What? Why? Do you have a warrant?' asked Mrs Smith. 'What's this about?'

'We do not need a warrant in such circumstances, madam. Section 32 of the Police and Criminal Evidence Act allows us to make a search at the home of a suspect if a life is in danger,' said Walker. 'And we believe it is. So, please step aside.' He'd not felt able to use a Section 32 to initially search Hawley's house, as he'd not had anything really concrete on him. But this time, he had a positive match on the description of the person seen in the woods, and confirmation of the use of earbuds, and this would be enough—or, at least, he hoped it would. It was time to take a few calculated risks.

The woman did as asked, accepting what he said, letting Walker, PC Briggs, and DI Riley through.

Walker went to the main bedroom, a large room with high ceilings. There were various units with drawers—one, a Georgian chest, had clothes in, another cheaper-looking unit had toiletries. He tried the desk in the corner instead, where he guessed Alan Smith conducted his work and made a living as a day trader. It had several smaller drawers, which appeared untidy and not in any particular order, with various bits and bobs being stuffed in each drawer. In one of them, Walker easily found a little bag full of earbud caps, the kind that manufacturers supply as replacements.

He pulled out the little bag and removed one of the earbud caps. It was familiar—*black on the top, but red underneath, round and about the size of a generously sized blueberry*. He'd got him.

'Briggs! Riley!' shouted Walker, and they came running in. 'We have a match on the earbud cap.'

PC Briggs held up the case of an IKEA Fixa Tool Kit that she'd found in the boiler room, one just like the coroner had showed them back in Burscough, this one with a hammer missing. 'And it looks like we have the murder weapon too,' she said.

'We need to find this guy, and fast,' said Walker. 'This is our man!'

* * *

'There's no sign of him,' said DI Riley. Him and the other officers had been frantically scouring the immediate countryside, trying to locate the whereabouts of Alan Smith before he could hurt anybody else. Only Walker and PC Briggs had stayed at the Smith family home, just in case Alan returned. They were sat in the living room, waiting and hoping.

'Mrs Smith, this is very important. What time was your husband due back?'

She looked at the time on her phone. 'About forty-five minutes ago,' she said. She was in shock, not quite sure how to process what was going on around her. She clearly had no clue as to what her husband had been doing, or what he was capable of.

'And is he usually late like this?' asked Walker.

'No. Not usually. Although he has been late a couple of times recently,' she said.

'Mrs Smith, there's a young girl, missing. We need to find her. Is there anywhere you could think of that Alan might have taken her to? Somewhere private?' asked Walker. 'Anywhere at all?'

'My Alan would never… He's not that kind of…' She was shaken, trying to convince herself of her husband's innocence, but not quite making it. 'He's…'

'Mrs Smith. Is there anywhere like that?' asked Walker, more firmly.

She thought about it. 'Well, there's the garage.'

'Where's that?' asked Walker, not knowing they even had a garage.

'It's in the main grounds, through the entrance to Rufford New Hall. We're in the first set of garages on the right. Ours is the third left in the block. I can give you the key, but there's nothing there. I was in there this morning, picking up some bread from the freezer we have in there.'

'Then is there anywhere else you can think of? Somewhere your husband has access to?' asked Walker. 'Somewhere private.'

A light bulb seemed to go off in Mrs Smith's head. 'Oh... of course. His father's house. He died a few months ago, you see, and we still haven't sold it. He checks on it about once per week, although he's been going a bit more recently, sorting a few things out there. At least, that's what he told me.'

Walker snapped his fingers, several times. 'Get the keys and the address and meet me in the car,' he said to PC Briggs. 'That's where we're going! Oh... and Mrs Smith, your father-in-law: was he buried?'

'Why, no. He was cremated,' she said, pointing up towards a vase on the top shelf of a large, almost ceiling high bookcase. 'The ashes are up there.'

'Grab that too,' said Walker. 'Sorry, but we need it. It's evidence now.'

* * *

'Now, go find him!' said Walker, issuing his final orders to the surrounding officers before heading off to the house of Alan Smith's deceased father. If they didn't find Alan Smith soon, he could go anywhere—anywhere in the country, or even beyond. He could kill again, multiple times. There was no telling what he might do. They simply had to find him, and quick. But in the meantime, Walker had to find that girl. She was *the* main priority now. She had been for some time.

Walker got in his unmarked Corsa with PC Briggs, leaving

the rest of the officers and DI Riley searching for Alan Smith. On the way out, Walker drove slowly, still looking out of the windows, seeing if he could spot anything in the surrounding foliage and large bushes that adjoined the road leading out from The Main Hall. As luck would have it, he did see something at the bend in the road, deep within the bushes, up ahead, moving, so he put the headlights on full beam and stopped, got out of the car, leaving the door wide open.

'Chief?' said PC Briggs.

It could have been an animal, but he wanted to see for himself, check it out. He got his torch out too, got closer to the bush, peered inside. It was a mixture of rhododendron plants that were just starting to flower, mixed in with various evergreens, all cut about ten feet tall to create a wall of shrubbery each side of the single lane road leading in and out. There was no noise except for the low hum of the car.

'Hello?' he said.

A branch snapped, like something, or someone, had just stood on it.

Walker got his baton out. 'It's the police. I'm coming in,' he said.

More branches and twigs started to move and snap, faster now, and a dark figure moved across, in front of Walker, and out through the back side of the bush.

'Mr Smith!' he shouted. Walker went in, got through the bush as quickly as he could, scratching up his face on the way, getting tangled on branches, here and there, before breaking free and getting out the other side.

Once out of the rear side of the shrubbery, Walker saw Alan jumping over one of the fences that kept the sheep in the Deer Park, which were just simple wooden stakes with wires running through them—not very sturdy, but enough to keep the sheep out, most of the time. Smith was running across the empty grazing fields now, headed towards a wooded area on the opposite side. The land here wasn't flat, and he kept slowing down, having to navigate around fallen trees or mounds of earth or grasses that were too tall. Walker soon got on his tail, jumping over the fence himself, and he started to make some ground. He had to. This was his chance. The thought that this could be the man who'd not only killed two people recently, and possibly some young girl as well, but who'd also murdered his sister, was more than enough to fuel him, to push him on, despite being near exhaustion already from the events of the last few days. He pumped his arms and legs like never before, taking in great gasps of air, pushing it out with the force of an air rifle, and then sucking in some more. He was moving like a man possessed, like someone chasing his own demons, desperately seeking retribution, hunting down the devil himself. When he'd been chasing Hawley, although he'd been pretty sure that was his guy at the time, there had been something niggling at him he'd been unwilling to fully admit, even to himself, creating some doubt. But this time there was an indubitable clarity that relentlessly drove him on.

He managed to catch up with Smith soon enough, who was moving without the benefit of a torch, which had slowed him down somewhat. Walker was still holding his baton in his dominant hand, and his torch in the other, and once close enough to his man, almost within touching distance, Walker whacked him on the shoulder with the baton and fell heavily on top of him, dropping the torch as he did so. He straddled the man now, still hanging on to the baton, ready to hit him again. But before he could, Walker took a hit in the face from his own torch, hard, on his left temple. Smith had grabbed it in the mayhem. The blow made Walker even dizzier than normal, made him feel nauseous, long enough for Smith to get up again, try to get away. But Walker grabbed his clothing, got dragged a few inches on his back and arse, through the sheep muck and mud, before the man kicked him in the head, not once, but twice. The second connection was solid, as firm as it possibly could be. Walker was taking a beating. He had to let go, or he'd soon be dead, and then he'd never catch the man. Smith got away from him again, obviously satisfied with the blow he'd landed, and ran off into the night.

CHAPTER THIRTY-NINE

'**G**od damn it,' said Walker, breathing heavily, feeling like he might pass out at any moment. He urged himself to get up but couldn't move. So, instead, he grabbed his radio and turned it on. 'Suspect heading south-east into a wooden area just the other side of Flash Lane. All units, get after him immediately.'

'Will do,' said a voice.

'On it,' said another.

'Sir? Are you okay?' It was PC Briggs.

'Not you, Constable. You stay exactly where you are. I'm coming back. We need to find the Watkins girl. Wait for me,' he said. He had to let Smith go, for now, trust the other officers to get after him, do their jobs. He'd done all he could here. He was physically spent.

He managed, with much effort, to pull himself to his knees, and grabbed a nearby crooked branch—the field fortuitously littered with them from a plethora of fallen trees—this one shaped enough for use as a makeshift crutch. He made his way back to the fence he'd jumped over, and this time carefully climbed over it to find PC Briggs waiting for him on the other side.

'Chief! You okay?' she asked, seeing the condition he was

in. 'I'm sorry. I couldn't find you. I didn't know where you'd gone.'

'I lost him. He got me, good and proper. We need to get to that house now, find Emily, see if she's there,' he said. 'Let the other officers do their job, chase him down. I'm finished. Let's go.'

They got back in the car, with Walker in the driver's seat again.

'How far is it?' he asked, while PC Briggs was still busy punching the address she'd got off Mrs Smith into the navigation system.

She paused, waiting for the system to calculate. 'It's just twelve minutes, Chief,' she said. It's just after Croston, on the way to Chorley.

'I'll get there in eight,' said Walker, hitting the accelerator. He was still a bit dizzy, but ready to go, find that girl. The adrenaline was kicking back in, refuelling him. It wasn't over until it was over, and he was still breathing—for now.

* * *

Arrived at the address of Mr Smith's deceased father, Walker pulled up into the gravel driveway of the secluded detached five-bedroom property. It would be worth quite a bit, probably more than half a million quid. Perhaps not enough for the Smiths to retire off entirely just yet, but certainly enough to make their lives easier, and for Alan to start to work on a part-time basis.

'Pitched roof,' said Walker. 'Large enough for an attic.

Check to see if there's a basement too—after checking all the rooms, that is. Any outbuildings as well. *Go!'*

They entered the abode, a dusty place with outdated 1970s décor, and started their search. PC Briggs looked downstairs, while Walker went higher. He did a quick search of the bedrooms and bathroom, but his main interest was in the step ladders that were folded at the top of the stairs. He located a loft hatch and found there was a sliding bolt lock on the *outside* of the hatch door. Not the norm.

'Constable! Up here!' shouted Walker.

He got the ladders and set them up under the hatch, and unlocked the door, pushing and then sliding the hatch door across into the converted attic. He pulled himself up to find a young girl lying in the corner, chained to one of the wooden rafters that held up the roof. It was her. It was the Watkins girl.

Walker got up into the loft and PC Briggs started to follow. 'Is she there?' she asked, urgently. Then she got high enough up the ladder to be able to see. 'Oh, my God. Is she alive?'

Emily Watkins wasn't conscious, so Walker checked the pulse on the side of her neck, in the soft hollow just below her windpipe.

She was alive.

'She has a pulse, but… it's weak. We need to get her to a hospital,' said Walker.

PC Briggs called it in, and they waited for help to arrive, silently praying and hoping she'd be okay.

'Chief, you did it. You found her,' said PC Briggs.

Walker scowled. He was beyond exhausted now, in danger of needing a stay at a hospital himself. *'We* found her,' he corrected. 'And this isn't over until we have Alan Smith in custody. He'll do it again if we don't catch him. He won't stop.'

PC Briggs got closer, and Emily stirred, just a touch, perhaps sensing their presence even if she wasn't fully conscious. PC Briggs held her hand. 'Hey. It's going to be okay,' she said. 'You're safe now. Help is coming. We're going to get you better.'

The attic, like most people's, had a fair bit of junk in there—some boxes full of stuff and various random items here and there: a synthetic Christmas tree in a box, a pile of jigsaw puzzles, and a bag full of musty old clothes. There was also a portable camping toilet near Emily though, with a toilet roll next to it on the floor and an empty bottle of water. If Alan hadn't been for a couple of days or more, she could be dehydrated, Walker thought. She needed fluids, and quick. She certainly looked dehydrated—her lips all cracked and dry. She also had some dried blood on her head and a wound that had started to heal.

'How long?' asked Walker.

'They said about ten minutes,' said PC Briggs. 'Hold on, Emily. Hold on.'

* * *

Walker and PC Briggs watched as Emily Watkins was loaded into an ambulance on the substantial driveway of Alan Smith's father's house. She was still unconscious, but now in the relatively safe hands of Chorley and South Ribble Hospital staff. She at least had a fighting chance now.

'Oh, please. I hope she's okay,' said PC Briggs. 'She has to be. She made it this far.'

'Well, that's out of our hands now,' said Walker, feeling disoriented again, his head still throbbing. He needed to take care of himself soon, or he'd be next. His symptoms were increasing, becoming more potent. He didn't have the luxury of being careful right now though, not right at this moment—not with a serial killer still on the loose, and one who could strike again at any moment. He'd have to take that chance, trust his body to do its thing. 'Let's get back to Rufford,' he said. 'I want to talk to Mrs Smith some more. She must know something about where her husband might be.'

CHAPTER FORTY

Mrs Smith's cup and saucer clinked against each other as she tried to drink. She was a nervous wreck, just barely hanging on, but she'd still managed to make Walker and PC Briggs a cup of tea—Walker agreeing to the offer of the drink, thinking that focussing on something normal might help her to calm her down. He wasn't going to drink it, though. It wasn't the right time to ask for a decaffeinated beverage.

'He had her, at Bob's place?' she said, finding it difficult to believe what her husband had done. Bob, they'd learned, was her father-in-law's name—Alan's father. 'In the attic? Oh, my God. *Alan!*' She slammed her fist down on the dining table in frustration and the noise woke her daughter up, who started to cry. And that was the cue for Mrs Smith to slump forward in defeat—full on meltdown—starting to weep.

Walker nodded in the direction of the crying. PC Briggs got the message and went off to attend to the girl, who'd been asleep in the bedroom, while Walker stayed with Mrs Smith. They weren't going to be able to talk properly until either the little girl was settled again, or until they had a babysitter and they could take Mrs Smith down to the station.

When Mrs Smith's tears had subsided a little, Walker said,

288

'Do you have anybody to take care of your girl, while we ask you a few questions?'

Mrs Smith shook her head. 'No. We've become more and more isolated over the years. We don't have any close family left to help out, or friends. Alan said we can't trust anybody else.'

They'd clearly been having a tough time of it, but, unfortunately, it was soon going to get a hell of a lot worse.

Thankfully, whatever PC Briggs was doing was helping the little girl, as she was starting to quieten down and settle.

'How is she doing that?' asked Mrs Smith, sounding more frustrated than grateful. 'It sometimes takes me hours to get her settled. I have to carry her around on my back sometimes. It's the only thing that stops her crying in the middle of the night. I'm no good at this. I can't do it anymore. Not on my own. Not without Alan. He always knew what to do, guided me. Not that he did much of the doing himself. *Bastard!*'

She was clearly furious with her husband, and rightly so. She might be for weeks, months, maybe for the rest of her life. When she'd calmed a little, Walker moved in.

'Mrs Smith, we need to find your husband before he does anything like this again. And to do that, we're going to need your help,' he said in as calm a tone as he could muster, despite his mind racing. She nodded her understanding, and looked him in the eyes, so Walker went on. 'Let's start at the beginning. Have you noticed anything unusual about your husband during the past week or so? Have you suspected anything untoward?'

'Well… he's been sleeping earlier than usual and getting up later. And he's been even moodier than normal, and that's saying something. But other than that, I didn't notice anything,' she said, exasperated. 'Nothing like this, anyway. Why didn't I know about this? How couldn't I know?'

'It's not your fault, Mrs Smith. But we need to find him, and fast. Now, tell me, how often has he been going out alone, and where did he say he was going?' asked Walker.

PC Briggs returned to the living room, alone. 'She's gone back to sleep,' she whispered, and sat down next to Walker.

'He goes for a walk every day,' said Mrs Smith. 'Alone. The time varies. Sometimes he goes out in the morning, sometimes in the afternoon or evening. This past week, he's been heading out later.'

'I see. And where does he go?' asked Walker.

'Just… all around here. The woods, the Deer Park, down to the canal and around the farmlands, and over at Mere Sands—the nature reserve just across the main road,' she said. 'I rarely ask, these days. He just walks and walks. I don't mind as usually it helps put him in a better mood, but recently, that's not been the case. Kept saying people were bothering him, driving him mad. Something about a dog jumping all over him one time. I don't know. I think I don't always listen properly if I'm dealing with Amy. He says I should listen better.'

'And how long does he go for?' asked Walker.

'Usually about an hour,' she said. 'Although one night, he was quite late, and it made me worry. We had an argument about it. That was one of the days he woke up really late—the next day, I mean. I felt like something was wrong but dismissed it. I shouldn't have, should I?'

'And you saw him, sleeping?' asked Walker, looking at a single bed that sat in the corner of the living room, wondering what their sleeping arrangements were.

'Oh, we don't sleep together,' she said. 'I sleep with our daughter in case she wakes up during the night. And he sleeps alone in the big bed—says it's important he sleeps well so he can work with a clear head. Says we'll be in real trouble if he blows his trading account. That single bed over there is just my daughter's old bed. I sometimes use that too, if she's sleeping well alone. But she rarely does these days, not since the accident.'

'I see,' said Walker. 'And does the main bedroom door have a lock? The room where Alan sleeps?'

'It does,' said Mrs Smith. 'I don't go in there when he's sleeping. He hates to be woken up. Gets angry about it. And if I disturb him while he's working too. So, he locks it when he doesn't want to be disturbed. It's easier that way, so I know, and because I sometimes forget and go in there to get something anyway, even if I do know. He says my memory is going, that I should take some omega-3 supplements, but I keep forgetting to get some, which kind of proves his point, I suppose.'

'And these windows,' said Walker, pointing at the three-metre-high Victorian wooden framed sliding windows that adorned the flat. 'Do they open wide enough to be able to climb out of?'

'Yes, I suppose,' said Mrs Smith, realising what Walker was getting at. 'If the jammer catch is disengaged.'

'So, theoretically, he could lock the bedroom door at night, climb out of the window, be out for several hours, and then come back, and you wouldn't be any the wiser?' he said.

Mrs Smith thought about it, and her shoulders slumped even more. 'Yes. I suppose so,' she said. 'I'd never considered that. He has some kind of sleeping app that makes soothing noises, so all I can hear coming from the bedroom is that. When it's on, I presume he's sleeping.'

'Is there anything else you remember? Dirty clothes? Anything like that?' asked Walker.

'No, not... Well, he did have some jeans go missing. I asked him where they were, and he said he'd thrown them away, that they'd gotten a hole in and he needed some new ones,' she said. 'I thought that was strange. He usually keeps everything and asks me to fix it if there's a hole or some damage. He's pretty tight with money, you see.'

Mrs Smith had now calmed down considerably, at least enough to talk, and Walker was confident she was now thinking clearly enough to be asked what he needed to know.

'Listen to me very carefully now. Does your husband, Alan, have any favourite places he likes to go to? Anywhere that he goes to think or calm down?' asked Walker. 'Anywhere like that?'

'Not really. He just likes to walk around,' said Mrs Smith. 'Although...'

'Although *what?*' asked Walker, right on the very precipice of losing his patience. His headache wasn't going away, his energy levels flatlining. 'Go on.'

'There is this one place: *Ashurst's Beacon*—over at Beacon Country Park, near the golf course. He used to like to go up there, sit on the tower. He brought us there a couple of times, me and our daughter, when she was a baby. Before... when we were happy,' she said. 'Before all this. You might find him there.'

Walker clicked his fingers, communicating to PC Briggs that he wanted to mobilise a fleet of cars ready to go to the Beacon Point. She got up and headed to the door.

'See you outside in a minute,' said Walker. 'Get them prepped and ready.'

PC Briggs nodded her understanding and exited the flat.

'I'm sorry. May I ask, more specifically, what happened to your daughter?' asked Walker. 'We need to know everything. PC Briggs mentioned your daughter is autistic?'

'Yes. When she was two, she was diagnosed with ASD—Autism Spectrum Disorder,' said Mrs Smith. 'And then she started to walk, and run, but had no sense of fear, you see. One day, she got away from me, slipped out of my hand, ran out into the road. A car hit her, broke her back. Now she's in a wheelchair, and she can't even speak to communicate how she feels. She's non-verbal, you see. It's incredibly frustrating for all of us. I can't tell you. And, even worse, the driver of that car had been drinking—failed a breathalyser test. He never went to prison either or anything like that as witnesses saw our daughter run out in front of the car. I often wonder, if he hadn't been drinking, maybe his reactions would have been better. But I suppose we'll never know. I don't think my husband ever really got over that. None of us did.'

'I see. And, as I understand it, this was a completely separate incident? Nothing to do with the Hawley kid,' asked Walker. 'That happened later, right?' He was beginning to see the extent of their bad luck, what they'd been through.

'That's right,' said Mrs Smith. 'A couple of years after Amy had been paralysed, just when we were starting to come to terms with everything, we almost got run over again by that Hawley boy. We couldn't believe it happened again. Another drunk driver. It's hard to believe, isn't it? Alan said the boy deserved to die. He was beyond furious, what with that being the second time. Said people were out of control, that someone should do something.' Her eyes went a little wider as the realisation hit. 'I think he once said it's about time people took the law into their own hands. I thought he was just venting.'

Walker got up. There was no more time to lose.

'One last question. How old is your husband, Mrs Smith?' asked Walker. He was thinking about the cold case again, whether Alan could also have been involved in his sister's murder all those years ago.

'Why, he's fifty-four. I'm his second wife. His first wife couldn't have kids. Amy is his only child,' she said. This meant he was in the right age range to be Mandy's killer too.

'Thank you, Mrs Smith. I have to go now,' said Walker, starting to leave, but Mrs Smith shouted after him.

'Detective. Please don't hurt him! Please don't hurt my Alan. He's not a bad man. He just lost his way at some point,' she said. 'He doesn't know what he's doing.'

'I'll do my best,' said Walker, before disappearing and closing the door behind him.

CHAPTER FORTY-ONE

'There he is,' said Walker. It was sunrise. They'd been out all night, looking for him, waiting, and Alan Smith was now, as hoped, finally sitting at the base of the Beacon Tower, which had a seating area all around it just as Mrs Smith had described. They'd been waiting camped out in the nearby woods, their cars parked out of sight behind a dilapidated old, abandoned pub just up the road. DCI Walker had got him surrounded, mobilising police on all sides of the hill the tower sat on. With everyone set, he checked to make sure he had some cuffs on his belt. He did. 'You wait here,' he said to PC Briggs, who was stood next to him. 'I'll arrest him.'

'Sir?' said PC Briggs, seeming concerned for Walker's safety again, probably thinking it prudent that more than one officer approached him this time. 'What if he's got one final move up his sleeve?'

'I've got this,' he said. 'If he was going to do something, he'd have done it already.' He just wanted to talk to the man, in private. Smith had clearly given up; he wasn't running this time. He'd just calmly watched them get into formation. Walker wanted to find out once and for all if the man had anything to do with the death of his sister. It didn't matter if Smith admitted it in court or not. He'd be sentenced for

295

a double homicide and one kidnapping anyway. They had enough for that. That would be enough to keep him behind bars for the rest of his life. But Walker needed to know, to put it to bed, once and for all. Maybe then he could go back to his wife and kids, finally be a better husband and father. Get some closure. Maybe he could get his life together. 'I want to try to convince him to come peacefully.' PC Briggs looked at him, frowning. 'I made a promise to his wife,' he said.

PC Briggs held an arm out to the other officers, gesturing for them to stay where they were, and Walker began to approach Alan Smith, alone. It was only when Walker was a few feet away that Alan looked up, really saw him for the first time, making eye contact.

'I just needed some peace and quiet,' he said. 'That's all. I just wanted to be left alone.'

'Mr Smith... *Alan*. Do you know what's happening? May I sit down, next to you?' asked Walker.

Alan nodded, reluctantly, so Walker sat a couple of feet away from him.

'You the guy I kicked in the head?' he asked. Walker nodded. 'Sorry about that.'

'What happened?' asked Walker. He'd been a cop for long enough to know when an offender was ready to talk. The man couldn't wait to explain, to try to cleanse his soul. 'We know what you did. I just want to know *why*?'

Alan gulped, hard, having difficulty swallowing. 'My daughter... you know... some guy broke her back, paralysed her. She'll be in a wheelchair for the rest of her life,' said Alan. 'Bastard had been drinking. As if she didn't have enough challenges already. She was diagnosed with ASD when she was little. She's non-verbal, you know. Can't even tell us when she's in pain, or when she's uncomfortable. It's been hell.'

Walker nodded. 'Your wife mentioned,' he said. 'I was sorry to hear that. Must have been tough.'

'It was. We were just trying to live our life, do our best to be happy with what we had, but it wasn't easy. We used to go for an evening stroll together, after our main meal. My daughter seemed to like it. I'd push her in her chair. She'd smile at the trees and the little bird noises. It was the only time she really looked at peace. Then one day, out of the blue, that arsehole Nick Hawley almost ran us over, hurtled right across the footpath in front of us,' he said, anger rising, the feelings of it all obviously coming back to him. 'He deserved to die. We haven't been for a stroll together since. My little girl starts to cry every time we try to take her out of the house now.'

'He did kill himself, though, didn't he?' asked Walker, sensing there was more to it. 'He committed suicide, right?'

Alan sighed and shook his head. He was ready to give everything up, without a fight. He was as spent as Walker was.

'After he crashed into that tree, I went over there. My wife said I should see if he was alive. So, she called 999, and I went over. I was fuming, beyond angry. I managed to open the car door, and he was wedged in by the steering wheel—no air bag. He was bleeding out, clearly injured, but still alive. He looked at me and started laughing. Can you believe that? *Laughing.* He smelled of alcohol, and there was a half empty bottle of Bell's whisky on the passenger's seat. I just lost it; went into a fog I couldn't find a way out of. I looked back at my wife, and she had her back to the car, on the phone. So, I…'

'What did you do, Mr Smith?' asked Walker.

'I...' Alan gave it some thought, just for a few seconds, and then smiled, giving up. He was going to prison. He knew that. It was too late. One more wouldn't make any difference. 'I pulled an old rag from the car door and stuffed it in his mouth. His arms were pinned; he couldn't move. Then I put my hand over his mouth and held his nose. It seemed to take forever, with him twitching and convulsing, probably a minute or so; but I kept checking my wife wasn't watching and carried on. After it was done, I put the rag in my pocket, got rid of it. It was easy. I felt so much better.'

'And everyone assumed he'd died in the crash,' said Walker. He knew that coroners didn't always carry out post-mortems on road traffic fatalities if the injuries were severe enough, and if families were opposed, and it seemed this was the case here.

Alan nodded. 'I thought I'd feel guilty, but I felt empowered. Things at home even got better for a while. I started having sex with my wife again. We even talked about trying for another child. I finally felt like I had some control back in my life. But then my father died, and things started to spiral out of control again.'

'Sounds like you've had a tough time of it,' said Walker, thinking that giving him a bit of sympathy might open him up even more. He needed to know everything.

'You've no idea,' said Alan. 'No idea at all. My dad had cancer—a rare form, a sarcoma of the kidney. They gave him six months, but he only lasted for three. It was hard to watch him go like that.'

'I bet,' said Walker, feeling impatient, but trying not to show it, knowing that patience was going to be key in getting all the facts. Patricia Robinson had been through a similar thing with her husband, had watched him die of a different type of cancer. They'd both been suffering, but Alan hadn't considered that other people had problems too. He'd been too self-absorbed, and so he'd killed the poor woman in cold blood, become something like a cancer himself.

'My relationship with my wife started to go downhill. We argued a lot,' he said. 'Stress seemed to come from everywhere—my job, the neighbours, trying to sell my father's house. And, of course, caring for my daughter is a twenty-four-hour affair, and it's tough. There's not really any respite. The only thing I had to relieve some of the pressure and stress was my daily walk. That was it. I don't have anything else. Sad, isn't it? My wife agreed I should have an hour to myself every day to get the blood moving, as I'm sitting for most of my work. I'd listen to music, try to turn off completely. I found a nice route, in the Deer Park, where nobody ever bothered me. But then that bloody dog walker started coming there,' he went on, with some disdain.

'Tom Woods?' said Walker.

'I never knew his name,' said Alan. 'He had this dog that would run at me, jump all over me, get me full of mud and muck. It was big, strong. It almost knocked me over one time, scratched me with its paws. He had no control over it. He'd chase it around, trying to catch it, trying to put it on a lead. But it was impossible. They shouldn't let them off the lead if they can't control them! I was furious. You have to understand how precious that time was for me. Without that, I felt like I was going insane.'

Walker wondered whether he was insane in the first place, or whether that had tipped him over the edge. 'So, you killed him?' he asked.

'No. Not just like that. The same thing happened a few times, and I got more and more angry about it each time. Even when he wasn't there, my walk wasn't the same anymore because I was looking around, expecting to be mauled by that bloody dog again. I started to fantasise about killing him at first. Then, the next time I saw them, I warned him, told him to his face that he'd better have his dog on the lead the next time I saw him. He told me he was training it, that he was taking advantage of the field as it didn't have any sheep in at the time—that he didn't know people walked there. I told him if he didn't keep the dog on the lead, he'd be sorry.' Alan shook his head, still annoyed about it. 'I couldn't sleep for thinking about it. It became an obsession. Then one evening, after dark, I killed a sheep. I wanted to know how it would feel. I wanted to practice killing. I did it with a knife, then shoved it in a big bag and put it in the water there. I had real trouble sinking it at first and getting it deep enough, so I decided there and then that I wouldn't be doing that again. So, I started to come up with other ideas.'

'That was you? So, you planned it then,' said Walker.

'I really believed he deserved to die, that actions have consequences. I saw him in the woods one day with the dog off the lead again, heading toward the Deer Park. They didn't see me, and I vowed to bring a hammer in my pocket the next time. I was incandescent with rage,' said Alan. 'I wasn't really sure that I'd do anything with it, when the time came. I just wanted to feel empowered. But, when that time did come, my rage took over, and I hit him. I'd got a taste for it.'

'And you took him to that old icehouse,' said Walker.

'I pulled him into some bushes at first, got him out of sight.

I thought he was already dead. Then I came back at night, a couple of hours later, with some equipment from my garage, dragged him towards the icehouse—which I'd seen many times. He even woke up at one stage, scared the shit out of me, and I panicked… finished him off. That was the hardest part. I had no choice at that point though. It was too late. Once I got him to the icehouse, I cut the padlock off with some bolt cutters I'd prepared, and put him in,' said Alan. 'Out of sight, out of mind. I'd been carrying a small bag of my father's ashes around with me ever since he died. I sometimes sprinkled some in a place I liked while out walking. That's what I used to mark the body. Then I put a new lock on the gate so nobody could get in and got rid of the old broken one in my garbage bin the next day. I'd always been drawn to that place, for some reason. Always wanted to see inside.'

Walker wanted to know more about the cross of ash—was desperate to know more—but he'd save that for last. He needed to get all the facts first, to make the case watertight. 'And the dog?' asked Walker.

'It was a stupid thing. I chased it off before I hid him in the bushes, and it just went running, all over the Deer Park, enjoying itself. Like it thought we were playing. So, I just left it to it,' said Alan. 'It wasn't its fault. It was its stupid owner.'

'And did doing this give you feelings of empowerment again?' asked Walker.

'It did. For a short while. But not as strong as the first time,' said Alan. 'I was getting addicted to that feeling, I think. I needed it more and more, just to survive, just to get through the day.'

'So, you killed again?' asked Walker.

'The old lady. She was mean. It wasn't planned. Wrong

place, wrong time. I was just trying to get some peace again, on my daily walk, get back to my baseline, and she started having a go at me. Said I shouldn't be there. Asked me where I lived, and said I had no right to be on that land. Told me to get out. That place is the only thing that's been keeping me sane for the past couple of years,' said Alan. 'It's my meditation. Without it... I'd have been lost.'

Walker once again wondered just how precarious Alan's mental health had been during that time, whether he might have been stark raving bonkers already, but he let him go on anyway. He didn't want to stop now. If he got him back to the station, Smith might have time to think, clam up, ask for a lawyer. So, it was better to get a full confession now, write it up at the station, and then get him to sign it in an official interview. Plus, he needed as much information as possible as soon as, to make sure they had every angle covered, and to make sure there had been no more murders.

'You hit her, with the same hammer?' asked Walker.

'Yes. I'd been carrying it in my pocket ever since. It gave me comfort, the same as my father's ashes. So, when she started shouting at me, I figured I had nothing else to lose. I'd already killed two people, had that on my conscience forever. One more didn't seem to make much difference, in the moment. When she turned to leave, I hit her on the back of the head, and then a couple times more once she was on the ground. She was gone in seconds. Her dog didn't even seem to care. I was going to whack the little mutt as well, but it kept licking the blood off her head, smacking its lips and looking at me with some kind of gratitude in its eyes, which seemed kind of funny, so I hesitated. But then it started yapping, so I tried to chase it off, but it was too quick and just kept on barking.

I knew it might attract attention, and it was such hard work to hide the first body, and I didn't have the strength to do it again, so, I just dragged the corpse off to one side; and after hastily marking the head with another cross of ash, I covered it with this piece of garbage I found. I knew it would be found soon, what with the dog still circling the body and barking like crazy, but I didn't care. Maybe I wanted to be caught,' he said.

'Why's that?' asked Walker.

'Because prison would be a holiday to me,' said Alan. 'No more responsibility. No more trying to earn a living. No more dealing with my wife and daughter. No more anything.'

'I see,' said Walker. 'And what happened with the Watkins girl—the sixteen-year-old that we found in your father's attic? Why did you do that?'

'Her. She was littering,' said Alan. 'I know that sounds ridiculous. But she left some dog crap near the footpath. Someone had been leaving shit in those dog poop bags there for years. One time, we accidentally ran over some with my daughter's wheelchair, and it got everywhere after she rolled the wheels—all over her hands and face. We worried she'd got some in her eyes, so we had to take her to A&E to check it out. She had to take antibiotics for it and getting her to take oral medication is a nightmare. We had to force feed her the stuff, hold her down. It was awful. Felt like we were abusing her. Sometimes, people leave the dog poop bags by the side of the road for cars to squish. It's criminal. Someone had to do something. People are out of control. Actions have consequences.'

'But she was just a young girl, Mr Smith. Still at school,' said Walker. 'A child.'

'Well, she was a lippy one, and she didn't look like a child. Her parents should have educated her better. I told her to pick it up—the dog shit—and she got abusive. So, I snapped again. Everything I'd held in over the years, all the frustrations, all the bitterness, came flooding out. I got out of the car and just hit her until she lost consciousness,' he said. 'The Cocker Spaniel she had was going nuts, even more than the old woman's little mutt. Barking and snarling, nipping at me—it even grabbed my clothes a couple of times while I was dragging the girl over to the car. I don't know what it is about people and their dogs around here? They must have nothing better to do. I swung at it a couple of times, trying to shut the thing up, but the bloody thing dodged out of the way. When I was driving off, it chased after us halfway along the main road, still yapping, stupid thing. Anyway, I took the girl to my father's place, thinking to bury her in the garden or something, but she was still alive. I couldn't do it. Not this time. I realised what I'd done once I'd calmed down. When I got a good look at her, I realised she wasn't much older than my daughter. So, I tied her up in the attic while I thought about what to do—tried to figure out what was best. I wasn't scared of being caught. My life was over already. I just wasn't sure what was best for my family. I had some life insurance, so thought maybe there might be a way to... Things just got out of control so quickly, and I couldn't find a way back. Is she okay? The girl? You found her?'

'She's in a critical condition, Mr Smith. But at least she's in safe hands now, at the hospital,' said Walker.

Alan nodded. 'That's good. I'm not a bad man, Detective. Life just got the better of me, that's all, and I got angry. Sometimes, people need to be angry. *Should* be. But it took over, became too strong, completely uncontrollable.'

'There's just one more thing I need to ask you,' said Walker. It was time. He steeled himself, wondering if this might be the moment he finally found out who'd killed his sister all those years ago. 'The cross of ash that you put on the forehead of the first two victims. Why did you do that?'

Alan took a deep breath and exhaled. 'I'd fantasised about using my father's ashes in that way for a while, had always had dark thoughts like that. My rage had been building for some time, getting out of control, hating everyone. The night I killed Tom Woods, I'd whipped myself up into a wrathful frenzy I suppose, and I went out into the woods and the Deer Park very much on edge. Looking back, I was just itching for an excuse to use that hammer on someone, anyone who proved themselves to be deserving of death—and in my mind, that guy was. He'd been ruining my walks for weeks. I was so angry I couldn't sleep. I think seeing him that night was fate. It was meant to be. I got the idea for the cross of ash from a book. You'll find it on a shelf in our main bedroom, where I work—a book about murders conducted in Lancashire. I'm a True Crime fan, you see. Some little girl was killed, back in the eighties, and the killer placed a cross of ash on her forehead. So, I used that. It seemed fitting, somehow—penance for his sins, or something—and I also thought if I copied it, it might throw the police off for a while.'

Walker felt deflated, like he'd just been gut-punched. 'So, you had nothing to do with the death of that little girl in 1987?' he asked.

'1987? You know the date. You're familiar with it? No, of course not, I spent my teenage years in South Africa in the late eighties. My father worked over there for a while,' said

Alan. 'He was an engineer.'

Walker had suspected, deep down, that it wasn't the same killer—the MO was just too different. But hearing it was still a crushing blow. He'd wanted it to be him, to put it to bed, once and for all, to get on with his life. But that wasn't going to happen now. It would have to be confirmed, but it seemed he'd reached yet another dead end on that.

'And the ashes?' asked Walker.

'My father's,' said Alan. *'For you were made from dust, and to dust you will return.'* Walker looked up at the night sky. So many stars. 'I suppose we're all just stardust,' he said. 'Life is fragile and precious. And you... have killed two people and kidnapped one. I'm arresting you now, Alan. I'm going to read you your rights.'

Alan nodded. He wasn't going to resist this time. Not at all. Walker took out his handcuffs and secured him ready for transit.

CHAPTER FORTY-TWO

'Chief! We have another one!' said one of the police officers who'd been helping to form a perimeter around the Beacon Point. It wasn't over. Not yet. 'Over here.'

Walker was escorting Alan Smith off the hill they were on, towards a squad car that had been moved a little closer at his command—to a public car park that fronted the golf course, just across from the main road at the bottom of Beacon Point. They hadn't used the car park earlier as they didn't want to alert Smith to their presence. But using it now would make escorting him easier, hence the order. They hadn't got very far before being called though.

'Hold him,' said Walker to a couple of the officers. 'Take him to the car. And make sure he doesn't get away.' There were more than enough officers around to make sure he gave them no more trouble, especially now his hands were cuffed.

Walker rocked his head toward a woodland off to one side—where the officer who'd called him had come out of—to communicate to PC Briggs to follow him. She did. When they got to the site in question, it was complete and utter carnage. A young girl, five years old, was quietly crying her heart out, being comforted by two of the female police officers.

Although she was physically unharmed, both her palms were covered in blood, and there was some on her face too. Her parents had been bludgeoned to death, hit repeatedly and violently with a crowbar that now sat to one side, clearly just thrown there after use for them to find. One of their heads had been hit so hard it had completely caved in.

'*Jesus!*' said PC Briggs. There was no doubt about what had happened, or who had done it. 'Why would he...?'

Walker got a little closer, surveyed the scene. This one wouldn't be difficult to solve. Smith hadn't been wearing any gloves—there'd be fingerprints all over the murder weapon: *his* fingerprints; although it wasn't yet clear where he'd got it from. And there were more crosses on the victims' foreheads, drawn on with dirt this time. He'd seen enough. These people had been at the wrong place at the wrong time, probably trying to catch the early morning sunrise from the viewpoint, while Walker and his crew had been hiding out in the opposite woodland, waiting for Smith to arrive, keeping their eyes on the Beacon Point. They'd seen and heard nothing of this. It had been done stealthily and the little girl was quietly weeping rather than wailing out loud, so they hadn't been alerted to the incident.

By the time they got down the hill to the car park across the main road, the whole convoy of marked and unmarked police vehicles were already there. Something else was going on too. There was frantic shouting and ambulances arriving, sirens blazing and lights flashing—too many for the latest victims they'd found. It was utter chaos. Some of the officers were jumping over the stone wall that fronted the golf course, down onto the field. Others were already out there, crouched down next to battered bodies on the grass, administering CPR, doing chest compressions and mouth-to-mouth. It seemed that before going to the Beacon Point, Mr Smith had gone on a killing spree. It was a bloodbath. There were six elderly golfers down—four male and two female, and only two of the males were still moving.

'Oh, my God. Chief? What has he done?' asked PC Briggs, in a state of shock. What she was seeing was now too much to comprehend, and even DCI Walker, with all of his decades of policing experience, was taken aback. He had no answer for her.

The only light at the end of this horrific tunnel was that Alan Smith was now safely locked inside a squad car. He'd already been ushered into it before Walker and PC Briggs had arrived, a car parked facing the panorama of the golf course, a normally tranquil recreational area that had been transformed by him into a killing field. The officer who'd seen the slaughter first had no doubt immediately alerted his colleagues, who'd already notified emergency services and started to help.

Smith stared at Walker and PC Briggs from the side window of the back seat of the car, watching them as they stood next to the vehicle looking out at his work and then back at him, dumbfounded. When they were done, they looked at Smith once more, who smiled. It was a smile Walker hadn't seen before, one that was somewhere between creepy and downright evil.

'Chief? I don't understand. Did he do this for fun, or because he was having some kind of a breakdown?' asked PC Briggs.

'I'm not sure,' said Walker, shaking his head. 'But in the end, what's done is done.'

CHAPTER FORTY-THREE

All the staff from the Incident Room at Skelmersdale Police Station had met at the Bull and Dog pub in Burscough to toast a drink to the arrest of Alan Smith. It was a station tradition for big cases like this, but this gathering was particularly subdued. What had happened had shocked them all. DCI Jonathan Walker in particular didn't feel much like celebrating. He wasn't a big fan of all this back-patting at the best of times, and this was far from the best of times. When the case had started, it looked like he might finally get on the trail of his sister's killer—the symbolic drawing of the cross on the foreheads of the first and second victims was uncannily similar to that case. But with Alan Smith being confirmed as being out of the country at the time of Walker's sister's death, it was impossible that Alan and the cold case killer were one and the same. It was a copycat, and Smith had admitted it. Walker was back to square one. Another dead end—one of many he'd had since beginning the arduous task of finding the person who'd killed his sister. It was why he carried on working for the Lancashire Constabulary, in spite of his declining health. There was always *some* hope, but on this occasion, he felt less optimistic than he had in a long time. In a word, he was feeling down.

They had two tables at the pub, which all the police staff squeezed around. Walker was on the same table as PC Briggs. All of them were off duty, but some had to start a shift soon; so, some were drinking alcoholic drinks, and some were not. Walker was not. He wasn't working soon. He just couldn't drink. Not with his meds. Also on PC Briggs's table was the box containing her birthday cake that the staff had rallied to buy, as yet untouched.

'I'll get the next ones,' said PC Briggs to her table. Despite the feeling amongst them, the gathering was helping. They needed a break and some downtime. 'DCI Walker, could you give me a hand?' Walker started a slow clap. He didn't like such jokes, but the other officers and detectives needed some small relief, and typically expected this kind of thing when they were winding down, so he went with it. They needed someone to lighten things up. Everyone had put a lot of work in to get the case to a conclusion, and a lot of overtime. Many of them had families of their own, so Walker appreciated the effort. It might not have been a great result, but it was a result, nonetheless; he thought they should celebrate that, try to get back to normal, try to get what they'd seen out of their heads.

'Very droll,' said PC Briggs, standing up to make her way to the bar. 'Come on.'

'Oh, alright then,' said Walker, standing up and following her.

When Walker's sister had died, young Jon had been just sixteen years old, and his sister only eight. They'd been playing at the local park and Jon was supposed to have been supervising her. He'd been playing football with his pals, while his sister had been playing on the swings and the slide, alone. She disappeared, went missing, and turned up dead a day later in a field a few miles away, having been beaten and strangled—the killer leaving a cross of ash on Amanda's forehead, drawn with a cigarette: a *Benson & Hedges* to be precise, something that had only recently been discovered via forensic analysis. He'd just got the result a few days back, in fact, had requested it a while ago after reading that article in the journal he'd bought. That gave him another avenue to follow, at least, though it wasn't much. The murder had been a brutal act that shocked the community at the time, and the killer was never found, of course—although someone was wrongly arrested to begin with. Walker had never forgiven himself for not taking better care of his kid sister, and he doubted he ever would. It was his fault she was dead.

They got to the bar and ordered the drinks, with Walker still struggling to appear to be pleased about the conclusion to the case. It had not gone as he'd hoped at all—eight people dead in the end, an orphaned little girl, four people seriously injured, including at least one probably traumatised for life in Emily Watkins, even if she did make a full physical recovery. Plus, a cold case that remained firmly in the freezer. It had been an unmitigated disaster.

'What is it, Chief?' asked PC Briggs, who'd remained remarkably upbeat after the initial shock of seeing everything had settled in. 'We did our best. We couldn't have done anything more to save those people. You have to let it go.'

She thought he was beating himself up because they hadn't been able to prevent Alan Smith's final few attacks, but it wasn't that. He'd seen it all before and wouldn't still be in the job if he held on to such things. Shit happened. Their job was simply to reduce the detritus as much as possible and help convict those who created it. He'd handle that, in time.

They did their best with the resources they had—followed procedure. What was really getting to him was his sister's case. It seemed like it would never end, and it was an obsession he just couldn't let go of. It defined him.

'It's not that,' said Walker. 'I mean, it's tragic, and I wish we could have done more, but wishing won't make it come true. I'm experienced enough to accept that. Although... *you* are not. You're handling this very well, Constable. Maybe you have the right stuff to be a DI one day.'

PC Briggs smiled a pained smile. 'Well, I have to admit, I have enjoyed the challenge of the case. It beats the day-to-day rounds as a PC, that's for sure. I'll think about it—look into it some more.'

Walker started to gather the drinks together on two trays while PC Briggs paid the bartender. A women came over and joined them at the bar. It was one of the journalists who'd accosted them at the station, the good looking one who'd got right up in Walker's face, the TV lady. She looked at him and smiled.

'Don't worry. I'm not working now,' she said. 'Congratulations on the arrest. I heard. I'm working on another story at the moment. One of my colleagues has taken over reporting on that one.'

Walker nodded. 'Thanks.'

She placed a folded napkin in front of him and walked away without even ordering a drink, her posture exemplary, head held high. Walker unfolded it to find a phone number written on it next to the name *Emma* and *Call Me*. PC Briggs saw it before Walker could think what to do.

'Nice. You pulled,' she said, smirking. 'You got kids?'

Walker sighed. 'Enough with the questions, Constable.

You're not a detective yet,' he said.

'Sorry, I... Just want to know who I've been working with, that's all,' said PC Briggs. 'I don't—have kids I mean, if you're interested at all. I'm single. I had a boyfriend, but... it wasn't good. So, now I'm on my own.'

'Well, good for you,' said Walker, feeling a tad uncomfortable, not quite sure if she was coming on to him or not too. Probably not, he thought. He was almost twice her age for a start. Then again, the journalist didn't look much older. 'I have two children. They're in their teens now. But I don't see them much.'

'Divorced?' asked PC Briggs. 'I'm *so* sorry. A bit on the nose. Too many questions, I know. I get like this in pubs after a drink. Start shooting my mouth off.'

'Then perhaps you shouldn't drink then,' said Walker, dryly. He crushed the napkin and pushed it across the bar, but PC Briggs quickly grabbed it and stuffed it in his suit jacket handkerchief pocket.

'You never know,' she said, patting the lump in the pocket. Walker didn't respond, stone faced, and instead began carrying the trays of drinks back to their table.

'Here they are!' said DI Riley. 'Where have you been? We're all parched here? Not been doing anything we wouldn't do, I hope!'

'We've been at the bar, Detective,' said PC Briggs, taking a pint of beer and being less than careful in handing it to the DI, spilling some of it on the table as she passed it over.

'Thanks,' he said, before raising the glass. 'Well done, everyone,' he said, in a muted tone, with everyone remaining a bit subdued. 'We got our man. Cheers.'

They all grabbed a drink and muttered cheers, clinking

glasses, before taking the customary sip.

'Come on, DCI Walker,' said DI Riley. 'You could look a bit happier about it. We've all worked very hard on this one. Really gone through the pain barrier.' He held his face where he'd had the wisdom tooth removed and smiled. He too was doing his best to lighten the mood in what were otherwise dire circumstances.

Walker held out an apologetic hand. 'I thank you for all the hard work you put in on the case,' he said. 'Really. I'm grateful that Alan Smith is now in custody, and the streets are that much safer. You did a great job, everyone.'

Superintendent Ronald Hughes was also there. He didn't usually come to these kinds of things, so Walker guessed he was trying to be supportive. He was the only one who knew of Walker's personal connection to the case, of course—how he'd been desperate for the Icehouse Killer to be the same person who'd murdered his sister all those years ago. He'd know how crushed Walker would be about the result, even though they'd not talked about it yet.

Superintendent Hughes slowly stood up, and his position was such that the others all looked at him, attentively, getting ready to listen to what he had to say.

'I think what DCI Walker is trying to say is that this has been an arduous case for everyone concerned, and while we're thankful for a relatively quick resolution, eight people have died, and so, in that sense, there is little to celebrate, as we all know. By all means congratulate yourselves for a job well done—you deserve that—but come tomorrow, there'll be more criminals to catch, and more people to keep safe. So, don't drink *too* much. But feel free to go mad with the birthday cake,' said DS Hughes, glancing across at PC Briggs and smiling. 'And DCI Walker, you take a good rest. Take a week off. Recuperate. You've been absent for a while, and you need to get your stamina back. But may I, on behalf of everyone, thank you for returning from your leave of absence early to work on this case, and seeing to its speedy resolution. What we can say, is that while the deaths of all those people *is* a tragedy, the work you've all done over the past few days may well have saved many more lives. So, well done for that.'

'Here, here,' said DI Riley. 'To DCI Walker. And with that, they all raised their glasses again, this time a little more upbeat, and collectively said, *'To DCI Walker,'* before drinking some more.

Walker appreciated it, but he was tired. He'd been tired before all of this even began. His illness had taken a toll on him, and he'd never quite got up to full strength. He suspected he never would. With the adrenaline of the case now subsiding, he felt drained, like his battery was almost flat. He just couldn't wait to climb into his nice warm bed and stay there for a while, recovering.

'Well, that's enough for me,' he said, abruptly, standing up. 'Thanks again, everyone. Enjoy the drinks.'

EPILOGUE

Around six months after arresting Alan Smith at the Beacon Point, Walker entered a secure room at HMP Garth, a prison just north-east of Croston, not too far from Smith's home. The prison officers had supplied a room so Walker could conduct a private interview with Smith. He'd got eight back-to-back life sentences for the eight murders he committed, including the one of Nick Hawley two years ago, plus an additional twelve years for the kidnapping of Emily Watkins. He'd never get out. That wasn't enough for Walker though. He needed to know *why*. If somebody didn't learn something from this whole sorry mess, from the tragedy of all those lives being ruined, then those people would have all died for nothing. At least, that's how he saw it—he had a responsibility to make sense of it. So, he sat, waiting for Alan Smith to be brought in, and he soon came.

Walker hardly recognised the man. He'd grown a beard, or something like that—wispy black hair covered his face, although it was notably thinner at the sides, and he'd put on a little weight. He seemed more comfortable, more at ease than before, and he now had a skinhead. He looked tougher—less domesticated. In short, he seemed like he'd found his natural habitat.

Alan sat down across from Walker, and the prison officer escorting him cuffed one of his hands to the table.

'That really necessary, Jack?' asked Alan to the prison officer.

'For a Chief of Police, yes,' said the man evidently called Jack. 'My boss would have me if anything happened.'

Alan nodded his understanding and accepted being shackled, before turning his attention toward Walker, staring him directly in the eyes for the first time.

Jack exited the room and closed the door, leaving them to it.

'What can I do for you?' asked Alan, trying to gesture with both hands, but forgetting one of them was cuffed for a second, making the chains rattle and clink.

'I... I'll get straight to the point, Mr Smith. I need to understand why you did what you did, personally—why you killed all those people,' said Walker. 'You gave a full confession of *what* you did in court, but you never really said why. I need to know.'

Alan Smith had admitted to killing Nick Hawley through asphyxiation, Tom Woods and Patricia Robinson by blunt force trauma with a hammer, and David and Sally Fielding—the two parents at Beacon Point who'd been with their young daughter—by blunt force trauma with a crowbar he'd found on his travels. He'd also confessed to killing three, and injuring three golfers at *Beacon Park Golf Club*, and attacking and kidnapping Emily Watkins.

'Why did you do these things?' asked Walker.

Alan rolled his eyes. 'I've had a couple of reporters here asking me the same thing. I told them to get lost.'

'And are you going to tell me to get lost too?' asked Walker.

Alan gave it some thought, before shaking his head.

'So?' asked Walker.

'Ever since I was little, I always had dark thoughts,' he said. 'I figured everyone did, but I'm not so sure now. I suppose you want to know that I was abused as a child, that I had a traumatic time, and what I did was the result of that. Would that make you feel better? Well, I'm sorry, Detective Walker, but that's not the case. My parents were wonderful. They couldn't have done a better job. I had a lovely childhood. But I was fascinated with death.' He picked up one of two plastic cups of water that had been placed there for them by the prison staff and took a sip. 'When I was a child, I used to visualise my mother dying, in great detail, to see how it felt, to prepare my emotions for when that day of grief finally came. I like to be prepared you see.'

'Go on,' said Walker.

'I also used to have a sibling—an older brother—but he died early in his twenties. I used to regularly fantasise about killing my brother when he was alive, whenever he did something to upset me; when we were kids, I mean. I had nothing to do with that, by the way. His death was an accident. It knocked me for six, actually. When I got older, I had similar dark fantasies, but with strangers or neighbours who'd angered me. I wanted to get revenge on certain people, or enact my own justice, but I never did anything, of course. I was a law-abiding citizen—a *model* citizen. I didn't so much as get three points on my license for speeding. Never. I'm usually a very careful person.'

'But you weren't careful when you killed those people,' said Walker. 'There was evidence everywhere.'

'I never intended not to be caught,' said Alan. 'Well, maybe

319

for the first one. But not the others.'

'You mean Nick Hawley, the young man who allegedly tried to kill himself?' asked Walker.

'No. He deserved to die. I wasn't going down for that. I'm not counting that one. He wanted to die anyway. I meant the dog walker, the one I put in that old building,' said Alan. 'Seeing him, decaying in that place, underground, out of sight, it gave me a sense of being in my own unconscious mind for a short time—of finally seeing the darkness and the horror there. It's like I had it safely padlocked up for so long, and then someone broke the lock. There was no going back after that.' Walker wasn't quite sure where the metaphors ended, and reality began.

'Do you think your family life had put an undue strain on you, psychologically, Mr Smith?' asked Walker. 'Did you just crack? That couple you killed up at Beacon Point, they had a little girl. She was just five. She's an orphan now, having to be fostered.'

'Just like my girl then,' said Alan. 'Look, they were shouting at her, smacking her bottom. They wouldn't have been good parents. I did her a favour.'

Walker had been biding his time to approach the subject of Smith's wife. In the weeks following his arrest, Alan's wife had committed suicide, took some pills and drank a large amount of gin, before getting into the bathtub. She'd done it on a Sunday night and left an email to be picked up by the local doctors on a Monday morning. Their daughter had still been sleeping when the emergency services arrived.

'I heard about what happened to your wife, and your daughter. I was very sorry to hear that,' said Walker.

'Well, don't be,' said Alan. 'We were in a living hell in

that place. My wife is free now, as am I, and our daughter is with people who are better equipped to handle her. It might seem strange to you, but *this* is my freedom—no more responsibilities, no more caring, no more stress, no more worry. And if someone angers me in here, I just let out the fury without worrying about the consequences. There's nothing more they can do to me. I'm truly free.'

'So, you did this as a way of escaping?' asked Walker.

Alan thought about it. 'That, and to vent, to let off some pressure and stress. We couldn't have carried on the way we were,' he said. 'We were going out of our minds.'

That much, Walker did agree with. 'Did you enjoy doing what you did, Mr Smith?' he asked, feeling his own anger bubbling, just below the surface, not being able to accept the pointlessness of it all. 'What about those poor people out playing golf? You battered half of them to death. One of them still can't walk. What did they do to you?'

Alan gave Walker that smile again—the one that had a certain malevolence to it, one devoid of soul or feeling. Walker wondered whether he was getting a glimpse of the real man behind the mask, the beast that resided within Alan Smith's unconscious mind, below the surface of social norms and etiquette: the animal within.

'You don't seem very happy with my explanation, Detective,' said Alan. 'Isn't what I experienced—all that stress—enough reason to crack, to do what I did?'

'Actually no. Not for most people,' said Walker, shaking his head and rubbing his stubble. 'I'm sorry. I'm just not buying it.'

Alan didn't react how Walker expected. He thought he'd go off the rails, start shouting or try to physically get at Walker.

He wanted to see that rage, up close, but he appeared almost pleased. 'You do seem intelligent. I'll give you that. Maybe I've finally found my equal. Would you like me to unpack an alternative version of events for you now?' he asked.

Walker didn't know if he was playing with him or not. 'I'm listening,' he said.

Alan took another sip of the water, rolled it around his mouth before swallowing.

'When my daughter was diagnosed with autism, all my wife's attention started going toward her. She was obsessed with teaching her to speak, kept singing the same songs over and over. It was excruciating. Life became unbearable, full of annoyances and inconvenience. Then later, when Amy was paralysed, that's when I became completely invisible. I was nothing—an afterthought. I kept our family going, financially I mean. I did everything. *Me*. I was working miracles, but all that went unnoticed,' he said, starting to spit out his words. 'It was all about Amy at that point. I fantasied about killing the man who ran her over, to avenge the harm done. But he disappeared—went abroad somewhere, I think. So, when it almost happened again, it was unreal, and I wasn't going to let that chance go this time.'

'So, you killed Nick Hawley,' said Walker.

Alan nodded. 'I'd always wanted to know what it feels like to kill a person, and I wasn't disappointed. Although my wife didn't know about it, what I did, she must have noticed some kind of change in me because she started to have sex with me again. I felt like a man again, for a short while at least. But it wasn't enough. The boy's father was responsible too, the one who kept sniffing around, coming to our home, wanting to know more about what happened. He had no right bothering us like that. If he'd have done a better job of being a dad, it could all have been avoided.' He took a breath, looked around the musty room. 'I suppose most people can't see what I can—the details, the consequences of actions, the probability of risk and reward. But that's really no excuse. He could still have tried harder, disciplined his kid better. So, I decided to find out more about the family, to get an idea of how to punish them properly for their laziness. To be honest, I wanted to annihilate them, wipe them off the face of the Earth. At first, I just thought I'd kill the father, so I went out practicing on a sheep, trying to hone my skills. It was too messy though and much too quick for the likes of him. I wanted him to suffer, like I had. I went to his house one night after dark, looked in through some of the windows, had a look around the garden. I found a shrine to his son containing a vase filled with ashes. I took some, filled an empty candy pack I had in my bum bag, and then urinated on the shrine. It was glorious, a real stress reliever. I thought I might set him up somehow, but the idea hadn't fully formed yet. I was just preparing what I could.'

Alan paused, took another breath. Walker knew he couldn't have known about the shrine in Darren Hawley's garden, not unless someone had told him—and that seemed unlikely. So, he'd probably been there and seen it for himself, like he said, at the very least.

'So, you had the ashes. And then what?' asked Walker, urging him on.

'Just about everyone was pissing me off at this point. Nobody has any common sense anymore. I was just itching for someone to give me an excuse to... You know. And then the Woods guy came along. I bashed his freakin' head in good and proper. He deserved it too. Idiot. That's when it all came together. I decided to set Hawley up. I'd frame him for the murder, for several even. He was a disgusting drunk. The world would be better off without him. I'd be doing everyone a favour and getting rid of some other scum to boot. It was win-win.'

'So, you planned everything from that point onwards?' asked Walker. Alan seemed to be enjoying himself now, showing off how clever he'd been to someone he seemed to respect, while also venting some of his frustrations at the same time and justifying his actions.

'I remembered the Amanda Morris case from one of my books and decided to use the cross of ash to mark the body. I knew the case was unsolved, so I thought I might frame him for that too. There was this other case too, one involving a serial killer called Hawley, of all names, so I had an idea to frame it as there being psychosis running in the family. It's often in the genes, isn't it?'

'Go on. And Patricia Robinson?' asked Walker.

'Patience, Detective,' said Alan, giving Walker some warning shots with his eyes. 'I was pretty much going out hunting at that point, I suppose, if I'm honest. I had a taste for it, you see, and I wanted more. I was just itching for someone, anyone, to wrong me so I could punish them, smite them off the face of the goddamned Earth. And this time, I was all prepared. I had the ash with me, and the hammer, and I did her in, before marking the body again.'

'And Emily?' asked Walker.

Alan leaned forward, seeming even more eager to reveal this part of his story. 'I learned of Nick Hawley's crush on Emily after seeing his Facebook page. Some of his friends were teasing him about it in some of their comments, long before he died. I thought I could abduct her, maybe tie her up and gag her in Hawley's shed and call it in anonymously, before killing her so she couldn't ID me. She even made it easy for me, leaving dog shit everywhere, stoking my rage. I actually wanted to kill her immediately after seeing that, but I managed to restrain myself, just knocked her unconscious—I thought moving her to the shed would have been easier if she was still alive, you see. But then you started sniffing around, spoiling everything for me before I could put my plan into action. When it became clear you were really on to me, when all those police cars showed up at my home, I figured, what the hell? I might as well go out in style, satisfy my craving once and for all.'

'You didn't want to run?' asked Walker. 'Why did you make it so easy for us like that?'

Alan thought about it. 'I thought the only reason I'd never done anything like that before was the fear of losing my freedom. But I came to realise that having your behaviour constrained, by not being able to do the things you really want to do, in your nature, I mean, is not freedom at all. I'd been trapped in a prison without walls all my life. I feel nothing for people, but I had to pretend I did, just to fit in. Finally doing what I wanted was emancipating, and in prison, with a life-sentence, I realised I'd be able to do whatever I wanted. There'd be nothing left to stop me. I stabbed a man last week with a weapon I made. It was beautiful. I can be as violent as I like in here, and I'm finally getting some respect, some notoriety,' said Alan.

'So, that's what really happened?' asked Walker. 'That's the truth?'

Alan shrugged his shoulders. 'You didn't seem happy with

my first explanation, so I offered you another.'

'Look, I just want to know the truth,' said Walker. He felt he was getting a handle on the man now, beginning to understand a little of what made him tick.

'Your truth is for you to decide,' said Alan. 'I think we're done here,' he said. 'It was a pleasure to see you again, Detective Walker.'

Walker didn't want to leave it like that. He wasn't often desperate, but this time, he yearned to understand why Smith had done what he did. If he could understand that, just a little, then maybe he could get an insight into the mind of his sister's killer too. 'Mr Smith, I... I just need to—'

'We're done,' said Alan, firmly. 'Jack!'

The interview was over and Walker knew it.

* * *

Walker got into his unmarked Audi A6, having now got dibs on a better car—the exact one he used to drive before his illness. Inside sat PC Briggs, only she wasn't a PC anymore. She was *DC* Briggs. She'd got qualified and become a detective, and, at her request, she'd partnered up with Walker, which Walker wasn't totally displeased about.

'Anything?' she asked.

'Some,' said Walker. 'Quite a bit, actually. He talked.'

'And did you get what you were looking for?' she asked.

Walker shook his head. 'Not really. Either he's an evil bastard, or life just got the better of him, or maybe it's a bit of both. He gave me an alternative version of events, but he may be delusional. Maybe he doesn't even know himself anymore.'

Walker was holding a brown A4 envelope that one of the prison staff had given him on the way out, a report written up by the prison psychiatrist.

'What's that?' asked DC Briggs.

Walker opened up the envelope, took a look, skimming through several pages. 'An assessment of Hawley's mental health,' he said. 'He's been claiming PTSD from prolonged stress from the start, but observations of him in prison, and I quote, *are suggestive of a narcissistic personality disorder with elements of malignant narcissism and psychopathy*. However, it also goes on to say, *his rage may be trigged by external events and past trauma, activating the fight or flight response, which could be indicative of post-traumatic stress.*'

'Maybe it's time to let this one go,' said DC Briggs. 'Move on.'

Walker chewed on his lower lip, breaking the skin. She was probably right. His thoughts dragged him back to that icehouse again. In its heyday, that place would have been filled with huge rocks of ice and darkness, the perfect manifestation of Alan Smith's utter lack of empathy and hollow soul. If what he said was true, he was a monster—a psychopath—end of. The hollowness of that underground space chimed with the unfillable emptiness of his narcissistic ego, an ego that would have required constant feeding—something Mrs Smith would no longer be doing. Walker took a moment to remember she was as a much a victim as anyone in all of this; and the memory of the inside of that icehouse, and of being inside Alan Smith's head, would no doubt haunt Walker for many years to come.

'Chief?' asked DC Briggs.

'Alright. Come on then. Let's go get something to eat. You

must be starving,' he said.

DC Briggs grimaced. 'I am hungry, but, er, no can do, Chief,' she said. 'We've just had a call come in. Some young woman has been found dead up on *Rivington Pike*. Gotta get over there ASAP, check it out. The Duty Officer is preparing things for us as we speak. We don't have long.'

Walker closed the door and put his belt on. DC Briggs was in the driver seat this time, giving him a well-earned break.

'After you then,' he said. 'Let's go.'

THE END

A Note From the Author

"Thanks so much for reading my book, *The Icehouse*. I hope you enjoyed it. Please could you be so kind as to leave a **review** on Amazon? I read *every* review and they help new readers discover my books. In fact, they're invaluable for my career and the continued lives of DCI Walker and the gang. So... please, do it now before you forget! (and I'll keep writing)"

J.J. Richards

Subscribe For More!

Finally, why not visit my website below and sign up to the newsletter for some freebies and news of any upcoming releases in the series.

J-J-Richards.com

Printed in Great Britain
by Amazon

25411505R00192